STAR PYRAMID

CHRONICLES OF THE CONCORDAT

Also by Ian Stewart from Elsewhen Press

Loophole

STAR PYRAMID

CHRONICLES OF THE CONCORDAT

IAN STEWART

Elsewhen Press

STAR PYRAMID
First published in Great Britain by Elsewhen Press, 2025
An imprint of Alnpete Limited

Elsewhen Press, PO Box 757, Dartford, Kent DA2 7TQ
www.elsewhen.press

British Library Cataloguing in Publication Data.
A catalogue record for this book is available from the British Library.

ISBN 978-1-915304-86-5 Print edition
ISBN 978-1-915304-96-4 eBook edition

Designed and formatted by Elsewhen Press

CONTENTS

*In memory of Tim Poston (19 June 1945 – 22 August 2017)
who helped to plot an early version of this novel in 1979.*

The pyramids of ancient Egypt were colossal machines
intended to carry powerful rulers to the stars.
The modern one was the same.

PART ONE

THE PROPHET

CHAPTER 1
ISLAND OF STABILITY
Dmitri Mendeleev
Saint Petersburg, Russia 1869

There is no beginning.

In ancient texts it is written that when the cosmos reformed and a lost soul fell from the World of Radiance to occupy the Palace of Brahma, taking the role of Brahma – 'all-creating Lord' – even that was not a beginning.

There is nowhere that the story really starts.

But we are finite, and we speak of beginnings.

* * *

Eka-plutonium.

Heavy plutonium.

Unbihexium.

Superheavy element 126.

As elusive as the Philosopher's Stone, and with the same overwhelming value – for the same reasons.

Johann Dobereiner took the first tentative steps in 1829, grouping elements into triads. Lothar Meyer plotted atomic weights against atomic volumes in 1864, and claimed to have seen patterns. John Alexander Reina Newlands saw the path in 1865 with his Law of Octaves, but the experts howled him down, in echoes of Johannes Kepler's Music of the Spheres. It had to be *eight*, of course...

Out of Russia came a prophet.

Dmitri Mendeleev did not scour the Earth for new minerals. He did point a spectroscope at the Sun, but that wasn't the breakthrough. His father Ivan taught in schools – fine arts, politics and philosophy. Despite many setbacks, Dmitri eventually went one better, becoming a chemistry professor at the Saint Petersburg Technological Institute in 1864, and at the Saint Petersburg State University a year later.

His mother had urged him to 'patiently search divine and

scientific truth'. He searched the divine and found it lacking, abandoning the Church for a vague belief in a supreme creator god that definitely existed – for how else could the universe exist? – but left that universe to its own devices, along with the tiny part of it that comprised the human race. He followed the other half of her advice, focusing on science that would explain those devices.

His passion for teaching led him along paths as unorthodox as his idiosyncratic take on Deist beliefs. His students were having trouble, and like any caring teacher he sympathised with their plight and sought to make learning simpler and easier to remember. *Fifty-six* chemical elements! Mendeleev was used to large numbers. He was from a family of 14 children; there would have been three more but they'd died before being baptised. In the Eastern Orthodox Church to which his parents belonged, that meant they'd died shortly after birth. But *this* family was four times the size, and unlike his, it was still growing. A new element discovered roughly every year, making matters even worse…

A strange brew. His god was imaginative but disorganised. Gases, liquids, solids. Metals. Burning, like chlorine and phosphorus. Metals that resisted acids, like gold; that burned brightly like magnesium; that ignited spontaneously like sodium and potassium, burning even underwater; that flowed like quicksilver. Fifty-six perfect individuals, whims of Mendeleev's disinterested deity. Many times fifty-six properties, almost impossible to remember.

Pity the poor students.

Yet there were family resemblances, tantalising hints of some hidden divine plan. Chlorine, fluorine: monovalent reactive gases. Carbon, silicon: tetravalent solids. Some mnemonic, at least, must surely be within reach.

Order them by atomic weight, from the lightest to the heaviest. Hydrogen, lithium, beryllium, boron, carbon, nitrogen, oxygen, fluorine… next sodium, a light metal similar to lithium. Then magnesium, resembling beryllium. Aluminium and boron, carbon and silicon. Periodicity? Or coincidence?

Next, phosphorus, 'corresponding' to nitrogen. Inert gas and inflammable solid? Maybe the pattern was no better than 'all odd numbers are prime', which works for seven out of the first nine numbers, but… Keep trying.

Oxygen and sulphur. Perhaps.

Fluorine and chlorine. Better.

Lithium, sodium, *potassium!*

There *was* a pattern; at least, enough to make life a lot easier for his students. Unaware of the work of his predecessors, he presented it to the Russian Chemical Society in 1869 under the title *The Dependence Between the Properties of the Atomic Weights of the Elements*. But the pattern with the best fits left gaps. He even juggled the order a bit, away from increasing atomic weight: 42 years later his order was a perfect fit to the sequence of the newly discovered nuclear charge. Choosing three gaps in particular, he described the properties that the 'missing' elements ought to have, interpolated from those of the elements above and below.

In 1875 Paul-Émile de Boisbaudran found what he called *gallium*. It was Mendeleev's 'eka-aluminium' to the last property. Lars Neilsen extracted *scandium* in 1879 from two minerals containing rare earth elements, and it fitted 'eka-boron'. And in 1886 Clemens Winkler isolated *germanium*, later much spread on silicon chips, from the newly discovered mineral argyrodite. It chimed in for 'eka-silicon'.

Eight of Mendeleev's ten gaps were finally filled; only dwi-caesium and eka-niobium declined to come to the party. Not bad for a chemist with no inkling of atomic theory, inspired by hope of a concealed divine order, working by thought alone.

* * *

Too far, perhaps, for a beginning…

Let us turn to the physicists, who tidied the picture with nuclear charge – the number of protons in an element's atomic nucleus. The same number of electrons vibrate in shells around it, giving the reactions that chemists see. Hidden from their view, the number of neutrons can differ, giving rise to distinct isotopes of the same element with confusing differences in atomic weight. Atomic number is much cleaner than atomic weight, the patterns clearer. The chemically stable, inert elements – helium, argon, neon – have neatly packed shells, as hard to disturb as an old maid's wedding-chest. Probing the nucleus showed that it, too, has shells, filled with protons and neutrons. 'Magic' numbers of these give neat shells again, and *atomically* stable elements: 2, 8, 20, 28, 50, 82. Helium has two protons and two neutrons: doubly magic, unusually stable. Lead has 82 protons: stable stuff, and a bad starting point if you want to make gold.

Beyond lead the elements become so unstable that they fall apart spontaneously. The radioactives: radium, thorium, uranium; even the chemically stable inert gas radon. Many are shorter-lived than human empires, even than human lives, and any of those on Earth came to pieces long ago. But men made them with excitement in particle accelerators, with grim satisfaction in bombs. Americium, curium, berkelium, californium, einsteinium, fermium, mendelevium, nobelium. In the 1960s and 70s nuclear physics was Big Money-Power Business, and Bigness doesn't concede its right to plant name flags. Traditional decencies broke down completely with element 106, which long remained unbaptised; in 1984 it was named 'orwellium', quite unofficially, and outside government reports the name stuck for a time. Finally, in 1997, the International Union of Pure and Applied Chemistry agreed to call it seaborgium.

By now the lifetimes were becoming so short that discovery claims rested on intricate inferences that the new elements *had* existed. New superheavy elements were endlessly claimed and denied as the 20th Century moved to its bloodstained close. The heaviest, the noble gas organesson, with 118 protons, was created in 2002 and named in 2016, on the basis of the five (or, controversially, six) atoms that had ever existed, and those for less than a millisecond. The properties of these elements were extrapolated or calculated; they would never exist long enough to have a chemistry.

Mendeleev's trail had petered out in what Russian physicists called the Bay of Pigs.

But, just as *chemical* stability blesses helium, argon, neon, krypton, skipping the violence of fluorine or sodium in between, perhaps *atomic* stability also picks up again later? Something between mathematics and a sense of numerical smell said that nuclear charges of 124, 126, and maybe (just maybe) 164, were the most likely candidates for an Island of Stability in the seething ocean of elements and their increasingly fragile isotopes.

In 1971 researchers at CERN tried to synthesise element 126 from thorium and krypton, but the results were unconvincing. As early as 1976, natural 126 was claimed, but disproved. Much later this claim turned out to have been prophetic, for a newer prophet than Dmitri Ivanovich Mendeleev.

In the 2030s there were theoretical hints of a transmutation process that could produce almost any element as quietly as yeast makes alcohol, without vast machines or energies – but a crucial catalyst was element 126: eka-plutonium. Fifty years later a new view of spacetime began to question the speed-of-light barrier, but again element 126 was essential. The alchemists of the 21st Century seemed as far from making heavy plutonium as those of the 12th were from turning lead into gold.

In 2092 an Indian team, using the big machine in recently-liberated Lhasa for parasoliton scattering experiments in search of a new ultra-massive fundamental particle that might revive the by-then-discredited theory of Dark Matter (nothing was further from their minds than the mere atomic nucleus) hit just the right energy, charge, and charm. Out coalesced three atoms of what they promptly named mahabhavium, reviving the Sanskrit from which Mendeleev drew 'eka'. Element ^{126}Mb was added to the periodic table.

'Maha' = great.

'Bhava' = stuff.

'-ium' = rigidly established dog-Latin for 'element'.

And that, perhaps, is where the story really starts.

PART TWO

MAHABHAVIUM BOONDOGGLE

CHAPTER 2

MONGREL GET OF A PARANOID CAMEL

Francis J. Simpson IV

*Global Union Astronautics Administration Building
Bayankhongor 2157*

The Vice President for Stress Computation dumped a stack of graphics holocopies on my desk and ran bony fingers through her shoulder-length blonde hair.

"There are times," she said, "when I think this mongrel get of a paranoid camel was designed by Hindus."

I can't say it made much sense to me, since the design had been a huge team effort involving at least seventy separate nationalities and cultural groups, but Hjördis seldom made sense when she was on a rant. Until you figured it out and everything fell into place.

At that point I hadn't, so I prevaricated.

"Almost certainly a racial slur, unbecoming of one in your position," I said, playing the PC bureaucrat. With a degree of honesty: I didn't want to be forced to issue a formal reprimand. It would look bad on her record. And mine. "Unless you mean that the *mandir* or *koil* has distinctive pyramidal elements, especially the one in Kerala– "

"Stop operating in default Coordinator mode, Frank, and *listen* to me!"

Well, I'd got her attention. Now she had to get mine.

I leaned across my desk, a huge slab of fake wood polished to a shine that would probably have been visible from Karoubi's Star – except that, in point of fact, it wasn't visible from a metre away. I'm not a great believer in a tidy desk: when I'm busy I like to pile stuff up everywhere. And I'm always busy. It looks a mess, but *I* know exactly where everything is. The random scatter of Hjördis's holocopies was negligible in comparison. The only surprise was that she'd found somewhere to dump them.

Still, it was disrespectful. But then, Hjördis generally was.

Unable to find anywhere to rest my elbows, I remained leaning, and locked my heavy-browed brown eyes with her pale blue ones until one of us blinked.

Not me. I never lose *those* battles.

"It's a quaint idea, Hjördis, at best. What's all this about?"

She shook her head, obviously frustrated. Eventually she'd calm down and tell me the real reason for this outburst. But, as I knew from long experience, not yet.

"It's like that Hindu cosmology with the Earth riding on four elephants, standing on the back of a turtle, swimming in a celestial ocean. Only more complicated."

It was my turn to shake the head. "I think the elephants were originally mistranslations of the word for 'snake'. Not that it makes much difference. *Four* elephants? Well, the fourfold symmetry suits *Star Pyramid*, and it's not my job to keep mythology straight. Or yours."

My attempt to lighten her mood had clearly failed. Still, I now understood where the Hindus had come from. I stared at her for a long moment, then sighed.

"If it's any consolation, Hjördis, I agree she's a bit of a lash-up."

I swear her eyes flashed. For a moment the room lit up like a pinball machine on *TILT*. But that was probably my visual cortex resonating with the vocal detonation.

"Lash-up? *Lash*-up? She makes the Apollo Program look like a Japanese flower arrangement! She's a megaton of chewing-gum wrapped up in a light year of string! She's the biggest mess of compromises since Henry Ford chose the gasoline engine. Nothing, *ekkert, nichts*, is straightforward. Do you realise that this bitch has *five* different propulsion systems?"

If there's anyone on the Project who does not *realise it*, I thought, *it's my job to fire them – yesterday.* I could have pointed out that actually there would be only four propulsion systems until – if – when – the mission succeeded. First, a lox/H rocket barrage to move her out of the construction zone. Second, an MHD booster to get her up to ramspeed. Third, an eka-Bussard, which will get her up to *light*speed if the thing manages to ignite. Fourth, the AMDrive to slow down and stop on arrival. *And, of course, the fifth…* But that, at least, wasn't Hjördis's problem.

"Technically," I pointed out, "the Da Silva drive won't work until they arrive. It's only four propulsion systems for now."

"That's if the damned thing works! *And* if they can produce enough mahabhavium at the other end. And even if that argument held water, four is still *too many*."

I spread my hands in surrender at that point, but continued to argue another. "They should only need two kilos of fuel for the Da Silva to get home. So the specialists tell me."

"Fine, that'll get it home. But we'll need more than *that* Frank. The plan calls for—"

"Fifty kilos, I know. We'll need it if we want to build a fleet."

"And we can't risk return flights on an untested engine to get more."

"Agreed. Still, even if they can't refine enough mahabhavium, they can still get home without it. They can light the eka-Bussard with the AMDrive, won't even need the MHD."

Hjordis was unimpressed.

"I know the contingency plans, Frank. And I also know it'll take another four hundred years for them to get back. Assuming they manage to light up the eka-Bussard again. That's impossible to test."

"No, but all the simulations show that the Matter Annihilation Drive is capable of igniting the eka-Bussard." Remembering I was supposed to be a bureaucrat, I added, "Remember, the official acronym is AMDrive, not MAD."

Hjördis was unimpressed. "I accept that by then they'll have plenty of stored antimatter, Frank. And *you* know full well that everyone calls it the MAD because *it fits*." We both know the contingency plan. The same engines that will slow them down for orbital insertion at Karoubi's star can accelerate them back up to ramspeed, bringing them home again after another 400 years. If *that's* not mad, tell me what is!"

Neither of us gave voice to the simple fact that none of the crew would survive *two* four-hundred year journeys, and that no one would welcome them back anyway if they didn't bring the much-needed magic element. *In fact*, I thought sourly, *by 2980 there probably wouldn't be anyone to deny them the welcome; Earth could only borrow so much time.*

To be frank – ha – I didn't even see them getting outside the Solar System. The whole idea of starflight was just too far-fetched. We didn't have the technology to do it sensibly. I wasn't sure we had the technology to do it at all, however clumsily. But it was my job to give it our best shot, and I would shoot myself rather than give voice to any private misgivings.

Focus on the positive. *The prize for success!*

If wishes were starships, there'd be new-agers on Proxima Centauri.

I was a professional. My personal opinions could not be permitted to interfere with doing my job. And my job was to keep *Star Pyramid*'s Design, Bio, Eco, Psych, SusAn, and above all Construction sections on a very tight and impossibly complex schedule.

Hjördis was still in full flame. "Then there's all the ancillary equipment! Ramscoops. Life-support. Antiproton confinement bottles. The antenna reversal system is needlessly complicated! Why didn't they–"

"Hjördis, we've been through that already. The ship has to reverse orientation to slow down. Turning the entire antenna would need a massive motor, too big to replace if it goes wrong. Turning each segment separately uses 24 smaller motors, and we can carry spares and replace any that fail preparatory tests. Engineering took the decision long ago and it's too late to change, even if it made sense."

She ignored me. "Magnetics. Electrics. Computers. The Da Silvas: the same lump of doped lead has to function in the communicator *and* the eka-Bussard! Instruments. Plumbing. Temperature control. And every time anyone gets a new bright idea, my section has to run all the structural stability programs *again!*"

I muttered sympathy noises, knowing they'd have no effect, and sighed. "It's the same for everyone, Hjördis. It's a rush job. If we'd started planning around the time Djoser had the first Egyptian pyramid erected, we might actually be on top of things. Do you know how much time I spend firefighting?"

A grudging nod. It encouraged me to press on with the same line of defence.

"Most of the ship is still at the design stage, even though much of it's already under construction. The overall design is flexible, lots of contingency and scenario planning. But we have to keep adapting the details. What else do you expect of a one-off project of this magnitude?"

No response. This was an improvement. I looked her in the eye.

"You can handle it."

She wasn't yet in the mood to concede.

"Oh, sure." Hands waving dismissively. "In a fifth-generation version, every component would do seventeen jobs, failsafed nine ways, and *like* it. But, win or lose, this will be the only sub-cee starflight ever, and the art is in no state to do it that way. Simplify, simplify, separate out what we can, till we *think* we know what it will do! But even so, the design problems are from Nifflheim. Half the components will still have to do two jobs, and most of the decel systems get rebuilt *en route*. It's like launching a winged battleship with no landing-gear, and rebuilding it in flight into a giant helicopter so it can land!"

* * *

Hjördis Sigmundsdóttir had finally run out of breath, and while she was getting it back I saw a chance to regulate the flow. Once she calmed down, she'd tell me what was *really* troubling her. The fireworks were her equivalent of anti-radar chaff. I thought about buying time by collecting together the scattered holocopies, but decided it would be interpreted as criticism. In any case, there was nowhere to put them except on the floor. Call for a coffee? No, that would be seen as a diversionary tactic. Correctly. Best just to wait for the storm to blow itself out.

"It'll be a long flight, Hjördis. It'll give them something to do. Dare I remind you that there are only *two* working onboard drives on the outward journey? The Da Silva can't be completed until they get there."

"Sure." Her tone was dismissive. "And even if they do, and complete it, there's no way to test the existing components under realistic conditions! That's over four thousand separate subsystems whose integrity I'm supposed to sign off on, but *can't test!*"

Give Hjördis credit, she was committed, a hundred and ten per cent. But she was getting herself all worked up about things over which she had no control.

I needed her to be fully functional.

"The Da Silva is the only system you're *not* responsible for," I said. "It will be the responsibility of whoever's in charge at the time. Whatever happens, it won't affect *us*. Maybe our great-great-great-whatever-grandchildren, if we have any."

She slumped in her chair. "I suppose."

Time to change tack. I gave her my best concerned-boss look.

"You need to lighten up. You're supposed to *compute* stresses, not suffer from them."

Wait a second, then show her I'm on her side.

"If I can offer you any extra support without breaking the budget, it's yours. What I want you to do is verify that the design remains within acceptable limits for structural stress – however the other guys decide to modify it. You can do it, you're the best in the business. That's why I hired you."

We batted it to and fro. Eventually Hjördis departed, only partially mollified, but before she left I'd flushed from cover her real grouse. She wanted more time on the Mahacitta 706 hypercomputer. *Everyone* wanted more time on the 706; I'd discovered that two months *before* starting my new job as Coordinator. The works in Liaoning were building two more as fast as the Ramaputta Orbital Factory could grow the components, but delivery was still two years away. It was likely to be set back further, because the latest shipment of praseodymium nitrate from São Paulo was impure. So I offered Hjördis overnight access to the Brathwait multiprocessor network, the best available alternative. I knew I'd have to spend two hours massaging egos and making wild promises to persuade the machine's minders to grant it, but there were deployable carrots and sticks. However, those would have to wait.

My desklight blinked: next customer. The never-ending stream of problems, demands, and whines would have given most people a nervous breakdown. They wouldn't have been willing to touch my job, even from the other end of Archimedes's lever, long enough to move the Earth. But I love being in the thick of the action. No chance of any great-great-great-whatever-grandchildren for me; no chance of any children. My paramour is my job, and it occupies my thoughts from dawn to dusk.

And many hours from dusk to dawn.

* * *

At least I didn't have to plan our public relations campaign. That was the purview of the Computational Psychonics team. They had a budget as large as Engineering's, not counting actual construction costs, and were angling for a 706 of their own. I had yet to convince the engineers that spacecraft design is a trivial problem compared to multibillion-variable human relationships. The engineers, for their part, referred to public relations as Thought Control.

It was, and it was working. CompPsych was doing a superb job. When the anti-GU guerrillas in Australia had been persuaded to lay down their Kalashnikovs because the war was hurting *Star Pyramid*'s crucial nickel supplies, I'd realised the strength of world feeling behind the Project. It was awe-inspiring.

Although I wasn't directly involved in *planning* the public relations campaign, I still had to make cameo appearances from time to time. Reassure the world that there was a firm hand on the tiller. Whatever. It made a break from endless meetings, even if press conferences were just another kind of meeting. For years, critical questions from the press has all been about *how*, not *whether*, to go to Karoubi's star. For instance, when I'd announced Berrios's selection…

* * *

I've always found Conference Room C in the GUAA Building reassuring. The décor is simple and slightly old-fashioned, with soft blue seats arranged in informal irregular rows and spaces for holovision camera tripods. The podium and platform at the front are more formal. Psychologically, the audience is pampered and lulled into a sense of comfort and complacency, and the speaker looks down on them, conveying a subtle sense of authority. All this is exactly what Computational Psychonics had intended when approving the design. The effect is enhanced by paintings (not photographs or holograms) of successful GU projects that line the walls, and a giant GU logo on the wall behind the platform. When, as now, Room C is hosting a press conference, these advantages come to the fore. Especially when the announcement is guaranteed to be contentious.

Today's topic was a pilot project for *Star Pyramid*: a small, specialist craft that would – we hoped – ensure that vital technology would actually work. We were building the ship, and had just chosen its pilot. But it was all very controversial.

The shortlist comprised eight test-pilots – four male, four female. I read out brief resumés of their careers, and told the assembled journalists (a word still used even though none of them worked for anything to do with paper) that the decision had been made on priority ranking, with 38-year-old Federico Berrios at the top of the list.

"Monsieur Simpson?"

I recognised the elfin face and dangling earrings of Nicole Dorier from HVQ, HoloVision Québecoise. Elfin but flushed, something must have pressed one of her buttons. This was predictable with Nicole, but which button, and what would press it, were not.

"I'm a little surprised that none of these persons are married. Surely space exploration requires the stable personalities who form secure bonds?"

"I'm glad you raised that issue, Nicole." *I'm not, particularly, but someone was going to.* "I agree entirely with you when it comes to short missions. When Armstrong leaped for Mankind he'd been married thirteen years, with two children. When Barrett and Makin went to Mars eighty-six years later, their wife was running Mission Control. Those were very careful, and correct, psychological choices. But long periods in space require a more self-contained personality, though of course without any tendency towards psychotic withdrawal."

Hope that heads off that particular line of questioning.

"Two people on the shortlist, in fact, regularly practice religious retreat: Thenmozhi Tambiah in a Buddhist convent and Berrios in one of the orbital monasteries. As you see from his resumé, he's Roman Catholic, like many Bolivians."

I paused, trying to gauge the mood of the room. This was one of the main reasons I preferred to hold press conferences in person. The other was that it made the press feel appreciated. That and the free alcohol afterwards.

I had one other point to make. As my media trainer had dinned into me years ago, the trick when dealing with the press is decide what answers you want to publicise and ignore the questions. Make the answer seem to fit if possible, but don't even try if you can't. *That's not the issue! The issue is…* But on this occasion, I could play it straight.

"In Berrios's case, the word 'retreat' isn't terribly appropriate. The orbital monasteries double as asteroid-mining corporations. The monkish lifestyle is well suited to that kind of work, on your own on a lump of rock a million kilometres from nowhere, drilling out valuable minerals. It's a hard life, and it's given Berrios even more valuable experience in deep space. That's one big tick beside his name."

Before anyone could follow up on that with awkward supplementaries, Delhi Broadcasting chipped in with a more technical query, if engineering is more technical than psych.

"Why do you need a manned flight? Mission Control works out of Bayankhongor through a freewave link. Why not test the Bussard by remote control? Or install an AI? Surely then the payload would be less, and a single test flight wouldn't use up one tenth of the entire Project budget."

Actually, 8.7%, but I mustn't quibble. He just rounded it up.

"True, Mr. Achathan, if we were testing only the Bussard," I said. "But *Star Pyramid* must be manned. Artificial Intelligence has its place, but rapid decisions in unexpected circumstances are not among its strengths. Many of the ship's systems will be rebuilt *en route*, the mahabhavium must be collected from a place we don't know enough about for reliable advance planning, and then the main Da Silva drive must be finished and configured for the return. Not to mention a hundred unexpected contingencies that could require human intervention. If the mission were purely automated, we might find that four hundred years of reports culminated in nothing more than an error message. So *people* have to be on board, which implies that it has to be either a generation ship or one whose crew spend most of their time in suspended animation, given the 98-year timespan–"

"Shouldn't that be 400 years?"

"In our frame of reference, yes. But *Star Pyramid* will spend most of the trip at just below the speed of light, and time dilation reduces the time it takes in the ship's frame of reference. Clear? Great.

"As I was saying, the only choices were a generation ship, with a few crew and a relatively large number of... well, basically, passengers; *or* a smaller contingent of the best people we can find, on a suspended animation sleep-wake rota. As you know, the generation ship idea was deemed impractical, and the development of reliable SusAn tech seventy years ago made the choice obvious. Even with a much smaller crew animate at any given moment, the presence of humans requires life support. So we're also testing various design features on *Tyger*, and we test them fully by supporting life. The presence of a human pilot opens up further opportunities, so we'll be testing many other new technologies that will be crucial for *Star Pyramid*."

A West African wearing an amazing scarlet kaftan and a multicoloured hat swallowed the bait I'd just dangled. "You're referring to the Da Silva communicator?"

"An excellent example, Alvin."

"I believe that requires *Tyger* to carry a substantial quantity of mahabhavium."

"That's one reason. Freewave depends on the stuff, as well you know. But the–"

"How can you possibly justify that when mahabhavium is so scarce?"

Big smile. Then look serious.

"It does look odd, doesn't it? But I can assure you that nothing involving *Star Pyramid* happens without very good reason, and after a lot of expert input and debate."

He shook his head. "Come on, Frank, you can do better than regurgitating a bland formula like that."

"Yes, I can. And I was about to do just that. The decision was forced upon us for three reasons.

"First, we need to keep an eye on everything that's happening on *Tyger*, in real time. Freewave is the only way to do that. Second, like I said, the flight isn't just about *Tyger*. It's about all of the tech that *Star Pyramid* will rely on. Which includes freewave. We have to be sure that Da Silva communication protocols will function correctly over much greater distances than have yet been explored. Admittedly, *Tyger* won't reach interstellar distances, but it will go further from Earth than any previous mission."

"Third—"

"That's all very well, but you're risking *four years'* production of a vital and very expensive resource!"

Alvin did rather tend to make a nuisance of himself, which was a pity because when off his hobby-horse he was good company, with an endless fund of amusing stories about celebrities he'd interviewed. Professionally, he was trying to make a name for himself as an abrasive scourge of bureaucracy, a stance that Lagos Newsline had taken from the day it launched. There were times I felt the same way.

In fact, this issue was one such. I'd never been fully convinced that we'd chosen the right candidate, but CompPsych had strong-armed me into it, assisted by pressure from above. *Way* above.

"I agree, it looks ridiculous. We'd much prefer not to take the risk. Unfortunately, we have to. And that's the *third* reason—" *pause to make it clear that I didn't like being interrupted* – "and it's by far the most significant.

"We've been referring to the Bussard ramscoop/ramrocket drive. Actually, technically it's the *eka*-Bussard. From an old Sanskrit name meaning 'one'. It started out as a tribute to Dmitri Mendeleev, who, as we discussed at last week's historical briefing, came up with the periodic table of the elements and indirectly led the world to discover mahabhavium. It's been repurposed since then: *e*fferent *k*armabhumic *a*ntistrophe.

"It's a mouthful, isn't it? That's why we say 'eka'. Don't blame me for the technical terms, Quade Kylie invented them years ago, long before any of his weird ideas became reality. Basically, it means 'pushing stuff away by using a *k*-field to reverse it'.

"The problem is easy to understand. When Robert Bussard came up with the ramscoop concept in 1960, the idea was that the spaceship would use vast electromagnetic fields to scoop up atoms of hydrogen as it moved through interstellar space. When compressed, the hydrogen would become fuel, undergoing nuclear fusion and generating power. However, the idea has a serious flaw, especially at speeds near that of light. Anyone like to guess what?"

A young woman I didn't recognise, presumably new to the job, put up her hand. "You have to slow the atoms down, don't you? You can't let them slam into the collecting… thing… at the speed of light, or it would get damaged." She paused. "Slow down *relative to the ship*, I mean. The atoms are stationary and the ship's moving. So I guess what really happens is, the atoms are pushed away in front of you."

"That's right. Any scooping device will pile stuff up ahead of it, creating drag and that opposes the thrust generated by the fuel. It's like trying to power an airplane by funnelling in pollution from the air: the funnel creates more drag than the thrust generated by the stuff it sucks in.

"I said '*any* scooping device' has this flaw. Wrong. But to avoid it you need mahabhavium. More than for freewave comm, less by far than you need to skip to a distant star in an instant. Da Silva linkage can transmit *any* physical quantity instantaneously. Freewave sends electromagnetic waves, just not by the usual route. Not by *any* route: just here/there and nothing in between. The extra bit of kit that turns a flawed Bussard into an entirely practical eka-Bussard is a Da Silva linkage that stops matter building up ahead of the ship by pushing it *backwards* into the throat of a conventional Bussard. In effect, it sucks the atoms in fast enough to use them as fuel, but slowly enough not to damage the ship. Any excess is just diverted past the ship.

"That's the idea. In theory it should work like a dream; in the lab, related nanoscale systems do what theory predicts. But we can't just carry on building *Star Pyramid*, blithely assuming its eka-Bussard will work as soon as it's switched on. We can't test it on the ship itself: the more massive the object, the more mahabhavium you need to get the eka-Bussard working, and we don't have enough. So we have to try it out on a smaller prototype, and that's the main reason for *Tyger*'s existence. The resonating cavity on *Tyger* has to be doped with at least 1.36 nanograms. Currently the three Lhasatrons generate a quarter of that every year. There's no other option."

Well, that's silenced them all.

Not for long. "Can I ask a supplementary, Coordinator?"

"Yes, Alvin, but please bear in mind that this press conference is scheduled to stop in… 23 minutes' time. And everyone else has questions too. Thirty seconds."

He nodded. "Will you also be testing the antimatter system?"

"Depends what you mean by that. *Tyger* isn't equipped with the matter-annihilation drive that *Star Pyramid* will use to slow down from eka-Bussard ignition speed, because she won't have time to accumulate fuel. We'll catch her and slow her down externally on her return. But it's only in interstellar space, with the tremendous energy output of Bussard fusion, that we can create and store antimatter in quantity. So *Tyger* will test the process, and the tenth of a kilo of antimatter she carries with her will be of great use to science when she brings it back.

"This also helps justify the budget." I grinned. Ripple of laughter.

"You won't be bringing it back to Earth?" the correspondent from one of the more excitable platforms exclaimed in alarm. "If it got out it would be like a, uh– a billion times the bomb that destroyed Jerusalem!"

"No, no," I reassured him. "In bulk, it will stay in solar orbit, never closer to the Earth than ten million kilometres. Any that's brought to Earth will be just a few atoms. Less bang than a New Year crackerjack, and it won't get out anyway. Remember, we're *already* making and storing the stuff.

"Next question?"

The discussion returned to Berrios's background, and the anxious topic of the End of the World faded from view.

"Is it wise even to contemplate using religious believers to play such a vital role? Their beliefs could cloud their judgment." That was Jenny Yang of Sumatra Holovision; very smart, dedicated, and quick on her feet. We'd crossed swords before and the score was roughly even. People in the region had bad memories of religious authorities in government, and after their successful revolution they were still sensitive to the issue.

My team had gone over that ground in considerable depth, and my answers were tried and tested for being candid, credible, and inoffensive – except to those determined to take offense no matter what.

"I wouldn't dream of employing fanatics, Jenny. Religious or secular. But a founding principle of the Global Union is to respect cultural belief systems. The other six people on the shortlist have no religious affiliation. It didn't count for them, and it didn't count against them either.

"Berrios tops the list on experience and merit. He's test-flown everything from Petrobrás jump-jets to MHDrive Jovian probes. The Jupiter mission in particular required lightning reflexes and correct decisions after a ten-month voyage that would have given an extrovert jail-fever. And, as I said, his mining experience in the asteroid belt is a big plus.

"We're convinced he's the best choice."

It never crossed my mind to mention it to the media, you appreciate, but Berry also possessed one other vital attribute: lack of imagination. There are too many things that can go wrong with a prototype starship, and nobody with a vivid imagination would survive the mental stresses of a *Tyger*-ride.

* * *

I usually emerge from these events having enjoyed the verbal fencing, but on this occasion I felt drained and apprehensive. Not because of how the discussion had gone; I'd given as good as I'd got. But the topic had revived some deep-seated doubts in my mind.

Ideal though Berrios seemed, there'd been one huge black mark against him, not mentioned in the resumé we'd made public. Not his fault in any way, but it had thrown him mentally and he was still suffering the consequences. The incident had been hushed up, but it had led him to retreat from wider society.

When he emerged as a potential front-runner, CompPysch had put him through a battery of tests, concluding that he'd come to terms with his past. If anything, the experience had made him mentally stronger: nothing to lose, everything to gain. That was why the Chief Psychologist, Kingsley Potter, had singled him out, despite his previous mental collapse and flight into obscurity.

I'd never been totally convinced. CompPsych's success in modelling large groups of people was phenomenal, but individuals were less predictable. I'd told Potter it was a gamble. He'd countered that it was a calculated risk, and explained one key step in the calculation. He'd placed the mental issue on the negative side of the balance, and the positives on the other.

Among the positives, outweighing everything else, was an essential attribute for *Tyger*'s planned excursion; Berrios had a freakish tolerance for sustained high g's. That, above anything else, had clinched it. There was really no other sensible choice.

Even so, I couldn't get rid of the sinking feeling that CompPsych had made a mistake.

CHAPTER 3

PARALLEL UNIVERSES (1)

Li Yingyue (李映月)

*Global Union Astronautics Administration Building,
Bayankhongor 2157*

"But why a pyramid, Sean?"

The Head of the Engineering Consultancy Group had been expecting my question, but he hesitated. He could give me the stock answer, of course: a bland two-liner that explained nothing. I'd heard it a thousand times. I was after something else, and it threw him off balance for a few seconds because he clearly understood that, but didn't know what it might be. He collected himself, and I could almost read his mind. It wouldn't do to treat me like an ignoramus, but he couldn't get too technical either because then I'd *feel* like an ignoramus. So he would have to settle for something in between.

He began cautiously.

"It pretty much has to be for the thing to work at all."

I gave him my thousand-kilometre stare. He knew what it meant. *You've got to do better than that.*

"It's – it's all tied up with the symmetries of the mass distribution about the principal – No, sorry, let me start again. Assessor Li: how much math background do you have?"

He looked uncomfortable even asking. He hadn't yet touched the coffee that Henry had brought for us. I picked up my cup and sipped. *Not bad. Pretty good, actually.*

"Don't let it get cold, Sean. I know you like coffee."

He actually flinched. I hadn't realised he was *that* nervous. He reached for the cup. His hand shook slightly as he took a mouthful. Put the cup down too quickly, making a noise when it hit the saucer.

He flushed, a band of pink around his collar. Despite his surname, he was pale-skinned and of German descent. Average height, bit of a paunch from his favourite exercise of beer drinking, A nice guy, but too timid for his own good, and all too obviously nervous around women.

Sean, we don't bite. Well, not in public.

I didn't let my amusement show; these scientific types have the sensitive temperament of a prima donna, particularly the men. I allowed the barest flicker of a smile at the corners of my mouth.

"Sean, I don't give a damn if you make me look ignorant. I *am* ignorant. That's why I'm asking you. If it helps: I never had time to specialise. I couldn't have been appointed to the Board of Project Assessors if I had. My background is as broad as the Sahara and as deep as a dried-up oasis."

He nodded, but I could see he needed more than that.

"I did have the usual two years of calculus, if that helps. And basic physics, concurrently." As he relaxed, I added: "All I need is a thumbnail sketch so I can explain it to the TOC on Thursday." That's the Technical Oversight Committee. "You simplify it for me, and I'll simplify that for *them*, OK? Yes, we'll lose some of the fine points, like validity, but the aim of the game is to bag that appropriation. Right?"

He nodded, but he still looked uncomfortable. It was a good job *I* was in charge of securing funding.

Henry had brought biscuits, too. I munched on one while Sean fiddled with his cup.

Drink or don't drink, I thought. *There is no try.*

Following my lead, he sipped at his coffee as if he thought it might bite him. Nibbled distractedly at a biscuit.

"Don't worry about oversimplifying, either," I said, hoping to reassure him. "Assume zero knowledge but infinite intelligence."

Sean Mobutu winced, but kept a brave face. I liked him, but he needed to loosen up.

"Fine," he said. "You know why the sky is blue?"

Easy. "Refraction."

The engineer looked pained. "Well, sort of. It's not like a rainbow, where your answer would be a big part of the story, Assessor Li. It's more of a statistical scattering effect in the upper atmosphere. *Fluctuations.* That's a good word to use for the Committee. They won't understand it, but they won't be willing to admit that."

"*Blue.*"

"Oh, yes, I'm getting to that. The fluctuations scatter the light, photons bouncing all over the place, and the blue ones come off best because their wavelength is shorter. Inverse fourth power of the wavelength… no, don't tell the TOC that."

I looked out of the window for a moment, towards the greyish-purple of the Hangayn Nuruu range, dimly visible through the morning mist. "OK so far, I'm following you."

"The Da Silva drive is like that. It needs a really rich fluctuation domain."

"In the upper atmosphere?"

"No, in the quantum states of spacetime."

"Right." I had no idea of what he was talking about, and my curt reply made that clear.

Doggedly, he ploughed ahead. "In terms of energy, that requires a really flat minimum, so the states can bounce around a lot without getting sucked back into the one with lowest energy. Like a frying pan rather than a spoon."

Mixed analogies, but I gave him credit for *trying*. Anyway, I understood that bit. "You mean like a fourth or sixth power graph, rather than an x-squared parabola?" His eyes nearly popped out of his head. "Like I said, two years of calculus."

A tentative smile showed relief. We might not be on the same wavelength, but we were at least in the same class of the electromagnetic spectrum. He was finally starting to relax.

"Ah. That's it, exactly, Assessor Li. A nearly flat floor, so that fluctuations away from the centre take a long time to roll back. But steep walls further out, so they don't escape entirely."

"Got it."

"Except we're not talking about numerical variables like temperature; we're looking at fluctuations in the topology of spacetime."

"*Not* got it."

He floundered around for a moment, then squared his shoulders and got back to business. "You're aware that on the smallest scales, space and time aren't like they seem on a human scale: calm and continuous? They're more like a kind of foam, lots of very, very tiny holes joined together by thin films, vibrating like – well, vibrating very fast. Merging and splitting apart and bursting and reforming.

"You're definitely aware that all Da Silva phenomena – drives, communicators, and the like – rely on some very strange properties of mahabhavium?"

"I'd better be, Sean, since that's what the project I'm assessing is all about."

To his credit, he didn't remind me I'd told him 'zero knowledge'. Instead, he said: "Mahabhavium does nothing left to its own devices. It lives on an island of stability in isotope-space."

I let that pass. I could just about work out what he meant.

"The trick with mahabhavium," he said, "is to sit it in that sort of fluctuation domain. Its nucleus is huge, 310 nucleons in the commonest isotope; that's an enormous energy concentration. So although we say it's stable, actually it's hovering on the ragged edge of instability the whole time.

"The next point is a bit counterintuitive, but I assure you it's true. When placed in a rich fluctuation domain, the mahabhavium nucleus becomes *more* stable."

I grabbed for something weird that I'd once been told. "Is that like an inverted pendulum, stable upside down as long as you vibrate it really fast?"

He helped himself to another biscuit, drained his coffee-cup. The cups were small and dainty, very Japanese. Imports, of course.

I caught his eye, inclined my head towards the coffee-pot. He nodded, so I poured us both another cup.

"Could be," he said. "I never took a course in classical physics. Only the liberal arts students did that. I prefer real science to ancient history."

Ah, the arrogance of the nerds.

Then his eyes went wide. "Does it *really*– anyway, we're drifting off topic. It's more like stochastic resonance. The math is horrendous, I can't imagine how Loon and Kylie ever thought of it. Strong fluctuations, outside the usual linear domain of quantum theory, allied to strong singularities. Anyway, the upshot is a kind of tunnelling effect."

That rang a bell. A chance to show some intelligence.

"Like a quantum particle passing through an energy barrier despite lacking the energy to go over the top?" I asked. "Borrowing energy and then paying it back before the universe notices? A free lunch even though we all know There Ain't No Such Thing?"

He put his mudskipper face back on, all bulging eyes at the waterline of an incredulous face. But only for an instant. He was learning.

"Uh-huh. But I'm talking about quanta of spacetime, not particles, and the barrier they tunnel through is the one that keeps them existing in the place and time that they are, rather than somewhere else. And somewhen, of course."

"Of course."

As he paused to regain his breath, I seized my opportunity.

"Let's keep it simple, Sean. Are you telling me you can move bits of spacetime around?"

His eyes opened wide as if he'd never thought of it that way. "Yes. Well, they… kind of *jump*. A to B without passing though anywhere in between. They borrow a new location and pay it back before the universe notices what they've done."

I thought about that for a long moment.

"OK, Sean; very, very tiny bits of spacetime can teleport. How does that move a spaceship? I mean, *at all*. Let alone faster than light."

"Oh that's easy. If it's a quantum of spacetime that you're shifting around, any physical entity whose probability peaks there, shifts with it."

Peaking probabilities were outside my comfort zone, but I grasped the gist. "You can move *things*."

"You can move things. Small things, like an atom of iron. Big things, like *Star Pyramid* – if you can get enough mahabhavium."

"About a kilo, I believe."

"Near enough, Assessor Li. But all we have right now is–"

"A hundred billion atoms. Plus another billion tomorrow, and another billion the day after. Courtesy of the big accelerator at Lhasa. That's a lot of atoms. But it takes two and a half trillion to make one nanogram. Not a lot of mahabhavium."

"True," Sean said. "But a hundred billion atoms at each end is enough to carry an electromagnetic signal. Just over six months' production."

"Faster-than-light communication. The Da Silva. Otherwise known as freewave, and no wonder."

He nodded. "Yup. We've got that. Costs a bomb, but it works. Which is why we're confident that the same principles will work for *Star Pyramid*. Give me a gram of the stuff and I could move a cat from here to *Valles Marineris* in a split second. But we don't have a gram of it. With today's technology, even allowing for improvements, we'd be talking a billion years or so to *make* that much, and even then it would only teleport one pussycat to the nearest planet. A ship? To a star? Lifetime of the Universe. So the only remotely feasible way to get enough is to wait until *Star Pyramid* goes out there, grabs a big chunk of it for us, and uses some of it to come back."

Which reminded me of my original question.

"Sean, like I asked just now: *why a pyramid?*"

He leaned forward, excited now. I was getting to his own speciality.

"Gently, OK? Keep it *simple*, Sean."

He drew a deep breath.

"You mentioned a sixth-degree energy minimum. That's flatter than a parabola, but not flat enough. In fact, no singularity in one dimension is flat enough. We tried it with the hypersignal experiments from Lhasa to Marsport, but the signal-to-noise ratio was *awful.* More noise-to-signal. Do Carmo's voice sounded like the original wax-cylinder gramophone record!"

"Phonograph, Sean. Invented by Thomas Alva Edison in 1887."

His face showed the bland expression of the historically unconcerned, though he didn't roll his eyes. "Whatever. I wouldn't want to send a human being through something that disruptive. I wouldn't want to send a cat."

"Scrambled cat?"

"You're telling me. No, to get real fidelity in transmission, the domain has to be flat in two different directions, and the only way to arrange that in any reliable manner is *symmetry.* In two dimensions. Along the third, though, we need asymmetry. Otherwise the ship would be just as likely to go backwards as forwards. Aim for Leo and wind up in Aquarius.

"Anyhow… square symmetry is good enough for the two-dimensional energy trough. Put that together with a heavy lack of symmetry along the axis, and… well, a pyramid is pretty obvious, isn't it?"

He went quiet as I digested the implications.

Eventually, I said: "What about *more* symmetry, like a cone? That would be more convenient for artificial gravity. Uniform at a given radius when they spin the ship."

He eased back into his chair.

"Absolutely," he said. "In theory. But we can't manufacture that shape to fine enough tolerances. The imperfection sensitivity is horrendous with a cone. Remember how the Norwegians lost sixteen giant wind turbines to a freak North Sea wave?"

"Leading to the 2041 bread riots and the European Secessional Wars. Of course I do. You mean *symmetries* caused that?"

"Yup. Big cylindrical struts, circular symmetry like your cone. Never tested in waves that high, no one expected them to be possible. Buckled at loads way below theory. All caused by tiny imperfections.

"Believe you me, Assessor Li, that problem is bad enough with a pyramid. But it's within our capabilities if we're really, really careful. Lasers go in straight lines. Dammit, the ancient Egyptians lined the things up with the stars using little more than string!

"If we had the level of control needed to make conical Da Silva ships, we could do even better with something simpler. A cube or octahedron would give *three* dimensions of flatness using straight components. It'd be worth it: it would need only 1/81 as much mahabhavium. A bugger to steer, though, more like a coracle than a canoe, but the forwards/backwards issue could be solved if we had enough experience with Da Silva drives.

"Thing is, we won't get that unless *Star Pyramid* returns from Karoubi's Star with a cargo of mahabhavium big enough to fill a wheelbarrow."

He'd answered my question, but opened up another.

"You mean," I said, "for our great-great-great-whatever grandchildren to fill an antigravity slingship. Well, I'll try to make sure we get it for them."

CHAPTER 4

PARALLEL UNIVERSES (2)

Thekla Maury

Global Union Forward Planning Section
Social Policy Unit, Tōkyō 2157

"But why a pyramid?"

I'd flown in that morning on the red-eye MHDrive saucer from Sumatra, where I was Director of the Psychosocial Dynamics Laboratory of the Pangkalpinang Institute for Advanced Study. I hadn't had much sleep, but I was used to that. I trotted out the usual answer.

"It pretty much has to be for the thing to work at all, Joel."

Joel Krantz, a senior manager in the GUFPS Social Policy Unit, gave a wry shake of the head. "You didn't come all that way just to tell me that."

No, I didn't.

He thought I was here at his request, to help with employees who had mental health problems. Which I would do, of course, but I was there for reasons of my own. Which he needed to know about, but wouldn't like.

He had a pleasant office, light and airy, with a tiled floor that was mostly covered by rugs. As rug collections go, it was an impressive one. The walls were bare; I would have expected original artwork, but the only things breaking the flat white surfaces were grilles for heating and cooling. Right now, cooling: Tōkyō was as hot and sticky as the inside of a marathon runner's shoe. I'd dressed for the climate, though you wouldn't have guessed it from the smart office suit, traditional navy blue skirt (yes, *skirt*) and jacket, and prim white blouse. I'd had it tailored in a back-street lean-to in Hong Kong, from the latest generation of self-cooling fabrics. The blouse was faux-silk, open neck. All very retro, every inch the power-dressing exec. Despite which, I'd been sweating like a— no, pigs *don't* sweat, god knows why we always imagine they do. Perspiring like the proverbial, OK? But it was comfortable in Krantz's office. Not aggressively cool, just... not too hot.

So I kept the jacket on.

Krantz couldn't have been a bigger contrast – brightly coloured loungewear and real leather cowboy boots. Heavily built with a neck like a bull, wide shoulders, muscular. I'd read his file, and knew he worked out regularly with weights, but not as a body-builder: just to improve his ability to intimidate. It worked with most people, but not with me: I could sense the deep insecurity that led him to behave that way.

The boots suited him, he was a bit of a cowboy in the derogatory sense, a sloppy worker at everything except weight training and office politics. As a result, he'd been promoted well above his comfort zone, and once you reach that level the sky's the limit, because they're nearly all like that. The last thing they want is a competitor with brains who puts serious effort into doing the work.

That sounds as though I dislike him. The paradox of Joel Krantz is that he's a really likeable guy. Right up to the moment the knife slides into you from behind. He has a charm that's very hard to resist, even when you know what he's really like.

We were eleven floors up, with a view of the bay area and part of the Tōkyō-Yokohama metropolis. Tall buildings hid much of the actual *bay*, but sunlight made patterns on the rippling water as passing cargo ships disturbed it with their wakes. In places the city had stolen from the bay great blocks of reclaimed land. This made the bay smaller than it had been a century earlier, and the dozen or so artificial islands were linked by overhead cable-cars, each the size of a bus. GU Headquarters was situated on one of them: an artificial island some five kilometres north-east of the Rokugō estuary, ten south of the Kōtō shoreline. It was an octagonal prism surmounted by a pyramid surmounted by a square tower, and it was half a kilometre high. Above the revolving observation deck a communication pylon thrust into the sky, budded with clustered bouquets of microwave antennas like a single delphinium stem only partly into bloom.

If I craned my neck I could see a splash of green – the geodomed gardens of the ancient Imperial Palace – between and over the massed monoliths of corporate commerce and global government that crowded the shores of Tōkyō-wan in a clambering ferroconcrete hubbub and sprawl.

I stopped gazing at the scenery and looked Joel in the eye.

"I'd like to answer your question in my own way," I said. "At first what I say will seem irrelevant. Then it will seem ridiculous and insulting. But if you hear me out, you'll not only understand, but there's a fair chance you'll agree."

87%, according to Computational Psychonics's 706.

He looked intrigued rather than annoyed. "I can tell you're a psychosocial dynamicist. I've set aside two hours for this meeting, Thekla. That may turn out to be one hour 59 minutes too long, but I'll suspend judgment until you get round to the punchline."

Krantz had placed his desk so that he sat with his back to the big window, as relaxed as a cat on a lambskin rug. The view could distract his visitors, like me, but not him. Not that I was going to let myself be distracted. Woman on a mission, that was me.

"Thanks. I'll go the historical route. Why were the *original* pyramids built?"

Krantz wasn't expecting this, but held his peace, and bit his lower lip, thinking. I knew his passion was football – watching, not playing – so he was unlikely to know much archaeology, but everyone had heard of the pyramids. Only surviving member of the Seven Wonders of the World. We were well into the construction of the eighth, and it dwarfed all the rest combined.

He blinked as recollection dawned.

"Tombs."

"Good. Anything else?"

"Weren't they... kind of... resurrection machines? To propel the dead pharaoh into the afterlife, up among the stars? Each pharaoh had one built–"

"Sneferu built *three*. The engineering data suggest that there were sometimes several being constructed at the same time."

I pulled my chair closer to his desk. It scraped uneasily against the tiled floor. Ignoring his pained look, I ploughed ahead with my prepared pitch.

"Do you know about the satellite archaeology revolution of the 2020s?"

"Saw something about it a year or two back. Didn't they find a lost city?"

"Several. Would've been more, but most ancient city sites are now *modern* city sites, and even a satellite can't see through six floors of solid concrete. Lots of villages, towns, temples large and small, palace or two, harbours, canals... The new methods more than tripled the known sites without turning a single spadeful of sand. It was controversial; Egyptological scholars were still wallowing in the comfortable mud of their old mindset. But it gave results that no one could deny. When the dust had settled, so to speak, Egyptologists realised that the Fourth Dynasty had built more pyramids than there were pharaohs to bury in them. And by

2100 that discovery had revived an earlier theory, long thought to have been discredited, but always teasingly plausible. You're right, of course, pyramids were *used* as tombs and believed to bring the occupant back to life among the circumpolar stars – but that was incidental to their main purpose."

Krantz pushed some datacubes into a rough pile, toyed with a ballpoint. Buying time to respond. I stared past him at a container ship, apparently floating half way between two tall spires, waiting for him to collect his thoughts.

"So why *did* they build them?" he said. "It must have used up an incredible amount of labour."

I grinned. He'd fed me the line I'd been fishing for. "Exactly."

His brow furrowed. "Not following you."

"They built them to use up an incredible amount of labour."

That woke him up. "Crap, Thekla. You work to produce things, to get things. Not just for the sake of working! Couldn't the pharaohs have made their slaves do something *useful?* Roads, irrigation schemes, things like that?"

I stared at him, aghast. "Slaves? That old lie was discredited centuries ago. Herodotus, a Greek historian, made it up. He made *everything* up. 'The Father of Lies', some called him. Though some of what he wrote was true. He was also called 'the Father of History'."

"I sometimes wonder whether lies and history are the same thing," Krantz said.

"Depends on who's telling the alleged lies and who's writing the alleged history," I said. "But facts can be objective, and the slave stuff wasn't. Not Herodotus's finest hour. Either he was sowing anti-Egyptian propaganda or just imagining that the rest of the world was like slave-owning Greece.

"No, the pharaoh's workforce was composed of peasant farmers, and they were well looked after. Food, drink, medical care. Some were allowed to build their own tombs in their spare time – so they must've *had* spare time. Thing was, they sometimes had too much. So they had to be kept busy when their fields were flooded by the annual Nile inundation. Upper and Lower Egypt had been unified five hundred years earlier, but politically the union was still very fragile. Up till then their flood-season pastime had been raiding their neighbours, but the new unified government didn't approve of anything that might destabilise its still-tenuous grasp of the Nile Valley and the Delta."

"So they had to keep the peasants busy?"

"They had to keep the peasant *men* busy. The women were always busy, of course. But the men would sit around talking and getting drunk, just like they do today. And that could've led to violence.

"Roads? Egypt had its own freeway system, the river Nile. It didn't need roads. Didn't use wheels, not then. Not much point with all that sand. Irrigation? They already had a vast system of canals, and the Nile floods did the irrigation donkey-work." I laughed. "And the donkeys, of course. When they needed to shift a lot of water they had donkey-powered lifting gear."

"They could have built dams to control the floods," he persisted, a glint in his eye. Krantz liked nothing better than a good argument. To his credit, always a polite one. Grizzly bear on its best behaviour.

Two could play that game. In fact, it needed at least two, and it always got hopelessly complicated with more. So I said:

"They had the good sense not to, Joel. The French dammed the Nile at Qalyūb in 1860 but the water just seeped round it. The British dammed it at Aswan around 1900, and the Russians financed the Aswan High Dam sixty years later, which was highly controversial and did huge ecological damage, whatever its advantages might have been.

"I'm not claiming the pharaohs were into ecology. They just considered it sacrilege to mess up the annual floods that the Pharaoh had kindly persuaded the gods to provide for the benefit of his people. You can sneer, but it was a more enlightened attitude than any government had in the 20th or early 21st. Anything you can figure out as *useful*, its use always has side effects that you *can't* figure out.

"It's a common thread throughout human history. Transformative tech always looks wonderful at first when all its advantages strike home. Then, just when it's infiltrated its seductive way into just about everything, we discover we've made a bargain with the Devil."

Krantz grunted. Scratched an earlobe. "Yeah, I know what you mean."

"Ancient Rome using lead pipes for its water supply. Easy to make, convenient, fulfilling a public need. Taking years off people's lives, damaging their brains–"

"And all those crises of the 21st century," he said. "Which no one saw coming. Coal, oil, plastic, unregulated AI–"

"Lots of people saw them coming, Joel. But the men with the moneybags muddied the waters enough to stop governments taking action, and the turkeys kept voting for Christmas until they were served up on plates with sage and onion stuffing and pigs in blankets, and *finally* realised they weren't on to a winner.

"Anyway, the Aswan High Dam raised water levels upstream, irrigated the desert all right, created vast new fields for farmers… and also sucked up salts from the ground, making many of the new fields unusable in the long run. Then Lake Nasser started to silt up."

"Dammed if they do, and dammed if they don't," he said. Krantz could never resist a joke, however feeble or predictable.

"Joel, please be serious. Pyramids, now – a different matter altogether." I was warming to my theme by then; the words were flowing like an undammed Nile. "Pyramids just sat there, on unproductive land, looking spectacular, and got thousands of northerners and southerners working together to build them. They worked in teams with names like 'The white crown of Khnum-Khufu is powerful' or 'Enduring gang', like the Maoist communists in the 1960s or the PanAfrican Sodality eighty years ago when it was first emerging. The point was *social* engineering, just like all the work the priests had been doing to turn two lots of gods into aspects of each other. It worked, too; Egypt was glued into a single nation, one that survived for thousands of years despite occasional hiccups. And the proof that it worked is that never again did they build anything that big."

His face was a picture as he mulled over what I'd said.

"There must be somewhere round here we can get a coffee," I said. "Let's break, and I'll explain where you're going wrong."

* * *

There was a café area two floors down, and we found a quiet corner where no one would overhear us. Joel got a flat white and a slice of cake for himself, and a long black for me.

On one wall a flatscreen HV projection was showing *Star Pyramid*, a half-finished frame of thousands of metal girders 293 metres long and 230 square at the base, being fussed over by ugly-looking construction craft, welding bots crawling along them throwing off showers of sparks, cylindrical barges bringing materials from the Belt, with a crescent Moon artistically poised in the background.

Joel stared at it. "Must be a historical channel," he said. "She's a lot more advanced than that. The outer skin went on twelve years ago. All the action now is inside."

He sipped his coffee and took a mouthful of cake.

"You were trying to convince me that the Egyptian pharaohs built pyramids to *use up* surplus labour. You *really* think that?"

Sometimes silence is best. I wanted him to convince himself. But he needed a bit of encouragement. "Uh-huh."

"What has this to do with the Project, anyway?" Then the light dawned. "Oh."

I nodded.

He didn't look happy. "That's crazy. You're telling me that *Star Pyramid* is that kind of project! But it's not! It's about giving humanity the stars. Infinite resources. Dealing with overpopulation."

"Yes. Just as the Great Pyramid was about propelling Khufu into the afterlife and bringing prosperity to the land."

"Oh."

"Joel, I understand your commitment to the Project, but humanity doesn't *need* the stars. The Solar System will give us boundless resources for the next million years."

He uncrossed his legs and sat up, stretching his shoulders back.

"Don't be so sure of that, Thekla. The global population settled down to a steady nine billion by the end of the 21st, but when new resources opened up in the Belt, everyone decided there was no more need for restraint, and it started to shoot up again. Asteroid mining made the problem *worse*. It's another example of what you were just describing, the great idea that turned out to be a total bummer."

It hadn't been quite that straightforward, but he had a point.

Which I evaded.

"Mining the asteroid belt will always be far more practical than interstellar commerce," I said, "even if Da Silva drives could be made as cheaply as cans of energy-drink."

He didn't say anything immediately, but he left me in no doubt that I was arguing with a very big male animal keeping its aggressive reflexes under tight control.

"All very well, Thekla, but that's only true if humanity gets its act together and we all *cooperate* instead of fighting each other over madcap ideologies and pointless toys."

"On *that* we agree, Joel. The Project isn't about economics, population growth, or resources. It's about politics. Even though we've got the Global Union now, its grasp on power is distinctly shaky, like early dynastic Egypt. The signs are everywhere. Half of NorMerica getting ready to secede, repressive religionists crawling back out of the woodwork, fossil fuel production *increasing* when we desperately need it to stop altogether… And the GU has stuck one hand up its arse by *defining* itself in terms of nations!

"We need a unification job, Joel. Far more than the Egyptians ever did. Our secular priesthood is doing its best, trying to convince hard-liners that capitalism is socialistic, true communism requires managerial enterprise, all the rest of it – fitting Seth and Horus into the same system, basically – but it's not enough.

"We need – and have now got – the biggest boondoggle of all time."

Well, I'd convinced myself, but convincing Joel Krantz wasn't going to be so easy.

He was getting angry. Good enough at his job to conceal it, but I'd pushed too many buttons for him to keep a poker face.

"Back to my earlier point, Thekla. Updated. If a massive project is needed to unite humanity – and I'm not conceding that it is, or that *Star Pyramid* is nothing more than a vanity project – why not choose one that achieves something *useful*? Eliminate poverty. Bring the Mediterranean back to life. Reforest the Amazon Dustbowl. Why *waste* all that labour, all those resources?"

The same objections always came up when I revealed the truth about *Star Pyramid*. Not that I did it very often, and only to people I knew could be trusted to keep it under wraps. Mind you, I did sometimes think that I could have shouted it from the rooftops, because no one would've believed it. That's because the scam was working. Anyway, I had the answers off pat.

"I didn't say it was a vanity project. Just that what you see is not what you get. The alternatives you mentioned are all very worthy, and we should be doing them too. But you can't wipe out poverty in a single big project. It's local and structural, not a shortage of resources. Remember Venezuela? Oil-rich back in the days when oil was seen as an asset, but it came to pieces completely because of corrupt leaders."

"You need resources to cure poverty, though."

Touché. "Agreed. But if all we do is pour in resources without targeting them, the rich get richer, the corrupt get… corrupter, if there's such a word, the poor get poorer, the sick get sicker. The GU's putting huge resources into the Amazon, and the benefits are universal – even politicians like to breathe – but you still hear people asking 'Why should we pay to clear up the Brazzies' mess?'. And if those same people ever learned the true cost, we'd never keep the homemade nukes out.

"The most damnable thing is that if the GU reaches for a proper grip, the local rich use local nationalism to fight it off, keeping *their* grip on the local poor. The problem is an exaggerated sense of local identity and entitlement. Not only that: War on Poverty noises would trigger nationalistic disputes about which resources went where. What's needed is a project so huge and monolithic that the entire world has to be in it up to its neck, *and* its successful conclusion will benefit *everyone*."

He stroked his square chin with an enormous hand. "Or they just need to *believe* that its successful conclusion will benefit *them*."

He was definitely getting it now.

"It's not exactly a lie, Joel. It *would* benefit everyone. But the real ways that would happen are far too subtle for a public relations campaign. The message has to be short, snappy, and simple. With enough truth to survive any counter-culture that tries to shoot it down, but not the *whole* truth. Oh no."

Even now, he wasn't willing to cave in. Mouth set, jaw jutting. Voice a low growl.

"What about scientific projects? Huge new particle accelerators…"

"Already being done. Don't you see? That's why the physicists keep getting their money. The biologists have never really figured it out; they think the GU is more *interested* in the fundamental units of matter than in genetic grafts of cancer immunity! No, it's another case of pyramid-building."

I could see him mulling it over. He was high enough in the GU hierarchy to distinguish truth from propaganda, and he'd seen enough horse-trading to know that the Project wasn't the marvel of sweetness and light that it was held up to be. He ran a hand through his thinning hair. Even in the 22nd Century no one had cracked male pattern baldness. Just slowed it down. Slid the hand over the back of his neck, gave it a scratch. The picture of a Deep Thinker. I suspected it was really just a subconscious distraction, trying to pretend he was about to come up with the killer put-down.

He did try.

"You do have an original way of thinking, Thekla. Aren't you just shoehorning in any evidence that can be distorted enough to fit your thesis?"

Feeble. I waved an airy hand as if batting away an errant fly. Batting away criticism. I had the measure of him, now.

"I'm being selective, yes. Building a case. This is politics, Joel, not a logical debate. But think about it. Accelerators are really pretty tiny, even the Lhasatron. A hundred-kilometre circle, sure, but all the expensive equipment is confined to the perimeter tunnel. You could build a city inside it, and they'd've done so by now if the vibrations from traffic wouldn't disrupt the beam's stability.

"Accelerators, even the larger ones, soak up a fraction of what the armaments budgets throw around, and that's in a world allegedly at peace. They don't give off that world-busting-a-gut feeling that's needed. And particle accelerators aren't *comprehensible*. The physicists have been down to three fundamental building blocks, and back up to a hundred, at least four times as their kit gets more energetic. The public hasn't been with it since the Dark Matter fiasco led to the demise of quarks. And now they've *really* messed up! To be fair, the Lhasatron was *almost* big enough to work as a pyramid; people got really excited just by the size of the beast. But now it's gone and produced something *useful!*"

Joel nodded. "And the adverse side effect is obvious, even to me. Not enough of it."

He was definitely coming round to my way of thinking.

I finished my coffee. He'd already polished off his, and the cake.

"Let's go back to your office," I said.

* * *

"You were saying that we don't have enough mahabhavium. Everyone knows that, of course, but it's the key to all of the politicking and economic horse-trading, and you're absolutely right to focus on it."

Joel laughed. "No need to butter me up, Thekla."

"I'm not. Never works on you, anyway. No, I was just picking up the thread. What we have is nowhere near enough, and it never will be. Even if we set the Lhasatron to full time production of mahabhavium – which would cause the physicists to go on strike, they think it's their toy for para-soliton scattering experiments – we might get the rate up to three billion atoms a day. There's no way we can distribute such a scarce resource fairly. It's enough to start a war on its own. Everyone wants it, no one can possibly get enough of it.

"We could build more accelerators, but that would take decades, and there still wouldn't be enough. It would just make the problem worse: more to fight over, not enough to keep everyone happy.

"OK, I get it. So what should we do with the stuff? Throw it away?"

I didn't think he meant it seriously, but it suited my purpose to pretend I did.

"If you want worldwide riots, sure," I said. Raised an admonitory finger. "No, we use it for *Star Pyramid*. All of it. If the production rate goes up, if and when more accelerators are built, we use more. We use the *whole* world production for a *world* project. We stockpile every atom of mahabhavium that can be created over the next forty years. That goes with the ship when she's ready to roll, to power her Da Silva comm, the *k*-field linkage used in the eka-Bussard, and the Impact Avoidance System. After she's gone we use the continuing production down here to build bigger and better freewave communicators to keep in touch with *Star Pyramid*."

Joel got up, pacing around the room like a caged tiger. Not a happy bunny.

I kept up the barrage.

"You starting to see why we need a pyramid? Anything we can't share out equally, we put it into the Project and it's no longer divisive: just part of the Great World Effort. Even the people who refuse to support space research as romantic exploration are jumping on board because *Star Pyramid* is going to bring back mahabhavium by the barrowload."

He stopped pacing, swept his pile of datacubes into a drawer, making room for him to perch on the edge of his desk, directly opposite me. Leaned forward, hands on knees. Pursed his lips, shook his head. You didn't need three degrees in Computational Psychonics to know he wasn't ready to concede.

"Doesn't that destroy your thesis?" he said quietly. "Isn't that *useful?*"

Joel might not have been bright, but he had a certain animal cunning that sometimes made him seem smart, though a little unimaginative. It didn't do him much good on this occasion, because, to a psychodynamicist like me, he was nowhere as intimidating as he imagined, nor as smart. I had the answer to that one off pat too, it always comes up eventually.

"It does, and it is – but not yet. She has to go to Karoubi's star at normal sublight speeds, and she'll take just over 400 years to get there. She'll come back, *zapppp!*, by Da Silva drive, but if we haven't got a stable World Government by then we'll all be dead.

"She'll bring back enough mahabhavium to require a global industrial makeover, which will be tricky, but it'll be enough to share round. She can go back again to get more mahabhavium, multiple trips. And of course, the main early use will be to build more Da Silva starships. Smaller ones, we won't need another giant pyramid. Quicker, smarter, cheaper. It's a self-sustaining virtuous circle. And people can grasp that.

"Forty years to build her, with every nation contributing people, components, things they can *see*. Then the hope for all Earth together heading out among the stars… We need that to turn everyone from local nationalists into world citizens, because without world citizens there'll be no chance of forming a World Government. The Global Union will remain a machine for spiky compromises. Like Common Europe and PanAfrica."

He walked round the desk to his chair and sat down.

"All very well, Thekla. You've done a beautiful job convincing me that it has to be a *metaphorical* pyramid. But my original question was actually a simpler one. *Why that shape?*"

I laughed. "Like I said, Joel, it pretty much has to be. Oh, I know the engineers say the shape is more or less inevitable for a Da Silva ship, but it's not the only shape with the right symmetries. Engineers always have engineering reasons for why their designs are inevitable, but they're the most psychosocially illiterate group on the planet and they have absolutely no insight into their own motives. Remember the old phallic airplanes and rockets? It was only when most engineers were women that we got rid of the aerodynamic penis thrusting through the air, in favour of MHD saucer shapes that pass the air around them and go supersonic without a shockwave. The basic principles had been around for fifty years, but the males couldn't give up raping the sky."

It was his turn to laugh. "OK, OK. But aren't the saucer shapes kind of – er – *female?*"

"Central cavity as womb? Not to mention– no, not to mention. It's not the shape as such, Sean; it's the hidden symbolism. I concede that the engineers' technical reasons for a design are usually valid, within their limits and given their unspoken assumptions, but they're never the real reason for building the object in that form. Trust me, Joel, I'm a psychosocial dynamicist."

Steepled fingers, now: he seemed to be buying it.

"You're saying that a pyramid is… a massive penis *and* a womb symbol! Male and female principles combined. The tomb, deep in the old ones, the hollow chamber of the Da Silva drive–"

I cut him short with a gesture. "Not exactly. It's subtler. Everything is either convex or concave. Sometimes a banana is just a banana. That old Freudian language is a very rough approximation to modern computational psychonics, and the psychic power of pyramids leads a bit further than from elementary psychoanalysis to aircraft design… but, yeah, you've got the basic idea. The pyramid shape checks out as a psychosocial unifying symbol to five decimal places, *and* it's been field-tested."

He chuckled. "*Field*-tested? You mean those idiots who claimed that putting razor blades inside cardboard pyramids would keep them sharp for years?"

"I'm not talking about alleged physical effects, Joel. Pyramids affect the human mind. That's why people believed the razor-blade claims. And the people pushing the idea weren't idiots. They understood how to leverage that symbolism into hard cash. Not very scrupulous, I admit, but capitalism never is."

He mulled it over. "So what *do* you mean by 'field-tested', then?"

Good. He's stopped arguing with me and started to ask questions. It's so much easier to get information across if the intended recipient isn't pushing back. Direct quote from CompPsych 1.01.

"All over the world, for millennia," I said. "It unified the Egyptians. It unified the Teotihuacanos a couple of thousand years later. Stupas all over the far East had pyramidal sacred stone umbrellas over them. A pagoda is just a temple for a god or a ruler, with a multi-pyramid umbrella over it for extra honour. The mandala base of the shape… and look how the cults that that Scottish astronomer royal – I forget his name – set rolling in the 19th Century, are still rolling. But I do remember the name for it: pyramidology. Mystic knowledge that the Egyptians supposedly had, alien visitations, secrets of the universe…"

"Sounds more like pyramidolatry." He held up his hands in mute surrender. "OK, OK, you've convinced me. It's a worthwhile project *and* a shameless boondoggle. But why are you telling me all this?"

I judged I'd softened him up enough to tell him the truth. Well, most of it.

"Because you're next in line to be promoted on to the Steering Committee for the entire Project. Don't try to look modest, everyone knows that. The bosses just need to rubber-stamp the decision. And I want someone on the committee to understand that *Star Pyramid* carries huge psychosocial baggage. Yes, the shape has already been fixed, but that's just the beginning. If they treat the Project purely as a resource-grab, *it will fail.*"

"And humanity will go down with it?" He was into the next stage now: acceptance giving way to worry. Starting to think the consequences through.

"That's what the psychosocial dynamics has been telling me for the past decade, yes. You see… Thing is, the cultists were *right*, in a backhanded sort of way: the psychic power of the pyramid is terrific. But that power applies not to things, but to where psychic power always operates: on the psyche.

"So, the ship that humanity sends to Karoubi's Star *had* to be a pyramid. A literal one. Nothing else would've done the job. If the engineers had come up with something less powerful – a saucer shape, say – it wouldn't have got built. The psychonic symbolism would've been too uncertain. And the surface function of *Star Pyramid* is beautifully comprehensible, so no one asks the awkward questions. We don't have to be public about the true motive: not accessing new resources, but absorbing existing ones to unify the human race."

I'd kept the best till last. "One other thing, which clinches it. Have you noticed what the dimensions of *Star Pyramid* are?"

"Uh– about 200 metres square and 300 long."

"Good enough for government work. More accurately, it's 230 metres square and 293 long."

"So?"

"The base is exactly the same size as that of Khufu's Great Pyramid. The height is exactly twice that of Khufu's Great Pyramid. There's no way that engineering considerations alone would've arrived at those dimensions! *The GU is trying to outdo Khufu.*

"Which reminds me. Don't talk to anyone about this – *especially* the engineers!"

CHAPTER 5

PARALLEL UNIVERSES (3)

Gordon Shapiro

Farflung episode #43, X-Stream HoloVision 2157

"But why a pyramid?"

Lucinda Gracewell, piece to camera.

"It pretty much had to be for the thing to work at all."

Pregnant pause.

"But why is that?"

She puts on a puzzled look.

"What's so special about a pyramid?

"Think of it *this* way. Why is a drinks can a tube? Why are chocolate boxes square? Why are footballs oval?"

Cylinder, I thought. *Rectangular. Spherical. No, she's referring to* American *football.* But hey.

You might have expected an explanation in terms of structural integrity, or some other techie thing.

The audience didn't.

I didn't.

I knew what was coming.

"Because those icons have instant recognition! They identify the brand, and consumers identify *with* the brand! But – even better – the *Star Pyramid* brand was *different!* Steeped in ancient mystic power, as familiar as the nose on your face, but unjustly neglected. *Nobody* packed things in *pyramids!*"

Well, there were once things called tetrapacks. But she was right enough for HV. On the whole, they didn't. Until the world went mad for pyramania. Pyramidiocy, I call it. Now *everything* is packed in pyramidal containers.

"Nobody. Nothing. Not until *Star Pyramid* came along. Now, of course…"

Montage: Pyramidal boxes rolling off production lines by the thousand. Pyramidal soap, pyramidal chocolate. Pyramidal perfume bottles. Models wearing pyramidal *dresses*. Female, male… indeterminate.

"Old and new both at the same time. A stroke of genius. And by now the brand is *so* firmly established that changing it would be like changing the recipe for hoka-kola!

"But first, fellow Earthlings, the ship had to be built!"

I groaned. After several decades of media treatment, the fashionably hairless HV presenter was obviously desperate.

Me even more so. *Fellow Earthlings.* I swore under my breath and gritted my teeth as the feed washed over my eyes and the laboured script assailed my ears. *Farflung's* ratings were already plummeting, and the saturation coverage of the formal commencement of *Star Pyramid's* construction hadn't helped. The ceremonies were colourful, but the content was zero.

We'd been doing so well. *Farflung* had made its mark by not insulting the viewers' intelligence. Well, not insulting it too much. But, like everyone else trying to make serious programmes, we'd had to move with the times. Come to terms with the limited attention-span. Find imaginative ways to engage with what little attention remained.

My job as producer was well paid, and I didn't want to lose it. But unless the ratings picked up, I'd be out on my ear.

Lucinda was doing her best. Her sparkly personality could make watching paint dry interesting. That and her see-through dress.

"A *quarter* of Earth's productive capacity was already being turned towards the Project."

Scan of toiling masses, orbital factory, patient monkish face tending chip growth, nodule mining on the Atlantic floor.

"But the world had to be *sure*. The eka-Bussard had to be *tested*."

A familiar image: against the starry background, a spear of blue light. A thousand kilometres behind the ship, the flow becomes turbulent, producing multicoloured flames at the spear's base as the roiling gases cool.

Pretty, but not exactly original. Well, that's archival material for you. Does the job, just about, and we can't afford to acquire more original footage.

"Robert Bussard's classic design proposed using vast magnetic scoops–"

Great curling lines superimpose on the picture.

"– to sweep up hydrogen ions from the interstellar void and fuel a fusion motor. Bussard argued that the faster the ship moved–"

Yeah, yeah... The science advisor had argued against visible motion relative to the stars, but what else could you do?

"– the faster it would scoop up fuel. So it would speed up *forever*, getting closer and closer to the speed of light."

The stars begin to whiz by.

"Unfortunately, it's not that simple."

The stars slow down with a jerk. *Yeah, that's the word.*

"A *tiny part* of the stuff that fills the emptiness can be used as fuel. The rest *piles up* ahead of the ship."

Old clips of an icebreaker in the Arctic pack-ice, struggling to break through a wall of displaced ice. A hand is trying to push an enormous funnel through water, wide end first. The muscles stand out like knots. A fish overtakes the funnel.

"The energy balances out at a *fraction* of lightspeed. *Any* scoop has that problem. Fusion drives aren't *powerful* enough. By the end of the Twentieth, the Bussard ramdrive was no more than a historical footnote in an obscure journal."

Shot of obsolete library disk.

"The great thing was –" big smile, one to melt the stoniest heart. Problem is, Marcia Aikwood is widely believed not to possess one, and she's Head of Programming. "– the discovery that told us we couldn't survive *without* starflight also revived the Bussard."

Clichéd shot of the seven Indian physicists – four women, three men – working at the hundred kilometre accelerator at Lhasa. Zoom in on one face.

"Nilakantashastri was from Sri Lanka, once called Serendip, where the Three Princes 'were always making discoveries, by accidents and sagacity, of things they were not in quest of.' What they were *not* looking for – what *nobody* was looking for – was the element we now call *mahabhavium*."

Montage of crock of gold at rainbow's end, alchemists seeing solutions turn to gold, a mare sitting in a huge bird's nest, intercut with neo-Zen image of sudden illumination, light breaking through clouds.

Desperate, desperate. Marcia will throw a fit. *I'd better start looking for alternative employment. My wives won't like it.*

"Element 126, the stuff that makes transmutation of elements *cheap* and *easy*, and moves matter from one place to another *without* the passing of time."

Lucinda's glossy head appears again, and she pouts prettily.

"You know why we can't show you any. The amount of mahabhavium in the Solar System wouldn't fill a teaspoon. Every atom is worth ten megacredits, and *every single one* is human-made."

Teaspoon? I wish. But we can't talk nanograms.

A pause: her voice becomes more serious.

"We know its spectrum. That's the kind of light it emits when it's a hot gas. but we've never put enough of it together in one place to know what colour it is when it's solid."

The view turns to the night sky, zooming in on a tiny region of the constellation Leo. The orange dwarf companion dominates the image. The gas clouds around Karoubi's Star, first found by Zelda Zimmermann's spectral survey, just barely show as a faint smudge. Karoubi's star itself is a pulsar, far too small to be visible except in the X-ray spectrum, and even then only as the origin of its plasma jets and the filamentary structure the astronomers had dubbed the Mare's Tail. So Graphics kindly overlays a small red dot.

"It's the spectrum that clinches it. The line *missing* from this light says that in the gasclouds around Karoubi's Star there is mahabhavium by the *megaton*.

"Unfortunately, it's nearly four hundred light years away. The only way to get there was a Bussard ramjet that worked. So the world's superboffins figured out how to fix it using realistic amounts of mahabhavium!"

She didn't explain how. But then, the only people in the audience who'd want to know already did. And 'efferent karmabhumic antistrophe' doesn't exactly roll off the tongue.

"And so *Star Pyramid*, the great Project, was conceived and born. Twenty years in the planning, forty more in the execution. If the Project succeeds, we'll walk among the stars."

The shot moves back, becoming an outside view of the whole galaxy.

"If not–"

Zoom in on the Solar System, to Earth, to an old man ploughing a dusty field with a pointed stick.

"– when the metals and the fluorine and the germanium are all *gone*, when it takes more energy to *recover* used materials from the environment than the environment can safely absorb –"

Lucinda is back. On a roll now, quality much improved. *Maybe I'll survive this fiasco.* Close-up on that dress. Stay just the right side of pornographic. Sexier that way.

So I'm told.

"– we *die*."

She morphs into the old man, and the viewpoint pans back to reveal that he is ploughing the remains of the World HV Centre.

Voiceover only: "The Global Union will preserve us for a few more centuries – but if *Star Pyramid* does not return laden with mahabhavium…"

The view rises in silence over the surrounding ruins, artistically computed, of the city of São Sebastião do Rio de Janeiro.

PART THREE

FLASHBACK: BEGINNINGS

CHAPTER 6

KARMABHUMI

Jayakatwang Loon

Stockholm 2083

I remembered vividly how it had all begun, years ago.

Now I was reaping the rewards.

"I'm honoured to accept the Nobel Prize in Physics for 'advancing the mathematics of twelve-dimensional space, reinterpreting the four forces of nature as phase resonances, and predicting new phenomena caused by existence waves'."

I read the words carefully from the teleprompter that projected them directly on to my retina. It would not be appropriate to stumble or garble the carefully constructed sentence. Not at the high point of my scientific career.

I'd never cared for awards and prizes, or so I'd told myself, until the fateful day when the message turned up in my inbox. Even then I assumed it was a prank, until a limousine arrived with the official letter. Can you believe it? A physical *letter*. On crisp headed notepaper, signed by all 63 members of the High Cabinet of Common Europe.

With real ink.

I contacted the Indonesian embassy, and after a nervous few hours they confirmed that it was true. I confess, I discovered I felt differently about prizes. If nothing else, the money would be good.

Anyway, back to the presentation ceremony. A citation, a medal, handshakes all round... and now I had to explain, to an audience of the great and the good, but unfortunately not primarily the scientific or the numerate, about the discovery/invention of what were already being called the Loon Equations.

While the chattering died down I ran my eyes over the rows of VIPs in their smart suits and expensive dresses, hems ranging from ankle-length to pelmet. Some would spot the half-truths and not-quite-analogies that let me avoid technical details that only a highly trained professional could even begin to understand. Most of them were there because, on that day and at that time, the vast and luxurious auditorium was *the* place to be if you were anybody who was anybody. But I'd be just as out of my depth in their worlds, whatever they might be, and in one way or another each of them had as much right as I did to be there. I owed it to them to reward their attendance and attention by making my story comprehensible, so I began with the history, which goes back to the great Dmitri Mendeleev. Indeed, much further, but I had to start somewhere. Aided and abetted by stunning graphics procured by my PR agent, I led my audience quickly through atomic theory, elements and their isotopes, how nuclei become less and less stable as the number of nucleons increases, until elements become radioactive, then so unstable that their lifetimes are measured in nanoseconds. About the suspected Island of Stability where no such thing ought to exist. About elements 124, 164, and – of course – 126.

"By 2037," I said, warming to my task as I saw that most of the audience were still awake, "the stable existence of element 126 had become a theoretical certainty. It should be produced by bombarding atoms of uranium 238 with xenon ions at enormous energies. However, the cost of building a suitable accelerator appeared out of all proportion to the likely benefit, and nothing was done at that time.

"Then came the economic crisis of the late 21st Century, as Earth-based resources began to run dry. Humanity turned to the solar system, directing its not inconsiderable energies at practical problems of spatial industrialisation. Theoretical physics went into a steep decline."

I paused, sipped from the glass of water beside the podium. Still water, not sparkling. Sparkling makes you belch.

"It all picked up again after 2070, though. The Lhasatron was in the late stages of construction, which kept the particle physicists happy and helped to get the global economy back on track by throwing government money at it. There was renewed interest in a unified theory of particle interactions, and an explanation of the four forces of nature: gravitational, electromagnetic, weak, strong. The early simple picture of electrons, protons, and neutrons had proliferated into an untamed jungle of neutrinos, pions, mesons, positrons, and innumerable outlandish particles. No sooner than these had been organised by taking a small number of quarks as basic building blocks, did the proliferation begin afresh: charmed quarks, coloured quarks, antiquarks, quirks, quasiquarks, and supersymmetric squawks."

That got a laugh, suggesting they were still listening, though more restrained than I'd hoped for.

"Whenever physicists thought they had tamed the subatomic world, it refused to remain caged. New experiments, at great cost, spent years confirming the existing theory; then one of them would throw a curveball that left the whole shebang up for grabs.

"In the Spring of 2067, I and my colleagues at the Universitas Gadjah Mahda in Jogjakarta – whose medal this is, as much as it is mine, even though their names are not engraved on it – realised that the right way to set up a unified theory of elementary particles and forces of nature was – paradoxically – to abolish the notions of particle and force altogether.

"Imagine a twelve-dimensional manifold–" Belatedly I remembered that I'd been advised not to use this term. For a moment I was forced to improvise. "Think of this as a sort of... jelly. 'Jello' for my American friends. Any flavour will do: what matters is that jelly *wobbles*."

I knew I was back on track because the overhead graphics were showing a jelly, wobbling fit to burst. This got a bigger laugh.

"Wobbles aren't like ordinary matter, even when they're happening in ordinary matter. They can pass through each other unhindered. In some places wobbles reinforce each other; in others a wobble in one direction cancels out one in the opposite direction. Like noise-cancelling ear-buds, yes?

"Now, you must stretch your imaginations to their limits. The wobbles that concern us today take place not in matter, but in a medium that consists only of possibilities. Wobbles in that medium constitute what, for lack of a better term, I call *existence waves*. At peaks, where waves of possibility reinforce each other, things exist; at troughs, where waves cancel, they do not.

"These waves are highly complex, being polarised in eight independent directions. Adding three dimensions of space and one of time – yes, those notions are retained – we obtain a twelve-dimensional space." I had the presence of mind to add: "As I mentioned earlier." *Well, I'd said 'manifold', but they wouldn't notice.*

Then back to the script.

"I was fortunate enough to stumble across a beautiful system of mathematical equations describing these wobbles and their interactions." *Like hell, I spent three years battling with the clumsy annoying things.* "As the waves propagate through the jelly, they're refracted, just like light passing through water. And, like light, they can pile up to create extremely bright shapes, known as *caustics*."

The graphics showed a lens focusing sunlight on to paper, and the paper starting to burn.

"You see where the name comes from. Caustics are where constructive interference occurs in a persistent fashion. A rainbow is a series of circular caustics, one for each colour in the spectrum.

"This focusing effect is what makes existence waves work. A single wobble peaks at isolated points. These correspond to what ancient physicists called instantons: particles that wink into existence and then disappear again. But at caustics, matter can exist along curves. More properly, along four-dimensional continua." *Oops. Ignore.* "A caustic of the – modesty cautions against, but the term has become established – of the Loon Equations is a model of spacetime. The curves are world-lines of travelling particles. If we assume the elasticity of the jelly to be infinite, making it rigid, we recover Einstein's General Theory of relativity, *exactly*. The true elasticity is very large – which is why light moves very fast – so this is an excellent approximation.

"All physical properties of particles, including position – this is important – are determined by the extra eight dimensions of polarisation of the incident waves. Conventional quantum theory is a linear approximation to the Loon Equations, valid on small scales of space and time, though with special exceptions. The four 'forces' of nature are nothing more than phase resonances in various of these dimensions."

And so on...

You can easily find the HV file. There's even a text transcript.

* * *

There was a reception after my acceptance lecture, and I confess I drank too much champagne. I think most people would understand.

Part way into my fifth glass, enthusiastically explaining wave motion to Alicia Berggren, a famous female HV actor – we had asked a waiter for a plate of jelly – a thin, rather drab individual emerged from the crowd and tapped my elbow. Not the one holding the champagne flute, thankfully.

"We need to talk," he said. "Excuse me for butting in–" this to Alicia– "but this is important. I'll bug off in a mo." Then he winked at her.

The accent was antipodean, probably Australian. His tuxedo looked brand new and uncomfortable. Hired for the occasion, I guessed. The clip-on bowtie was at a slight slant. Hair of the Albert Einstein variety, though going thin on the top.

Given the company I was in, I remained polite. "Now?"

"No, not now mate. Course not! But drop by before you go, OK? Anaconda Hotel, tomorrow, breakfast?"

"Well, I–"

"My card." He pressed a rectangle of cardboard into my hand. A real, physical *card*. Printed. With ink. "Call me later to confirm. I promise you won't regret it." He winked at Alicia again. "Loved your performance in *Cuckoo Crazy*."

He disappeared back into the crowd.

"What a strange man," Alicia said. "Bit of a throwback to earlier times. Though I confess I do like his hair. Wild and untamed."

"Also slightly balding," I said, patting my own full head of dark brown hair. "You know, Alicia, he seemed kind of familiar…"

"Look at his card, maybe?"

"Good idea." I took it out of my pocket, and we both peered at it. I was suddenly aware of her perfume, as subtle and seductive as her elegantly coutured dress and the body within.

"Quade Kylie," she said. "Never heard of him."

But I had. "He's an Australian mathematician."

"Strange name."

"Well, 'Kylie' means 'boomerang'."

"And Quade?"

"I think it means 'destroy', actually. Not that people who use it to name their kids realise that. But it sort of fits. He's a bit of an eccentric, lots of weird ideas. Most are mad, but every so often one of them turns out to be a stroke of genius. It's dangerous to underestimate Quade Kylie." I sipped my champagne. "Unfortunately, it's just as dangerous to overestimate Quade Kylie."

She licked her lips. It was fun to watch. "You should take him up on the offer. Maybe this will be one of the strokes of genius."

"I doubt it. But you're right, it would be stupid to turn it down. If it turns out to be nonsense, all I'll waste is an hour or so. Which I'd be spending having breakfast anyway. Thank you."

She took my elbow. "Mr. Loon–""

"Call me Jaya. My friends do."

"Gay or straight, Jaya?"

The question, coming from what I believe is called left field, floored me. When I figured out what she was asking, I said: "Straight."

"Me too. Are you married?"

"No."

"Steady partner? Girlfriend?"

"No. None at all, steady or shaky. Too busy doing physics."

A smile lit up her face, a star going nova. "Well, Jaya my friend, I think you've talked enough physics for tonight. Here's another offer you should take up. This party's winding down. Let's go somewhere else."

I was drunk enough to agree at once. And she *was* attractive. And that *smile*…

"Where?" I asked. Stupidly.

"Would you like to see my hotel?"

"Well, uh–"

"My hotel *room*, silly. And I think you should send Mr. Kylie a text to suggest meeting him for lunch. Not breakfast."

Sweden.

* * *

"You're my first Nobel prize-winner."

"I bet you say that to all the boys."

"Only those who win Nobels."

"Maybe you should collect the set."

"Maybe that's exactly what I'm doing."

* * *

Next morning, over room-service breakfast, Alicia and I looked for news reports of my Nobel lecture.

She found one. It read, in its entirety:

"A new theory of particles has been created by Dr. Jayakatwang Loon. It is revolutionary in principle and mathematically complex."

"You shouldn't have called it a twelve-dimensional manifold, Jaya," Alicia said. "I'm sure your fellow mathematicians and theoretical physicists like that kind of thing, but it puts the newshounds off." She paused to stretch; it looked *wonderful,* even with her clothes on. "Puts *me* off, to be honest," she said.

"What should I call it, then? An existence wave field?"

"Something a lot sexier than 'existence wave', too. Hmmm. Let me call my publicity people."

She dug her phone out from under the bed where it had fallen during the previous night's romp. It was one of the new hPhones with a 3D hologram display. Hugely expensive right now, but the price would soon start to plummet if the things caught on. It was flat and round, like a large biscuit. That, I'd read somewhere, was called a 'dais'. A tiny stage with the hologram images playing the role of actors. She did something with her finger and a single rose blossom appeared. Another flick of a finger and she had a short, animated conversation with someone called Casper.

"Something with Buddhist resonances, you think? Oh, I see. All the rage right now. So kind of Indian? Ah, Sanskrit. And what precisely would you suggest? How d'you spell that? Better still, text me."

Her hPhone pinged and she studied the text panel sprouting from the dais.

"Thanks, Casper. Looks good. What does it mean?"

I waited while whoever she was talking to explained. I couldn't quite hear that end of the conversation. She tossed the phone to the end of the bed.

"Karmabhumi," she said.

I stroked her shoulder, which happened to be the nearest part of her.

"And now you're going to tell me what it means," I cajoled.

"Mmm. Yes. It's Sanskrit. That's– "

"An ancient language from the Indian subcontinent. And it means?

"'Destiny of the Earth', so Casper says."

"Nice."

"Well, near enough. 'Karma' is the universal law of causality that determines everyone's fate. 'Bhumi' is Earth, more significantly the Earth goddess. Specifically, it refers to the ground as opposed to the heavens."

"So I should call it a karmabhumi field? You're telling me that's sexier than the existence wave manifold?"

"Jaya, *anything* is sexier than 'existence wave manifold'."

"I'm not convinced it'll fly with the mathematicians. For a start, they'll spell it all wrong."

"Then shorten it. Call it a k-field."

I rolled the name around on my tongue.

"You know, Alicia, that's not bad."

* * *

Kylie was sitting in the lobby when I walked into the Anaconda hotel. With that profusion of wiry white hair it was impossible to miss him. In many ways the room was like any lobby of any upmarket hotel anywhere in the world: as wide as a baseball field with plush armchairs and couches arranged around low tables, tall plants in huge ceramic pots, a giant HV dais next to a big wall with display facilities, small repeaters on the tables. But busts of former Nobel prize-winners lined the walls on high shelves, and the adjacent bar area formed a circular depression lined with steps, like an ancient amphitheatre. The bar, like the lobby and restaurant, was staffed by men and women.

I waved and took a seat opposite him.

"I've booked lunch for 12.45, like we agreed yesterday," he told me. "There's a restaurant on the mezzo floor, lifts over there." He gestured vaguely at a dark corner of the lobby.

'Mezzo' was obvious, but *lifts?* Ah, elevators. I'd learned my English in Santa Fe.

"But before we eat, I'd like to talk here for a bit if you're OK with that."

I muttered something inane to affirm my willingness to talk.

"I've discovered something surprising about your equations," he said. "Well, it surprised *me*. If you know it already, this'll be a short discussion, but I've not seen it in any of the papers your group's been producing over the years. Not even the most recent ePrints."

"You've been reading our work, then."

He gave me a broad grin. "Lapping it up, mate. It's brillo. The only thing the Nobel committee got wrong was not giving it to you ten years ago."

A waiter materialised beside us and took our lunch orders. A human, not a rowaiter: nowadays you only ran into bots at the bottom end of the hospitality market. He was back two minutes later with our drinks.

Kylie had ordered a beer, I'd gone for a margarita, crushed ice, salt on the rim.

"Brillo,' he repeated. "Also, incomplete."

When I didn't reply immediately, he added, "Sorry, where I come from we say what we mean. I can tell you what's missing."

"Fire away," I said, as I sipped the tequila concoction. "Convince me."

He downed half of his beer in a single gulp, put down the mug, wiped froth off his upper lip. "I'm going to ask you a very basic question, and you'll probably think it's a silly one. What's the most important feature of any physics equation?"

Easy. "Its symmetries. Symmetries imply conserved quantities. Well, continuous ones do."

"Fine. What are the symmetries of the Loon Equations?"

Well, I'd established that six years ago in joint work with Bagaskoro and Ningrum. "Lorentz symmetries of the four spacetime dimensions. Gauge symmetries of the 8-dimensional fibres, extending those of the standard model of particle physics. Those are symplectic, so we're looking at Sp(8) combined with the Lorentz group."

"That's six dimensions for the Lorentz," he said, "plus 8 x 17 for Sp(8) – it's the *compact* symplectic group, yes? – making 142."

"Correct."

"So, if I told you it's actually 144, you'd think I was a few stubbies short of a six-pack."

No, I wouldn't. I wondered where all this was leading. But I like to think I keep an open mind, and I remembered Kylie's reputation: an eccentric maverick whose wild ideas seldom paid off, but when they did: *jackpot!* Could be dross, could be gold. So I hesitated, then hedged my bets.

"I'd be surprised if we'd missed two dimensions of symmetries, certainly. Ningrum was very careful."

"She's a physicist, right?"

"One of the best."

"I read the paper. You classified the *physical* symmetries. Those with clear physical interpretations. Somewhere in the middle of the proof an assumption crept in. I'll show you the exact place later. 'Property P3', it was called. What if there are continuous symmetries lacking Property P3?"

I tried to recall the discussions of three years ago. "Was that the equiconvergence condition?"

Kylie nodded.

"Ah, then we thought about that. It was Ningrum's idea, actually. She pointed out that without P3, any new solution would violate locality."

Kylie nodded again. "But you didn't try to find any extra symmetries, P3 or not?"

I laughed. "Why would we? Locality violation would imply a dozen unphysical features. Relativistic violation, multivalued location... I'm a physicist. I don't chase unphysical ideas out of mathematical curiosity."

"Uh-huh. Fair enough. But– I'm a mathematician, Dr. Loon."

"Jaya, please."

"Jaya. I chase any idea that tickles my fancy. My instinct is to find the symmetries first, and *then* worry about physicality. If they're not there, no worries. If they are there... well, maybe they have physical implications. I prefer not to pre-judge."

I now saw where he was going. "You're going to remind me that it's worked in the past. Dirac and the positron."

"That was a discrete symmetry, and the story's more complicated than it's usually made out to be, but – yeah. Dirac said he preferred a beautiful false theory to an ugly accurate one. I wouldn't go that far, but, like Dirac, I prefer to explore what's tucked away in the maths, and interpret it later."

"And you found two dimensions worth of extra symmetry. But – now that you come to mention it, my recollection is that Bagaskoro and Ningrum looked for unphysical symmetries too. Didn't find any. I'm pretty sure they proved they didn't exist."

I was expecting him to look worried, but he grinned. "You physicists don't know what 'proof' means. Perturbation expansion?"

What else? Boussin-Platt's non-perturbative methods were impractical. "Yes."

"Ah. Did they try eleventh order nonlinearities?"

I nearly dropped my margarita, it was such an absurd question. "*Eleventh?* Why the– why on Earth do you want to look for eleventh order effects?"

His grin got bigger. "Because they're there?" He laughed. "No, there's a better reason, Jaya. That's the lowest order in which modal parameters turn up in the singularities."

"Sorry, I'm not familiar with that concept."

"No worries, I'll clue you in." He pulled out a notepad and was opening a file when the waiter reappeared.

"Lunch is served, gentlemen."

"I'll show you afterwards," he said. "The food here's too good to let talk get in the way of eating."

* * *

An hour and twenty minutes later, equipped with another beer and margarita, we had decamped to the business lounge on the 27th floor, with a spectacular view over the city. And the rest of the story came out.

Kylie had discovered a two-parameter family of nonlinear transformations that preserved several key mathematical constructs related to my equations. If you ignored eleventh-order effects, they reduced to two of the known 'physical' symmetries. So the differences would only show up at high energies.

"What matters most," he explained, "is the physical interpretation of the extra symmetries. It's extremely counterintuitive. They permit the *instantaneous* exchange of existence-wave singularities between points in the universal caustic."

It sounded like gold but it *had* to be dross. *Surely*. It was disappointing, I'd hoped for something sensible, not this insanity.

"You mean, matter-transmission?"

A shake of the head. "Not exactly transmission, mate. More go from A to B without passing through anything in between. Total time: as close to zero as anyone can measure."

This was sounding more and more like crackpottery, and my reply was curt and dismissive. "Like I said: unphysical. Now, I really must–"

If he found that offensive, he didn't show it. "Only if matter-transmission is a physical impossibility, Jaya. But that's an assumption, not a fact."

Touché. The conventional wisdom isn't always wise. There's no ox like the orthodox. But–

"It's a sensible assumption," I replied. "Nothing in conventional physics allows it."

He leaned back in his chair, shaking with mirth.

"Just listen to yourself, mate. Dr Jayakatwang Loon, resting his argument on *conventional* physics! Bugger me, mate, that's rich!"

Skewered. I started laughing too, the other guests must have thought us mad. Maybe they'd be right.

"OK, Quade. If you want me to take this idea seriously, there are obvious objections, to which you've got to supply some pretty convincing answers."

I probed. Asked the hard questions. He had answers to them all. We batted it to and fro. I pointed out that the practical consequences, aside from matter-transmission, would include faster-than-light travel, antigravity, total conversion of matter to energy, and total conversion of energy to matter. Kylie responded with the same point as before: we didn't *know* these things were impossible, we just believed they were.

The more he explained, the more plausible he became. He didn't sound like a crank: his evident enthusiasm was tempered with healthy scepticism and he knew the literature backwards, even if he disagreed with much of it. Despite myself, I was warming to his ideas. I didn't think they were *right*, but I did think they were interesting.

However, you have to be realistic.

"You're talking total revolution in the physical sciences," I said. "But right now, Quade, it's all pie in the sky. Words are not enough. *Nullius in verbum*, right? If you want anyone to believe you, you'll have to come up with physical analogues of your unphysical transformations, and show experimentally that they're not any of the known 142 types."

He sighed. "I know. I hoped you'd show more imagination than all the other drongos, but–"

"Actually," I added, "you might get away with describing how an experiment like that might be done. The experimentalists are always on the lookout for a new theory to confirm or deny.

"If you can do that, the reviewers will at least let you publish."

He gave me an earnest look. "Any ideas?"

I hadn't thought very hard about it, to be honest. It was all too speculative for me to take seriously. But he was smart and keen, and he'd read our papers a lot more carefully than anyone else I'd met, *and* understood them.

Abruptly changing the topic, Quade enquired delicately about Alicia. I said we'd got on well and were going to meet up again later.

"She says we shouldn't call them existence waves," I said, when there was a lull in the conversation. "Too dull."

"Y'know, mate, that sheila could well be right."

"Alicia."

"I can see I need to teach you some Aussie slang. No matter. What did Alicia suggest?"

"Some guy called Casper who's her publicist came up with it. Karmabhumi."

He tossed back his beer, ordered another. "'Karma' I know, something Buddhist, right?"

"'Destiny', she said. So Casper told her."

"Good strong word. And 'bhumi'?"

"Earth. Ground. The Earth goddess."

"Mm-hmm. Bit of a mouthful, though."

"Less so than 'twelve-dimensional manifold', they both felt."

"True." He still looked sceptical.

"Shorten it, she said. To k-field."

Kylie gave a great guffaw. "Oh, yes! Now *that*, I like!"

I stared at him. "Why?"

"Everyone'll think it's named after *me!*"

After a moment I twigged. "The k stands for Kylie?"

He shook his head. "Course not. It stands for 'karmabhumi', you just said so." Then he was off into peals of laughter again.

Some sort of connection assembled itself in my head. Buddhism… religion… *not* religion. Wise advice from my first PhD thesis advisor bubbled up from my subconscious. *Physics isn't a religion. There's no place for dogma. It's the crazy ideas that overturn paradigms.*

It would be fairly easy to get Ningrum to check Kylie's sums. If he hadn't made a mistake, it was an impressive piece of pure math, whatever the physics might be. And– well, he might just be right. If extra symmetries showed up in the math, they might just have physical meaning.

I'd look an awful fool if I dismissed it out of hand and missed out on *the* transformative technology of the 21st century.

So I sat sipping my drink, and a vague hint of an idea bubbled up in my mind. Little more than a throwaway remark.

"Quade: you might try thinking about the anomalous particle resonances that Alain Guevremont claims to have found at the Gammatron."

"The accelerator at Falaise d'Angamma?"

"Yes."

He grimaced, a quick twitch of his mouth. "Haven't come across his work. Why those?"

I shrugged. "Just a vague feeling. In my theory, the true forces of nature are particle resonances. Everything you're telling me would make a lot more sense if there were a fifth force. And that would show up as an unexpected resonance."

He downed what was left of his beer in a single gulp, and I got up to leave.

He shook me by the hand. "Thanks for the tip. I'll follow it up."

"Let me know if anything comes of it." But I didn't expect anything would.

* * *

A year later to the day, a link to an ePrint arrived in my inbox with a covering note. From Quade Kylie.

You were right.

I assumed he meant that he now accepted that his transformations were unphysical and therefore meaningless.

Not at all. He'd come up with an experimental design to test his theory. The required conditions could indeed be produced by particle resonances, in a suitably designed cavity. He'd worked out the design. But – and he said as much in the paper – there was a snag. The material surrounding the cavity had to be incredibly dense, as well as possessing a number of properties that, between them, ruled out all known materials and metamaterials. In a subsequent paper that later became a classic, he demonstrated that the stable superheavy element 126 should possess the desired properties.

That paper came to me as a reviewer, and I recommended publication. A Nobel prize counts for a lot, and the editor ignored the other three negative reviews. It caused quite a stir, but despite strong initial resistance the idea slowly gained support. Around 2090 the GU long-term planning group foresaw the depletion of the solar system's raw materials, leading to economic and social collapse within a millennium.

Critics argued that this figure was absurd – a million years would be a better estimate. But the GU remained adamant. The problem wasn't resources as such, it was accessible ones. And the GU got to define 'accessible'.

Kylie's ideas were the only ones that offered a long-term solution acceptable to the GU.

By 2094 the Lhasatron had shown that element 126 could be made artificially in very small quantities. Three atoms at first, upgraded to thousands every run. Then millions, with more upgrades on the way. Kylie tweaked his design and calculated that 600 million atoms would suffice to perform his experiment. A group in Reunified Tibet agreed to create them. Ramon Gómez Da Silva's group from Peru had the right lab equipment to do the experiment – and four years later a single charmed quark was teleported half way round the world in a time too short to measure.

The usual claims of error, and counterclaims, delayed acceptance until the Tibetan group upgraded their accelerator to increase the production rate. Five independent experiments then confirmed the Peruvian result, and Kylie became a media sensation overnight.

Casper turned out to be right. *Karmabhumi* became the new word of the year. I called Alicia to tell her. She replied that 'superheavy element 126' was just as unsexy as 'twelve-dimensional manifold of existence waves'.

"I'll put Casper on to it," she said.

Even such tiny quantities of the new element had physicists and chemists in raptures, and for a time the media made hay with the potential for new applications and new technologies. Then, inevitably, the backlash set in. If any of those applications were ever to become practical, the world would need to increase the production rate by a factor of trillions. And even the most optimistic advocate for the benefits of element 126 baulked at the construction of a trillion accelerators.

What was really needed was a faster method of production.

Much faster.

CHAPTER 7
BEYOND THE NEUTRON DRIP LINE

Zelda Zimmermann
Université Paris-Saclay, Paris 2099

When I was seven years old I decided I wanted to be a vet when I grew up. I loved animals – all animals, not just the cuddly furry ones with big kitten-eyes. I *had* a kitten, of course; in fact I had six cats of various ages and degrees of cuteness and scruffiness. But my pride and joy was my pet spider, a pink toe tarantula, species *Avicularia versicolor*, not that you probably want to know that.

I called her Tänzerin, which is German for a female dancer. Why? Because she wore pretty pink shoes? Well, she did, but no. Because she kind of scuttled about the floor? Not exactly – though she did that too, of course, when I let her. But you're not far off. The German word for 'tarantula' is 'Tarantel', and there's a dance called the Tarantella, in both German and English... well, the word is Italian, and so is the dance. The dance first appeared in the Italian province of Taranto, where there lived a species of wolf spider (*Lycosa tarantula*, not actually a tarantula, you appreciate) that was widely believed to be extremely venomous (even though its venom is actually quite mild, no worse than a bee sting). The spider was called the tarantula, after the province, and the dance was called the tarantella, after the spider, because people who'd been bitten often developed symptoms of hysteria. And *they* scuttled about a lot. For two reasons, actually. *One*: they thought they were going to die. *Two*: the belief arose that the best way to stay alive, if you were bitten by a wolf spider, was to dance energetically, on your own.

Whoever'd come up with that one must've laughed themself silly.

It evolved, of course, and in the Kingdom of the Two Sicilies it became a romantic courtship dance, which quite possibly originated in an earlier fusion of the Spanish fandango and the *ballo di sfessartia*, or Moresca, a 15th century dance enacting medieval wars between Moors and Christians, in which dancers blackened their faces and wore bells sewn to their costumes.

Sometimes men dressed up in drag, apparently in order to be taken for fools – in which, of course, they succeeded.

Possibly, there was a third reason. It could be that the dance goes back to a Dionysian cult that went underground when Christianity took over.

Anyway, that's how the tarantella was born, and how Tänzerin the spider with pink toes acquired her name, because Tarantel seemed a bit obvious to me at the time. Like naming your cat Cat.

Anyway, I had this cute little tarantula, right? I fed her on crickets. Live ones, tarantulas hunt their prey in the wild, and it seemed to me then, and still does, that it would be cruel to feed them dead meat. I wasn't sure what the crickets thought about the arrangement, to be honest, but nature red in tooth and claw and all that.

Spiders gross a lot of people out, especially big ones. My parents didn't have any issues; well, not any they revealed to me. But my Aunt Gisela couldn't stand poor little Tänzerin, and thereby hangs a tale.

You have to be careful when handling tarantulas. They like to sit in your hand, provided you Keep Calm and Carry On and don't mind a bit of tickling. But pink toe tarantulas can be distinctly skittish, and they often jump out of your hand. My advice, if you're handling a tarantula, is to sit on the floor. Spiders can be injured even by a very short fall, so the closer to the ground they are, the less danger they're in. And pink toe tarantulas bite if they get nervous. Like I said, you have to be careful when handling tarantulas–

Oh, you thought I was worried about *you*? No, it's the spider I worry about. *You're* big enough and ugly enough to take care of yourself.

That said, some people warn us not to handle tarantulas at all, because they have stiff hairs called urticating bristles on their undersides. These can irritate your skin, and if (when!) they fall out they can get into your eyes and that can be really nasty, so you should always wash your hands after touching a tarantula and avoid rubbing your eyes–

You probably don't want to know that either, but stay with me on this, it's important. It's also one reason why I never let the cats play with Tänzerin. You can guess the other one.

As tarantulas go, this one is fairly small, about ten centimetres across with its legs spread out. And as tarantulas go, Tänzerin went. (Not via the cats.) One day when Aunt Gisela and Uncle Friedrich were visiting, Gisela developed an eye irritation and they had to rush off to the local hospital. They treated her with eye drops – she had to put them in her eyes four times a day for three weeks, tailing off slowly – and she got it into her head that Tänzerin's bristles had been the cause. So my father insisted that I had to get rid of my spider, and I spent the next week weeping considerably more tears than my aunt had done. It was all so traumatic that I went right off the idea of becoming a vet.

Several years later we discovered that Aunt Gisela was allergic to cats, and that was by far the most likely reason for her eye inflammation. But by then I'd gone off spiders as well. I still love cats. But I spend so much time working that it wouldn't be fair to the cat.

Until recently I did most of that work observing with BART, the Big Aperture Radio Telescope in the Atacama Desert. I don't actually go to Chile, you appreciate: I logon from my rented apartment in central Paris. It's really quite nice, but cramped. I can't afford anything bigger, not within fifty kilometres. But that's no place for a cat anyway, and I don't have time to deal with *la nourriture* and *litière pour chat*. So I've been a cat-free zone for the last six years.

BART, being ground-based, is becoming ever more limited by mega-constellations of low-orbit satellites lighting up the night sky like dazzling swarms of fireflies, and in the last few months I followed most astronomers by switching to space telescopes...

Oh. Yes. I should explain. *Observing*. I skipped something important, sorry and all that.

It was like this. Having decided not to become a vet, I toyed with a few dozen potential career-tracks – HV influencer, neurosurgeon, wildfire drench pilot, things like that – and eventually settled on astrophysics. As one does. I did my first degree at Heidelberg, and then a doctorate at UKZN. That's KwaZulu-Natal in South Africa. After that, I was lucky enough to land a postdoc with *Professeur* Jason Karoubi at the Université Paris-Saclay. And then–

Hmmm. You've probably noticed that I tend to branch off into irrelevant details. A lot, I'm told. *I* don't think they're irrelevant, actually, but most people who know me are absolutely convinced– well, sorry, I'm doing it *again*. Let me put it bluntly: I'm some way along the spectrum. The ASD, I mean – Autism Spectrum Disorder. My condition is related to what used to be called Asperger's, but it's more sociable. I call it Attention to Significant Details, and it's those apparently irrelevant details that fascinate me. It's the opposite of what psychologists call 'selective attention', which is filtering information to stay within your comfort zone. I tend to filter information like a baleen whale: take a huge gulp of everything, comfortable or not, and hope there's something good in there somewhere. When I find it, *then* I focus. Until the next gulp.

Still, I do find it amusing that I'm not just *on* a spectrum, I'm analysing the things by the million. Stellar spectra, not neurodevelopmental disorders. Right now I'm working on pulsar-black hole interactions, and Jason managed to get me time on EROS, the Extreme Resolution Orbital Spectroscope that's part of the science complex at Earth's L2 point. I'm scanning the spectra of faint stars in the constellation Leo – the only cat in my life right now – at a rate of fifty thousand a night.

Anyway, it's been great talking to you, but I've got to sign off now. To see a spectroscope about a cat.

* * *

I have vivid memories of my first day in Jason's lab.

His office door was open. I knocked, was invited in. He stood up and we shook hands.

"Welcome to the team, Zelda. Call me Jason."

"Thank you, Prof– I mean, thank you, uh, Jason." My Asperger-like condition doesn't protect me from embarrassment, unfortunately; it just gets me into embarrassing situations. I could feel my cheeks blushing. Fortunately the current trend in makeup would not just conceal it, but bury it deeper than the Mariana trench.

I'd already moved into my *réduit* at Paris-Saclay, sorted out logons and passwords, and met several junior members of Karoubi's research group, but the boss had been away at a meeting in Valparaiso. His almost godlike stature in the astrophysics community was matched by his height of 205 centimetres – about six feet nine in American – but not by his manner, which to my surprise was open and friendly.

"Maurice tells me he's filled you in on the current state of the project," he said.

"Yes, he's been really helpful."

"What do you think of the overall plan?"

That stopped me dead for a moment. I'd just arrived, and the PI was asking me to criticise the project I'd been hired for. I stalled while my brain kicked in.

"I agree that we need a better understanding of the r-process," I said. That's rapid neutron capture. As opposed to the s-process. You can probably figure out what the 's' stands for.

You may have come across an old phrase: *we are stardust*. Trite but true. You see, three minutes after the Big Bang – bear with me, I promise to skip quite a lot – there were three elements in the universe: hydrogen, helium, and lithium. That was it. Old Mendeleev wouldn't've had much trouble working out his periodic table, except there were no periods.

They're still around, of course. Tarantulas, cats, and thee and me contain a lot of hydrogen atoms, and trace amounts of lithium. Much of that is probably just ingested from the environment – pollution, basically – but lithium is widely used to treat mental disorders, and some neurologists think we need it to regulate the brain's moods.

We don't, as far as I'm aware, have any helium, except when we inhale some and start speaking like a cartoon character on kids' HV.

What we do have, however, is a lot more than three elements. Carbon, oxygen, nitrogen, calcium, potassium, sodium, chlorine, magnesium, phosphorus, sulphur, fluorine, zinc, iron…

We're a periodic table in our own right!

Oxygen, 65%; carbon, 18.5%; hydrogen 9.5%; nitrogen 3.5%; the rest 3.5%; that's us. Of these elements, only hydrogen was created in the Big Bang. So where did the rest come from?

It's the philosophical mega-question. Why are we here?

Stardust.

Stars condensed out of the primal soup of the Big Bang when the universe was a hundred million years old, collected by gravity. These Population III stars were made from hydrogen and helium, only. Atomic nuclei are made from protons and neutrons. They can break up (fission) or combine (fusion). Helium is made by fusing hydrogen nuclei.

As their nuclear fusion reactions ran down, those first stars collapsed and exploded as supernovas. These massive explosions forced atomic nuclei together, leading to ever more complex elements.

The debris of these first stars also condensed, and the explosions continued. Eventually the atomic nuclei worked their way up the periodic table to iron. And got stuck. The nuclear reactions that would create even heavier elements from iron require more energy than they would produce.

But, we're here, and so are copper, zinc, and iodine, which we need in trace amounts, not to mention a lot of other elements with more protons than iron's 26. So nature must have found a clever trick to get beyond iron. Two tricks, actually: the r-process and the s-process.

Both of these processes add a neutron to an existing element's nucleus. That doesn't of itself make a new element, just a different isotope. In slow neutron capture – the s-process, right? – everything happens so slowly that the neutron has time to decay into a proton, which it does by spitting out an electron and a neutrino. That's called beta-minus decay, and it creates an element one step up the periodic table.

With me so far? Good. Hang in, guys, we're almost there.

The r-process is much more exciting. In the space of a second, it can create the entire panoply of heavy elements. It produces so many neutrons that they smash into each other faster than they can decay, all the way up to the neutron drip-line. This is the limiting ratio of neutrons to protons. Beyond that – and initially that's possible – the new nucleus is unstable, and its excess neutrons turn into protons, again via beta-minus. It can also break up into smaller nuclei, giving other elements entirely. So it was kind of obvious that mother nature had exploited the r-process to make tarantulas and humans existable – if there's such a word.

If not, there should be.

The evidence is everywhere. And that was a problem, not a solution. Which is what I told Jason.

"Interesting," he replied. "Why do you think that?"

"Because, although the evidence seems overwhelming, it's all circumstantial. We know heavy elements must have been created somehow, we know supernovae don't hack it, and rapid neutron capture is the only process we can think of that can do the job in the short time required."

He nodded, waiting.

"It looks like a slam-dunk. Except– well, maybe there's a totally different way for nature to have done it."

He pushed back, just a little. "The elemental proportions fit almost perfectly, Zelda."

I made my patent disbeliever's face. Scepticism incarnate.

"I'm not sure how strong that is, Jason. I know what everyone *says*, but– I've read about two hundred of the original papers, and what strikes me is that everyone knew the answer they were looking for. Agreement for the lighter elements is irrelevant; they don't need the r-process. For heavier ones – well, if the predicted proportion is too small everyone searches for a new nuclear reaction, and they stop when they get the numbers they want. Hardly anyone is trying to *break* the theory!"

He nodded, slowly. I couldn't work out his expression. "And that bothers you because…?"

I pounced, tarantula spotting fat, juicy cricket. "Because the essence of science is trying to prove that the prevailing wisdom's *wrong!*" I paused for breath. "Hoping to fail, of course, because that adds confidence that the theory's right."

He gave me a penetrating stare. "Do you really mean that? Hoping to fail?"

I laughed. "You got me. No, what I really want is to prove that everyone else is wrong. Because that's how the big advances in science come about. But – I don't want that yet. No one will listen to a postdoc with weird ideas. I need to establish myself first as a conventional scientist. Then I might be able to play the maverick and get away with it. Like Loon did."

He stroked his chin. "Yes, Loon went the conventional route first. But Quade Kylie didn't. He was a maverick from day one."

I laughed again. "Kylie didn't just work on the forces of nature: he *was* a force of nature."

"True. Uh– Zelda, one of my strongest principles is to encourage independent thinking. I'm not an empire-builder, I don't want my team to just follow my instructions. I want them to argue with me, and with each other. When they find it necessary. I don't even mind if the arguments get heated: emotional commitment is the basis of rationality. I *will* mind if people on my team let a scientific disagreement spill over into their social relations. I've watched mathematicians fight like rabid dogs about some obscure point of logic, giving the impression that they'll never be on speaking terms again. Then one of them suddenly says, 'Oh, *that's* what you've been trying to tell me! Of course, you're right, I hadn't thought of it that way.' And then they go off to a bar for a drink, best of friends.

"So what's your role in my project?"

The abrupt change of topic caught me by surprise.

"Uh– Analysing stellar spectra for evidence of the r-process."

"And?"

"Sorry, I didn't think there was anything else."

"Cast your mind back over what you just said."

It was my turn to be slow. "Oh. Analysing stellar spectra for evidence *against* the r-process."

"That'll do for now. But cast your net wider, Zelda. If you come up with a crazy idea, one that *you* think could be important, that might just break a conventional theory… Let me know.

"I promise not to steal it."

* * *

Six months passed. Jason had grown a beard, one of those trim little ones like a small hedgehog doing rock-climbing on your chin, and I'd settled in as if I'd been part of the team for years. Some postdocs left, either having landed better academic jobs or deciding to quit science for something less precarious and more lucrative. New ones arrived and were integrated into the team. My EROS scans had given us a database of seven million spectra. Various members of the team were analysing the data, running searches for patterns or anomalies. We'd found some interesting stars, published three papers in high-prestige journals (Karoubi only went for those), batted a hundred weird ideas around, flagged a few as promising but half-baked.

I'd developed a habit of attending seminars in other departments, mainly Theoretical Physics, Math, and Infotech, to broaden my mind. That particular week, one caught my eye. Translated from the French, it went like this:

MACHINE LEARNING METHODS FOR COMPUTING SPECTRA OF SUPERHEAVY ELEMENTS

Dr. Virginia Vo (Võ Vân Yên),
Hanoi University of Science and Technology

Lecture Room B.07, Infotech Building,
16.00-17.00, 11 October

The only element whose spectrum is explicitly computable is hydrogen, a result that was pivotal in the early days of classical quantum theory. Conventional numerical methods have since provided highly accurate theoretical spectra for all elements with atomic number up to ^{36}Kr. We report new computations for all known elements, including the highly unstable superheavy elements from ^{104}Rf to ^{121}Wx, using machine learning techniques.

I checked my diary and it said I had an informal group meeting then. I stuck my nose into half a dozen offices and rescheduled it an hour earlier.

I was getting a crazy idea.

* * *

After Vo's talk there was cheese and wine in the Common Room, and I managed to have a few words with her before the Head of Infotech whisked her away to talk to some visiting luminaries.

It was enough. I left with my mind awhirl.

The superheavy elements – *aka* transactinides – are anything with atomic number 104 or higher. That's 104 protons, the same number of electrons, and a range of neutrons, roughly comparable to the atomic number. Vo was a member of a group of 271 people who had cracked the problem of computing the spectrum of every known element. Including some so unstable that the spectrum had never been measured.

I mulled it over for two days, and then hotfooted it to Jason's office.

The door was shut. This meant that he was either in a meeting, attending a seminar, or away.

I scooted down to Reception and one of the secretaries told me he was in a meeting until mid-afternoon. I parked my butt on a rather hard bench in the corridor and waited, trying my best to be patient. Watched stuff on my tab's tiny HV dais.

He turned up just after 15.30.

"Jason – can I have a quick word? I think it could be important."

"I can give you ten minutes."

One should be enough, I thought. "Thanks."

As soon as we were both in the room I told him that he might want to shut the door. For security. After a short hesitation, no doubt worrying about potential charges of sexual harassment and then deciding I wasn't like that, he did.

"You said to let you know if I ever had a crazy idea," I said. "Well, I've had one."

"I hope it's crazy *enough*," he said.

"I want to look for mahabhavium in stellar spectra."

He nodded. "That fits the bill."

I was expecting him to argue, but all he said was: "But no one knows the spectrum of mahabhavium, Zelda."

I grinned. "Not yet. But Virginia Vo knows how to do it."

"Who is– no, don't tell me, I remember now. Vietnamese, on a whirlwind tour of France's Infotech departments."

"That's her. It's a huge group, and it computes spectra. They've done them all up to Wiwaxium. Uh, that's–"

"Element 121."

Me and my mouth. "Sorry, of course you'd know that. So I asked her–"

"Whether they could do it for element 126, obviously. Can they?"

By then I was chattering nineteen to the dozen and trying not to jump up and down with excitement. "She couldn't see why not! The only reason they'd stopped at 121 was because that's the heaviest element ever observed. They didn't see any point in spending a lot of money calculating spectra of elements beyond the neutron drip line."

"Because those can't exist, no doubt. Except–"

"Except, Jason, they *can* exist if they *do!* If they're stable! And that's what many physicists are convinced is true."

He shook his head; in pity, no doubt.

"Zelda, that's not a crazy idea." He muttered something to his diary.

My disappointment must have been obvious, because he immediately added:

"It's a brilliant idea."

"You really think so?"

"Enough to cancel every remaining appointment this afternoon. Now, tell me the rest. Vo left two days ago heading for Nice, I believe. You've been incubating this ever since. What's your plan?"

Time to put my cards on the table. Make or break time. *Go for it, girl!*

"Like I said, I want to look for mahabhavium in stellar spectra."

"Why do you think it could be there?"

I'd thought this bit through at length.

"I'll run through the reasoning, even though you'll know most of what I'm saying."

"Of course. If I have any questions I'll save them for when you've finished."

I swallowed hard and launched into my pre-prepared spiel.

"There's a huge database of spectra now – mostly stars, but other objects too. My job is to verify it, correct errors, and add to it. Any spectroscopist knows that there are all sorts of weird anomalies buried in the data. Unidentified spectral lines, things like that.

"Historically, helium was first identified in the spectrum of the Sun, but it remained an unverified hypothesis until it was found on

Earth and its spectrum was observed in a lab. There are 7,142 papers on SpecNet with observations like that. About half of them speculate about potential new isotopes of known elements, previously unknown nuclear resonances, radical new physics. A few predict unknown *elements*."

"Any of which imply unknown spectral lines, otherwise they'd've identified the source," he said, deep in thought. "And since we know all of the naturally occurring elements, anything new has to be superheavy."

"That's what many of them suggest. Actually, I reckon that most of them are just bad science, poor calibration, basic mistakes. But about a hundred seem credible.

"Not surprisingly, every one of those papers laments the impossibility of calculating spectra for unknown elements. The sums are just too complex. But Vo's group has changed all that."

Worry-lines creased his face. "You said her code is open access."

"So you think all those authors will have started computing spectra a month ago when it was first released? Beaten us to it?"

He shook his head. "No. There can't be any results like that in published or ePrint form; we'd know about them." The worry-lines vanished.

"Agreed. They'll've noticed the breakthrough, and figured out what they need to do. But the computations are ferocious. Most of these guys are fringe eccentrics, much of their equipment is poor — like I said, speculations based on dodgy measurements. Most won't have access to a hypercomputer and won't be able to get it. Their research will look outlandish to funding bodies. Their ideas will seem crazy. If they do manage to calculate the spectrum, they won't be able to publish anything until they've confirmed their spectral data with better equipment. They won't have access to EROS. And for any chance of spotting spectral lines of mahabhavium, that's what they'll need.

"Jason: this is a golden opportunity. *We can do this!* Hardly anyone else can. Hardly anyone else would give the idea a second thought."

He nodded, looking slightly stunned.

"If there's mahabhavium out there, Zelda, how is it generated?"

Well. I hid my surprise that he needed to ask. Even gods stumble.

"The r-process. Evidence *for*, I'm afraid. Not against. Hardly a surprise: it generates everything else! Astronomers detected plutonium in space more than a century ago, and that has atomic number 94. That can't possibly be the upper limit. The r-process probably generates Wiwaxium, too, but that has a half-life of zeptoseconds. If it can generate plutonium, why not eka-plutonium? If it can create nuclei with 121 protons, why not 126?"

He stroked his beard. "The difference being, that one's stable. Yes, I see."

"Finding the right spectral lines ought to be easy once you know what to look for – but there's a snag."

This time he was right there with me. "It won't be easy to spot it."

"No. The conditions to create it are rare – the main ones being neutron star collisions, with each other or black holes. Most of those won't be energetic enough to produce enough mahabhavium to detect. We'd see very faint lines, at best. But that gives us an advantage. We've got the best spectroscope in the world. EROS."

"And you think EROS can find it?"

I shook my head. "Probs not, to be honest; most likely, there's nothing to find. If it does exist out there, though, I'm sure we can find it. And if we do, that'll prove it's stable. It will vindicate both the existing stability calculations *and* Vo's code. There'll be at least two papers in it, both good enough to be published in *Nature Breakthroughs*."

It was his turn to shake his head. "Aim higher, Zelda."

"The *Proceedings*?" I squeaked. APGAS is *the* top journal on the planet in my subject. That's the *Astrophysical Proceedings of the Global Academy of Science*, OK?

"Where else? And I reckon it would be at least six papers." He leaned forward and stared at me. "Erasmus Darwin always said that every so often you should do a damn-fool experiment. So he did."

"What?"

"Played the trombone to his tulips."

"And what was the result?"

"Nothing. Let's be very clear, Zelda: this is a tulip trombone serenade experiment."

"Not at all," I said. "It's far less likely to give a result than that."

He chuckled, then pursed his lips. "The spectrum of mahbhavium would be a pretty good result, whatever we do or don't find in the stars. A shoo-in for *Nature Breakthroughs*.

"What do you need?"

I flicked a list to his diary. "This. Vo says she's sure we can get hold of their code. There's an Open Access version, but we'll need one optimised for the 707, and that's not been released yet. If I get in touch, she'll try to persuade their Oversight Committee to let us use it. We might have to pay a fee to cover the work involved, but 1200 Euros ought to be ample."

He bit his lip. "How long will it take on the 707?"

"It's a big nucleus. If we go for the simplest isotope, with 184 neutrons, about two hours. If we want the other most stable isotope, with 228… three and a half more."

"And the cost of using the 707?"

"There's a fund specifically for postdocs to get access. There's a fair chance I could get it from that. The main obstacle isn't money, Jason. It's getting a time-slot on the 707. There's a huge queue."

He thought about that.

"I may be able to pull a few strings. Give me two days."

* * *

I never did find out what strings Jason pulled. Presumably calling in a few favours from people with clout. Or offering *them* favours.

We got very little sleep, but we had the spectra four days later – for *both* isotopes. Wouldn't do to miss one, he reckoned.

"Now we need some funding for a thorough survey," Jason said. "Zelda: get your team to put their heads together and draft a proposal."

"Which grant agency?" I asked. It matters, it affects how you spin the description and who's likely to be on the review panel. You think scientists are unbiased and objective? Think again. It's *science* that's unbiased and objective, because it's what survives the emotional dust-up between opposing forces that all *know* what the answer should be.

"I'd try the European Research Agency."

"Wow! You think it's that good?"

"Yes," he said. "I do."

So the team and I did. We burned the midnight oil – well, kept the wind-powered lights bright – and sent him a polished proposal within 48 hours.

Two hours later he sent it back with 156 comments, everything from typos to new ideas. Chastened, though encouraged that he hadn't scrapped it entirely, we edited it and sent it back.

"This," he pronounced, "is brilliant."

He submitted it, with himself as Principal Investigator. It was going to be a shoo-in.

We waited.

Six weeks later we learned the outcome.

"I can't believe it!" I cried. "How could they reject something of that potential importance?" We were all upset. All except Jason Karoubi.

"It was worth a try," he said, "because ERA grants don't have many strings attached. But I'm not surprised they rejected it."

I flicked up the rejection letter so we could all see it. "Too speculative. Not enough citations of the current literature. No mechanism suggested for mahabhavium creation… Jason, it doesn't matter how it *gets* there, what's important is to find out whether it is!"

He stroked his curious little beard. I think he grew it for exactly that purpose. "I know that. You know that. *They* don't know that."

I was almost screeching at him. "But we *told* them!"

"Yes. Uh– Zelda, do you think the job of the review panel is to believe everything the investigators tell them?"

Reluctantly I conceded the point.

"So what do we do *now*?" I wailed.

He went into avuncular PI mode. "Simple. You go through the proposal taking out everything referring explicitly to mahabhavium–"

"*What?* But that's the whole point of–"

"It's the point of the *research*. It doesn't have to be the point of the *proposal*."

"Oh."

"As I was saying, cut out mahabhavium, but leave plenty of references to anomalous spectral lines. Shove in a dozen citations of the works of Lawrence, of – er – Kapoor and Smith, isn't it?"

"Kapoor and Smithies."

"Right. And *definitely* cite everything you can find by Halkett and Middleton."

"But their stuff is just lists of strange spectra," Jimmy Robison said. "With no clear purpose except butterfly-collecting. They make no attempt to figure out *why* their spectra look weird."

"Jimmy's right. It's all boring and routine!" Elvira Rodriguez complained.

Jason nodded. "Uh-huh. Of course it is. But what you don't know – because only now am I telling you – is that I strongly suspect they were on the review panel. So here's the plan. We'll resubmit to another agency, but Halkett and Middleton may well end up on the panel again. So we grit our teeth and put those citations in. And this time we send it to… the Observational

Astronomy Commission, under their Young Researcher programme. With Dr. Z. Zimmermann as PI."

So we did, in another two days.

After biting our nails for twelve weeks, we got the funding! The reviewers were extremely positive and went out of their way to praise our solidly realistic objectives and our comprehensive grasp of the mainstream literature.

"Always happens," Jason said ruefully. "Anything truly novel falls at one of the hurdles, because at least one reviewer doesn't understand it, doesn't believe it can work, or realises that if it *does* work it torpedoes the pet theory that their reputation rests on. Anything sufficiently dull, boring, and orthodox gets waved through without the slightest objection because everyone can see not just what it's trying to find out, but what it *will* find out. No one feels threatened and everyone can justify funding it. It's risk-free."

"But science advances by *taking* risks!" I objected.

He laughed. "Zelda: all of my best and most original papers were rejected initially."

I was so incensed I all but shouted at him. "So why did you let us submit the *first* version?"

"Calm down, Zelda. You've got the grant, remember? I let you submit it to make sure you all learned a vital lesson."

Bastard.

I added the spectral data to the master program for my sky survey, and carried on collecting 50,000 more spectra every night. Two people from the data analysis team, one of them a PhD student, were set to work combing the existing spectral database for signs of mahabhavium. That would now be automatic for any new data, but there could be $^{126}Mb^{310}$ or $^{126}Mb^{354}$ lines in previous observations.

We concentrated solely on EROS data. Nothing else would be sensitive enough.

We couldn't get any more time on the 707: this idea was far too speculative, not like computing the spectrum of an element that many physicists thought might possibly exist. Anyway, Jason had used up whatever favours he'd called in, or promised. So the trawl through the data would take months.

We crossed our fingers and hoped.

* * *

Jimmy came up with a clever algorithm to enhance selected spectral lines, and several candidate stars crawled out of the data swamp, covered in mud and weeds – by which I mean all sorts of random noise, you appreciate. Elvira Rodriguez cleaned it up, and then we tossed it back in the swamp.

False alarm.

According to my diary, it wasn't until day 72 that we saw a more convincing hint of mahabhavium in the spectrum of Pulsar 7731FQ in Leo. It was $^{126}Mb^{310}$, the most plausible isotope.

More precisely, it seemed to be in gas clouds surrounding the pulsar, between it and its companion star koppa Leonis 662. Pulsar 7731FQ is one star in a binary, and the other one is an orange dwarf, more properly a K-type main sequence star. Not dissimilar to our own G-type main sequence Sun. A bit smaller and cooler, mostly.

The gas clouds were a mixed blessing. Neutron star explosions produce a lot of gas, and that's where the r-process can generate new elements. But a pulsar *is* a neutron star, one that spins very fast, in which case it can't have exploded.

But it did have gas clouds.

It was all a bit of a puzzle.

Jason came up with more funding, now that we had semi-convincing preliminary data. Jimmy improved his algorithm, Elvira got her hands on the latest software for extracting signals from noise, and the significance level passed 5-sigma.

We had a result.

* * *

It was two weeks later, after the initial excitement had died down, that Jason finally asked the obvious question.

"Assuming what we've done is correct – and it might not be, the spectra are based on machine learning calculations, not controlled experiments, though to be frank that doesn't worry me – there's a question we've not even begun to answer."

"How the mahabhavium got there," I said.

"Ah. You've been thinking about that."

I nodded. "I started thinking about it ten minutes after we spotted the first $^{126}Mb^{310}$ spectral line."

Jason grunted. "You would." After a long silence he said: "Did your thoughts lead anywhere interesting?"

"Oh, yes. Very interesting. And mostly very wrong." More silence.

"You're keeping something back, Zelda."

"Sorry. Yes, I am. It's so half-baked that I didn't–"

He leaped to his feet, towering over me. He towered over *everyone*. "Out with it! The rest of us will decide how well baked it is."

So I trotted out a fairy story about how I'd started out thinking I had evidence *against* the r-process, which would've been really interesting, but then I'd spotted a loophole. The r-process could create mahabhavium only when local energy densities were far outside the normal range of a supernova. So there had to be something extra, something no longer in the binary system, to provide all that energy in a sufficiently compact form. Which led me to contemplate...

"A black hole," Jason beat me to the punchline.

"But that wouldn't–" Elvira began.

"It would if it–" Jimmy butted in.

"If it skimmed the surface of the pulsar and headed off into deep space again," Jason finished for us all.

I nodded vigorously. "Uh-huh. That was about the size of it. Silly idea, I shouldn't've–"

"The only thing you shouldn't have done, Zelda, is wait this long to tell us. What I said about crazy ideas doesn't only apply *once*! Write it up as an ePrint and we'll stick it on SpecNet and see if anyone salutes."

So we did.

And after the first ten comments were posted, we decided not to send it to a journal.

Too unorthodox and speculative.

But we left it on SpecNet, just in case.

* * *

To cut a long story short: anything about mahabhavium rapidly spreads all over the media. This one caused a feeding frenzy. Small sharks make a lot of noise and get blood in the water; then the big sharks smell it from kilometres away and move in, teeth bared. Within a week of our paper being published, the politicos took over.

At first their enthusiasm was lukewarm. We had to explain that although the spectral lines were very faint, that was because mahabhavium made up a very small *proportion* of the atoms in the gas clouds. But the clouds were gigantic, so the actual *quantity* of the stuff was quite big.

"How big?" one of them asked.

"Oooh... several million tonnes," Jason replied.

That woke them up.

A feasibility study by the Combined Space Agency showed that the techniques they were developing for proposed orbital colonies would suffice to construct a deep space ramrocket capable of making the voyage to what quickly became known as Karoubi's Star in an elapsed time of 400–500 years. There was the usual problem of matter piling up ahead of the scoop, but Quade Kylie had published an obscure paper suggesting a way to prevent that using a small amount of – you guessed it – mahabhavium. Small enough to create down here on good old planet Earth, given a few decades.

Extracting the mahabhavium also turned out to be feasible, at least in principle. A combination of ramscoop tech and mass spectrometry ought to be able to suck the atoms up selectively.

Jason apologised to me for the star's nickname. As head of the group and a prominent figure in scientific circles he became the natural target for the media, and they invented the name. I got plenty of credit in the astrophysics community and was lead author on two of our papers; it wasn't his fault that the media wanted a snappy name. Can't put Pulsar 7731FQ in a headline. It could have been Zimmermann's Star, I suppose – more likely Zelda's – and then I'd've had to apologise to *him*. Maybe I should've been more annoyed, but life's too short. I was too busy doing science to flog a dead horse.

Everything snowballed.

As the fledgling Project began to lumber its way off the ground, the Peruvians developed their breadboard circuits into a freewave system that was usable over terrestrial distances. The presence of a large part of the planet between source and receiver caused no difficulties. This was true Instant Messaging, and it turned informed speculation into established fact. The tech was limited to a small number of governments, because the quantities of mahabhavium being created were still very small, and likely to stay that way, but it had become mainstream science.

The advantages of instant communication were obvious. The rest of Kylie's predictions would have to wait for a decent supply of the superheavy element, but the more spectacular effects that he'd predicted, if real, would open up a practical route to the stars.

It just had to be pioneered by a hopelessly impractical route.

And that would need a concerted effort by the entire world.

The politicos took deep breaths… and gave the Project the go-ahead.

They could always cancel it later.

CHAPTER 8

THE RAIN DOES NOT WAIT

Alfonsina Shegwada

Katavi Regional Territories, PanAfrica 2138

When I first went to school, at the age of eight, they taught me to read, write, and count. And to worship *Star Pyramid*.

I should have started school when I was five, but my mother forebade it. And in our house – well, we called it a house, and as a young child in an isolated rural area next to a disputed land border I'd never seen anything to disabuse me of that belief – my mother's word was law. As I grew up, I realised that a cityman would have sneered at our humble dwelling, built as it was from mud and sticks and reeds and leaves, but by then I'd also realised that the citymen had sold their souls to Western colonialism.

"*Hiari yashinda utumwa*," she would say. *Freedom is better than slavery.*

Mother was always quoting proverbs. Lacking any formal education, she had made them her source of wisdom. This one doesn't mean what its literal translation suggests. 'Slavery' means being a slave to money, and 'freedom' is the freedom to live a life of poverty.

If *anyone* was free, it was us.

My parents had built our house – well, hut – on rented land with their own bare hands, using wood from what was left of the forest and mud from a nearby lake. There were thirteen other huts in our village, all built that way, and when I was small I assumed everyone lived like that. My father died soon after I was born; it was years later that I found out how. Like our neighbours, my mother worked our tiny vegetable plot and earned a pittance 'recycling' electronic waste in a large building with a corrugated iron roof and concrete walls. I later discovered that the air inside was contaminated with heavy metals and noxious chemicals, released when the workers took devices apart to reclaim valuable and often rare metals. That was undoubtedly what killed her at the age of 38.

When she died I was eight years old. I was moved in with an uncle whose house was several kilometres away from the recycling workshop. It had a corrugated iron roof and was on a long street at the edge of a substantial town. He promptly sent me to school, which worked out well, though not in the way Uncle Sadeeki was expecting. I grew up with robust health, a burning hatred of the so-called 'developed' world, and an instinctive ability to hide my true feelings.

Oh, no one *called* it colonialism. The PanAfrican Sodality is an autonomous, self-governing federation of former nation states. So its corrupt pro-Western officials told us, and still do.

My first week at school, I learned this wasn't true.

* * *

They put me in with the five-year-olds because, although my mother had taught me to read and write, my pinnacle of numeracy was counting to twenty on my fingers and toes. Even then, the other kids were ahead of me. They were doing 'take away', and most of the numbers were a lot bigger than my mother's flock of guinea-fowl had ever reached.

I stared at the question on the chalkboard.

If Guguklethu has 14 mangoes and eats 3, how many will she have left?

Well, I could do that one. Two hands and four toes; then forget three toes. *Eleven*. But I learned something new: to write it like this: 11.

The same number, *twice*? Confusing.

I'd sort it out. What I *really* couldn't wrap my head round was that anyone would have *fourteen* mangoes! Let alone get to eat three of them in one sitting.

Two days later: *If Faraji has 35 mangoes and Zendaya gives him 3, how many will he have?*

It was possible to do that one with fingers and toes, but I'd already come to appreciate the advantages of tens and units. Five plus three units, three tens… 38! What puzzled me was why anyone would give three whole mangoes to someone who already had 35. Faraji was clearly a greedy little sod, and Zendaya needed her head examined.

By the end of the month we'd moved on to harder sums. We'd done hundreds and thousands as well as tens and units, and the advantages of this 'decimal system' were now blindingly obvious. I could see that the real-world social settings were intended to help students, but to me they were totally detached from any world I was familiar with. *Alfonsina's mother has no mangoes and the rent-man is coming. What can she do?*

Nothing.

I stopped daydreaming and turned back to the board. *If planning for Star Pyramid began in 2106, and lasted 19 years, when did it end?*

I didn't have trouble getting the answer, even though it did involve knowing that six plus nine is five-carry-one, and what to do with the carry, which, by then, I did. It was easy. But once more the question itself baffled me.

I put my hand up.

"Yes, Alfonsina?"

"What is a star pyramid?"

Everyone else started talking in whispers. A few of my classmates stifled giggles.

Ms. Owusu told the class to be quiet. "You must remember that Alfonsina has only been with us for a month. She's from a deprived background and doesn't know a lot of things that the rest of you have grown up with."

Already I hated this star pyramid, whatever it was.

"Masego, please tell the class what *Star Pyramid* is."

I could see she was trying to be inclusive, by addressing the entire class, but they all knew she was speaking to me, so it came over as patronising and insincere.

A short girl in long braids tied with yellow bows stood up. "*Star Pyramid* is the most important thing in the world," she said.

This girl is so stupid, I thought. *If you ask someone what is the most important thing in the world, and they actually tell you, they're hopelessly simple-minded.*

"And why is that?" Ms. Owusu asked her.

"Because *Star Pyramid* will make everybody in the world rich!"

Stupid, simple-minded, and greedy.

Ms. Owusu nodded. "That's one way to put it, Masego." She turned to speak to me directly.

"*Star Pyramid* is a spaceship, Alfonsina. It's being built right now, and when it's ready it's going to visit a star. And bring back something very, very precious; something the world needs but doesn't have. The government says it will bring universal prosperity."

When I stared at her, she misinterpreted my silence. "Uh– like Masego said, that means it will make everyone rich."

She's stupid and greedy too, I thought. *So is our government. Fedha fedheha. Money is a disgrace.* My mother, when she was alive and working for money at the recycling workshop, had to explain that one to me. It doesn't mean that money *itself* is a disgrace – just people who desire more of it than they really need.

We'd never had enough. But we'd managed. Just. So why want more?

I could tell that everyone in the class had bought into this idiotic story, and it was equally obvious that our government officials had been bought by Western colonialists. I didn't know the word 'scam' then, but I did know that *kweli iliyo uchungu, si uwongo ulio mtamu. A bitter truth is better than a sweet lie.* And I knew better than to show them all how I felt.

"We'll be studying *Star Pyramid* next term," the teacher said. "But I can tell you a bit about it after class, Alfonsina, if you wish."

Ukifunga kinywa, nzi hakiingii. If you keep your mouth shut, it won't catch flies.

I told her that would be wonderful.

* * *

Just before my mother died, I asked her what my name meant. Not the family name: my first name, Alfonsina.

By then it was hard for her to talk, but she hadn't let that stop her. After she was taken to the company hospice I visited every day, and in fits and starts, interrupted by coughs, I'd learned a lot of family history that I'd never known before. Like how my father died.

Shot for elephant poaching.

Put baldly like that, it sounds like he was a bad man who deserved everything he got. Actually, he was just trying to feed his family. He hadn't intended to harm the elephant.

It happened like this.

The village where we lived had a communal plot where we grew maize. The village was just outside a Nature Park, which is an area that rich Westerners visit to watch animals. There were antelopes and giraffes and crocodiles in the river, and a lot of other animals whose names I forget… Oh, lions, there were a few of those.

And elephants. Not a name I'd be likely to forget.

The foreign visitors are only interested in the animals. They pay no attention to the people who need the same land to survive. To keep the Westerners happy, the Sodality government protects the animals with laws and ranger patrols. There are no laws or patrols to protect the people.

Some of the laws make sense. The one to prevent poaching, for instance. Killing an elephant just to cut off its tusks is cruel and selfish, not to say pointless. The only thing those people do with tusks is to sell them for money. They don't even know how to carve them. And as for their stupid uses in so-called 'medicine'...

Anyway, the rangers have the right, by law, to shoot poachers on sight. If you try to capture or harm an elephant, that makes you a poacher. And so it should, unless you have good reasons for your actions.

My father did. So did a dozen men in the village. Elephants were escaping from the Park though a damaged section of fence, and the rangers were being very lazy about mending it. A few elephants kept raiding our maize patch. The men drove them away with loud noises and fire, but the next night they'd be back. So my father decided to trap them. He didn't plan to kill them, just to keep them penned up until the rangers had repaired the fence and taken them back into the Park. He was laying snares – loops of heavy wire cable attached to a big, solid tree.

The rangers caught him, and shot him dead without even asking why he was doing that.

"Damn fool," my mother said. "The elephant would just have pushed the tree over. But he was desperate, we were all starving."

Afterwards a man from the government visited the village and found out about the broken fence. It was mended the next day, and apparently several rangers lost their jobs. A truck turned up with food parcels from some foreign aid agency. None of that would bring my father back.

But I was telling you about something else, wasn't I?

"Your name?" my mother said, her breathing laboured. I wiped away the spittle from the corner of her mouth with a tissue. "Why do you– think your– name has a meaning?"

"Most names do," I said.

She nodded. "Yes, they do. Though no one ever seems to ask. Why –" she coughed. "Why do you want to know?"

"Just wondered."

"You wonder about everything, girl. Always did, always will."

"I have an enquiring mind, mother."

She coughed again. "Never was a truer word– spoken. But– take care that your enquiries don't– don't– don't lead you into trouble."

"Don't worry, I won't."

She gave me that hard stare, hard enough to stop a rampaging elephant in its tracks.

"I don't believe you." She tried to smile, but it came out all lopsided because her mouth was droopy on one side. "No, I'm not saying you're lying. I just know how that– mind of yours works. And what I said was– was wrong. What I meant was… when it leads you into trouble, make sure– it's– the right *kind* of trouble."

"I don't understand."

"You will. When the time comes."

We sat for five minutes, not saying a word, withered hand resting on mine, the silence broken only by my mother coughing.

The spasm passed.

"The meaning?" I reminded her. "Of my name?"

She managed a faint smile amid a renewed bout of coughing. "It has– has many meanings. 'Noble warrior', that's one."

"That's a good meaning. Too flattering, though."

"Another is 'prepared for battle'."

"I would be, but I'm not sure which battle, yet."

"You will be." *Cough.* "There's a– a third. 'Willing to– to do anything'."

I thought about that. "*Anything?*"

"Anything you feel is necessary, girl."

I thought some more. "I like that one."

* * *

For years, seething inside but with a calm exterior, I sat through idiotic lessons on the amazing benefits that *Star Pyramid* was going to bring, and why we all had to endure harsh conditions and make huge sacrifices for the common good. The Global Union propaganda machine was relentless and all-encompassing. Every week we were given a 'progress report' which consisted largely of homilies on the importance of supporting the Project and exhortations to conform to authority. Brainwashing innocent children was only one tiny strand in the GU's web of disinformation. We had to learn and chant a slogan: *Earth first*.

The GU was as simple-minded as Masego.

Early in my education I discovered that the metals my mother had been recovering were destined to go to *Star Pyramid*. Not the ship itself, but support equipment on the ground.

The Project killed my mother.

Ironically, it was her death that had removed me from our village and saved me from the same fate. That and Uncle Sadeeki. I took this as an omen that my life had been preserved to avenge my mother's death.

"Everyone is united behind *Star Pyramid*," the teachers insisted.

"Everyone in the entire world! It has brought us all together as never before." And I nodded, and made the notes the teacher wanted me to make, and thought: *not everyone.*

I enjoyed the other classes, though. I romped through the mathematics lessons, absorbing it all like a sponge, never understanding why my classmates were having such difficulty. To be honest, I got a bit bored; it was too easy. But I was saved from boredom when I discovered that I had a rare talent for coding software. Just as I'd grasped decimal notation within a few hours when I'd first begun my education, and understood how to manipulate decision matrices before the teacher had finished defining them, I sucked up programming languages like an elephant at a waterhole. I navigated my way around the OuterNet as easily as a baboon scampering up a tree, and gradually my dying mother's advice took root in my agile mind.

Make sure it's the right kind of trouble.

In a moment of total clarity, I saw *exactly* what kind of trouble.

Now it was just a matter of getting into it.

For a time I considered setting up my own organisation – what the authorities would have called a terrorist cell. But my mother's words reverberated in my brain: *Hapana siri ya watu wawili. There is no secret if two people share it.*

The colonialists have a similar proverb: *Three can keep a secret if two of them are dead.* Pithy, and typically focused on killing; I preferred my mother's version. But both offered excellent advice, and I decided to heed it.

I doubled down on my infotech studies. I spent some of my spare time playing games and going out with my friends, to avoid exciting suspicion, but every night I forewent a few hours' sleep in favour of digging my way into ever more obscure regions of the UnderNet. I absorbed hacking techniques from expert criminals and quickly learned how to cover my tracks. I avoided joining any subversive groups, however carefully they guarded their secrets, but I used their sites to explore a hundred anti-globalist ideologies, taking inspiration wherever and whenever I found it. I learned how to use weapons, how to build bombs, and where to plant them for greatest effect. I learned how to fool all but the deepest lie-detection brain scans with a combination of Zen-like meditation and what I thought of as 'mindlessness'.

I put my hacking abilities to work, making subtle but vital changes to my past. At that point the only official records that mentioned me were lodged with the Education Ministry. There were more files on my parents, mainly at the Employment Centre and the Recycling Plant, but very few, because we were poor. The firewalls and password protections were, to put it bluntly, pathetic. Officialdom always thinks that their employees obey rules and regulations, so once they impose a rule, they don't stop to think how criminals could get round it. There are dozens of methods – impersonating other individuals to gain unauthorised access, pleading forgotten passwords, that kind of thing. The more complex the system, the more bugs it will have.

The time to make those changes was *now*, before making any contact with the people running the Project. They had learned the hard way to protect their systems against cyberattacks. The Project had unlimited funds, it didn't keep obsolete equipment or run old software. So I deleted some key information about me and my parents, to ensure that when the GU looked into my background, they found no hint that I might not approve of the Project. I covered my tracks completely, which would not have been possible with Project records.

I didn't portray myself as squeaky-clean. Just not as anyone with a grudge against *Star Pyramid*.

While I was engaged in all of these activities, I worked my way through the educational system with top grades all the way – even in the ubiquitous *Star Pyramid* propaganda classes. *Keep your friends close, and your enemies closer*, another Western proverb but none the worse for that. I enrolled at a Community College, wangled myself a bursary to take a degree in Software Systems Analysis at the Nelson Mandela Institute, won a scholarship to CalTech in the United States for my PhD, and – to my thesis advisor's despair – rejected the offered postdoc position in favour of a *much* better-paid job at a small start-up.

It suited my purposes perfectly.

It coded operational software for *Star Pyramid*.

* * *

Within five years that small company had grown to a major corporation employing 87,000 people worldwide. It had been bought out four times, every time by a larger organisation, and finally spun off as an independent operation for tax purposes. By then it had been rebranded as KarouBiz, and it was awash with *Star Pyramid* money.

I lack natural modesty, so I have no reservations about telling you that the company's success owed a great deal to my own efforts. That part of my long-term plan could now be considered a success. I mostly worked on software development, but towards the end I was promoted to Deputy Head of Cryptography with a six-figure salary and share options. To the outside world I was a wealthy professional whose commitment to the Project was unquestioned.

It was excellent cover. *Fimbo iliyo mkononi, ndiyo iuayo nyoka. A stick in the hand is the one that kills a snake.*

Now it was time to start on the final phase of my plan. I'd remained a lone wolf, for security. In my mind, and only there, my one-person revenge squad had a name. A name that my mother would have recognised instantly. *Mvua haina hodi.* Literally, 'rain does not wait to be invited.' What it means is: trouble comes when you don't expect it.

I was going to be that uninvited rain.

PART FOUR

TYGER, TYGER

CHAPTER 9

FORESTS OF THE NIGHT

Federico Berrios

Global Union Astronautics Administration Building, Bayankhongor 2159

As I walked out of the elevator and along the corridor, my mind went back to how my life had suddenly changed.

Again.

* * *

I'd sought peace in the twilight of the asteroids, where tumbling rocks and dustclouds dimmed the already enfeebled sun. I hid from light – not because it hurt my eyes, but because it hurt my soul.

I crossed myself and murmured a silent prayer. To hate God's perfect light was a sin. On Sunday I would confess that sin, but for now I took comfort in the twilight of the Belt. And in my guitar, my nightly accompaniment to the old songs of Earth.

I checked my oxygen supply: still half full. That was enough to start the lengthy task of aligning the drilling-machine to sample another core of rock, seeking seams of valuable metal ore. Metal for Earth. Metal for the Project.

It was out there in abundance. My task, and that of my brethren, was to locate it. This rock was thought to hold several hundred tonnes of assorted metals, predominately cobalt.

The radio crackled: Brother Cassio. The Abbot wanted to see me, urgently.

I wondered why.

Urgency was an unheard-of concept in the Athanasius Orbital Monastery. But I'd sworn obedience, so I strapped my rocket-pack back on. A brief spurt of reaction-mass and the rocky surface dropped away behind me. In the distance I saw the familiar green light blink, and aimed just to one side of it. Beyond, fainter, was a second green light. Ten such lay between me and the monastery.

I followed the beacons home.

There was definitely an unusual feeling in the air; I noticed it the moment I emerged from the airlock to stow my backpack in one of the lockers. An excitement just below the surface, quite unlike anything I'd encountered before.

An agitated novice grabbed me by the arm. "Is it true, Brother? Is it true?"

I gently detached the hand. "I've just got back from the rockface," I said. "I'm not aware of any new truth."

'But– but– what they're saying–"

I was the one who'd been mining metals with a heavy drill and jetting back to the Monastery, but he was the one out of breath.

"But the Abbot wants to see you *urgently*?"

"If that's your truth, I can confirm it. I know little else."

He tugged at my captive arm in a proprietary manner, but we always cut the novices some slack. And whatever was going on, it was a big break from our daily routine. I could understand his excitement.

"I'll lead you to him, Brother Berry, if I may."

I knew the route backwards, but I didn't want to disappoint the youth. So I followed him through the maze of tunnels that led from docking bays to living quarters, knocked on the Abbot's door, and went in.

"Brother Berry." The familiar figure, slightly stooped with osteoporosis from a lifetime in zero gravity, had a quiet, high-pitched voice. Like all of us, he wore a simple robe in a neutral colour, but his superior status still shone through his entirely genuine air of humility. He had charisma, he had six decades of experience, and nothing could change those.

"Father Abbot," I replied, inclining my head in deference. "I don't know why I've been the cause of such unseemly excitement, but I will spend my nights in penance and prayer, I will–"

"You will be silent and do as I instruct you, Brother Berry."

I swallowed, embarrassed, and complied. Suddenly *I* felt like a novice.

Despite his stoop, the Abbot was a compact, vigorous man, and an unusual one. As he often told visitors, he had to be both spiritual guide and CEO. If the Monastery had been a for-profit corporation, it would've been worth half a trillion, at least. He trod the thin line between those roles like a high-wire artiste.

"You seem to be causing a lot of fuss, Brother Berry."

I hadn't been aware that I was causing anything. The fuss – whatever it was – was causing *me*. Causing me to rush back from a good seam while I had plenty of air left.

No doubt some previous sin had caught up with me.

He seemed to be sizing me up, weighing me up. I'm short, and I have to admit that I'm running slightly to fat. One of the better aspects of monastic life is the food. At least, it is at the Athanasius Orbital Monastery. Brother Valeri is a magician. But I digress.

After a moment that seemed to drag out forever, he said: "There is a task for you, Brother. A vital task. God's work."

Not a previous sin, then. There'd have been plenty to choose from.

I'd hoped this day would come. I'd also hoped to go into it with my eyes open. "Am I to be told what this task is?"

"I've told you it's God's work. Do you ask for more?"

I was humbled. "I'll do it." *Whatever it is.*

The Abbot smiled, but the smile seemed forced. "I knew you would. But I warn you: it will be the hardest thing you've ever done."

I very much doubt that. Living with a past like mine is the hardest thing anyone could ever do. Yet I'd found a degree of peace in the Belt. The Abbot knew this, which made his next words all the more cruel.

"You will return to Earth."

"*No!*" The cry was torn from me against my will. I fell to my knees. "Father, forgive me. I didn't mean–" My fingers went in reflex to my rosary as I sought control. "Father, since God asks it, I will go to Earth." *Earth. Flames. Death.*

The Abbot knew the reasons for my inadvertent outburst. To be human is to suffer, and I'd suffered more than my share, though less than my victims. But life was never meant to be fair.

"An hour ago I received a communication from Her Holiness." Pope Matilda. "About a mission whose importance for the people of Earth is greater than any other except salvation itself."

I nodded, my mind blank. *What do I have to offer my fellows?*

"Federico Berrios: the Global Union has need of your former skills as a test pilot."

I froze. The Abbott had called me by my secular name, a name I was desperate to forget. But it was the memories that the name evoked that unmanned me. Tears welled from my eyes. "Father – I – *I can't.*"

Everything came back in a rush. The blinding light of the sun as my visor polarity failed. The flock of geese that I never saw. I only knew they'd been there because my controller told me afterwards. The engine casing ripping back like the lid of a beer-can. My finger stabbing at the panel. The explosion beneath me as my seat smashed through the cockpit.

I heard again the rush of wind as I tumbled out of control, the sharp tug as the parachute opened… I relived for a second my relief at survival. Then the sickening moment when I looked down and saw where my wrecked aircraft's plunging descent would end.

"You can." The voice was taut and vibrant as a guitar string. "You must." The Abbot's voice sank to a whisper. "Brother, it wasn't *your* fault that the dispossessed had built their homes in line with the airstrip."

"It wasn't their fault, either," I croaked.

"I know. All the good land had been taken."

I tried to regain some composure. "Father, I'm responsible for the death of two hundred people. I should have stayed with the plane, tried to direct its flight away–"

"No. The plane was uncontrollable."

I sank to the floor, sobbing. "The plane crashed on takeoff, Father. It was fully fuelled. They– they burned. Like sinners in hell, but they were innocent–"

"And now they're safe and happy in God's care," said the Abbot. "And God has given you a chance to redeem yourself in your own eyes. Your accident killed two hundred. Your skills can save twelve billion."

* * *

That had been nine weeks ago.

Soon, I'd be streaking towards Pi Arietis at three-quarter lightspeed. Then around a two-year circle, most of it superfluous from the engineering point of view but necessary to return me, and more importantly the precious human-made mahabhavium, to the home system. Along with any antimatter I'd managed to make along the way.

Now… was now. Stay in the moment.

I followed the yellow line on the wall along the maze of corridors until I arrived outside Coordinator Simpson's office. So the small screen at the door told me.

I hesitated. Took a deep breath. No longer a monk, once more a test-pilot, deep into my training for the new vehicle that God in His infinite wisdom had created me to fly, I continued to seek the same spiritual calm in the secular world. It was a world I had known well, and had fled from. Now I was back. Back in the hot seat. Back in the morass of human emotion and conflict. But my beliefs had come back with me, and that was a comfort and a strength.

I knocked, was invited in, complied.

Simpson was standing beside his desk, cool and calm as ever in suit and tie, even if the suit looked like it had seen better days a decade before and the tie was loose. Beetle brows above eyes the colour of antique furniture pierced my soul. I gave a slight, formal bow, shook hands, and took the indicated seat.

They say that a tidy desk indicates a tidy mind. Simpson's mind, apparently, resembled a farmyard. The deep litter filing system. I approved. A tidy mind, I've always felt, is a *tiny* mind, and a narrow one. I prefer minds that sprawl, that are too busy taking on the next task to squirrel away the refuse of old ones.

The Coordinator would clearly agree. He smiled, sat down behind his untidy desk, and inclined his head questioningly.

"Berry." He said it as though the nickname alone gave him great satisfaction. I couldn't for the life of me imagine why. "Call me Frank, I prefer informality. Problems with the sims?"

I shook my head. "For once, Coordinator Simp– uh, Frank – no. The paper tigers are fully functional. It's with *herself* that the problems will arise."

Rearranging piles of paper documents (paper is recyclable, you don't need electricity to access it, and it doesn't vanish if you poke a finger into the display in the wrong place) and rummaging through a box of datacubes, Frank nodded. "And you have a new problem for me."

"I do, but not with *herself* – except once again to register my protest at the new experimental package that's been shoehorned into the design."

"Module K? It's harmless."

"I've no reason to doubt that its *contents* – whatever they may be – are harmless. What I'm unhappy about is the secrecy that surrounds it. But that's by the by, Frank. What I wish to protest, yet again, is its potential effect on the integrity of *Tyger*."

I knew from previous discussions of this very controversial decision that Frank shared some of my misgivings, but he clearly wasn't about to admit it.

He coughed, scratched his rather large nose.

"All we've done is delegate some of the onboard functions to ground devices, uplinked through the existing, and essential, Da Silva freewave. That *improves* the integrity, Berry. Ground-based equipment can be repaired. It's efficient, too: letting an existing component do double duty. Anyway, if the Da Silva fails, we've got much bigger trouble than inadequate onboard computing power."

I shrugged. "What happens with double duty if the two duties conflict? Resilience is more important than efficiency. *Tyger* is highly complex – antimatter power supply, the Da Silva, the eka-Bussard, the antimatter generator and collector. Much of the technology has never been field-tested."

Simpson gave me a friendly grin. "That, Berry, is why we hired you."

I still felt more press-ganged than hired, but that wasn't his fault. If anything, it was the Abbot's. *No, not his fault either. God's will.* I decided not to continue that train of thought to its logical conclusion, which would have been blasphemous, and confined myself to immediate practicalities. "I just have a feeling that we should keep the onboard options as robust and flexible as possible." It sounded feeble, even to me.

Frank laughed. "Flexibility cuts two ways, Berry. You just don't like last-minute design changes, that's all. Neither do I. But they've been checked every which way and the engineers are adamant that they don't compromise *Tyger's* integrity in any manner or form. They've run hundreds of simulations to check that. I believe them."

I stared into his eyes, seeking... who knew what? Honesty? Reassurance? Redemption? I had no idea, I just sought. And I must have seen what I sought, because I found myself saying:

"Very well. I accept your assurances. With reservations." I smiled. "Test pilots always have reservations, Frank. That's how they stay alive. But there's another reason I came to see you, aside from trying to revive a lost cause. I have a new request."

His instant reaction was apprehension, but he smoothed it over immediately. "What?"

I gestured with my left hand. "Nothing serious. But I keep thinking about that two-year journey. Even with time-dilation, it's too long. I was wondering whether it would be possible for me to have a guitar on board."

"Hymns?"

"No. I have traditional tastes in religious music, and plain chant was perfected before the guitar. The ships of space have never generated their own songs, not with Mission Control always on the beam, so I play the music of the ancient ships of the sea. It's not recorded what songs the sailors of Columbus and Magellan sang, but those of the English-speaking period are magnificent."

Frank put on his best apologetic look. "Berry, we'd do anything to make those two years more pleasant for you. I know that a guitar would weigh only a kilo or so, but we can't afford a superfluous–"

"I'm well aware of that, Frank. But I want to propose a workaround, one that your technicians might be able to develop. Once the initial flight-tests of the eka-Bussard have been completed, the onboard computer won't need all of its processor units to interface with the 706. At that stage, for the first time in the flight–" I gave him a meaningful look "– there will be some spare capacity. The same applies to the physiological monitors. They're mostly remote, not all over wires like they used to be. I wonder if there's some way for the monitors to detect my finger-movements and feed the data to the computer so that it can simulate the sounds of a guitar."

Frank was impressed. "A virtual guitar. I don't see why not. Software doesn't weigh a thing. Especially when it can stay on the ground."

* * *

Later I asked one of the engineers. Apparently, one binary digit of data has an effective mass of 3×10^{-36} kilograms.

I don't think that would worry Frank.

* * *

I took *Tyger* away from the L5 industrial zone on old-fashioned chemical rockets and floated her out to the unstable L2 Lagrange point beyond the Earth's orbit, where the MHDrive booster *Womera* had been assembled.

Unlike the compact MHDrive saucers that murmur through Earth's atmosphere, *Womera* was a three-dimensional spiderweb, vast and invisible. From ten kilometres away, as I nudged *Tyger* towards her central docking cavity, I could just make out the thicker superconducting girders; but from a far enough distance to give her 600-kilometre disc a comprehensible shape, not even the fusion reactor nodes would have been visible to the naked eye. *Womera* was mostly empty space.

Undaunted, the HV camera crews were using photon resonance and real-time image enhancement to show their viewers what could never really be seen: *Womera*'s ghostly outline, her billions of coil windings and current enhancement spikes. I watched the scenes, relayed to me by freewave.

She would have to grow considerably before she could die in boosting *Star Pyramid*. But she was already big enough to accept into her womb the tiny *Tyger*, bear that egg to the edge of the Solar nest, and match speeds with it upon its return.

At the heart: me and the mahabhavium core. Around us, *Tyger*. Around *Tyger*, the ghostly scaffolding of *Womera*. And around *Womera*, wide as the Moon, the invisible fields of her magnetohydrodynamic drive.

Beyond the Moon is a vacuum superior to anything achieved on Earth, but to *Womera* space was filled by the solar wind, the violent breath of ionised gas driven out constantly by the sun. As the solar plasma streamed outwards from a flare that could have enveloped Earth and Moon together, the ghost came to life. Enormous electrical currents began to flow through her turret, through hundreds of kilometres of gas, down to the anode web at her base. The great coils within her created complex magnetic fields; the thin plasma began to flow, spiralling outwards to her upper face, inward below, always down.

Reaction matching action, *Womera* rose steadily in her self-defined 'up'. As the solar wind blew thicker, her acceleration grew.

Tiny inside her, I lay unmoving.

Tyger, too, was tiny. *Womera*, even though it was nowhere near its final size, was not. The combination had caused headaches for the mission controllers, because it was like attaching a rocket engine to a bicycle. When completed, *Womera* would accelerate *Star Pyramid* at a comfortable $0.5g$, thanks to the starship's huge mass. But the half-finished version had to be run at full power, for engineering reasons, so the lightweight *Tyger* would accelerate at $5g$. Not a problem for the ship, but an insuperable obstacle for most human pilots.

Not me. I could tolerate $5g$ for days on end. A gift, and a curse.

It was the real reason they'd chosen *me*. The rest of the selection performance had been a sham.

The vacuum of the inner Solar System is pea soup compared to the interstellar wastes; to astronomers, the Earth is inside the Sun's outermost layer. As *Womera* moved outwards, her acceleration dropped. It took her just seventeen days to reach *Tyger*'s ignition speed – a twentieth of the speed of light, Rio to Lunabase in half a minute. By now the thrust was down to an Earth-normal $1g$; even so it would take *Womera* months to kill her velocity and work her way back from the empty desert where *Tyger* thrived.

Far behind me: the orbit of Pluto. Ahead: what the poet William Blake might have called the Forests of the Night.

The Loon Equations provided the fearful symmetry.

I released the bars that restrained *Tyger*, and reversed *Womera*'s drive so that she fell away from her thousand-tonne passenger. *Tyger* rose through a ghostly birth-canal, watched by observation rockets launched years beforehand. By the time their signals reached Earth, *Tyger* would be further from them than the Earth is from the Sun.

* * *

The voices and images from the Astronautics Centre at Bayankhongor came over the Da Silva communicator with no crackle of interference, no flaw in the video feed. The bandwidth was too limited for HV, but compression coding allowed two-dimensional colour images. The crisp articulation and the absence of any timelag gave the eerie impression that I was in the same room as my controllers. I knew the experience would be the same for them. It was scientifically superfluous, but it was needed for the HV viewers, and it was good psychology for everyone. Especially me.

I confirmed that all onboard systems were in order, and readied *Tyger* for ram ignition.

The Mission Controller that day was Angélique Frazier. Her voice was calm and reassuring, her face serene. "All well groundside, Berry."

On my board, the summary window glowed a uniform green. "Ditto here, Angi."

"Ignition sequence starts in thirty seconds." As the ignition sequence proceeded, sections of my summary window changed colour to match its progress.

"Generators on. Magnetics on.

"Momentum transfer initiated. Hydrogen intake rising… stable.

"Berry, there's a touch of preturbulence in coil six. Can you keep an eye on that? Tuning now…

"Eject ramcasing. Power lasers.

"Laser ignition in ten seconds."

I crossed myself and began to pray – not for me, but for the future of humanity.

My board flashed yellow as the eka-Bussard lit. The video feed would show viewers, for the first time in reality rather than endless sims, the blue needle that was to become as much a symbol of the 22nd Century as the mushroom cloud had been of the 20th.

Angi kept talking, mainly for the benefit of the viewers.

"Plasma pressure increasing... Temperature a shade cool, half a billion degrees. Screw ripple instabilities setting in – stabilising.

"Berry: congratulations. Smooth as silk. How does it feel?"

Relaxing. Now that the moment of terror had passed, my voice was confident and controlled. "Silent. Slight vibration. I'm starting to feel the acceleration now, first time since leaving *Womera*. The computer is learning to control the intake rate by momentum feedback from the Da Silva – it knows how much mass we're encountering, and adjusts what it collects or diverts. The plasma is rock stable, which is a relief."

"So do you have a message for the people of Earth?" asked Frazier.

There was a scripted message asking for a prayer, but I tore up the script. "Tell them: *Tyger* is burning bright."

* * *

"*...brave boys,*
And to Greenland bore away.
Oh, the lookout up on the mainmast stood,
With a spyglass in his hand.
'There's a whale, there's a whale, and a whale-fish,' he cried,
And she blows at every span, brave boys,
And she blows at every span.
The captain stood on the quarterdeck..."

I was a thousand times farther than the Earth is from the Sun, a moderate star now dimmed a millionfold – yet still the brightest in the sky.

And I was singing.

I'd had to adjust my playing style to take account of the absence of resistance from the strings, but the virtual guitar worked well enough, and I whiled away many a tiresome hour strumming my invisible instrument. Apparently a live-recorded optical bubble of my performances, put out by a Korean recording company, had gone to number three in the folk charts.

I'd donated all royalties to a charity for the Bolivian poor.

Now, though, my performances were rarely broadcast live. At eighteen per cent of lightspeed my time was slowed enough to lower my pitch by a sixth of a semitone, and the HV engineers were now transmitting speeded-up recordings.

Nine weeks after ignition, Frank Simpson was in Bayankhongor on a routine visit. Again, Angi Frazier was Mission Controller. I'd just begun the sixth stanza of *The Greenland Whale Fishery* when I stopped abruptly.

One corner of my board flashed brilliant blue. The same would be happening in Mission Control, but I reported it anyway.

"Angi, something's going haywire in the antimatter system – the antiproton beam's oscillating at the entrance to the neutralisation chamber."

"Yeah, we saw it too."

I never did like the distance that mass had to go. But the antiparticle storage had to be ahead of the Da Silva, so we didn't have much choice.

I could hear Angi alerting all Controllers and putting herself in direct contact with the Power Systems group leader. "Morgan, I imagine you've noticed those beam readings? What's causing them?"

"Not sure, Angi, we need more data." A lilting voice attested to Welsh origins. "Could be a relativistic resonance effect in the Da Silva. We don't really know how time dilation affects synchronization... Yes, that's probably the cause. Pity we downgraded the onboard computing to make room for that last-minute science module – we could do with a lot more computing power to predict the instabilities."

"But surely the Da Silva link– oh."

I butted in. "I don't want to carp, but I kept warning everyone about that. 'It's just as good as having the equipment on *Tyger* itself'. That's the story we all told ourselves. But now the flaw's obvious. Da Silva linkage is fine for most tasks, but *not* when something's wrong with the Da Silva."

Angi's voice remained calm. "We'll review later. But don't worry, Berry, it's under control. We'll just reduce the antimatter flow rate, power down anything inessential. Then find a way to upgrade the software and damp out the instability.

"Stand by to cut the antimatter creation fifty per cent and dump the energy–

A shriek of static made my ears ring, and as I pulled my earbuds out, I heard her shouting.

"Morgan! Get that under control, whatev–"

The section of my board that reported on the Da Silva glowed a baleful orange.

I managed to maintain an unnatural composure and kept the information flowing.

"The beam's growing, Angi," I told her, though she no doubt knew that already. "It's developing a secondary mode. It's going to hit the–"

The static vanished off the top of the audible range. The board flickered crazily, and for a heart-stopping moment it went totally black. Then reluctant wedges of light returned, the reassuring green now spattered with diseased orange patches, scarlet at the core, slowly collapsing upon themselves like a decaying fungal rust, until only a few isolated spots remained on an otherwise normal board.

I found I could move again. But my heart was racing and tears were streaming down my face.

"That was rough," I said. "But it seems that God does not yet wish to claim me." Then the message screaming from the displays hit me. No doubt having the same effect at Bayankhongor.

Don't be too sure about that.

CHAPTER 10

GREAT WHALE-FISH

Francis J. Simpson IV

*Global Union Astronautics Administration Building,
Bayankhongor 2159*

What made the worst day of my life all the more cold-blooded was the absence of any sense of urgency.

Tyger had survived a miniature nuclear explosion. A few thousand antiprotons had touched the channel walls and annihilated themselves against ordinary matter. Instability in the Da Silva had caused the problem, but the Da Silva itself was OK. The power storage chamber and its nineteen grams of antihydrogen were untouched, but the antimatter guide tubes were wrecked.

The antiproton collection system was no longer essential, so I authorised an immediate shutdown. But other things *were* essential.

"So the lateral controls are no longer working, Mr. Simpson?"

Boris Rutzkoi was Undersecretary for Space, and he had stepped in – literally, in person – as soon as the scale of the disaster became apparent. He was one of those Russians who look quintessentially *Russian*. Thick-set body, shoulders broad and square as a wardrobe, medium height, all held with a stiff military bearing. Immaculate dark suit, white shirt, plain dark blue tie. Jet-black hair, not *too* short, no parting. Thick black eyebrows above eyes that never looked remotely like smiling, flatlined mouth. Square jaw, face permanently set in a look of vague distaste. Deep voice to match the face.

No informality for him; I'd tried once and been slapped down.

"Not exactly, Dr. Rutzkoi," I said carefully. "The eka-Bussard and the momentum transfer systems are completely undamaged, and in principle it's still possible to divert the ship from a straight line course." I paused to swallow. "Trouble is, guiding interstellar hydrogen into a *turning* ramjet is more intricate, by orders of magnitude, than proceeding in a straight line. The onboard computer can't perform the necessary calculations. Without those, the fuel supply will be so erratic that the ship will shake itself to pieces."

Rutzkoi wasn't buying it. "Da Silva communicator is *instantaneous*," he growled. "Can do calculations *here*." He thrust a pugnacious jaw perilously close to my nose. He spoke excellent accent-free English (American), but with the common Russian tendency to omit articles, be they definite or indefinite.

If only. I took a step back to get his face out of mine.

"It's not that simple, Dr. Rutzkoi. The communicator is instantaneous, yes, but the circuitry for encoding and decoding the data isn't. Unfortunately, the density fluctuations must be cancelled out in real time, and the coding step creates too much delay."

"That," Rutzkoi said, "is just complicated way to tell me *Tyger* isn't coming home."

I tried to swallow, my mouth suddenly dry, and nodded. It takes a lot to intimidate me, and Rutzkoi did it effortlessly.

"*Tyger* carries four year's global production of mahabhavium, Simpson. Whose return is essential to *Star Pyramid*," he growled.

"I can't work miracles. That's gone. It'll have to be replaced."

He thumped a clenched fist against his palm. "After four-year delay, monumental rescheduling, and worldwide panic."

"That was always the risk," I said. "A calculated risk."

The Undersecretary glared at me. "Not calculated *enough*."

Hell, it's not my *fault.* Time to fight back.

"Be fair, Dr. Rutzkoi." *We can't study relativistic Da Silva physics in the laboratory– No, that sounds too defensive.* "It's not my function to cast blame, but if I did, it would be upon those senior managers who decided, for reasons that were never explained, to delegate major computing functions to Ground Control. If they'd not done that, making everything depend on the freewave link, we wouldn't be in this position. When you go for broke, don't make side bets against yourself."

Rutzkoi's face was unreadable. "It's all very well trying to blame me, Simpson, but it achieves nothing. Listen to me. There's more to this than you know. There was another side bet. Overriding reason *why* you were forced to delegate computing functions groundside was to make room for emergency mahabhavium recovery system."

I leaped to my feet. "*What?* So *that's* what Module K was for! Jesus H. Christ, Rutzkoi, how am I supposed to keep the engineering decisions compatible with each other when I don't even know what's in the goddamned ship? Sigmundsdóttir will throw a fit when I tell her; she signed off on the design variation plans."

"*Dr.* Rutzkoi, Simpson. Reason is simple: need to know. And now you *do* need to know. What I'm telling you is that, thanks to imaginative forward planning, we can still get mahabhavium back. But–"

"But what?"

"To do that, we have to kill Berrios."

* * *

As Rutzkoi explained, I began to realise the extent of the betrayal. Now I knew what had been in the secret experimental package, the one that was so important that the design integrity of *Tyger* had been fatally compromised in order to include it.

The Global Union had been determined to get its mahabhavium back, at *any* cost. Officials way above my pay grade had contrived a mechanism that would dump those precious atoms into a container strong enough to survive a nuclear blast. Then the antimatter in its storage chamber would be brought into contact with ordinary matter, and the resulting explosion would be channelled to hurl the mahabhavium container back towards the inner Solar System, where a conventional ship would pick it up. The technology involved was crude, but it didn't have to be very accurate.

The pilot would be killed, of course, but we all knew how to rationalise that. Berrios was a dead man anyway. Better to give him a quick, painless death. Sheer hypocrisy; that wasn't the real reason. But it offered a moral fig-leaf.

If that had been the *only* problem, I could have lived with the decision. But I now knew – or at any rate strongly suspected – there was more. I glared at the Undersecretary. As far as I was concerned, he was responsible for this catastrophe, and my face showed it.

"You realise that the addition of Module K probably caused the very accident that it was intended to guard against?"

Rutzkoi stiffened. "That's pure conjecture, Simpson. In any case, it's irrelevant. Accident has happened. We must activate return system."

"And Berry must die."

Rutzkoi had faced that moral dilemma long ago, right back when Module K was being mooted. He trotted out the face-saving formula. "Federico Berrios is as good as dead already, Simpson. It will be act of humanity to put him out of his misery. *Earth first.*"

I sneered. "Yeah. An act of humanity that just happens to let the

GU get its mahabhavium back. You confuse humanity with expediency."

Rutzkoi shrugged. "In this instance, two coincide."

But I suddenly realised that they didn't. *Dear God in Heaven.*

Betrayal and anger were just two of the mixture of emotions that coursed through my mind. "Rutzkoi, you do realise that although the trip was planned to last only two years, the recycling systems are so good that they'd probably last indefinitely?"

Rutzkoi was scornful. "To keep Berrios alive in his condemned cell until he dies of old age? Are you suggesting we torture poor devil?"

"No. I'm suggesting we try to rescue him."

The Undersecretary wasn't expecting this. "Simpson, is this macabre joke?"

If only it was. "Think of it this way. The eka-Bussard is still working. Berry can't turn, but he *can* continue straight ahead. He can keep accelerating at a comfortable 1*g*."

"Into deep space. So what?"

"Think about his speed. At the end of a year he'll be travelling at three quarters the speed of light, and for him time will pass at half the rate it does for us. After two years by our reckoning, he will be only seventeen months older. By the time he's survived two years in *his* frame of reference, he'll be within four per cent of lightspeed, and forty-four months will have gone by on Earth. After that the calculations become even simpler. To a very good approximation, for every thirty-six of his weeks, the elapsed time on Earth doubles. For every two years of his subjective life, it *octuples*." Any GU official *must* understand exponential growth, it sleeps on the sidewalks of every city on Earth. "Five *Tyger* years from now, you and I will be dead. Six years for Berry is two centuries for us; eight's a millennium and a half.

"If he lives to be fifty, the combined efforts of the entire human race will've had *fifty thousand years* to rescue him." I could see my words were striking home. "There *has* to be a way."

Rutzkoi sank back into his chair, eyes staring.

"If *Star Pyramid* succeeds," I continued, "she'll open up the Galaxy to instantaneous travel. Do you not think, Undersecretary, that posterity will be grateful enough, to the man who made it possible, to go out and collect him somewhere down the millennia?"

The Undersecretary's resolve had vanished. "Why has nobody told me this before?" He looked weary and dispirited. "Scientific

Advisory Committee must have realised such scenario was possible, however unlikely." Then he shrugged. "Unfortunately, it changes nothing. Coordinator, I'll be frank. Nobody warned me of such eventuality. But – we must be realistic. Decision would have been same, even if they had done. Success of what you propose is highly improbable. *Tyger* is damaged, and its systems no longer possess their full design integrity. Until mahabhavium is plentiful – which will be *after* return of *Star Pyramid* – we simply cannot afford to lose four years' production."

He sighed and slumped back into his seat; and I had a momentary glimpse of the human being behind the granite crenellations.

"Yes, yes, I know, it would only set Project back four years. *No*, it wouldn't. Project is dynamic, operates to tight schedule, and is most complex operation this planet has ever contemplated. It's organised around return of four year's supply of mahabhavium, two years from now. It has too much momentum to be placed on hold.

"Some processes can't be paused. Some materials can't be stockpiled. Key personnel will age; some may die. You know how chaos spreads through complex system, amplifying, spawning more chaos. Any unexpected change in plan will ripple through entire Project with effects no one can anticipate. And if we can't anticipate them, we can't take steps to prevent or mitigate them."

"We'd find a way," I objected. "The Project has to be resilient, there are always unanticipated problems. We can't predict what they'll be, but we can predict they'll happen. It will be a struggle, I admit; a perpetual firefight. But we *can* reschedule."

He couldn't look me in the eye. "If absolutely necessary," he mumbled, "yes. But–" He banged a fist on my desk – "Only as last resort! *Any* other solution is preferable. *Any*."

I wanted to strangle him with my bare hands. He must have realised how I felt, you don't rise that high by being unaware of people's hidden emotions. And I wasn't hiding mine very effectively.

He softened his tone.

"Coordinator Simpson... Frank. Believe me when I say that in my heart I have deepest sympathy for your views. Berrios should be treated like hero he is, not condemned like criminal.

"But it is destiny of heroes to die, should that be necessary for greater good. That is what makes them heroic. So our heads must rule our hearts.

"I'm sorry."

I could understand where he was coming from, but I refused to accept that he was right.

"Our priority should be for Berry's welfare," I said. "An empty apology is just words. You'd say anything to justify what you consider expedient."

He hesitated. "That… is true," he said. "I would. Project is too big to be sacrificed for sake of one individual. Too important. But expediency is only part of highly complex tangle of issues.

"You talk of priorities. Global Union allocates priorities for *entire planet*. Project is largest single factor in economy of every member state. That is *reason* for Project, at political level. Not to rescue Earth in four centuries' time, but to rescue it *now*. To unify world *this* century, to avoid atomic war *this* century. Remember how Amazon conservationists sanctioned destruction of areas of rainforest to produce wood to make huts for tens of millions of *Star Pyramid* related personnel to live and work in? How dozens of world religions rewrote their holy books and began to preach zero population growth, just to conserve resources for Project? World is united behind *Star Pyramid*. Perhaps in long run Project will indeed save humanity, but as Lenin said, 'in long run we are all dead.' It's intended to save humanity *now*, and that's exactly what it's doing.

"So, before you urge me to rescue Berrios at any cost, I ask you to contemplate just how great that cost will be."

In my mind I began to follow the network of interlocking economic chains that was centred on *Star Pyramid*. I closed my eyes in defeat. I still thought I was right, but *I won't win this one. They'll override me. Kick me out and put a GU poodle in my place.*

The Undersecretary became businesslike again. "Have you discussed your rescue plan with Berrios?"

I shook my head. "I didn't want to raise false hopes. But I can't guarantee that he won't think of the idea for himself."

Rutzkoi's eyes and their beetle brows narrowed. "From this moment, you're forbidden to tell him. If you discuss idea with anyone I'll have you shot. And your death will not be reported in any media."

"Jesus, Rutzkoi, you don't need to threaten me. I understand the need for silence."

The pugnacious jaw and deep growl were back. "I want you to *be* silent, not just understand need."

His speed of recovery was impressive. I saw how he'd attained his exalted status. The decision seemed beyond question.

"So Berry must die."

"Regrettably, he must. And now I must inform you that we face even worse moral dilemma. Antimatter explosion has damaged several of *Tyger*'s systems. It's no longer possible to trigger blast remotely; it must be done manually. And for that, we need Berrios's cooperation."

"Dear God. You mean *Berrios* has to push the button that blows him to atoms?"

Rutzkoi nodded.

"That," I said, "is the sickest thing I've ever heard. What a horrible world we've created."

He nodded. "With its own horrible logic. I agree. But *he won't know that*. Krantz's people in the SPU have been working on scenario—"

"Yes, Joel would be just the right person to concoct a suitable pack of lies."

"*Scenario*. Krantz is a realist, he understands exactly what's at stake."

Sure. Promotion. Another heave up the slippery pole. But Rutzkoi would've twisted Krantz's arm, just like he was twisting mine.

"Arming sequence will be represented to Berrios as routine technical reprogramming task," Rutzkoi said. He sighed; it looked genuine. "I'm sorry, Simpson, I really am. But we can't risk him refusing."

* * *

Rutzkoi wouldn't even let me do the dirty deed myself. I could watch, but not speak. I might inadvertently give something away by my voice or manner. They delegated the task to Kingsley Potter, Chief Psychologist, whose team had recommended Berrios in the first place.

Over the faulty but still operational freewave link, the test pilot listened to the broadcast instructions, the code-groups and passwords. We watched the erratic video feed as he entered them carefully into the computer.

We waited.

The physiological monitors continued to show heartbeat and brainwaves.

"You've forgotten to initiate program," Rutzkoi pronounced.

There was a lengthy silence. Then Berrios spoke. His voice sounded infinitely sad and withdrawn.

"I know all about this new 'program', Mr Undersecretary. I know exactly what it's for. I've spent many days with little to do but think, and I've been looking into a few things that have always puzzled me. Last night I had a dream, in which I came to realise that I was to undergo a test. I would be offered a terrible temptation."

Rutzkoi didn't react. The Chief Psychologist shook his head. "Berry, you're just–"

"No. The dream was true: I believe it came from God. I've traced the circuits, and I know why Module K was foisted on me. A controlled explosion of the antimatter chamber, to direct the mahabhavium core back towards Earth, yes?"

"Nonsense. It's just an obscure experimen–"

"Please don't lie to me, Kingsley. Admit the truth, *please*. You owe me that."

I took a quick decision. It would probably mean my career, but – well, right now I wasn't greatly concerned. I turned off the sound channel for a moment.

"Let me speak to him. He knows; it won't give anything away. But he's more likely to cooperate if he hears it from me."

Rutzkoi pursed his lips, exhaled slowly. Glanced towards Potter, who nodded. "Very well, Simpson. Someone has to. You may as well be the bearer of bad news."

The bad news has already been borne.

I turned the sound back on and confirmed Berrios's suspicions. Then I explained why it was absolutely necessary for him to set off the explosion, and why I hated asking.

The pilot had listened patiently. "Frank: you don't have to argue the case so eloquently. I see the reasons perfectly. I understand why you have no choice but to insist, despite your own wishes. And I admit it: I'm tempted. I'd welcome oblivion. Then I'd be able to stop thinking about the terrible blinding sunlight and my people in flames."

Potter thought he saw some leverage, and jumped in before I could warn him. "Then why not redeem–"

Berry's reply was measured and calm. "I repeat: I'm tempted. But it's not oblivion that I'll face. It's God."

We all realised that now was not the time to argue religion. Whatever we personally believed, we knew what Berrios believed. Deeply, sincerely, and immovably.

All we could do was take it into account. Persuade him to sacrifice himself for the greater good.

"He'll understand," said the psychologist. "The accident wasn't your fault."

Berrios's voice sank to a whisper. "I don't fear meeting God on that account, Kingsley. But you ask me to commit a mortal sin."

The psychologist couldn't follow the reasoning. "It's a sin to die in order to save the human race?"

"No. *That* I'd do without hesitation. But it *is* a sin to commit suicide."

I glanced at Potter's stricken face. *That* wasn't why his Psych Team had chosen a religious man. They'd seen religion as just one more lever to manipulate. They'd forgotten that to Berrios it was something to live by.

The psychologist tried to regain the initiative.

"Federico, it's not suicide. It's a supreme act of self-sacrifice. When Christ went to the cross without protest, when He could save Himself but chose not to, was that suicide?" It was a cogent argument, but also a bad mistake, as I saw at once, despite being an atheist. I'd been exposed to the teachings, and after I'd rejected the supernatural elements, what remained was no more than the common currency of human morality in virtually every culture. We didn't need an omnipotent deity to tell us what was good and what was not. Especially not if millions were willing to go against their innate humanity and do whatever deed the priests announced that their god considered good. That's the problem with relying on authority instead of your own conscience. You sacrifice the ability to choose the right path. Sacrifice the ability to choose.

Like many atheists, I had a very clear idea of what I didn't believe in. Clearer, I venture to suggest, than that of many believers. Believers never ask the hard questions, never face up to uncomfortable inconsistencies.

I remembered what the priests had tried to teach me. The Chief Psychologist didn't have a religious bone in his body, and he clearly lacked my grasp of Berry's position as the test-pilot saw it. In those terms, Potter's argument was blasphemous. Christ was the Son of God; Berrios was not. It was as simple as that.

So I wasn't surprised when Berrios replied, coldly clear across the empty gulf, "It is expedient for us, that one man should die for the people?"

The psychologist, unfamiliar with the Gospel of Saint John, agreed with the words of Caiaphas.

Rutzkoi raged and blustered, but Berry was unmoved. As a monk, he had no family to threaten. When Rutzkoi hinted that he would blow up the Athanasius Orbital Monastery unless Berrios complied with GU orders, he remained unmoved. "Suicide is a mortal sin, even if carried out under coercion. You tempt me, but I will not yield. I can't stop you, but I don't believe you would carry out such a threat. If you did, you too would answer to God."

"Psych Team should have foreseen this!" Rutzkoi screeched. "Heads will roll!"

"As you just told me," I said, "that achieves nothing." As he glared at me I added: "No, I'm wrong. I'll tell you exactly what it will achieve. It will ensure that whichever heads roll, they won't include yours.

"What it *won't* achieve is getting the mahabhavium back. That's gone."

The monitors were still showing *Tyger*'s cramped cabin. We saw Berrios remove his headphones, leaving them squawking Rutzkoi's futile threats to the empty air. The pilot felt for his rosary. Then he changed his mind and reached out to the console, calling up the virtual guitar program. Continuing from where he had left off when disaster struck, he strummed the air. He began to sing, waveringly at first but gaining strength at each word. We all heard them, and could not look at each other.

"Now the losing of those half-dozen men,
It grieved our Captain sore.
But the losing of that great whale-fish,
It grieved him ten times more, brave boys,
It grieved him ten times more."

We heard him laugh, with neither rancour nor humour. He spoke the words he had originally been scheduled to say when *Tyger*'s ramscoop ignited and Angi Frazier asked him for a message.

"Tell the people of Earth to pray," he said quietly. "Not for me, but for themselves."

Then he switched off the freewave link and left us in stunned silence.

CHAPTER 11

EIGHT ISN'T LUCKY

Reynheiður Sigmundsdóttir

China-Kyrgyzstan Border Zone 2163

I know this isn't possible, but I swear I felt the eyes burning into the back of my neck before I heard the approaching footsteps. There was something about the rhythm of her gait – even through my drug-addled stupor I knew it was a woman – that reminded me…

Shit. I don't want to be reminded, thank you very much.

I'd seated myself on an upturned crate with my back to the side entrance of the bar. From here I could see out through the grimy front window, with a spiky zigzag crack where someone had tried to throw someone else through it and failed. There were old posters on the walls advertising Ladies of the Night. They were faded and torn. The posters weren't in great shape either.

The trouble was, I couldn't watch the side entrance without swivelling my neck like a barn owl triangulating a tasty vole. It had been, I belatedly recognised, a foolish choice of seat, Kong's Bar being deep in the decaying rat-runs of Shuidaoyuanzhongchang, close by the border between Kyrgyzstan and the Democratic Republic of Free China, where no man dared to tread without a gang of mercenary bodyguards.

But then, I was no man. Just as the DRFC, though undeniably Chinese, was neither democratic nor free. It was arguably a Republic, unless you thought that President Wu Qiángdé was a monarch of Sun King style in all but name; and if you did think that, you were careful to keep it to yourself.

It was, however, the ideal place to hide from an uncaring world; the arse-end of the universe, about as accessible as the south face of Nanga Parbat, ten times as dangerous, and the embodiment of anarchy but less organised. Which, to be honest, I found refreshing, compared to where I'd been four years ago.

I'd had a good job, then; money, expensive clothes, a pleasant house in a quiet suburb of Outer Tōkyō. Well, I'd *thought* it was a good job. I still had money, though I had to access it in untraceable ways, which required a great deal of bargaining and paranoia. No house – I was renting a room in a tin shack in an alley in Aikenboyicun – and my clothes hadn't been removed, let alone washed, for a week.

I was a mess. A self-inflicted mess. But in a funny way I was happy, mistress of my own destiny. A destiny that wasn't going to lead to much more than an early grave, assuming anyone bothered to dig me one. Probably left in the street to be eaten by one of the numerous packs of feral dogs, that was my destiny.

It felt nice to be useful for a change.

A foolish choice my seat might have been, but it was the only unoccupied one, the other patrons would have killed me as soon as looked at me if I caused the slightest trouble or looked at anyone sideways, and I was too tired, bored, or drunk to consider finding another bar. To be honest, all of the above. Anyway, I know how to take care of myself. I've been trained. That, in a roundabout way, was how I'd ended up in this dump. But it was *my* dump, and I was a bit miffed, to say the least, that someone was invading it uninvited.

My hand crept to the flechette-gun in my left boot and I turned to find out who was sneaking up on me.

"You won't be needing that, Reynheiður." The voice was female and familiar. "At least, not to shoot *me*."

A name struggled out of my messed-up brain, still high on gnathroprine liberally dosed with the raw alcohol that was the closest thing to a real drink you could find in Aksu Prefecture. Distilled from anything that stood still too long.

My voice shook. "Zanna?"

"Hole in one." A tall woman in her late thirties reached past my shoulder, picked up my glass, and drained it. "You won't be needing that, either. God, this moonshine tastes like kerosene mixed with antifreeze."

"That may well be an accurate recipe, Zanna. But you must admit it does have a kick."

"Like a train of mules on steroids. Take this."

She placed a glass of water in front of me, and a small green pill.

The room was spinning like a carousel, I'd turned round too quickly for my vestibular system to keep up with the rest of my head. My voice slurred. "Why should I sober up?"

"Because, like you, I wouldn't dream of coming to a place like this – hell, to a *country* like this – without a weapon. Along with a private goon squad who've been shadowing you for a week until I could spare the time to come and get you. Oh, and my gun is currently pointing at your spine. So take that pill."

I left pill and glass on the table. "Zanna, I don't want to sober up, and I don't want to come back to the Project. If I *did* come back, the first thing I'd do would be to shoot Krantz. Shoot *me* if you must, I'd prefer it."

Colonel Suzanna Mardeen walked round to face me across the filthy table that had previously supported my seventh drink that evening. She didn't look angry. Zanna never needed to, she could be devastatingly effective while wearing a bland, unreadable, expression. The gun, a nasty little thing no larger than a key-fob, was peeping out from her clenched fist. I recognised it as a poison-tipped needle-gun, illegal on the street unless you were in one of the Services. Which of course Zanna was.

"It's still pointing at your spine, just from the other direction," she told me.

"I see that."

Zanna and I had never seen eye to eye, but circumstances had forced us to work together, until Krantz–

Don't go there. It's what she wants.

I feigned calm. "Put your little toy back where no one can see it," I told her. "Find yourself a seat and a drink, pull the seat over next to mine, and we'll talk about it like civilised thugs."

Zanna nodded. She cast her eyes over the room, spotted a suitable chair and drink. Both were occupied, but that didn't bother her. In my experience very little ever did. She whispered something in the ear of the occupant, a huge man with muscles the size of tree-trunks and a long salt-and-pepper beard, who promptly shot out of the chair like a scalded cat and offered her his drink.

She dragged the chair over, perched herself elegantly upon it, and put the drink on the table. Unbuttoned her grubby coat to reveal faded denim jacket and jeans.

"You told him you're RAG," I said.

"Obviously."

"With your own goon squad, like you said. I don't see any of them."

Zanna laughed. "You're too smashed to notice."

"I've only had seven drinks!"

"Then you're losing your edge. A year ago you'd've spotted them a kilometre away. Half the men in this room are RAG Suppression Squad."

I glared at her. "I don't care if they're Tooth Fairies. I'm not rejoining the Project!" I knew why she was here, there was only one possible reason.

"Reynheiður, your special talents are needed."

"It would have been good if someone had remembered that before kicking me out."

Her voice softened. "The powers that be have remembered *now*. But after what Joel did to you, no one is surprised you're taking that line."

"Krantz threw me to the wolves." I looked at the drink she'd liberated. "Eight is lucky in China," I muttered, as I picked up the glass and tossed the hooch down.

Zanna gave me a calculating look. "He had no choice. You've always known that."

Same old bullshit. "There's always a choice, Zanna."

She shook her head. "I'm afraid that's not always true. As I'm about to prove to you."

It was my turn to brandish a weapon. "Really?"

Zanna gave me a pitiful look. "Really. You're slipping, Reynheiður. And eight isn't lucky. Didn't you notice I'd spiked that drink?"

CHAPTER 12

ONE WHO WALKS CAREFULLY

Alfonsina Shegwada

Project Unit M14, Guayaquil, Ecuador 2163

I'd prepared an elaborate plan to get myself on the *Star Pyramid* crew list by hacking into the GU's systems. In the event, I didn't need it.

They called me.

Mkono usioweza kuukata, ubusu. Kiss the hand you cannot cut off. In modern terms: If you can't beat them, join them.

Better still: join them, *then* beat them.

It wasn't exactly the *hand* I was having to kiss, but some things are necessary.

It was fate. My destiny. But I'd never believed that sort of bullshit. It was blind luck. Or maybe I really *was* that good. I certainly thought I was. I mean, look at how I'd risen through the ranks at KarouBiz.

Having been offered my life's desire, I played hard to get. Didn't want to seem over-keen, someone might get suspicious. Asked a lot of hard questions, raised potential problems. Eventually, giving every outward appearance of satisfaction, I agreed.

Apparently I'd done such a wonderful job with the Project's food preparation software that they wanted me around to look after it if anything went adrift. It hadn't occurred to them that this also put me in a great position to make sure it did.

It did pose some potential problems, though. I'd convinced myself long ago that there was no reliable way to destroy *Star Pyramid* remotely in the early stages of her voyage. That was why I had to be on board. Even then, it would have to be done in stages, disabling vital systems before striking the killer blow.

I had to tread a tightrope. The only way I could get on board, legit or hacked, would be to paint myself indispensable. And it had to be in some area of computer tech because changing my entire life story would require such a huge set of linked falsehoods that I'd almost certainly trip up and get caught.

I'd deliberately aimed low. The infotech on *Star Pyramid* has four security levels. Level Z is for Flight Controllers only. Level Y is technical mission-critical equipment: fusion reactors, the eka-Bussard and its ramscoop fields and engines, the Impact Avoidance System, the MAD and antimatter storage, that kind of thing. Level X is human-related equipment: SusAn, air, water, food, and by extension Hydroponics. Level W is everything else, from cleaning bots to decisions about the menus in restaurants.

My work at KarouBiz qualified me for clearance level W. It would've been easy to get that raised, so I'd worked very hard not to. My hidden hacking abilities and crypto experience would be enough to let me gain access to anything needing X or Y. Either would do. I wouldn't need level Z.

The trick, as I figured it, was to lay enough decoys to bury my tracks. And the time to do that was to set up a few key features *now*, and complete the job no more than a week before I contrived to make something go horribly adrift. That is, several centuries Earth time into the voyage. That way I wouldn't be leaving clues lying around for a similar time period.

When I did hack in, though, I'd need to cover up my new tracks. And the way to do that, I'd decided, was to fool them into thinking that the problem was an old one that hadn't been spotted. A subtle error that had inserted itself into legacy software from the time when *Star Pyramid* was little more than a rapidly growing jumble of steel girders and plates in a station-keeping orbit at the L2 point on the opposite side of Earth to the Sun. Well, that *looked* like it had.

Done sufficiently carefully, this would head off any kind of witch-hunt for an onboard saboteur. Not just looking in the wrong place: looking in the wrong *time*.

Tawala ngumi, linda ulimi. Control your fists, guard your tongue.

* * *

First step: a medical examination.

It could all have fizzled out right then, before I'd even begun my training. The GU was expecting a few natural deaths to occur during the voyage. To minimise the number, only fairly young people would be selected, and they'd be chosen for robust health and a low prospect of developing any serious complaints.

I was a bit nervous, because my childhood hadn't exactly been the kind that produced vigorous, healthy adults. I was short, the result of never having enough food to eat. If I'd been a few years older when my mother died, I'd have been working in the recycling plant like her, and my body would be riddled with cancer and Lord knows what else.

I'd avoided voluntary medical tests because those might look suspicious. I'd been exercising regularly: long-distance running, weights, martial arts. Building up my strength and stamina. I wasn't aware of any health conditions.

But then, you never are until you find out.

The examination took the best part of a day. A series of doctors and nurses poked and prodded every part of my body, some extremely intimate. They put me through endless tests: eyesight, hearing, breathing, heartbeat, muscular control. They took six sample tubes of my blood. *Six!*

I passed muster, by a wide margin. My small size didn't cause any concern.

Then they sent me for surgery to have my appendix removed. A standard precaution, and one that told me I was well on the way to being accepted.

They sent me home, to rest after the ordeal, and to let the traces of keyhole surgery heal. That took four weeks.

The day after, I received my marching orders.

* * *

Guayaquil is in Ecuador, two degrees south of the equator, straddling the Guayas river, about 80 kilometres upstream from the Gulf of Guayaquil and the open sea. The coastal land is an ancient river delta nestling against foothills of the Andes mountains, backbone of South America. It was the nearest city to the Project's Intensive Training Unit. The ITU was tucked away on the lower slopes of the mountains, deep within a reforested area.

We drove there from the airport in a mud-spattered ORV – off-road vehicle. A robust four-wheel drive car that seated six people: four passengers in two pairs of seats at the back, the driver and another escort in the front. The journey would take between eight and ten hours, depending on road conditions.

Road? Ha.

Both GU officers looked SouMerican, with coffee-coloured skin and thick black hair. When we were climbing in I'd noticed that both had neatly cut moustaches. A few grey hairs poked out from under the driver's cap, and I'd also spotted some in his moustache. I reckoned he was about thirty-five years old, and his companion ten years younger. Both wore dark grey-green uniforms: baggy trousers with wide belts, heavy tunics, leather boots. Peaked cap with some kind of insignia. Each of them had a pistol in a holster strapped to his waist, and there were two automatic rifles in the footwell. The driver was a rather surly man who reluctantly admitted to the name Edwardo Jaramillo Solorzano and thereafter said very little. The younger officer, a talkative man named Edison Zambrano Rodríguez, seemed more friendly.

It was a long, bumpy ride, along narrow tracks walled in by thick rainforest. I surreptitiously sized up my fellow passengers: one male trainee, two female. We'd be joining several hundred other trainees, at different stages of their training and with different specialities.

"Simone Dupuy," the woman sitting next to me in the first row behind the driver said.

It took me a moment to realise she was introducing herself.

"We'll be spending a lot of time together, I think," she went on, a deep throaty voice, the kind that men seem to imagine is sexy. I doubted it would work for her, she was rather plain and distinctly overweight. But then, what did I know about men? Her café-au-lait skin was smooth and unblemished, not like mine, which was darker and sun-damaged. And she had beautiful auburn hair, whereas mine was short, mousey, and curly. She was tall, too; if we were standing, I wouldn't come up to her shoulders. I hadn't been a pretty child and I was definitely not a pretty woman. Neither in body nor mind. A robust and determined one, though. Woman on a mission. But not the mission the GU had presented me with.

"Both of us being in Infotech, I mean," she said.

"Ah. You know who I am."

"You're Shegweda, aren't you?"

"Shegwada. Alfonsina Shegwada."

Dupuy ducked her head in apology. "Sorry, I'm terrible with names."

The man in the seat behind leaned over and offered a hand to shake, so we did. "Rowley Pollard. I'm in Comm."

"Ah. Then you know all about... *k*-fields," Simone said.

Big grin. "Karmabhumi? 'Course. Can't run freewave without that stuff."

"They tell me the math's very hard."

"Not really. There's good analogies with classical physics, they help. Anyway, Gayl will tell you: astrophysics equations, they far worse."

The blonde woman beside him nodded. "Yup. The Loon

Equations are child's play compared to compressible plasma flows in free boundary magnetic fields. Even *without* the quantum effects."

Pollard was a typically laid-back 'Bajan' – a West Indian from Barbados – with a soft drawling voice, extremely dark skin attesting his African origin and slave ancestry, and finely chiselled features. Many a fashion model would have paid a fortune for Rowley Pollard's cheekbones. Born in Marley Vale at the south-east corner of the island, he told us. He'd started out helping his father, a fisherman, which got him interested in satellite navigation. He built his own GPS receivers and sold them to augment his family's income from fishing, which eventually came to the attention of the Electronics Department at the University of the West Indies in the Bridgetown suburbs. Ten years and fourteen patents later, the Project snapped him up.

He was even taller than the two women, probably about 1.8 metres, hard to be sure when he was sitting. I couldn't see his legs but his posture told me he was a bit cramped, so they had to be quite long. Athletic build, he would surely have made a demon fast bowler at cricket – though later he told me that he'd always hated organised sports.

"This is Gayl. Gayl Goodenough," he said, waving a splayed hand towards the fourth trainee, a slim, slightly nervous woman with hazel eyes and a figure to die for. "One o' *Star Pyramid's* astrophysicists."

Science, not technists, then.

We had a short but animated conversation, interrupted when the ORV ran over a stone or a rut, which was too often for my liking. When the track was free of ruts it was corrugated by what had to be a lot of local traffic, so we were all getting a free massage, like it or not. I was tempted to check my teeth to make sure they'd remained in their sockets.

Despite her name, Dupuy wasn't French, nor even from a former French colony like Canada. Her father was from what formerly was Burkina Faso in PanAfrica, her mother from Louisiana in the United States, and she'd been born in Poland. Diplomatic Corps. Goodenough was slim and cool, even in the sweltering rainforest heat and humidity, with blonde hair tied in a ponytail and piercing green eyes.

We didn't say much about our specialities. Not so much because we didn't want to talk shop, but because Edison now took it upon himself to act as tour guide and no one else could get a word in edgewise. It was clearly a routine he'd followed many times, but it was interesting in its own way. And it helped to distract us from the bumpy, muddy track.

"Three hundred years ago, this area was rainforest, like now," he said, swivelling in his dilapidated seat to face us. No grey in his hair or moustache. His cap was worn at a tilt and his eyes were a penetrating blue. "Two hundred years ago the trees had been cut down and sold, the brush and branches burned, and it was farmland. Cattle, maize. A hundred years ago it was little more than desolate scrubland, ruined by slash-and-burn agriculture. Sixty-four years ago the Ecuadorian government began reforestation, funded by the GU Rewilding Programme. They took advice from Costa Rica, which has a long track record of protecting its wilderness areas, especially rainforest."

"It worked," Pollard said.

"Sure did. The advice was good. The programme's been a huge success."

My cover was now so deeply ingrained that I had no difficulty looking enthusiastic about the GU's generosity and asking Edison questions. So did the other three trainees as we bumped and juddered our way along the muddy trails that served as roads.

At first, the forest appeared much the same in whichever direction I looked, but with Edison's voluble help I began to pick out different kinds of trees. They were liberally decorated with vines, some with large leaves and thick ropy stalks, others small-leafed and clinging with multiply dividing roots. The vines wound their way up and around the trunks, while the lower regions of the forest were filled with ferns and bushes and shrubs, grasses, brilliant flowers in every colour of the rainbow.

Speaking of which, the rain now started falling in torrents.

That's why they call them rainforests. Right now the rain was so heavy you saw more of it than you did of the forest.

Mvua haina hodi.

* * *

We bounced on, the track now becoming more like a stream as the path developed a distinct upward gradient. The ORV slithered from side to side as its tyres lost their grip in the increasingly glutinous mud.

"Don't worry," Edison told us. "The treads are cut very deep. With luck, we might not have to get out and push."

We moved more slowly now, in fits and starts, and the passing trees stopped being green blurs and began to take on definite shapes.

"What are those?" Rowley asked him, pointing to a cluster of green-grey trunks that disappeared into the heavy canopy. They all had thick triangular buttresses that made them resemble the early conceptions of space rockets; tall upright cylinders with protruding fins at the base. "They look like some of the trees back home. Flamboyant trees, we call them."

"Ah. These are different, but you've picked a good one. Always impresses visitors. The Kichwa tribe of the Amazon call them *ceibo*. I doubt you'll know that name, but you've probably heard of their most useful product."

"Kapok," Gayl said.

Surprise clouded Edison's usually sunny visage. "Oh. You know about them, then?"

"I thought you were an astrophysicist," Simone said. "Not a botanist."

"Yup."

"While we *travel* to the stars, Gayl will be delvin' into their innards," Rowley said. "Nuclear reactions, gravitational collapse, cool stuff like that."

I was forming the distinct impression that Gayl and Rowley had known each other for a long time. Didn't behave like an item: just friends.

"The surfaces of stars are just as interesting as their guts, Rowley," Gayl said. "Magnetohydrodynamics. MHD for short. How the magnetic fields twist and writhe and snap causing huge prominences. Solar mass ejections. But you're right; my favourite area is neutron stars."

"Like Karoubi's Star," Simone said. "And that's why you're here."

"Why we all here," Rowley said.

"So how do you know about *ceibo* trees, Gayl?"

"*Ceibo pentandra*," she said. "And Rowley's trees are *Delonix regia*. I have a mind like an elephant's attic, stuffed with all the junk and souvenirs of a lifetime."

"I never knew elephants had attics," Simone said with a smile.

"If they did, they'd resemble my memory. Like a memory palace but less orderly."

"Elephants never forget. She got an eidetic memory," Rowley clarified.

And it all came rushing back. I had never forgotten, either.
The elephant.
My father.

The GU had spent a fortune reforesting Ecuador. But they'd done nothing to help my village, in what I now knew had been the ten-kilometre demilitarised zone between Tanzania and Zambia. All they'd done was to use us as slaves and kill us.

And there was another thought. *Eidetic memory. I must be very careful around this woman.* People like that can notice mistakes months after you've made them. However careful you thought you'd been. Or, as Mother would no doubt have said, *chura mzuia maji ndovu. A frog can stop an elephant drinking water.*

What it means is: Don't underestimate your enemy.

Some of this must have shown in my face, because Edison asked "Are you all right, Alfonsina?"

"Uh– I feel a bit sick, actually," I said, to cover the emotional disturbance unleashed by the casual reference to elephants. "It's all this bouncing."

Edison made a sympathetic face. "The rain should stop in fifteen minutes, and there's a clearing in the forest. Can you hold on till then?"

"I think so."

"Then we'll have a half-hour break."

* * *

There was a *ceibo* tree near the clearing.

Muttering to himself, Edwardo checked the vehicle over, kicking tyres and inspecting the suspension, which was thickly encrusted with mud.

The rest of us followed Edison as he swung an old but sharp machete to clear a path through soaking wet vegetation to give us a closer view. Lizards scuttled away as we approached, and we tried to avoid the profusion of spiders' webs and their resident spiders. The fin-like roots were *huge*. You could hide between them if you wanted.

"Don't let it scratch you," Edison warned us, pointing at the short thick thorns in the tree's broad trunk, which was much the same colour as his uniform. Its clusters of shield-shaped scarlet petals were in blossom and gave off a sweet perfume. "They can grow to 70 metres," he said. "But not yet in this forest. Another century should do it."

At Simone's urging he pointed out a few other species. The straggly trees with a profusion of thin trunks and pale grey bark were palo santo. Edison was especially proud of them, because you seldom find them outside established old-growth forests. "Only an expert in horticulture can persuade them to thrive in reforested areas," he said. "It takes care, hard work, and a lot of clever techniques that the Costa Ricans invented."

You couldn't miss the guayacan tree, more a large shrub crowned with spectacular lemon-yellow flowers shaped like tiny trumpets. These were still in the early stages of their very slow growth, the tallest rising about 12 metres. "Wait a century and they'll be three times that," Edison said.

"Aside from monkeys and lizards, I haven't seen any animals," Simone said. "Are there any others?"

"Nothing dangerous," Edison replied, baring his teeth, then grinning.

"Oh! No, I wasn't worried. I love wild animals. I was hoping to see a jaguar."

He shook his head. "Not a chance. They're around, but elusive at the best of times. They'd never be within five kilometres of a noisy machine like ours."

Even the monkeys were so high in the treetops that we got little more than fleeting glimpses. We might have spotted a few sloths hanging lazily from branches, if we'd used Edison's binoculars and known where to look, but they'd be well camouflaged by algae in their fur. No jaguars, no tapirs, not even an iguana; but they were all there, Edison said, and their numbers were increasing. Unlike most of SouMerica's rainforest remnants.

What we did see were *birds*. Birds on branches, high or low; birds flitting between trees, expertly dodging the bushes. Birds in small groups, solitary birds, brightly coloured birds, dull birds.

"No surprise, all those birds," Edison said, after we'd got back in the ORV and were once more bouncing up and down as we traversed an especially rutted section of track. He enquired solicitously after my health, and I told him that the break had settled my stomach and I was fine. We'd turned off what counted for the main drag in these parts, and the trail was winding its way up into the foothills. We couldn't see much ahead because of the trees, but the zigzag path suggested we'd keep going uphill for some time.

While Edwardo grappled with the ORV, Edison resumed his mission to educate us about Ecuadorian birdlife. "There are over 1600 species of bird in Ecuador, and we have 600 of them in the reforested area now. As much variety and colour as you'll see anywhere in the Amazon. See that one with the white beak, black head, and brown body? That's–"

"An olive oropendola," Gayl said. "And the short fat black one with a bright green mask and iridescent blue underbelly is a paradise tanager."

"What's that multicoloured one with a long curved beak?" Pollard asked.

"Point it out. Oh, over there. That's a golden-collared toucanet."

"You know birds as well?" Edison said.

"Yeah. Unlike the trees, though, it's a hobby of mine. Birdwatching."

I must definitely *be very careful around this woman. She'll be unusually observant, as well.*

We saw macaws and hoatzins and toucans, more monkeys, and more trees than I'd seen in my entire life. Edison prattled happily on, and I leaned back and closed my eyes.

* * *

"Are we nearly there yet?" Rowley asked, grinning broadly. Gayl sniggered. I didn't get the joke, if there was one. It seemed a sensible enough question to me.

"Ten minutes," Edwardo said, breaking his habitual silence.

And without warning, the sky opened up above us and the rays of the setting sun bathed the landscape in rose-coloured light, the irregular shadows of the forest seeming to lengthen as we watched. The muddy track ended in a huge puddle and morphed into a narrow tarmac road.

The clearing was human-made, but it hadn't been hacked out of the forest. Instead, it was an area where reforestation had been confined to orderly clumps of shrub and long grasses. A garden. In the centre of the open area – it must have been at least five hectares – was a walled compound topped with razorwire. Inside it was a building.

And what a building.

I heard Simone gasp. Rowley muttered something under his breath.

"I can't believe it," Gayl said. "They've re-created the Step Pyramid!"

Rowley shook his head – in wonderment, I thought. I wanted to shake mine, too, but for a different reason. "They've re-created the entire complex," he said. "Enclosure wall, Step Pyramid… all of it." He shook his head again. "I detect the heavy hand of the Marketing Department. The *Star Pyramid* brand, embodied in stone. Someone paid an architect *millions* to design this! And millions more for someone to build it."

I began to take a shine to Rowley. His mind and mine worked along similar lines.

The ORV trundled along the road towards a gated entrance. The outer wall was at least half a kilometre long. Behind it, the pyramid rose in five stages, each step ten metres or more high.

"I don't think Djoser's pyramid had windows," Rowley said. "Or satellite dishes on top."

In the centre of the wall the tarmac thrust its way between two widely spaced gateposts. Atop the pyramid, the GU flag flew proudly. There was a guards' hut beside the gateposts, with at least twenty soldiers, all carrying automatic weapons.

We stopped just inside the wall, where a solid barrier blocked the road. Edwardo produced documentation, two of the soldiers inspected it closely.

Now we could see other modern embellishments. Instead of a large open space and a few small temples nestling against the walls, as in Djoser's day, the interior was crammed with a maze of single-storey outbuildings. The road ended in a perfect circle surrounding a large pool with fountains. The central pyramid dominated the complex. An impressive collection of modernistic columns and swooping arches fronted what was clearly its main entrance, a series of six enormous doors, side by side. The entire building was clad in beautifully cut stone, inset with huge windows. The stone glowed an ever-deeper red as the sun sank below the treeline.

It had obviously been built to impress, but all I could see was money wasted on a colossal scale. Money that could have been spent helping my village, or a million other underprivileged people who had been slaving to make *Star Pyramid* a reality. *Jumbe mroho hufilisi wenzake. A greedy chief impoverishes the people.* I was tempted to spit, but gasped with fake astonishment instead.

The barrier sank into the ground and they waved us through.

I'm in.

* * *

Two hundred-plus trainees, evenly divided by sex, less evenly by gender identity. Fifty instructors: 27 identifying as male, 19 as female, two non-binary, two declined to specify. In my childhood village, everything had been straightforward: men were men, women women, girls girls, and boys would always be boys. This, I now understood, was convenient for 95 per cent of the population, but hell for the other five per cent; even so, I'd never quite adjusted to the complex sexuality of the outside world, where virtually everyone had at least three identities: biological sex, gender, and sexual proclivity. Which seemed to occur in every possible combination, making the *Kama Sutra* seem like an infant school primer.

Don't get me wrong: I'm no prude, and no virgin either. But such relationships hold little interest for me. They'd just distract from my sole objective in life. Which you already know about. Since I had no intention of entering into any kind of relationship, I couldn't've cared less who was doing what with which to whom. The only relationship that interested me was the one I was already in; unflinching hatred towards the Global Union. It was also a relationship that I concealed so successfully that most of the time I managed to hide it from myself.

Except when someone mentioned elephants.

Our first week was spent in various orientation exercises. Aims of the Project, history of the Project, current state of the Project. I rejected the aims, considered the history to be propaganda, rapidly knew a lot more about the current state than my instructors did, and passed every test with flying colours by regurgitating what they'd been teaching me. That was important; they could still bump me off the roster if I didn't measure up.

Then GU Law, space law, international treaties, job descriptions, chains of command, chains of reporting, mission terms of reference, what we weren't allowed to do, what we were supposed to do.

I've never worked harder in my life.

More interesting was the comprehensive, though superficial, survey of *Star Pyramid*'s onboard systems. Layout of the ship, all 24 decks of it. Propulsion: ramscoop, antimatter, and – so the GU hoped – Da Silva. Fusion generators for power. Lateral jets to create spin. Communications: some radio, but mainly concentrating on Da Silva freewave. Life support, breaking down into air and heating. Suspended Animation caskets (I privately thought of SusAn as 'death support'). Medicine, from analgesics to brain surgery. Food and water, coming together in Hydroponics, a polite name for endless arrays of slimy green algal vats, whose product would be flavoured, textured, and printed into foodstuffs indistinguishable from the real thing. Recycling, of *everything*. Computer systems, heavy machinery, lightweight equipment. OWLLs, shuttles, drones. Security systems: cameras in every public space, transmitting all data back to Earth in real time by freewave, with a copy kept on the ship. But no cameras in recreational areas and restaurants, and none in the crew's private quarters. Illegal surveillance, apparently, and counterproductive by implying a lack of trust. So the psychologists said.

Oh, yes, that reminds me: introduction to human psychology. How to look out for danger signs of incipient psychosis in your fellow crew members.

And those weren't a tenth of it. It was a crash course, with emphasis on the crash: intensive periods of study separated by 'rest days' when we did physical activities instead. Twenty-kilometre runs through the mountains, weight-lifting, rowing boats. Cycling, mobile and static. Physical strength, stamina, and agility were, they told us, just as important as mental strength, stamina, and agility.

No one told us, but obviously training was only one part of this. The GU was putting us all through the wringer to find out how we'd react to stress. The weak shall inherit the Earth; the strong will go to the stars.

I studied everything, remembered most of it for long enough to pass the test, suppressed all signs of weakness, and focused on a number of key areas, notably Security.

As an infotech trainee I spent a lot of my time at an HV dais learning everything that was relevant to level W clearance, such as how to program the food printers for new recipes. I breezed through all of this, absorbing along the way a hundred methods to wriggle past what the GU's coders naively thought to be unbreachable firewalls. Not an official part of the course, you appreciate, and not anything I'd make my instructors aware of. But I'd already done my apprenticeship on the UnderNet, and the only tricks I didn't know were those that hadn't yet been invented.

With enormous care, I put some of them into practice, laying the groundwork for the apparent error in legacy code. Not the error itself; I'd sort that out much later when *Star Pyramid* was several centuries into its voyage and I knew the lie of the land. My plan now was to set up some back doors where traces of an error could retrospectively be inserted, so that someone *really* clever would believe they'd uncovered a mistake everyone else had missed, all those years ago.

I was a bit worried when Gayl walked in unexpectedly when I was working my way through a short pile of holocopies of the most crucial operational overviews. I'd made them so that I could access the information without logging into the system over and over again. With my level of clearance I couldn't edit the underlying code, but as a minor member of the Infotech section I was permitted to read it. We worked in open areas so anyone could walk by, but I'd tucked myself away on a corner behind a screen of tall rainforest plants in big terracotta pots. It was just bad luck that she happened to poke her nose in before I could slip the holocopies into a drawer for later private perusal.

As soon as she saw I was working, she apologised for intruding and backed away. I was a bit nervous for the next few days, because she might mention it to someone higher up the food chain who'd turn up unannounced and ask awkward questions. But that was always on the cards anyway, and I had good answers ready.

Twenty seconds on a terminal, in the middle of a complicated series of commands relating to an obscure part of the code for food preparation, and the back door was safely inserted where no one would ever expect it. Another thirty and all traces of my access had been erased. In a few days' time I'd hand in the holocopies for recycling. That would go on record, along with their original creation. Proving I had nothing to hide, should anyone decide to look into what I'd been doing.

A week went past, and no one had come to question me. I was in the clear.

Outwardly, I remained calm. Inwardly, I was singing. It had been a risk, but a calculated one that would simplify things a great deal when it really mattered, more than two hundred years into an unknowable future.

It never rains in space. But rain will come.

CHAPTER 13

IDENTICAL TWINS

Colonel Suzanna Mardeen

Rapid Action Group, Cairo, Egypt 2163

The dossier appeared in flatscreen projection on the HV dais in the office I was currently occupying. Outside, in the bustling streets, the people of Cairo went about their business. Inside, I went about mine.

Everything we do in RAG is important, not that most of the world ever gets to find out about it. We're the eyes, ears, and nose of the GU, and, when needed, its fists. Without us the Project would've collapsed into a smouldering heap of rubble decades ago. We operate across national boundaries... no, we don't bother to recognise national boundaries.

My task for the next few days was doubly important. So although I knew the dossiers by heart, I was– no, I *didn't* know them by heart, I just thought I did. That's why I'd pulled them up for review.

I turned my attention to the first one. There was all the usual guff about name, date of birth, place of birth, and so on and so on and so on. What I wanted to refresh my memory on was the recorded HV personal statement, where the subject talked about himself. Or, in this case, herself.

I flicked it to 'play', and after a few minutes of rather dull introduction I leaned forward for a closer view...

* * *

"Hjördis and I are twins," Reynheiður Sigmundsdóttir said. Only her head was visible, life size. Nordic features; her Scandinavian ancestry had won out over the Celtic. Well-defined cheekbones. Very short dark hair, but that was dyed from her natural blonde. Dark blue eyes. No makeup. An intense stare.

I could zoom out to watch the rest of her, but at this point it was what she was saying that I wanted to hear again, and see if her expression matched the words.

"Genetically, we're identical. We *look* identical. Well, we did at first, and we still would if we didn't wear very different clothes, cut and dye our hair differently, wear different makeup or none. She likes flamboyant jewellery; I seldom wear any. It tends to get in the way of the AK-53. We behave differently, too: I'm introverted and she's outgoing.

"We grew up in Iceland on a farm near Sauðárkrókur, about 250 kilometres north-east of Reykjavik, on the coast at the top of Skagafjörða. Our father was Sigmund Gunnarsson, our mother Sigríður Vilhjálmsson. They owned a herd of sixty horses. Yes, those archetypal Icelandic horses. We both loved them.

"Don't *ever* call them 'ponies', Íslendingar find that insulting.

"An íslenski hesturinn is small, to be sure, with a thick mane, but it's a true horse. One of its unusual characteristics is its gait. Rather, gaits. Most horses can walk, trot, and gallop. Many can canter, or be taught to. The Icelandic horse has two more, so it's called the five-gaited horse. We *can* count: we just consider the canter and gallop to be variations on the same gait. The other two are the tölt, an ambling gait that's similar to a pace, like a camel or a giraffe, and the flugskeið, also a bit like a pace, but faster. It's used for pace races. Only the best breeds can do both of those, our horses among them.

"When we were young, our mother always dressed us in identical clothing, usually practical farm stuff, trousers and shirts. Even in those we were real cuties; strangers were always cooing over us. But Hjördis wanted to wear pretty, girly clothes like most of the other girls at school, so mother gave in and dressed her differently. She was the bubbly, flighty one who got all the boyfriends; I was the studious one, not that interested in boys and them not much interested in me. Lots of self-control until someone pushed me too far; then I'd explode with no prior warning. She looked mild and friendly, but she had serious anger issues. Temper like a wolverine when aroused. Didn't happen often, but when it did, it was like being hit by a tsunami.

"As we got older, we both changed. We started out very close but drifted apart. I still love her, she's my twin sister. But I'm not sure whether I *like* her. It's an abstract arms-length sort of love and we hardly ever see each other. Not even electronically.

"When we were in our late teens, Hjördis stopped playing around and started studying as though her life depended on it. We both went to the Taekniskóllin in Reykjavik, and then to the University there. We had very different preferences. Hjördis got a top degree, made a career as an engineer, then slid sideways into Structural Certification. I started out in agriculture, then chucked it in after a year and a half at University and joined the Marine Corps. I wanted more action and less thinking, missions rather than assignments and examinations. I fought three campaigns in central Africa and was head-hunted by RAG. Specifically, Lieutenant Suzanna Mardeen. A real bitch, hard as flint. I kind of liked her, but she was scary."

* * *

You hid both well, I thought. *I found* you *scary.*
  I hid that well too, apparently.
  She was right, though. I was a hard bitch. So was she.
  At that time I'd climbed the ranks to Lieutenant, on the staff of Brigadier General Vassily Ivanovich Popov. He was always on the lookout for suitable people, but he didn't have time to read all the personnel reports and other bumf, so he assigned the task to his staff. Most of the time, that was me.
  I spotted Reynheiður Sigmundsdóttir's potential immediately. Anyone would. It was the combination of talents that stood out. Always in the top two or three, no matter what. Second with a sniper rifle, third in weapons training with a variety of hardware from pistols to anti-tank missiles. Second in e-warfare, from hacking to drone surveillance. Spoke six languages fluently and could make her way in six more. Proficient in all forms of unarmed combat. Proficient in all forms of armed combat. Highly intelligent; top of the class by a wide margin in psychological profiling. And that was what *really* caught my eye. She was brilliant at it. With one exception: she'd never managed to profile herself. She hadn't a clue what she was really like, it had all been submerged for so long that she'd built a wall around herself. Not just a defensive wall: this one had turrets with cannon and murder-holes to drop molten lead on your enemies.
  Her later record, especially under fire, was impeccable. Cool and calm when everything around her was disintegrating. Could spot an IED a kilometre away. Tackled a suicide bomber in Ombella-M'poko Prefecture, who was driving a jeep stuffed full of explosives into the biggest city, Bangui; shot her through the head three times and defused the bomb before the timer (set to two minutes) tripped the detonator.
  When I drew Popov's attention to her, he immediately hired her

for the Project and had her earmarked for *Star Pyramid*. He'd been looking for just such a person.

She was delighted, and took to her role like a duck to water, impressing everyone she worked with.

Five months later, with no warning, the GU kicked her out.

Now, they wanted her back. But that wasn't going to be easy.

I flicked off her file and flicked on her sister's.

* * *

"Reynheiður and I are twins."

Unlike her sister, Hjördis Sigmundsdóttir had retained her natural blonde hair, and wore it shoulder length. That aside, their faces were the same. But Hjördis didn't stare into the camera; she looked totally relaxed.

"At birth we looked identical, and Mamma liked to dress us alike, until we started school. One day Reynheiður flatly refused to wear the same clothes I did, which at that point was pretty flowery dresses. It was what Mamma used to wear whenever she got the chance, which wasn't all that often, living on a farm. About once a month, except in the depth of winter when the roads were often impassable, she'd swap the jeans and sweater for a long dress and put on big, dangly earrings and a pendant or two. Pabbi would change into a smart jacket and trousers, and they'd drive into town for a meal at the best restaurant. Mamma worked hard on the farm, but there was a feminine side to her that was just below the surface when it wasn't on it. And she was determined to raise her twin daughters to be feminine too, until Reynheiður put a stop to her plans, ripping her dress and screaming her head off.

"We were both blonde, and Mamma liked us with shoulder-length hair. So naturally Reynheiður 'borrowed' Pabbi's beard-trimmer and gave herself a crew-cut, dyed bright purple. Could've been worse, I guess: she could have shaved her head bald. Then again, it might've looked better that way.

"Secretly I envied her. I wanted to be a tomboy, too, and there were plenty of opportunities on our farm. But the disappointment on Mamma's face when Reynheiður threw her tantrum got to me, and I didn't want to see it again. So I gave in, dressed the way she wanted me to, and pretended to like it.

"It had an unwanted side effect. When we reached puberty, the boys were always pestering the pretty little twin in the flowery dress. Reynheiður was such a miserable little– well, so gloomy and introverted– that they stayed well clear of her. Good idea, she'd have felled them with a right hook if they'd dared to get within reach. Though I had a feeling she was jealous of all the attention I was getting. They crowded round me like bears round a honey-pot. Ironically, I didn't want it, but I'd found early on that the best way to keep the randy little sods at arm's length was to lead them on and then throw a huff and dump them if they tried anything.

"Yes, I was a prick-tease. The pricks deserved it.

"Our parents owned horses– oh, my sister must've told you about those already, she was obsessed with them. I helped round them up in the autumn when the cold weather was setting in, bringing them down from the highlands where they'd been running free and grazing the lush grass. Laufskálarétt, that's what it's called. Thousands of people come from far and wide to watch. But I never felt that way about them, cute though they were. I don't know why. Most girls go through a horsey phase, but I never did. Did she tell you not to– right, yes. 'Ponies' is a no-no.

"I got fed up being chased by the boys, so as soon as I turned 18 I told my parents that now I had reached the age of majority I was in charge of my own affairs. I wore more sober clothing, trousers rather than skirts and dresses, and enrolled at Reykjavik University to get a degree. I really wanted to go into management, and thought about Business Studies, but Pabbi persuaded me that a background in something more solid would be an advantage in the long run, when I was competing with people who'd never actually *done* anything at the sharp end. So I took an Engineering degree, part mechanical and part electronic. Later I segued into a more managerial role certifying structural integrity, where I could use my practical expertise as well.

"I never noticed the lack of qualifications in Business Studies.

"Reynheiður, typically, insisted on doing the exact opposite. Dropped out and joined the *army*, for heaven's sake! Mind you, she was always the aggressive one. Not like me, I wouldn't boo a goose. We all thought she was mad, but she lucked out when some high-ranking officer offered her a job in– well, actually, I have no idea, because she wouldn't say. I think it was in covert ops and she *couldn't* say without ending up behind bars for ten years. Meanwhile, I'd climbed the greasy pole into a senior position on the Project. That's right, *Star Pyramid*.

"Reynheiður and I were as close as a clam at first, but then we both began to change. She went her way, I went mine. I still love her, I suppose, but she's not an easy person to love. Doesn't show much emotion. I'd like to have seen more of her, still do. But she's seldom on the same continent as me and half the time there's no way to contact her, So I've... well, given up on her, basically."

* * *

The contrast between the similarities and the differences was striking. It was clear to me that even if they *had* once been as close as a clam, neither understood the other as well as they imagined. And their parents had understood neither of them.

I thought about my own file. It, too, had a recorded personal statement, but mine was far less revealing than those of Sigmund Gunnarsson's twin daughters. Just a bland recital of things that were on public record.

If I'd recorded something more personal in nature, I suppose it might have gone like this...

* * *

"I was born Solana Zaneta Martínez on 9 July 2129 in a tiny ramshackle hut in a stinking *cinturón de miséria* that sprawled up hillside on the outskirts of Guamúchil, Mexico. These rings of slums surrounding towns and cities had all been demolished a hundred years before, but after asteroid mining triggered a new population boom they'd returned, an untreatable cancer. There was no doctor, only an old woman from higher up the hill who acted as an untrained – though very experienced – midwife. I was the sixth child in a family that eventually reached nine, not counting my parents.

"Life in the *cinturón* was basic but tolerable – once you got used to the smell, the close proximity of unwashed humans, the screaming babies, the rainwater running down the walls, and the ubiquitous rats and roaches – except when the gangs and drug dealers threw their weight around, which was pretty often. Growing up in that atmosphere you either learned to look after yourself, or you got squashed.

"I made sure no one squashed *me*. I cultivated a hair-trigger temper and a reputation for never backing down, even if it killed me. What I *wanted* was an AK-53, like the gangs, but I always knew that was unrealistic. I settled for a knife with a twenty-centimetre blade, and knew how to use it. I left scars on a dozen idiots who hadn't got the message.

"When I was fifteen years old my father somehow managed to get that rarest of the rare, a *genuine* immigrant visa for the United States. Along with a job servicing garbage trucks in Tucson, Arizona. We ran the usual gauntlet across the land border and within a week he'd changed his name to Mardeen and mine to Suzanna. I don't know where he got the family name from.

"We all found jobs, and my father insisted they had to be legal: having managed to gain legal entry into the USA he had no intention of being deported, along with the rest of his family. We worked hard, and after a few years my father bought a small wood-framed house in the suburbs. It needed a lot of work, but my eldest brother Joe (born José Miguel) had by then become a skilled carpenter, and he and my father fixed it up, with the rest of us helping as best we could.

"When I turned sixteen I decided to join the military. My street-fighting abilities would help me gain entry, and I'd realised long before that I had a natural inclination for violence. Better to channel it into a respectable profession than to risk falling in with criminals.

"And that's how I ended up in RAG."

* * *

There'd have been more, of course, as I climbed the promotion ladder to my current rank as Colonel. But the early days were the formative ones, and they're why I'm a hard bitch.

. Works for me.

Anyway, enough about me. Having refreshed my memory about the twins, I was confident that the plan ought to work. I ordered my team to make the opening moves in the Gemini Gambit.

The first was to taper off Reynheiður Sigmundsdóttir's sedatives.

CHAPTER 14
THE GEMINI GAMBIT
Reynheiður Sigmundsdóttir

*Global Union Anti-Terrorism Section,
Cairo, Egypt 2163*

"I know you're awake, Reynheiður," the voice said. "You can stop trying to fake unconsciousness."

I lay still, trying to persuade my brain to start thinking. It was struggling.

"You drugged me," I mumbled.

"Technically, you drugged yourself, since it was you who picked up the glass and drained it."

"You were the one who laced it."

I'd remembered that, but I couldn't for the life of me remember who I was talking to. Then I placed the voice, and events started to fall into place.

Zanna.

Colonel Suzanna Mardeen. Rapid Action Group. RAG.

"Guilty as charged," she said. "It was necessary. The GU wants you back."

I remembered that, too, now. "Back in the Project? No way." I proceeded to instruct her to perform several indecent acts that were almost certainly logical impossibilities, let alone biological ones.

"The Project needs you."

That's rich. "I don't give a shit what the Project needs." I wriggled around as if my back hurt and I was seeking a more comfortable position, but actually I was testing for the presence of restraints. *None.* Then I realised they weren't required; the drug had left me as weak as a newborn kitten.

But I could speak. "No one cared what *I* needed. You should have left me in Shuidaoyuanzhongchang. I was happy there."

"Drinking yourself to death in Kong's Bar, high on a gnathroprine overdose? You have a strange idea of happiness."

"Let me clarify. Happier than I would've been if I'd stayed sober."

"Fat chance of that. But there's no point wasting our breath on recriminations, Reynheiður."

"*You're* wasting your breath. *I'm* targeting it where it will have the most impact."

She laughed. "To wit: *zero*. Now, stop being childish and listen to me. Something's come up that could do serious damage to *Star Pyramid*. That's the future of humanity, not just some vanity project for GU bureaucrats. I know what Krantz did, and if it makes you feel better, I'm sorry."

"Nope. Doesn't."

"Well, I'm sorry anyway, and that's not something you'll often hear from me. So is Joel, it may surprise you to learn."

"I don't give a fuck how Joel feels."

"Sit up, it'll help you think straight."

I decided that that was probably sound advice, whatever else I thought about Krantz and Mardeen. My strength was starting to improve as the drug wore off, but Zanna had to call a couple of robonurses to lever my upper body into an upright posture, propped up by pillows. I was wearing some sort of pyjamas, pale blue, thick material but soft. What I took to be medical gear was attached to the walls or on free-standing trolleys with tiny wheels. All the usual bleeps and blinks and wiggly traces.

"Where am I?" I asked.

"Gwats." Well, that's what it sounded like.

"Shit. You've brought me to Cairo." GUATS was the Global Union Anti-Terrorism Section.

"Well done."

"It looks like a private room in a hospital."

"It is. GUATS has a small clinic."

"Why am I here?"

"You know perfectly well. The GU wants you to rejoin the Project. And Krantz is on the Steering Committee, so in this matter he speaks for the GU."

That threw me, and I tried to recover some poise.

"Fuck. He got that promotion. I thought Krantz was based in Tōkyō."

"He was when he threw you out. Right now he's in Cairo, liaising with the Egyptian counter-terror agencies. Next week he might be anywhere."

I was getting angry again. "Well, you can tell him I'm not willing to help him stop maniacs and fanatics damaging *Star Pyramid* before she's ready to launch."

Zanna gave a rueful smile. "That's not what he wants you to do, Reynheiður."

"Then what the fuck *does* he want me to do?"

"Stop maniacs and fanatics damaging the ship *after* she's launched."

* * *

It was evening in Cairo and the atmosphere was hot and humid. The proximity of the Nile was the cause of much of the moisture, and the throngs of humanity were the cause of the rest.

I'd changed into street clothes, courtesy of GUATS, and Zanna escorted me to a small restaurant at the northern end of Mohammed Mazhar, a street running parallel to the river on Zamalek, a large island in the river in the centre of the city.

"There's someone I want you to meet, and I don't want it to happen in this building," Zanna said. "Somewhere less formal, where you can relax."

"Krantz? If it's Krantz, I'll relax all right. I'll find a relaxing way to kill him."

She shook her head. "Don't be childish. Anyway, it's not Krantz. You'll meet *him* tomorrow. You know it's unavoidable."

"So are death and taxes, but I don't want to make it easy for either of them." It was a half-hearted reply. She was right, and I didn't really see any point in arguing.

Save that for Krantz.

I'd thought of escaping, of course, but they'd let me out on a leash, and tugging at it would only give me a sore neck. Zanna was armed, the place was surrounded by RAG operatives, and I'd undoubtedly been given an implant that would let satellites track my every move. There are ways to deal with all of those, but they're risky, so I decided to wait for whatever Zanna was going to spring on me unannounced, and enjoy a stylish evening out. The first for a long, long time.

I'd been expecting something expensive, but the Nefertari was just an ordinary café with a typically touristy name. Not even worthy of the title 'restaurant'. Yet it had human waiters. Very attentive human waiters. There had once been air-con, but typically for Cairo it didn't work; however, the waiters rushed off and came back with two huge fans. They kept the ubiquitous flies away, too. Compared to Kong's Bar in the CKBZ, it was the Ritz.

We'd hardly sat down – on plump scarlet cushions fringed with gold braid and tassels – when small cups of dark brown liquid materialised in front of us. Egyptian coffee, strong, hot, and mindbendingly sweet. Poured by the café owner in person, whose name was – guess – Mohammed.

I'd been trained to eat and drink just about anything without complaint, and I saw no need to offend Mohammed, or risk getting him into trouble with RAG, so I tossed it down like a shot of moonshine and was unsurprised when he promptly presented me with another. There was no menu, and Zanna told him to serve whatever he thought would be best.

I had my back to the door; not something I've ever been comfortable with, but it let Zanna sit facing it and she was the one with the portable armoury. I heard footsteps behind me, and she said: "Ah. There you are."

She gestured to the visitor to join us, and she did.

When I realised who it was, I gaped like a mouth-breeding cichlid hiding her young from predators.

"My god. Hjördis!"

We both stood up, and embraced, awkwardly. I hadn't seen my twin sister for four years. As kids we'd been inseparable; as adults we'd kept in touch. Sort of.

It was embarrassingly emotional and I emerged from her arms in a state of shock. I knew she was working for the Project – hell, everyone was working for the Project – but I thought she was in Bayankhongor.

"I thought you were in Bayankhongor," I said.

"I am. But not today. Arrived an hour ago on a government saucer. Urgent, they said. They only told me I was meeting you on the way to this restaurant."

She looked good, in an emerald green trouser suit and sandals a similar shade but darker. The colour suited her blonde hair. She also looked tired, which I put down to her flight.

It was all very obvious, and I said so. "You're here to persuade me to rejoin the Project and fly on *Star Pyramid*."

She made no attempt to deny it. "Yes."

"You know all about it?"

"Only what they told me before I left the airport to come here."

"We want Reynheiður to be a security mole on the flight to Karoubi's Star," Zanna said. "We have good reason to believe that the sabotage attempts we're currently preventing, pretty much every day, won't end when *Womera* lights up its engines. Unfortunately the intelligence names no names, presumably because no names are known."

"And Reynheiður is the best qualified person on the entire planet to go along for the ride and deal with any security issues that arise," Hjördis said.

Zanna nodded. "She has the full package of skills: physical, virtual, and psychological."

Hjördis feigned amusement. "Then you shouldn't have let Krantz scapegoat her for the *Tyger* fiasco."

"I didn't *let* him. I was too low in the pecking order for that. *No one* in Security let him, he went over our heads. But it wasn't even his idea. I'm pretty sure it was down to Rutzkoi: he had no intention of carrying the can for the loss of four years' production of mahabhavium and the ensuing panic. But that's not based on hard intel, it was all covered up extremely tightly. And – well, sorry, but it's true – your sister was the prime goat to scape."

"In the right place–" Hjördis began.

"At precisely the wrong time," I finished for her.

"I don't want to start an argument," Zanna said. "I've already told you, Reynheiður, I sympathise with your views. But you *were* in charge of all psychological profiling for test-pilot selection."

"Yes, but–"

Plates began to appear on the table. Flat bread, hummus, olives, some sort of aubergine concoction.

"Eat," Zanna said.

* * *

It seemed good advice, the smells were delicious. More dishes arrived, and a bottle of wine: Mohammed didn't drink himself, but he had no qualms about serving alcohol to infidels. By the time we reached the dessert course, all three of us were far more relaxed than we had any right to be, given the circumstances.

Zanna's faithful goon squad watching the back and front of the building helped, of course. Not that she told me they were out there. It was obvious.

Syrupy basbousa, wonderful as long as you like honey – dripping all over your fingers. Feteer meshaltet, thin crispy pastry in layers. Baklava, of course, made 'to my grandmother's secret recipe'. Every Egyptian has a grandmother with a secret baklava recipe, every one of them is different, and every one of them works perfectly.

Another bottle of wine. I knew I was being softened up, but being plied with wine and honey was a far cry from the mess I'd been in in Shuidaoyuanzhongchang. Plus, if I was on board *Star Pyramid* I wouldn't run into–

Oops.

"Zanna, tell me that Krantz isn't going to be on *Star Pyramid*."

"Krantz isn't going to be on *Star Pyramid*. Truly. You wouldn't find him within a hundred kilometres of it. He *hates* spaceflight."

One worry ticked off.

"You were talking about test-pilot selection," I said, deciding to face my fears head-on.

Zanna pursed her lips– deciding, I suspected, what line to take. After a few seconds she said: "Yes. The selection. The advice that tipped the balance in favour of Federico Berrios. You were in charge of the psychological profiling."

True. Also irrelevant. "Yes. Under the direct command of Kingsley Potter."

Zanna twitched her mouth knowingly. "Who delegated all major decisions to you."

I emitted a strangled snort. "The bastard did, yes. At the time I was pleased. When Krantz fired me I figured out why."

"The Psych Team did fail to spot the dangers of Berrios's beliefs," Zanna pointed out.

"Yes. The Psych *Team*. All of it."

"Run by you."

I was running out of self-justifications, and said nothing.

Hjördis reached across and took my hand. "Reynheiður, we're the little people. The big ones are happy to let us reach for the stars, but if it works they accept the plaudits, and if we miss and hit the ground head first we suffer the bruises. That's how it is; how it's always been and always will be.

"I talked to Joel afterwards. He was distraught. I think he wanted to strangle Rutzkoi with his bare hands. But he didn't dare risk the cancellation of *Star Pyramid,* and right at that moment it was a very real danger."

"The politicos might've got cold feet," I said.

"They were barefoot in a blizzard," Hjördis said. "The expense, the risk of failure, the need to compromise, the imperative of placing the future of humanity above petty ideology… Krantz was focused solely on heading them off, organising his little part of the complete rescheduling of the Project that Berrios's refusal to kill himself had precipitated. Heads had to roll, yours was neatly adjacent to the chopping-block, and *you* had just become dispensable.

"He was in the process of finding you a new job when you took off for unknown parts. It took years to track you down to the CKBZ. By then it was too late."

"Until the Services got wind of a sleeper plot," Zanna said, "and decided you were indispensable again."

I was still angry, but despite my best intentions I was starting to see it through Project-coloured glasses.

"You're telling me it was just bad luck?"

"It wasn't *just* anything," Hjördis said. "It was a betrayal. But sometimes–"

"Sometimes these things are necessary," I finished for her. "So here we are. Are you trying to tell me to accept the offer and go on *Star Pyramid?*"

Silence. Then a nod.

"Easy for you," I told her. "You're not the one who's being sent on a trip to Karoubi's Star, and getting back four centuries into the future. If at all."

She tilted her glass and drank the last of the wine.

"Actually, sister dear, that's *exactly* what I'm going to do."

* * *

"You've come up in the world," I said.

The office was lavishly furnished with a huge window. If you squinted through the pollution haze, you could see two of the pyramids, bright triangles against a grey sky.

"You're not here to discuss me," Krantz said, making it clear who we *were* here to discuss. He looked older, more time-worn, probably ground down trying to hang on to a job that was well above his level of competence. Not running to fat, though, despite all the formal dinners that undoubtedly came his way. Still a big man with a muscular physique. Still capable of charming the pants off you while undermining the ground you stood on. Still Joel Krantz.

I'll give him credit, he made no attempt to patronise me, or to justify his decision. He did say he was sorry that he'd been the one to convey the bad news, but the decision had been taken at the highest levels.

"If you want me to kiss and make up," I told him, "you're off your head."

"I don't expect forgiveness. What I want, Reynheiður, is you on board *Star Pyramid.* Nothing personal, this is business. Hjördis has already agreed to go, and you know that. I want you to go with her."

It'd be one way to get away from <u>*you,*</u> I thought. But I kept the thought to myself.

"What sort of business? No, don't tell me, stupid question. This

153

is the Anti-Terrorism Section. There's been a terrorist threat to *Star Pyramid*, and you want me to fix it for you."

He shrugged. "There's never been a day *without* a terrorist threat to *Star Pyramid*. The public may believe the Project has united the entire planet, as the GU keeps proclaiming… and, to be fair, humanity is probably more united today than it's ever been. But that's a very low bar, and there are plenty of dissident groups and individuals hiding in the woodwork, ready to crawl out if they sense an opening.

"No, I don't have any specific threat in mind. What worries me – and those above me – is that once the ship's on its way, the only people who can deal with any subsequent threats are those on board her."

"So we need some of our own people to go along for the ride," Zanna said.

"Nice to know I'm back to being one of 'your' people," I sulked.

"Reynheiður, you never left. Not permanently, not as far as Joel and I were concerned. We always knew the GU would want you back."

News to me. "Why?"

"Because you were the best counter-terror agent they had, and you still are once we get you trained up again."

She saw the look on my face, and before I could explode she added: "That's why they made you the scapegoat. It had to be one hundred per cent credible. They couldn't get away with throwing a small fish to the wolves. They had to throw a big fish."

The absurdity of it all hit me. "Zanna, you don't throw fish to wolves. Well, you *could*, but the metaphor's about throwing people. Dump them off the sleigh before the wolf pack attacks it and kills everyone else."

She gave a slow nod. "Exactly."

The word hung in the air.

"You're telling me I was fired because I was brilliant at my job?"

Krantz nodded. "Yes. Absolutely. You were so brilliant that you were handling all of the psychological profiling for *Tyger*. When it blew up in everyone's faces, you were standing in front of the wall when the firing-squad turned up."

This is too much. I swore, briefly and obscenely. "I don't know whether your security clearance was high enough then, Joel, but I *warned* them not to give the job to Federico Berrios."

A half-smile. "I assure you my clearance is quite sufficient, and I've read your report. You didn't warn them because of his religious beliefs."

True. But that's only part of it.

I walked across to the window. Sixteen floors down, traffic on a four-lane overhead ramp had invented two more lanes and clogged solid. If I listened hard I could hear blaring horns through the triple glazing.

"Not directly," I said over my shoulder. Turned to face them both. "I warned Kingsley Potter *and* Frank Simpson that Berrios was a bomb waiting to go off if someone tripped the detonator. He had a guilt complex the size of Manhattan. His religion was his refuge. So we pulled him out of his hidey-hole and put him right back where he never wanted to be. Piloting a priceless machine, responsible for a huge disaster if he made the tiniest mistake. He was terrified history would repeat itself."

Even now I felt myself growing angry because of the stupidity of it all. The unavoidable stupidity. *Stay calm.*

"Potter insisted I was wrong. Pooh-poohed the whole idea. Told me I'd be convicted of treason and spend the rest of my life in solitary if I made my misgivings public. As if I'd not read the NDA. Prat."

Joel nodded. "Reynheiður, I didn't know about that threat until now. I wouldn't have thought Potter had the guts, to be honest."

"Why break the habit of a lifetime? Honesty doesn't suit you."

Zanna was right, I was being childish. He ignored the jibe. "But I knew the rest," he said. "Agreed with your assessment. Said so. But Simpson overruled me. He was adamant that it had to be Berrios. And we both know why."

It's what made the stupidity unavoidable. "Hi-grav tolerance."

"Berrios was a freak. No one else could've withstood the *g*-forces. They were wasting their time even *considering* any other candidates. That overrode every other consideration. They'd have given him the job even if he'd been proclaiming himself the Son of God and running around stark naked."

I digested this. *Put-up job.* Not just Rutzkoi protecting his own back; Simpson, too. A double betrayal. They'd put pressure on Potter, and he'd caved in. Krantz was right, Potter wouldn't have had the guts to dump me off his own bat.

It all made sense, now.

I hauled my mind back into the present. "So you don't know of any specific threat involving on-board personnel, but you suspect there could be one. *Might* be one. So you're using me to hedge your bets."

"We're asking you to accept," Zanna said. "For the benefit of humanity."

"Oh, save me the bleeding heart."

She shook her head. "For once, Reynheiður, it's not an act. We want you to do what you do best."

"Snooping around digging for terrorists."

"Actually," Krantz said, "it's not just terrorist activity. I want you on board to ensure mission compliance."

Ominous. Not sure I approve of where this is heading.

"Unwrap the bureaucrap, Joel."

Krantz straightened his shoulders. My psychological training told me that this was an unconscious admission that he was under severe pressure from higher echelons. Or maybe that was just obvious.

"The GU is… concerned… that the *Star Pyramid* contingent could go off-mission. Could happen in lots of ways. Go stir-crazy, cooped up in a tin can for a century while everything they knew and loved ages by four times that. Trap themselves in political speculations. Start an onboard civil war over a triviality.

"So the plan is to include a small team of trained operatives under your command. If you're needed, they'll use the freewave to have you woken up. Then you deal with the insurgency, be it a terror group or the people on *Star Pyramid* throwing a collective paddy."

"Ah. You want me to be the GU's spy."

He shook his head. "Enforcer. Would you want *Star Pyramid* to fail?"

To his credit, he didn't point out that if it did, and I'd turned down this security role, I'd be partially responsible. First *Tyger*, then *Star Pyramid*. Another case of history repeating itself.

Not something I'd want on my headstone.

I sensed I was wavering. If I didn't take it on they'd just find someone else. Someone less qualified. But I still needed to clear the air.

"And my sister's part in this? She has no anti-terrorist experience whatsoever. Are you using *her* to snare *me*? Is that what yesterday's social event was all about?"

"Why don't you ask her?" Zanna said.

She waved the door open and Hjördis walked in.

* * *

"I'm not going on the ship because of you," Hjördis said. "I signed up years ago, long before Rutzkoi made Joel fire you. I was involved in the Project all along, it became my life. My baby."

"And when Baby grew up, you didn't want her to leave home?" I meant it as sarcasm, but she took it at face value.

"Pretty much, yes. So I decided to go with her."

I was baffled. "I don't believe this. You're telling me you're bunking off to a distant star because of some misplaced maternal instinct?"

She shook her head, long dangly earrings flashing silver and pink in the sunlit room. "I'm going because *I have to*. I've devoted my life to the Project because I believe in it. I'm *committed*. And – well, dear sister, I think you're equally committed. I'm your twin. I know how your mind works, because deep down it's just like mine. We've been shaped by different life experiences, we're not the same people. But underneath the civilised facade we think the same way.

"This is not an offer you can refuse. You'd spend the rest of your life regretting it – though it wouldn't be a very long life."

I thought back to the last few years, drinking myself to death in a run-down shack at the back of beyond, high on makeshift drugs, not caring I was ruining my life because I didn't think I had one any more. *Anything* would be better than that. And now Fate was offering me a meaningful job for which I was totally suited.

I could see only two downsides.

First, I was letting Rutzkoi and Simpson off the hook. *Tough.* This is too important for petty grievances. Set them aside.

Second: the location.

On the other hand, Mother Earth wasn't a great place to be any more. Lurching from crisis to crisis, clinging on by her ragged-nailed fingertips.

Shit.

"I'm in."

CHAPTER 15

FROM LEO TO L2

Alfonsina Shegwada

Star Pyramid embarkation 2169

Packing my bag was easy. It took precisely eight minutes, because I didn't own much beyond a few clothes and a tab. Plus a wooden carving of a hippopotamus that my mother had given me when I was four. My baggage allowance was five times what I actually took. The main limitation wasn't storage on *Star Pyramid*; it was how much mass I would be allowed when climbing out of Earth's gravity-well.

My particular intake to ITU Guayaquil had comprised 61 students. The 22 of us that had survived the course took a standard hydrox lifter to Low Earth Orbit. We all knew each other by then, of course, having been cooped up in the same building for five months. Some of the training had been standard for everyone; some more specialised, depending on the skills that we had and the skills that the GU wanted us to acquire.

The lifter had eight rows of seats, six in each row divided by a central aisle. I was sitting in between Michael Clapham, a math whiz, and Georgina Maxwell, a nurse. Gayl Goodenough was one row in front of us. I'd spent quite a lot of time with Michael, there being a lot of overlap between math and infotech. I'd mainly run into Gayl and Georgina during physical training and mealtimes. I'd never actually spoken to either of them beyond a perfunctory "hi".

When he'd first arrived at ITU, Clapham had been distinctly rotund, though not actually obese. Like Simone Dupuy, he'd been under notice that unless he lost at least 12 kilos he'd be out on his ear, and he'd spent almost all of his spare time (what little there was) working out in the gym. Now he was almost as slim as Gayl, but much shorter. A benevolent hobbit with not much chin. Simone had managed to slim down enough to keep her place on the flight, but not by much.

We were all about to get our first taste of 5*g* acceleration followed by the unsettling onset of zero-*g*. And, for some, the all too familiar taste and smell of human vomit. We all wore extraction helmets in case the falling sensation made us throw up.

A disembodied voice ran through the usual instructions about how to sit during acceleration phases, how to adjust the retractable earmuffs, how to breathe as normally as possible when an elephant was sitting on your chest...

I wished they hadn't mentioned elephants. But I was getting less sensitive about that. Battle-hardened.

There was no countdown, just a five-second warning and five bleeps. The last one coincided with said elephant settling itself down on your ribcage, as the lifter's four engines lit up and the clamps released it. With a noise that would have woken the dead we departed *terra firma* and ascended on a pillar of flame towards an increasingly dark sky.

It should have been exciting, but the discomfort damped down any such feeling. At best, it was a relief to be on our way at last.

After three minutes the elephant lost interest and went away. Five minutes after that, we slid smoothly into Low Earth Orbit. It was my first time in LEO; my first time in space. It was the same for nearly all of us, although Yamazaki Kazuko had served as a Space Cadet and made five flights to LEO, twice going on to one of the spaceports 60,000 kilometres from the Moon at the Earth-Moon Lagrange point EM-L1, between Earth and Moon where their gravitational pulls cancel out. She'd never made a lunar landing, and neither would we.

It did seem a bit strange to be heading off to a far star when we'd never been to the Moon. Like taking a round-the-world saucer trip when you'd never left your house before.

We circled the Earth six times before the pilot and ground staff decided everything was in order for insertion to EM-L1. The view, of the planet beneath us, as expected, was amazing, when we could see it. Another elephant experience, shorter this time, and we were on our way, coasting in zero gravity.

Those of us who didn't throw up were allowed to play some floating games in a padded compartment at the rear of the shuttle. Michael turned out to be rather good at zero-*g* handball, with a soft, squishy ball that was made from some kind of foam, and Gayl beat us all at ten-pin bowling. Not the usual groundbait arrangement in a triangle: a pyramid – three-sided, not four like *Star Pyramid* – with a base of six pins in a triangle, surmounted by another triangle of three, with one perched on top. The 'pins' were shorter and fatter than those down on the ground, and they were arranged with their wide bases pointing away from the bowler and the tip of the pyramid pointing towards them. The ball was surprisingly solid, so you had to watch out for rebounds, and of course you didn't actually bowl it. You set it up hovering in front of you, and hit it with the flat of your hand.

I asked Gayl if she'd played it before.

"Nope."

Like most of us, she was in space for the first time. But she'd watched an HV of a professional match when she was eleven years old, so she'd dredged it up from her memory and copied the tactics.

Now we could see the Earth as a complete sphere, in greens, browns, and above all blue and white. From this distance it looked idyllic. But I remembered what it looked like close up.

A day into the trip (it would last two and a half) the cabin crew distracted us with all the usual demonstrations with balls of water hovering in mid-air and zero-*g* juggling (which involved bouncing soft balls off the walls).

We also watched ourselves lifting off on HV. Everything about *Star Pyramid* was media fodder. As usual with mass communications, they all copied each other. There was never more than one story at any time – two would frighten the horses – and right now, we were that story. Because *Star Pyramid* was keyed up, teed up, psyched up, all set, and raring to go. Not to mention cocked, primed, and loaded, and a hundred other clichés. And we, its crew, were the most interesting feature of the load, because we were *people*, not things, and if there's anything the media love it's a human interest story.

They interviewed three of us; the lifter had its own HV camera. I made sure that I wasn't chosen, to maintain my low profile, but there was no shortage of volunteers, all eager to impress family and friends. I had no family – Uncle Sadeeki had died of an aneurysm two years earlier and Auntie Hawa had followed him six months later with bone cancer – and no friends. Not anyone close enough to call a friend. Never had one. Lots of acquaintances, though; that had been unavoidable. So no one to impress, not that I'd have wanted to if there had been.

I took care to stay away from the camera, just in case some bright spark wondered who the rough-skinned little woman with the crazy hair was and decided that another interview would be a good idea.

There was much talk of how great it was that the GU had allowed the media to film us.

Apparently I was the only person on or off the planet to realise that actually, all of us were *things* to the GU. *Earth first*. We were little better than cannon-fodder.

Things improved a bit at EM-L1, which was a fully-fledged spaceport with entertainment zones and facilities equivalent to those of a three-star hotel. Like most space stations it was a toroid. This one was shaped like a short, wide cylinder from which a smaller cylinder down the middle had been removed. Like any sensible wheel it had a central hub, where visiting spacecraft docked, and spokes, so that the people in the spacecraft could make their way into the main toroid.

Which we duly did. The trickiest part was when the pilot spun the lifter about its axis to match the spin of the station, having lined us up with the hub; and then adding a small forward vector to engage our nose with the docking ring.

This caused three people who'd been perfectly fine up to that point to make use of their extraction helmets.

The spin gave an illusion of gravity in the main toroid, about $0.6g$. We stood or walked with our heads pointing towards the hub, and the floors were curved. There were three separate storeys, with decreasing gravity as you went 'up'; that is, towards the hub. Accommodation was on the top floor (in hotels I always like not having anyone above me to keep me awake by trampling around overhead, so this was pleasant); two restaurants and a bar (yes, bar, though one with a low alcohol limit per customer) on the middle floor; recreation and technical areas on the 'ground' floor.

We spent five days sampling the rather limited delights of a standard orbital space station while more of the crew were ferried up. We soon tired of the cratered plains and jagged mountains as they passed slowly across the HV dais in the lounge; to me the lunar surface resembled nothing other than a war zone, a leaden landscape riddled with shell-holes, splashed with rays of blast-shattered rock and ash.

We gave heartfelt thanks when we were transferred to a shuttle for our onward journey. By then we were all hardened spacefarers, but they still insisted that we wear extraction helmets, an insistence that quickly proved to be wise. The transport's destination was the Sun-Earth Lagrange point L2, where we would board *Star Pyramid*. The starship was undergoing her final stages of commissioning, and when the final item on the checklist of 17 million was ticked she would be inserted into *Womera*, a massive but near-invisible cage waiting patiently for her moment of glory. The L2 Lagrange Zone, once the province of only the science complex, was getting rather crowded, but space is big. L2 is unstable, but it takes very little energy to keep station near it, and 'near' is several thousand kilometres. *Womera* was about 3,000 kilometres distant, well away from the current centre of activity.

We could see out of the shuttle's heavy glass windows, and when we got near enough the pilot obligingly rolled the ship to give us views of our future home. *Star Pyramid* looked like a rather squat and ill-proportioned version of every sci-fi cliché from the time when they first discovered CGI, all flat planes studded with mysterious protrusions, all of it high-contrast in the unfiltered starlight of vacuum. The only difference was that instead of being gun-metal grey, the ship had been painted a deep green.

It was totally uninspiring until your brain figured out how big it was.

The tip of the pyramid was pointing away from us, and we were approaching from the side, so the view was dominated by the square base and its five huge ramrocket exhausts. I craned my neck trying to see the massive comm antenna, with its 24 independently manoeuvrable segments, which was of particular interest, but saw nothing. It must have been there, but the ship wasn't spinning and it was tucked away on the far side, hidden from my view. It would be folded flat to the hull at this stage of deployment, in any case.

The name STAR PYRAMID was emblazoned along all four of its triangular sides in huge sans serif capital letters, as if anyone could possibly fail to be aware of what the thing was. More accurately, the name was written as **STAR PYRAMID**, no doubt because some bright spark in PR though that the upside down V's looked cute.

At least they hadn't used two of them for the M.

Several smaller vessels were huddled against its hull, attached by appropriate docking gear. Some had nosed up to hatches and stuck out like piglets suckling at a sow; some were linked by flexible tubes large enough to carry people or equipment. One of the huge shuttle bays was wide open and inside I could see the front of a dumpy OWLL with the angular outline of a much larger shuttle behind it. Another shuttle hovered just outside, unattached, presumably being loaded on board.

The ship was no doubt a hive of activity, but most of the action would be going on behind those thick hull plates. Outside, everything looked calm and orderly, proceeding at a glacial pace. Only when she had been fully commissioned, her crew embarked, and every item of cargo secured, would the next stage of the complex departure sequence begin. Tugs would tow *Star Pyramid* into the centre of a huge ring of chemical rockets, currently floating ten kilometres away and visible only as a stack of thin semicircles of reflected sunlight. This clumsy but reliable device would carry the starship to where *Womera* waited; then more tugs would secure her in *Womera*'s ghostly womb, ready for the first stage of her long and perilous journey.

More perilous than they know.

Our transport completed a careful approach and docked with one of the shuttle bays, part way along one edge of *Star Pyramid*. A series of loud bangs announced our safe arrival as clamps closed around our docking ring.

The connecting tube opened, and we made our cautious way along it.

Mwenda pole, haumii miguu. One who walks carefully, does not hurt his foot.

You can figure out what that one means. It's not about walking. I resolved to bow to its wisdom. *Thank you, Mother.*

As we passed through the entrance in the three-metre thick hull, I took a deep breath.

Star Pyramid smelled… *new.*

I'm in.

PART FIVE

LIGHTSPEED CRAWL

CHAPTER 16

PYRAMIDOLATRY

Rowley Pollard

Star Pyramid 2169

The missile came screaming up from the general direction of Mars and smashed into *Star Pyramid*'s bow in a spectacular explosion of glass and foam.

"I name this ship… *Star Pyramid!*"

Rosalind Newberry, Secretary-General of the Global Union, watched as the spray of champagne dissipated. A slow-motion replay from one of the three authorised media bots that had been deployed for exactly this event showed the six-metre long pyramidal bottle, specially manufactured for the occasion, impacting the ship's steel hull. The sponsor's label, edited in as a graphic because the precise attitude of the bottle could not be controlled, was prominent.

Newberry removed her hand from the HV dais, which still displayed the large and purely ceremonial button at which she had waved a casual hand to launch the champagne missile from a military cruiser ten kilometres distant. She smiled for the cameras, and her entourage of dignitaries applauded. The whole event had been a security nightmare from the time said dignitaries had travelled to the launchpad in Florida to the time their shuttle docked with *Star Pyramid*; in fact, it would remain a security nightmare until they were all safely back on Earth in their own countries. It had also been unavoidable: such a momentous occasion demanded that tradition be followed.

"You wouldn't think her name has been painted on the hull for the last decade," Michael Clapham whispered to Simone Dupuy. They were sitting just behind me.

"Michael, *behave!*" Simone whispered back. "This is the *official* naming ceremony and launch, it doesn't matter when the paint was applied."

"Doesn't matter when she'll actually *launch*, either," he grumped, unabashed. "That's months away."

Making sure no cameras were pointing our way, Fiona turned and glared at them. They shut up.

I was included because everything was being beamed to Earth by freewave, and it was my job to ensure that the linkup went without a hitch. Everyone thinks that freewave is straightforward, once you have the right equipment, but anyone familiar with karmabhumi fields knows that's optimistic. The main potential issue is k-weather, erratic flows in the k-field. The greater the distance between transmitter and receiver, the worse the problem becomes. Short-range: no prob, which is why Quade Kylie hadn't realised it might be an issue. But this broadcast was between L2 and Earth: just about the tipping point where occasional disruption might just possibly happen. The math of k-weather is horrendous, and also something of a black art. So I trusted to luck and prepared to improvise if we lost the link.

I had the whole system on my tab. In principle I was just as much in control wandering around chatting to the visitors as I would have been back in my nice quiet cabin. And protocol demanded that senior crew absolutely *had* to attend to our prestigious guests, in person. I would have been happier without all the distractions, but the truth was that my people were perfectly capable of running the whole show without me.

I checked the cues on the tab. Next up was a surprise, arranged in secret by the HV people. Even Fiona didn't know about it.

"Distinguished guests, ladies and gentlemen, and viewers all over our beautiful planet," I announced. Heads turned. Fiona stared at me as if she thought I'd gone mad. I winked at her.

"Before you begin inspectin' our wonderful ship, ladies and gentlemen, there's some messages for us all."

If there's a k-storm glitch now, I'll be toast.

"Please look at the main HV dais."

After a heart-stopping flicker, an image stabilised. An elderly woman peered at the camera through old-fashioned spectacles, composed and relaxed, sitting on a chair beside an elegant Japanese moss garden. Two cats perched on her knees: one an unusual auburn colour, not a typical ginger cat; the other, a pure white longhair.

"Is that... *Zelda Zimmermann?*" Newberry whispered. Before I could answer, a caption confirmed her suspicion.

"I apologise for not being present in person on this momentous occasion," Zimmermann said. "But my doctors won't let me. Something silly about me being 94 years old. Too frail for the g-forces, they say. *Me? Frail?*"

She paused to stroke the cats. "This one," she said, scratching the auburn cat between the ears, "is Copper. The white one's Lioness."

I couldn't help laughing. It took a few seconds before any of the dignitaries got it.

"Copper's actually a Suphalak. That's a natural Thai breed, first mentioned by Buddhist monks in the *Tamra Maew* over four hundred years ago. Not to be confused with the Burmese, which is a created breed that expresses the colorpoint gene–"

"An appropriate choice of names," Newberry put in quickly, before Zimmermann could continue her characteristic ASD ramble. "I'm delighted you're with us, Professor Zimmermann, if only by freewave. We all are."

"Thank you, Secretary-General. It's an honour and a privilege. Since I'm not allowed to be present in person, I'm doing the next best thing. I just want to wish *Star Pyramid's* courageous crew–"

Don't say 'good luck', Zelda.

"–good hunting! Stay safe, bring back my mahabhavium. I know you can do it."

There were other messages from VIPs who had either been unable to make the trip to L2 or hadn't been invited. Pope Matilda III gave us her blessing and led a global prayer for our safety and success. I don't really hold with that kind of thing, despite – more likely because of – being brought up in the Church of God the Baptist. Lots of baptists in Barbados, goes back to the slave trade. Which says a lot about true Christian white gentlefolk. Still, I suppose the prayer showed that people cared. At worst, it would do no harm. At best–

Face it, Rowley: we need all the help we can get.

* * *

When the naming ceremony and messages from the great and the good had finished, it was time for the dignitaries to inspect the ship's facilities. Aided by a dozen senior crew, Fiona shepherded them through the door that opened on to the central concourse, a tube six metres wide that ran along most of the ship's axis. Hovering HV bots followed every move, patched into the ship's freewave antenna.

It was a curious procession. Secretary-General Newberry had elected to wear standard crew coveralls, though hers were tailored to fit her slightly overripe figure. In compensation, her hair stylist had gone over the top with the multicoloured tinting and intricate braiding that was the fashion of the day. The dignitaries wore anything from sober suits to brightly coloured national costume. All of this in zero gravity.

As we made our way up and down the concourse, Fiona filled them in on the ship's basic layout.

"I'm sure you all know this," she said, "but our audience back home may not. *Star Pyramid* has 24 decks, stacked along the main axis from A Deck at the bow to Z Deck at the stern. This concourse runs through the middle of them. There are four moving cars. Depending on the direction of the artificial gravity – when we have any, which right now we don't – they either act like elevators or trains."

The President-for-life of PanAfrica, resplendent in scarlet and sky-blue, commented: "That's very organised, Admiral."

"Less so than it sounds, Mr President. That was a very rough description of a complex reality. Practical issues have demanded innumerable compromises. The decks aren't equally spaced: those for the ramscoop engines and Matter Annihilation Drive are spaced thirty metres apart – that's one tenth of the ship's length – whereas those intended for human occupation have only three metres headroom."

At a sideways flick of her eyes her second-in-command, Assistant Flight Controller Wisdom Makumba, smoothly took over.

"Some decks have multiple levels, Mr President," he said, "and some protrude into the space nominally occupied by their neighbours. Not all are accessible directly from the central concourse; those that are include living quarters, kitchens, restaurants, and recreational facilities.

"Others require appropriate authorisation. Some are accessible only indirectly and with suitable protective equipment, and a few areas – such as the interiors of the fusion reactors – can be accessed only by bots. We have twenty antimatter storage tori, and those are out of bounds to everyone and everything."

"What if one of them fails?" the Chair of the European Assembly asked. "Wouldn't you need to do some maintenance?"

Makumba shook his head vehemently. "If one of the storage tori shows signs of incipient failure, there won't be time to tinker with it. We'll eject it."

Automated, less than a millisecond, or we're all dead, I thought. Not that any of us would tell that to the dignitaries.

Fiona sensibly didn't take them through the list of which deck was what, but she explained that each deck had a primary purpose and innumerable secondary ones, in order to squeeze every required system in.

"You said there are 24 decks, labelled A to Z," the Japanese

Premier mused. He was a compact, wiry little man with sparse greying hair and a subtle air of perpetual amusement. By reputation, sharp as a samurai sword, but more deadly. "Yet the English alphabet had 26 letters when I last looked."

"Well spotted, Sukimoto-san," Fiona said. "Decks I and O are missing."

His eyes widened; in surprise, I assumed.

"Oh. Why?"

She shrugged. "Probably because the design has only 24 decks."

"The official explanation is to avoid confusion with the numbers 1 and 0," Makumba said.

The Premier thought about that. "Would there be any confusion? There are no decks 0 or 1, are there?"

"No," Fiona said. "No numbered decks at all, only letters. I agree entirely. It makes no sense."

"Bureaucracy," the Egyptian President said flatly.

You should know, I thought. *Egypt had bureaucracy down to a fine art at least five thousand years ago, and nothing has changed since.* But, like the others, I nodded: he was, of course, right.

Fiona tapped my shoulder. "Mr. Pollard: perhaps you'd like to tell our guests a little about your contribution."

"My job's comms," I said. "Communications. At the moment that include laser and radio, but the main medium is freewave. That's how everyone watchin' on Earth can witness this pivotal event in human history –" we'd been primed to work such phrases in whenever possible – "with zero comm-lag. Uh, what I mean is, instantly."

Fiona nodded. She turned to the Japanese Premier. "All senior crew are trained to play any role, should that become necessary. Tell them how we control the ship, Rowley."

This caught me by surprise, but I realised that the Admiral was trying to inject some spontaneity into the proceedings.

"Uh– well, it's pretty straightforward, really. When we are on duty, senior crew mostly hangs out on D Deck. That's Command and Control, you get? From there we monitor and operate all of *Star Pyramid*'s systems: comms (my baby), collision avoidance, ramscoops, antimatter collection and storage, ramrocket and" – *don't call it the MAD, Rowley* – "Matter Annihilation Drive; life support and SusAn, and much, much more."

"We don't *expect* anything to go wrong," Fiona put in, "but we have to assume it could, so Assistant Flight Controller Makumba and other crew occupy the backup Command and Control suite on

G Deck. He shadows my every move, taking command himself from time to time."

The procession floated on, visiting random parts of the ship in no particular order, depending on what the delegates wanted to look at next. The GU had made it clear that we had to let *them* decide what to see. Or at least make everyone think they were deciding. Occasionally we made a brief side trip into a deck that one of the visitors decided might be of interest.

Most of the ship was starkly functional: corridors and rooms with exposed girders encased in plastic cladding (and sometimes padding). We didn't think they'd want to see those, so we surreptitiously herded them into the areas where we ate, drank, slept, and relaxed.

Those were very different.

"You live well, Admiral," the President-for-life of PanAfrica said. "These facilities would do credit to a luxury hotel."

"Very kind of you, President Onyango," she replied. "Most parts of the ship are somewhat spartan, but since we'll be spending about a century, subjective time, on board, the Psychosocial Unit insisted that a bit of luxury and comfort was in order. It causes no problems: unlike most vessels designed for spaceflight, saving weight isn't a major consideration. And the expense is tiny by comparison with the Project as a whole."

"Money well spent?" he asked, sceptically.

"Money well spent," she agreed, pretending to take the comment at face value.

The Maltese Ambassador to Outer Space insisted on inspecting a shuttle bay. We have four, with huge doors that open into vacuum. They hold eight shuttles, four OWLLs, and several hundred drones.

"What is an OWLL?" a SouMerican diplomat asked.

Fiona gestured to Salomé Blanchet, from Engineering.

"The name stand for 'Orbit-World Launch and Landing'," she said. "They do what their name suggests. Each OWLL can carry a 1500-kilogram payload, including any human occupants."

"Do they need a pilot?"

"No, they're fully automated. But there are controls for a pilot and a copilot, if needed. The shuttles are different: they function only in space. At the start of the voyage we used them to ferry personnel from lunar orbit to *Star Pyramid,* the same way you arrived here. By the end of the trip we'll have modified them to secure mahabhavium from the gas clouds surrounding Karoubi's Star."

"And the drones?"

"They're piloted remotely, powered by miniaturised fusion cells. They have numerous uses: hull inspections during the voyage, simple repair work, things like that. In that environment they're reusable. They can also be dropped into atmosphere using re-entry cocoons with disposable parachutes, but they can't return to orbit under their own power. There are larger cocoons and chutes to drop heavier equipment, but we're not expecting to use them. Purely precautionary."

Next, again at the dignitaries' insistence, was SusAn. That was the cue for Dr William Horatio Amblesyde, Chief Medic, to put his oar in. After they'd stared goggle-eyed at the rows of coffin-like caskets and the complex equipment attached to them, and he'd summarised the complex procedures for deanimating and reanimating the human body safely, he explained that SusAn, for all its benefits, had a difficult downside.

"Once someone's been woken up, it's dangerous to suspend them again until at least two and a half years have passed."

"Why?" one of the party asked. I didn't spot who.

Amblesyde spread his hands wide. "For reasons we don't fully understand despite decades of intensive research, the chance of surviving reanimation goes down rapidly as the period between successive reanimations gets shorter. Two years: 15% chance of death plus 12% chance of irreversible brain damage. One year: 60% death plus 25% brain damage. Six months: 100% death. So, to leave a safety margin, the minimal period of reanimation has been set at three years per stint. That's a legal limit imposed by the GU."

"So each of you is – uh – animate for how long altogether?" President Onyango asked.

"About twelve years in total," Amblesyde said. "Except for Admiral Rickart."

"I'll be animate for the first year of the voyage and the last," she explained. "Plus five three-year periods surrounding the most crucial operations: flypasts of Wolf 359 and Regulus, shutdown, turnover, and braking point."

Onyango nodded sagely. "Of course. Your presence will be necessary at such crucial events. But what happens in between?"

"Other ex-naval crew take charge," Fiona said. "They're just as experienced as I am. If something sufficiently nasty blows up they're authorised to have me reanimated. Which would take another three years off my projected lifespan after *Star Pyramid*'s return, so the threat level has to be high." She gave the rest of us a meaningful look. "Wake me up *without* good reason and I'll make your life hell!"

The dignitaries all laughed, and so did we. But *we* knew she meant it.

After three hours of this kind of thing the tour ended up on H Deck for a reception and the HV bots quietly withdrew. This part of the ceremony was private. Champagne flowed, for those who wanted it, with alternatives for those who didn't, or were from cultures where alcohol was forbidden. Plus assorted nibbles, of course. Real food transported to us along with the dignitaries, not printed from textured and flavoured algae as all our meals would be on the voyage.

Eventually, Security deftly herded our high-level visitors back into their shuttle and it headed back towards the Moon.

No disasters. Smooth as silk, considering.

It was a relief to get that particular event out of the way. Now most of us could breathe again and get on with more important things.

"You know," Fiona said to our small select group, "It still amazes me that right at the start I *applied* for this job. It amazes me more that so far I've not regretted accepting."

"That," I told her, "is because you got the full support of a wonderful, expert crew."

Fiona shook her head, but there was a twinkle in her eye. "What I've got, Rowley, is a disruptive bunch of highly talented overgrown schoolkids. You people scare the life out of me. Though not as much as this voyage does."

She had a point.

A hundred years from Earth to Karoubi's Star; four hundred in Earth's reference frame. I'd be frozen solid for most of it, on duty 24/7 for the rest. (We measured time subjectively in familiar units, even though it would be out of sync with Earth. The Psychosocial Unit had insisted on it for our mental health.)

Coming back would take so little time that no one would be able to measure it, in either frame.

If we succeeded.

If not, we'd be coming back the hard way.

Or not at all.

* * *

For a few of us, official duties still hadn't finished. The media people were still hanging around doing interviews, of just about anyone they could persuade to speak to them. I was still in charge of the HV-freewave hookup. Clapham hung around too, in case *k*-weather caused problems and we needed some smart math quickly. I hoped he'd keep a civil tongue in his head. At least I'd had a chance to remind him of what Fiona would do if he didn't.

One of the media guys sat Fiona in the command chair and arranged his cameras to make the most of our picturesque old-fashioned array of screens and our state-of-the-art HV daises. The rest of us were allowed to stay provided we kept quiet and didn't move a muscle.

Fiona looked confident and relaxed. You don't reach her level of seniority without learning how to handle the media. Despite her impeccably smart uniform, donned specially for the launch ceremony, she resembled everyone's favourite auntie, which made it easy to underestimate her.

"I gather you come from a military family." He was suave and well-groomed, at his ease despite the location, and his name was Nigel. He didn't tell us his surname. He had no human assistants, just a swarm of bots. Very specialised bots. They set themselves up to film enough angles to get the high-resolution 3D effect that HV viewers demanded.

"That's true," she said, managing to give the impression that she had thought about the question before answering. "My family's been military through and through for at least five generations. Navy, Marines, Air Corps. My grandfather flew fighter jets in the Kamchatka insurgency, his brother was a helicopter pilot."

Nigel did something with his fingers and the bots assumed a new configuration. "How did you end up in command of a starship?"

Fiona arched one eyebrow. "Well, Nigel: when the action moved into space, both the Navy and the Air Force moved with it. I'd started out as an LTJG on a destroyer in the Indian Ocean, and graduated to FADM: admiral of a fleet of heavily armed cruisers patrolling the asteroid belt. I'd been lucky to make the shortlist for *Star Pyramid*, and more than a little surprised when I was offered the post of Flight Controller, one of ten places for overall command."

The topic switched to suspended animation. Unless you've become a hermit and escaped all the *Star Pyramid* ballyhoo fomented by the Global Union, you can hardly fail to be aware that everyone on board was to spend 90 per cent of their time in SusAn.

Fiona didn't quite put it that way, but she did get over the point that she wouldn't be animate for the entire hundred-year trip. That would've made her about 150 years old when we finally arrived, and despite medical advances, no one lives that long. So the ten Flight Controllers would timeshare the responsibilities of high command: ten years subjective time each, on average.

Nigel nodded sagely. "Share them, yes, But you're first among equals, aren't you?"

"You could put it that way. I'm Flight Director, one level up from Flight Controller. It was only after I'd accepted the posting that they told me that. It means I have to be in charge of all mission-critical manoeuvres."

"Including the return to Earth under the first working Da Silva drive in history."

"Yes, if all goes to plan."

Nigel pounced, probably thinking she'd made a mistake.

"Do you have any reason to suppose it won't?"

"No, Nigel, but I'm being realistic. No major project ever goes exactly to plan. There are no guarantees." She paused, then trotted out one of our pre-prepared pledges. "Well, one, actually. I personally guarantee that every single person on this ship will strive to their utmost to make sure we achieve our prime objective."

To his credit, he didn't say 'mahabhavium'. Everyone knew that.

She did it for him. "The plan, as we all know, is to extract mahabhavium from the gas clouds, atom by atom."

"But quickly?"

"Oh, yes. Very. And in huge quantities." For the first time during the interview a faint smile lit up her face. "We'll be using shuttles equipped with an adaptation of the eka-Bussard's Da Silva-linked ramfield, hybridised with a mass spectrometer to channel the atoms of mahabhavium, and only those, into carefully designed collection vessels. The enormous capacity of the adapted ramscoop fields, the speed with which the eight shuttles can gobble up kilometres by the thousand, and above all the atomic selectivity of the Da Silva-linkage, will combine to let us gather the required amount of mahabhavium in under three weeks."

"That quickly? Impressive," he said, sounding sincere. "And you bear the ultimate responsibility for the mission."

Fiona nodded. "It's a hands-on job, Nigel, despite SusAn."

"I see. You'll spend more time reanimated than most of your crew?"

"Yes, it comes with the territory. But only for mission-critical manoeuvres. The three-year safety period between reanimation and deanimation means I've got to be animate for seventeen years rather than the normal ten."

He looked her in the eye, inquisitor mode. "Are you happy with that?"

She returned the look, no longer in favourite auntie mode. "Well, they did offer me the option of backing out *after* they explained that," she said lightly. Mona Lisa smile. Enigmatic.

Nigel looked serious. "But you didn't."

Obviously not. "No. Rickarts never refuse a challenge."

Nigel recognised the perfect exit line. "Thank you, Admiral Fiona Rickart."

After filming a few more bits and pieces to help with the editing, Nigel had what he wanted. He gestured at the hovering cambots.

"That's a wrap, guys."

Nigel and his bots left in search of other victims.

But his questions had left us all wondering, yet again, what we'd let ourselves in for.

Humanity was pushing its technological know-how to, perhaps beyond, the limit. Two things were obvious from the start: it was going to be complicated, and it was going to be hair-raising.

CHAPTER 17

FROM L2 TO LEO

Fiona Rickart

Star Pyramid 2169

Two months later…

I could access all the ship's systems from any location, but it felt right to sit in the Flight Controller's chair in Command and Control and carry out exactly that duty. D Deck was one of the smaller ones; the nearer the front of the alphabet, the nearer the bow of *Star Pyramid,* and elementary geometry meant that space was more limited.

D Deck was perhaps the only part of the ship that looked almost exactly like anyone would expect from watching old HV space operas. Wall-to-wall screens showing the ship's interior and exterior in real time, scrolling code and engineering schematics, innumerable matrices of lights blinking in innumerable colours, deeply upholstered swivel-mounted seats with retractable acceleration restraints… the works.

I'd been surprised that the HV people hadn't asked why, when everyone's been using HV dais tech for donkeys' years. Probably they'd *expected* it to look like old HV space operas. Actually, it's an excellent question. The answer is that D Deck has an extensive battery of HV tech, which is what I mainly use, but it *also* has simpler and therefore more reliable equipment as backup. We don't use voice commands because voices are easily spoofed, and (very rarely) an offhand remark about something innocuous might be misinterpreted. Humanity has learned the hard way not to trust AI except for very specialist applications, mainly scientific ones.

So far, we'd made it from LEO to L2. Now came the hard bit: from L2 to Leo.

Mission Control gave the signal, and we went live.

Time to hitch a ride.

* * *

I fired up the massive ring of old-fashioned rockets, a slow but reliable way to conduct *Star Pyramid* from the L2 construction zone to where *Womera* waited, three thousand kilometres away. *Womera* was gigantic, a flattish disc a thousand kilometres across; tilted at right angles to the ecliptic, her axis already aimed towards Leo. Even when her central hub was no more than twenty kilometres away, the vast booster was almost invisible to the unaided eye, except when sunlight reflected off one of her superconducting girders. In enhanced reality she looked like a frisbee stuffed with chickenwire, but each wire was the width of a subway tunnel. Her ten thousand fusion reactor nodes, linked by those girders, would make their presence known only when they ignited.

On 24 October 2169, guided by automated machinery that knew the precise location of every girder, reactor, current enhancement spike, and coil winding, the tugs edged slowly through the central tube of this ghostly maze and *Star Pyramid* was implanted into *Womera*'s capacious womb. Once the two ships were linked up, a complex operation in its own right, we headed away from the solar system in the general direction of the constellation Leo at $0.5g$ acceleration, the most that *Womera* could safely withstand when it was carrying a payload of one and a half million tonnes.

On D Deck everything *seemed* calm, but below the surface there was a mixture of tension and elation.

"We on our way," Rowley drawled.

"Humanity's greatest adventure." Gayl sounded unusually subdued. "It's really happening." She shook her head, awed. "I never really believed it would. It was too... *outrageous*."

Even I could hardly believe it, after all the complex preparations, the four-year delay and ensuing panic, and a general feeling that a project as complicated as *Star Pyramid* could never actually happen. Almost the entire population of the Earth was watching each stage of our launch sequence. The crew made valiant efforts to remain in the acceptable range between stage fright and over-excitement. It may have helped that there wasn't a lot for them to do at that point.

"Fuel levels nominal," Salomé told me. "Power stable."

Until the ramscoop came online and trapped enough hydrogen to fuel all of the ship's fusion generators, *Star Pyramid* was running on pre-loaded fuel, enough to power one of them. The SusAn caskets were empty, and they'd stay that way until the eka-Bussard kicked in with a continuous and inexhaustible supply of hydrogen. The restaurants were running multiple shifts, their tables a hubbub of chat and laughter; the low-*g* recreational facilities were fully booked days ahead. You couldn't travel along the central concourse without encountering friends or colleagues.

All this was soon to change.

Thirty billion kilometres from the Sun, where the Öpik-Oort cloud – a silly name for something consisting of so much empty space – no longer threatened the faintest chance of a collision, *Womera* and *Star Pyramid* parted company. We'd reached ramscoop ignition speed, with an ample margin. Now the eka-Bussard just had to ignite.

It did, so smoothly that you couldn't feel the jolt. Half a million tonnes of cargo contained in a million tonnes of metal mined in the asteroid belt, shaped in the Earth-Moon L1 foundry habitat and assembled at Earth-Sun L2, began to accelerate – imperceptibly at first, but faster as the scooped-up hydrogen began to fuse and the ship's momentum slowly built. Vibrations from the engines had been suppressed to the best of the designers' abilities, but a low background thrum perfused every corner of the ship. We quickly got used to it, and would notice it only if it stopped.

I gave silent thanks to Federico Berrios and *Tyger* for pioneering the eka-Bussard. Belatedly realised that unless he'd died, he was *still out there*, nine light years from Earth and having aged only four years. He'd never renewed contact. It must be awful… no, maybe not. He'd been a monk in the Belt, he *liked* solitude. Even so, stuck in a small ship with nothing but vacuum within light years might be too much solitude, even for him.

Would anyone ever rescue him?

Difficult enough if *Star Pyramid* succeeded.

Impossible if we failed.

* * *

Everything about *Star Pyramid* was complicated, and everything was interlinked with everything else. The source of these technical complications was, as always in spaceflight, the presence of human beings. Bots would have been less fragile and less demanding, but also too risky. Humans could adapt and improvise in ways no machine yet built could match. But humans need air, food, water – and, on a voyage of this length, gravity.

The day Salomé Blanchet had arrived on board and reported to me, she had expressed her views about gravity concisely and pertinently.

"It's a pig."

She was right, and I said so. The multiple propulsion systems that were the only way to make the ridiculous thing work created multiple gravitational scenarios, and the ship and its crew had to keep functioning in all of them.

During most of this initial booster stage of the voyage, we'd effectively been working in $0.5g$, with the deck partitions horizontal and the central concourse a vertical elevator shaft lined with four independent elevators. Now the ship's acceleration would give the illusion of normal gravity. This would gradually tail off as we attained maximum velocity and stopped accelerating. At shutdown, in 2396, the eka-Bussard would be turned off and the ship would coast. The sense of artificial gravity would remain, however; by then, attitude jets powered by our fusion generators would have set the massive pyramid spinning.

This would lead to significant variations in the apparent force: the further away from the central axis, the greater the apparent force of gravity. It would take weeks to get anywhere near the required spin rate, but eventually the whole vessel would become a giant gyroscope, ensuring massive stability.

Clapham and Pallendorf had briefed us all on what to expect. We'd been told many times already, but Mission Control had insisted on a recap. Never misses a trick, Mission Control.

"When the ship's spinning on its axis," Clapham had told us, "it creates what's conventionally known as 'artificial gravity'. We all know that.

"What only some of us know is, that's a very bad name.

"'Pseudogravity', that's what we mathematicians and physicists call it, and we're probably the only people who find it inspirational.

"Artificial gravity is directed *radially*. That feels fairly normal when you're standing or walking, but it can affect freely moving objects in very strange ways. The problem is that real gravity acts on everything, whereas pseudogravity acts only on objects that are in contact with a spinning surface. So, if you drop something, or throw it, it doesn't do what you expect. The object travels in a straight line, but *you* are moving in a circle. In your frame of reference, which is the only one human beings are used to, it's as if the object combines the straight-line motion with a *backwards* rotation.

"I can show you the equations if anyone– no, fine, fair enough. But I *will* show you some simulations."

Did you know that if you hit a golf ball in a spinning space habitat, it can follow a path shaped like a heart? Fortunately we can't play golf on *Star Pyramid*. Not enough open space. But even if you just drop an object it seldom ends up where you expect. It's one reason that crew are forbidden to float along the concourse, even though the force of pseudogravity there is tiny.

That's not the only issue. Spin-induced gravity would require major psychological adjustments. Floors and ceilings would swap roles with walls. The central concourse would become a longitudinal passage, its elevators now running like trains. It would also be the only place on the ship that effectively had no gravity. In principle, people could fly along it if they were careful not to bump into anything, but in practice this was all too likely, so it was forbidden except in an emergency.

This state of affairs would persist until braking point, when the MAD kicked in to slow us down and the effective gravitational field reverted to what it had been with the eka-Bussard in operation.

Most of the ship's machinery was designed to be independent of the direction or strength of artificial gravity. The rest of it, mainly anything to do with the crew, would be reconfigured as necessary. So, for example, H Deck, where the restaurants, bars, lounges, and recreational facilities were located, was partitioned into innumerable small rooms, with furnishings that could be relocated when the floor changed position. The same went for N Deck, which contained all the SusAn caskets and their support equipment.

Those changes were still to come, but it was encouraging to see that everything was within design parameters. So far. The GU's engineers had done an amazing job. Now it was up to me, as Flight Director, to build on their work. With the ship no longer safe in *Womera*'s embrace but proceeding under its own power, I finally felt that I merited the title.

My main problem wasn't hardware – I had staff for that. It was wetware. People. Infinitely more complex, infinitely more prone to unpredictable malfunctions. I had 739 of them, plus me, to keep under control, and I had the distinct feeling that the one who'd cause me the most difficulty was me. Why? Easy. I can't be objective about myself.

* * *

There were five main categories of crew: support, technists, medics, scientists, flight. Normally, each crew member would get three periods of animation, each three years long.

The support staff handled day-to-day tasks – cooking, cleaning, even laundry. But most of it was automated, and there would seldom be more than seventy human beings animate and carrying out the tasks that couldn't safely be assigned to bots.

The technists – which included engineering, infotech, and comms, along with much else – assisted the flight crew during the voyage by testing and maintaining essential equipment. They also operated the freewave link and kept it working. Their most crucial task would come when we got to Karoubi's Star, when they'd be in charge of the detection, location, and collection of mahabhavium. Along the way they would rebuild the shuttles for that purpose.

The medics did what medics have always done – tend the sick, lay out the dead, and occasionally play God. If *Star Pyramid* had been a generation ship a substantial part of their job would have been delivering babies, but mercifully we had SusAn, making everything far simpler. All personnel had reversible contraceptive implants, making everything simpler still. The medics also dealt with the effects of suspended animation on the human body. Deanimation and reanimation are complex and delicate tasks.

The scientists made observations, theorised, and followed their noses wherever their thoughts might lead them. You can do quite a bit of science in nine years. Enough to keep them happy.

The flight crew did what it said on the tin: fly *Star Pyramid* and kept her flying. They operated the ramdrive, antimatter creation and storage, the MAD, and the Impact Avoidance System. They considered everyone else to be passengers, and everyone else considered themselves to be crew, their official designation. Every one of them had survived the most rigorous selection process in history. Qualifications, track record, psych profile. Balanced for gender, ethnicity, nationality, political inclination. The only kind of balance the GU hadn't gone for was religion. After Berrios, they preferred people of a more secular disposition.

According to the manifests I was flight crew, indeed Flight Director, but no one called me that. To keep command lines clear, there was a paramilitary pecking order for administrative staff, though no official ranks. More like a line management tree. I could peck anyone, no one could peck me. Uniquely among the crew, I'd kept my old Navy rank, so technically I was an admiral, and that's what everyone else called me when they were being formal. Which was seldom.

Admiral.

Most days I felt more like a cross between matriarch and doormat.

Relativistic time dilation meant that the faster we went, the slower ship's time passed compared to Earth time. So, in subjective time, it would take us only a hundred years to reach our destination while four hundred years passed back home.

Unlike *Tyger*, which was light enough never to stop accelerating, *Star Pyramid* would tail off its ramrocket power before it reached its theoretical maximum velocity. The ship was so massive that the rocket exhausts might start to deteriorate at any higher speed. Balancing the probability of failure against the time taken to get to Karoubi's star, the designers had settled for a conservative 98.41% lightspeed.

Not bad for something massing one and a half million tonnes.

Without suspended animation even a hundred-year trip would have required a generation ship, and the complexities of life support would have been daunting. They were daunting enough *with* SusAn. Most of the crew would be animate only for nine or ten years, so the mission planners didn't expect there to be much work for the medics, but as a precaution at least two of them were on duty at any given time. The rest could be reanimated within a few hours, should their services be needed, but once reanimated they would have to stay that way for the statutory three-year safety period.

The starship's 740 personnel had been selected for psychological resilience, adaptability, the ability to improvise, and raw courage. Unfortunately, these characteristics conflicted with another desirable one: conformity to authority.

You can't have everything.

Star Pyramid had been a mess of compromises from the day she was no more than a gleam in Ramon Gómez Da Silva's eye. One more would hardly hurt.

* * *

Pushing negative thoughts aside, I wandered through the ship, making my presence felt, checking that the crew were in good spirits and performing their assigned tasks. You have to be careful with this. 'Management by walking around' can all too easily morph into micromanagement, and instead of reassuring everyone it can make them feel spied on.

I'd walked that tightrope for long enough to be confident I was getting it right, but no one was likely to tell me otherwise unless I was getting it badly wrong. Even on a civilian vessel, you don't criticise an Admiral without very good reason.

High command is a lonely place, however much support you have.

A few of the more uptight crew members saluted as I passed. Later I'd have a private word, asking them not to. A few gave me a friendly wave. Most acknowledged my presence and quietly carried on with their duties.

I poked my nose into Hydroponics. I hadn't announced the visit, but they were expecting me anyway, having kept an eye on my progress through the ship. Surprise inspections are possible, but they require concealing my location, which warns everyone to expect a surprise inspection. In any case, surprise inspections suggest a lack of confidence in my crew, so I avoid them.

"Admiral Rickart."

"Marina."

I knew who she was – I make a point of knowing everyone, and she had a very recognisable face, square-jawed with freckles. In any case, like everyone animate, she was wearing coveralls with an ID badge. Hers read: Marina Gottlieb, hydroponics hygienist, Y. The 'Y' was her security clearance level; you can work the rest out. We used the same ID system for everyone, even me: Fiona Rickart, flight crew, Z. Her coveralls were pale green, which I suppose was appropriate, but the colour was optional. Mine were usually black. Off duty most of us went for informal outfits, even me, but our wardrobe was limited by our weight allowance, which was the same for everyone. Democracy in action. More clothes meant less of everything else. However, clothing was recyclable and printable. As the voyage progressed I expected more inventive costumes.

"This is an unexpected pleasure," she said.

"Unexpected? Do you really think I'd believe that?" I smiled to show it was a joke.

Marina laughed. "Last time I checked where you'd got to you were stuck on M Deck with the technists. I figured that would keep you, uh, *entertained,* for an hour at least. So actually it is unexpected."

"I cut the show-and-tell short."

She nodded. "Very wise. Technists are always keen to show off their gadgets." She introduced me to her assistants. At this point there were 22 of them, but soon that number would be reduced to three. They all looked keen and energetic. I wondered how long it would take for that to be reduced, too. Everything tends to slip on a long voyage, and this one was longer than anyone had ever endured before, even with SusAn. One of the disconcerting features of suspended animation is that waking up after a century would feel much like waking up after one night's sleep – aside from the grogginess, discomfort, weakness of the muscles, and discontinuity of the surrounding culture, of course. So you don't feel as though you've had a long break between successive reanimations. More like taking an overnight saucer to a foreign land, flying cattle class.

"I realise you know every centimetre of the ship like the back of your hand, Admiral, but would you like to look around our little garden?"

The little garden occupied about 30,000 square metres, stacked in racks on four levels, arranged on a grid. Most of it was hidden behind other racks, much like an old-fashioned library where you can't see most of the bookshelves because the other shelves get in the way. It was split into hundreds of separate sectors by barriers with micropore filters, to prevent the spread of potential viral infections. The smell was more like an aquarium than a farmer's field, faintly astringent. There were pipes and banks of lighting everywhere. The racks were full of green goo. Delicious. Eventually.

"You have more faith in my powers of recall than I do," I said. "This is just a flying visit. Not to check up on your work; to make sure there's nothing else you need."

She ran fingers through her curly brown hair. "We're good. The most critical parts are the nutrient delivery system and the lighting, and Roger here–" she nodded at a ginger-haired young man clad in grey coveralls – "is in the middle of a routine inspection."

Roger pulled his shoulders straight. "No problems so far, Admiral. All major subsystems check out."

"And the minor ones?" It's always the tiny things that kill you.

"They're fine too." He paused. "Well... I'm keeping an eye on one bank of algae that look a little yellow, to be honest. The instruments say everything's normal, but– well, I grew up on a 'ponics farm in Nebraska and I trust my instincts more than I trust instruments." He paused, wondered if he'd gone too far, and added "not that I've got anything against instruments–"

Marina rescued him before his face became even redder. "Roger's doing spot checks on the ionic balances for optimal photosynthesis," Marina said. "If he finds an issue, he'll be on top of it. No one here wants to risk damaging the mission by being sloppy."

"Or in any other way," Roger said quickly. "We know how vital *Star Pyramid* is for Earth's future."

He'd clearly bought into the official reasons for the Project, and I had no wish to disillusion him, because they were true. Just not, perhaps, the whole truth. But then, whenever does any of us face up to the whole truth?

I wondered why I was having more of those negative thoughts. Worried that it was all going too smoothly? Well, I was, because nothing ever goes exactly to plan, but I didn't think that was the only reason. I would have faced up to the whole truth if I'd known what it was. Just… vague disquiet.

I brushed the thoughts aside. Worry when you know what to worry about, I told myself.

While everyone else got back to their assigned tasks, Marina showed me round her domain, one of the largest operations on the ship. It occupied two decks, Q and S, separated by recycling. A complex but organised mass of vats and tubes to grow the algae, harvesting robots, a preparation area where the food printers turned the bland substance into everything from a bowl of lentil soup to a five-course meal – and countless subsidiary operations.

Next, T Deck, and an hour or so with our engineers. Nearly done.

Back in my quarters, I tried to gauge what I'd learned.

The main thing that had left a lasting impression on me was the extent to which everyone on board exuded energy and commitment. My crew were mostly young, idealists who had bought into the importance of the Project for the future of humanity. You don't sign up for a 400-year trip on a whim.

I was tempted to view their attitude as naivety, but if it was, I'd been equally naive. I wondered how long this positive attitude would last. The start of a journey is usually the easiest part.

The level of activity on board was far from representative of the remainder of the voyage. At this stage everyone was animate, but now that the ramscoops were assuring us of ample fuel it was time to reduce the numbers to about a hundred. Everyone else had to go into SusAn for somewhere between 60 and 120 years, depending on their duty rota.

The surplus crew were deanimated over a period of two weeks, about forty people every day. It could have been done faster, but I wanted to spend quality time with every one of them before the medics began their intricate preparations. I didn't want the medics to feel hurried. I wanted every member of my crew to know that those of us who remained animate were dedicated to the safety of everyone on board. That they weren't just names on a list. Amblesyde did the same, answering any questions they had about the procedure. It had been covered a dozen times during training, but that was just theory: now it was shortly to become reality. He balanced a professional manner with a natural friendliness that surely had to be genuine. If not, he was an impressive actor.

The last to go under were the other nine Flight Controllers. At that stage the ship had attained its long-term configuration, both of equipment and personnel, and the seventy of us who remained animate settled into a regular routine. It wasn't boring; there was always plenty to do, especially for the scientists; but everywhere seemed *empty*.

Star Pyramid, formerly a high-tech village, was now little more than a ghost town with a slowly changing roster of ghosts.

CHAPTER 18

THE WOLF AND THE PRINCE

Kyril Pallendorf

Star Pyramid 2187 and 2268

It had been sheer luck that Karoubi's Star was close to the plane of the ecliptic, or we'd never have had a chance of getting there with the available technology. But *Star Pyramid* would still need a couple of carefully calculated boosts away from that plane to reach its destination. As a bonus, they offered unprecedented chances to observe stars from distances of light hours rather than light years.

As Chief Scientist, I was determined that my teams would make the most of these opportunities, which implied that I must be animate for both flypasts to keep everyone on their toes.

I had tried to explain this to the Flight Director.

"Admiral Rickart?"

"Yes, Kyril?"

"I prefer to be addressed as 'Professor Pallendorf', Admiral."

"And I prefer to be addressed as 'Fiona', but nobody seems to pay much attention, Kyril."

The Admiral seems touchy today, I thought, wondering what might have been the cause. However, there were more important issues that I wished to bring to her attention, as I tactfully explained. After reminding her of the general outline of the science programme, to establish the context, I made my wishes clear.

"I recommend, in the strongest possible terms, that everyone on my science teams should be reanimated for the two flypast events."

"Everyone?"

"Yes. I also recommend extending the animation period to four years: from two years before each event to two years after."

I was expecting her to give the suggestion the careful thought it deserved, but her reply was immediate.

"No. Mission guidelines mandate that no crew member should be continuously animate for more than the statutory three years, unless there is an overriding reason to extend that period."

"But there is! The science team needs more time to prepare, and–"

"*No*, Kyril. Three years is ample. You're just trying to get special treatment."

My protests fell on stony ground, and after some rather unsatisfactory discussion I was forced to accept a compromise: all key science personnel would be animate for at least one of the flypasts. To the Admiral's credit, she did accept my proposal that most members of the science team should be reanimated two years ahead of the events, rather than the usual eighteen months. That would give me enough time to make sure they were prepared for the vital few days of intensive activity, and the usual three-year period would give me another twelve months to organise the analysis of our results and the publication of our reports, which the astronomical community back on Earth would be anxious to examine.

Afterwards I reflected that the discussion had gone much the way I'd expected, but it was disappointing that the Admiral had not simply accepted my advice. I sent a strong protest to the GU asking them to override her decision, but they took no action. They didn't even reply, which was strange, because my opinion ought to have carried considerable weight. I've always been a talented organiser.

When I was eight years old, at my school in Geneva, I was put in charge of rehearsals for the school play. Many of the parents complimented me on how slick the performance was – the reward for a great deal of hard work. Later, at the Kantonsschule, I specialised in science and organised science fairs. I've always had a flair for science; I like its precision, logical inference, and the use of experiments to verify hypotheses. In my teens I gravitated towards the physical sciences, and when Uncle Simeon gave me a high-powered and rather expensive telescope I spent many hours either side of midnight observing planets, moons, and above all, stars. Stars were less spectacular than closer bodies, but their mystery spoke to me. It was fun to time occultations and use them to calculate the orbits of planets and moons, to check for myself what the OuterNet said. I saved my allowance and bought a spectroscope accessory, and made numerous logs of which elements were present in which stars. I still have them, lodged in a safety deposit box back on Earth.

Later, I secured remote access to more professional equipment, at first through citizen science programmes, then in my own right as a qualified scientist. As my academic career progressed I found ways to combine real scientific work with administration, which appealed to me because I could ensure that all procedures were being carried out in adherence to the regulations. If there's one thing I can't stand, it's sloppy science based on hunches and guesswork.

It was this attention to detail and precision that secured me a prestigious appointment to oversee the science programme during the planning stage of the Project which I'd spent years angling for. In due course, thanks no doubt to my diligence and hard-won expertise, I was selected for the same role on board *Star Pyramid* itself.

This made it all the more annoying that Admiral Rickart had not accepted my advice. Still, we all have our cross to bear.

* * *

In 2187, when time-dilation had lost the ship's clocks two years in comparison to Earth time and we'd covered just under eight light years, *Star Pyramid* made its first course-correction: a flypast encounter with the flare star Wolf 359. The plan was to zip past the star at 97.32% light speed, still accelerating, using its gravity to change direction slightly. Not a slingshot, just a mild deflection.

For those of us who were animate, the flypast would be the first departure from daily routine in anything up to three years. Everyone had been talking about it for ages, and I'd made sure that my science team was as well prepared as humanly possible. The flypast was also a major event back on Earth, so the GU had lined up a multimedia jamboree with a live freewave broadcast. Most of it was automated – feed from the scientific instruments, that kind of thing – and much of it happened on Earth, with historical footage, interviews of experts, discussions with sceptics who still seemed to imagine the Project could be cancelled.

There was also a live freewave interview. I delegated it to Václav Rádsetoulal, deputy head of Astrophysics, who'd had years of media experience back on Earth. The rest of my scientists were too busy to spare the time from their preparations, and so was I. In any case, I dislike being in the limelight. It distracts from the serious business of science.

For atmosphere, Václav suggested that we stage the interview in a small studio next to the auditorium and provide a local audience, who would watch the proceedings on a large HV dais. We could film them for audience reaction and do some vox-pops. He seemed pleased when I approved of this idea.

I gave him a few pointers on what to do and what not to do. I joined the audience for the HV broadcast, to check that he'd complied with my instructions, and I was pleased to observe that he had. As a result, his interview was organised and successful.

The usual introductions over, the presenter back in Los Angeles – Samantha Dennis, that was her name, a rather fluffy young woman – got down to business.

"Why is the star named after a wolf," she asked, "when it's in the constellation Leo, the lion?"

I had primed Václav for stupid questions like this one, and he didn't bat an eyelid.

"It's a historical accident, Samantha. It's not the animal, it's someone's name. Max Wolf." (He pronounced it with a 'V' – 'Volff'.) "His full name is a mouthful, Maximilian Franz Joseph Cornelius Wolf. He was German, and he worked in the city of Heidelberg, one of the first astronomers in the world to use photography to study stars. He started out hunting comets, but then he got interested in finding which stars were nearest to the Sun."

The HV flicked up an old photograph, black-and-white; a greying man with a dark beard and moustache, prominent ears and a very direct stare that was probably just the pose the photographer had insisted he should adopt.

The presenter pursed her surgically enhanced lips, feigning puzzlement. "*Finding* them? Didn't he know where they were?"

"Ah. I meant, he was finding out how close they were. The science was rudimentary, so he couldn't do what we'd do now, running through all the brighter stars to discover how far away they were. He figured that anything moving across the night sky quickly enough to measure would have to be close by, in astronomical terms."

She adjusted her wide-brimmed conical hat, the latest fashion in indoor wear.

"Don't they all move?"

Time-lapse graphic of the Milky Way spinning behind silhouetted trees.

"Well, yes, but that's because the Earth rotates. Stars also move relative to each other, and that's what Wolf was looking for. The closer they are to us, the faster they appear to move."

Commercial MHD saucers in the distance, small dots wandering lazily across the sky. One comes in to land, close up, moving fast.

"But stars are so far away that the apparent movement is tiny, even for the closer ones," Václav explained. "So we only notice they're moving if we make very accurate observations over long periods of time. Wolf 359 is only 7.8 light years away – the eighth nearest star, bearing in mind that alpha Centauri is a triple star and Luhman 16 is a double star. Counting brown dwarfs, of course."

"Of course," Samantha said. I doubted she'd know a brown dwarf from a pink elephant, but she managed to look intelligent and knowledgeable. "And the number? 359?"

"It was the 359th star in a catalogue that Wolf published in 1919. Its more conventional name is CN Leonis. In the constellation Leo, like you said."

"Which is where *Star Pyramid* is heading?"

"Exactly. Karoubi's Star is in much the same direction, so we're taking a look at Wolf 359 as we go past."

Stock image of red dwarf star. Too bright to be Wolf 359.

Samantha adjusted a strand of hair that was poking out from under the brim of her hat. "You're not just taking a look, though are you?"

Václav shook his head. "We're going to use the star's gravitational field to give the ship's course a nudge."

Samantha nodded vigorously, and had to lift the hat and brush her hair away from her eyes again. "We'll be talking about that later, to the Flight Controller, folks, so don't hop channels... Now, Wolf 359. It's not a normal star, is it, Václav?"

"No. That's an extra reason for observing it. It's what astronomers call a flare star."

An animation, now: a dim speckly red ball, its edges flickering sporadically; then, without warning, throwing off a huge loop of bright gas, expanding to half the size of the star, breaking away, dying down, everything quiet again... then another loop.

"Its brightness can increase dramatically in a few minutes, across the entire electromagnetic spectrum. That's what we might see if we get lucky. The flares are caused by dynamic behaviour in its photosphere – like solar flares in our own Sun, but far more energetic."

"Photosphere? Is that related to Wolf's use of photography?"

That nearly floored him, but he recovered. "Uh – sorry. The photosphere is the lowest layer of the star's atmosphere. To us it looks like the star's surface. Where its light appears to come from."

She let that 'appears to' pass. "'Dynamic behaviour' – can you be more specific, Václav?"

"Ah. The, uh– the star's magnetic field lines are swirling around, and sometimes they get so tangled and compressed that they break. Like an elastic band that's simultaneously being twisted and stretched so tightly that it eventually snaps, releasing most of the stored energy in a single burst."

"And that's going to be really spectacular?"

Archive material of solar flares.

"Let me put it this way, Samantha: the flares are almost as big as the star."

"Wow!"

Václav held up one hand, pointing a finger skywards. "But... I don't want to mislead our audience, Samantha. As I said, it will only be spectacular if we get lucky and there's a flare while we're nearby."

"And will we get lucky?"

Václav grimaced. "The probabilities say not, sorry. But we can hope."

There were more questions, and Václav did his best to answer them, until Samantha thanked him and announced the next item: an interview with a baseball pitcher who'd just broken the record for intentional walks in one game.

Yes, I was very satisfied with the interview, as I told Václav when I debriefed him immediately the interview had finished. He had made a few minor slips, of course, and I pointed those out in my usual friendly and helpful manner.

* * *

The Wolf 359 flypast was the first break in the monotony of the voyage, and we were all looking forward to a change of routine. Even me. Ordinarily I dislike breaking routine because routines encourage firm discipline, but on this occasion there was a solid reason for the changes. They were necessary to organise the ship's scientific activities.

Admiral Rickart decided – in my view an error – to make an occasion out of it, with a flypast party, a special flare star cake, and other sillinesses, leading up to the flypast itself. Most of the crew let their hair down, metaphorically speaking; those who could let it down literally. I made a brief public appearance, for form's sake, and then went back to my cabin to polish my plans for the flypast.

I don't really care for parties. Too noisy and disorganised. Anyway, I wanted to check that my team had calibrated their instruments correctly. I always check: however competent subordinates may appear, they sometimes screw up.

Fortunately, after that it all got more serious. Whatever the experience for the viewers back home, dull or exciting, the science would be humanity's first close-up view of any star except the Sun. A historic first, and a definite contender for a Nobel Prize.

While the science team pointed its instruments and made its observations, I and the rest of the animate crew watched the spectacle – well, we were hoping for a spectacle – as it started to unfold in video feed from the scopes. Back on Earth, the show was being broadcast planetwide in real time, thanks to the miracle of freewave. So, ironically, the only humans in the Galaxy who would not have an opportunity to watch the flypast live were those on *Star Pyramid* who were deanimate. It was a pity we couldn't have reanimated the entire crew, but then hundreds of surplus beings would've been knocking around the ship for the next three years consuming limited resources with nothing worthwhile to do. Hopelessly inefficient.

Anyway, it wasn't in the mission plan.

I did point out that those who'd missed the live event would be able to enjoy very detailed recordings when they next reanimated, and since everything was relayed from the scopes anyway, the visual experience would be identical. I couldn't help thinking that the psychological one would not. Being there *when it really happens* is always different from watching recordings afterwards. No matter how accurately they replicate the real thing. But there was no need to admit that.

I'd arranged to co-opt the theatre on K Deck, usually the scene of entertainment modules, from classics – *Romeo and Juliet*, *Game of Thrones*, *War of the Six Deserts* – to modern offerings like *Muriel and Amy Go Back to School*, *Pterodactyl II*, and *Seven Brides for Seven Sisters*.

My astronomy team relayed the more interesting parts of their observations to the big HV dais there. We'd been hoping to observe a flare during the flypast. The Admiral had confirmed that this would be perfectly safe, because our closest approach would be 7.5 billion kilometres, about six light hours. However, the star wasn't playing ball. Or, rather, it *was* playing ball: a dim red ball, round and quiescent.

Not spectacular enough to interest Samantha Dennis's producer.

My team did spot three planets, two of them far too small to have been observed from Earth. None habitable, but one had a comparatively large icy moon, raising the possibility of an under-ice ocean. So my scientists were excited, despite the absence of flare fireworks.

For everyone else, Wolf 359 was a bit of a damp squib.

For the next year my team worked all hours to extract scientific knowledge from the flypast observations. Then they were deanimated, as was I. Other members of the science team would continue working on our trove of data while we slept.

Admiral Rickart had presided over that first flypast, and in the fullness of time would preside over the second, but in between her replacements would take charge, following each at three-year intervals. Each overlapping their predecessor for a month to ensure a smooth transition.

Between the encounters with Wolf 359 and Regulus, the most significant event would be shutdown, scheduled for 2211 when the ship reached its maximum design speed. Of all our major manoeuvres this would be by far the simplest, though not without its dangers. Rickart wouldn't be needed to keep an eye on it, and most of the science team could sleep on, untroubled by any significant tasks. The duty Flight Controller would put the eka-Bussard into a lower power mode, most of that power being diverted into antimatter production. The rest would be used in occasional bursts to keep our speed at maximum. The flight crew would reconfigure the ramscoop fields and k-field linkage for impact avoidance only, power down the eka-Bussard engines, and convert *Star Pyramid* to coast mode. Occasionally they would turn on the ramrocket fusion motors to compensate for friction with the interstellar medium and to align our trajectory even more perfectly. Life on board *Star Pyramid* would once more settle into a regular routine.

* * *

I had higher hopes for my next reanimation. In 2268, now 80 light years away from Earth and 81 years after the Wolf flypast as measured by GU timekeepers but only 28 on *Star Pyramid*, the ship was scheduled to whip past Regulus in a second course-correction manoeuvre, still travelling at its maximum speed.

As before, I was reanimated two years ahead. Six months later, Admiral Rickart joined me, ready to take command again during the flypast period.

The first official task for a newly animate Flight Controller is to reassess the overall state of the ship and its mission. That meant a long series of briefings, all of which I attended *ex officio*. The

Medical Officer notified us of two deaths: one from an undiagnosed and very rare heart condition, the other from a head-on collision between two over-keen handball players on K Deck, resulting in a broken neck.

Both bodies had been recycled. We recycled *everything*.

My scientists were torn between delight at getting such a close-up view of this complex four-star system, and sadness that the encounter would be so short. *Star Pyramid* would never get closer than four light minutes to any of the stars, which gave them only a one-day window for extremely high resolution observations with the ship's seven telescopes, a two-day window either side for high resolution, and a few weeks before and after when it would still be possible to make out fine detail.

The Admiral authorised another flypast party and another cake. As she and I had agreed, the SusAn schedule was arranged so that, apart from me and a dozen other key personnel, a different group of people would have the opportunity to witness a sight never before seen by human eyes.

We organised everything in exactly the same way. No point reinventing the wheel. So once more the animate crew watched HV feed in the K Deck theatre. It was the second break in the monotony of the voyage, 28 ship's years after Wolf 359, and as before, Earth's masses could watch the same show in real time, assuming they could tear their eyes away from reality HV or the stock market feeds.

There'd been the same slew of media interviews as for the Wolf 359 flypast, and the crew performed to the best of their variable abilities. What they didn't know was that the interviews had been commissioned by the GU, which had paid the HV companies large sums of cash to set them up. Previously it had been the other way round. The painful truth was that this time no one wanted to interview us, a sign that Earth was fast losing interest. Naturally, it was a truth the GU preferred to hide from us, and the interviewers, being professionals, gave the impression that the entire population of the planet was hanging on our every word.

Rickart and I knew better. Like the GU, we didn't tell anyone.

A week before the encounter, Regulus looked like a single slightly bluish, fairly bright, star. Nothing much to write home about. But this time, my scientists were confident of a more impressive spectacle, and they weren't disappointed.

I'd selected Max Clark, the currently animate head of Astronomy, to act as commentator. Which, to be fair, he did pretty well, provided you compared his performance to someone giving a not very exciting lecture.

"The name 'Regulus' is Latin for 'prince'," he began. "And the name is appropriate, as I'll explain. What we're looking at right now is Regulus A," Clark continued in his slightly reedy voice. "A blue-white subgiant star of spectral type B8. Mass about 3.8 times that of our own Sun. What you're seeing is a composite image from three of our telescopes: one in the visual range, one infra-red, and one x-ray.

"Notice its shape, flattened like a satsuma rather than round like an orange. Technically, it's an oblate spheroid. It bulges at the equator because it spins very fast, about once every 16 hours. Basically it's a big ball of gas, so it deforms under the enormous centrifugal forces created by its spin."

I was sitting next to Rickart in the front row. At this point she turned in her seat, presumably to gauge how the rest of the audience was responding; I did the same. On the whole, they were attentive and quiet, though two had already gone to sleep. She signalled one of her staff to give them a poke. Wouldn't want anyone to miss the show.

"It looks like a single star from this distance," Clark explained. "But when we switch the scopes to higher levels of magnification, we can pick up a companion. I should add that you are among the very first people to see the companion. It's not visible from Earth, not even with the most powerful telescopes. We knew it must be there, because it affects the spectrum of Regulus A. It was thought to be a white dwarf – the mass of the Sun compressed within the volume of the Earth. Once it was a conventional star, not especially large, so when its nuclear reactions started to run down it wasn't massive enough to create a supernova. Instead, it... died. It collapsed in on itself when the radiation pressure from the core could no longer overcome the pull of gravity. We call it a stellar core remnant, which you can probably guess means 'remains of a star's core'."

He paused, picked up a glass of water, drank a mouthful. Back on Earth that would no doubt be edited out. Replaced by some graphic.

"Well, now we know that the deduction was right! That's exactly what we're observing, as I speak, in the companion star.

"All the matter inside it is highly compressed – though not as much as in a neutron star. The atoms still have electrons. Now, I'm sure you all remember the old model of an atom as a nucleus composed of protons and neutrons, surrounded by electrons, which settle into a series of concentric *shells*. Not how we think of atoms today, of course, but not a bad picture for present purposes.

"In an isolated atom, many of the shells are incomplete. Like the seating in a half-empty sports stadium. But when a star collapses to a white dwarf, more and more spectators come into the stadium, filling up all the seats. So electrons fill up all of the low-energy shells surrounding the nucleus. At that stage the matter resists compression very strongly, because there's no easy way for the electrons to move. It's called 'electron-degenerate matter'."

Rickart and I turned round again. Audience still attentive, except for a couple in the back row who were interested only in each other. Not doing any harm, I suppose, though it was highly unprofessional. Not members of my team, I was pleased to note. But then, they were too busy making observations for such frivolities.

"The astronomers of the 20th century knew early on that Regulus isn't one star; it's two very close together. *But*: they didn't suspect the existence of the white dwarf you're looking at. Instead, they'd discovered an orange dwarf companion, much further away. About 0.8 times the mass of the Sun. And that, it soon turned out, is also a double star, with its own companion: a red dwarf, less than half as massive.

"So, ladies and gentlemen: Regulus is a *double* double star! Truly a prince among stars. The blue-white subgiant and the white dwarf circle each other like two folk dancers holding hands and swinging each other around. The orange and red dwarfs do the same. But now the two couples also follow each other round and round at opposite sides of a bigger circle. So each dancer traces a complex path of Ptolemaic epicycles."

He had to explain that last bit, of course, when we got to the Q&A.

CHAPTER 19

MESSAGE FROM HOME

Eileen Myazaki

Floor B10, Global Union Tower, Tōkyō 2420

Above ground, the GU Tower In Tōkyō has 138 floors. My boss's office is on the 135th. Below ground, according to the guidebooks and city planning records, are eight more.

His other office is on the tenth.

Below the eighth basement floor is a layer of concrete. It's the lid of a concrete box that contains two more floors. The lid, walls, and floor of the box are thick enough to survive a 100-megaton nuclear blast, immediately above them at the surface.

Liancy Tampling, my boss's Chief of Staff, runs the ninth floor, where information from all over the world, and beyond, is collected, stored, analysed, and digested into briefings for the GU's executives. It's a warren of dimly-lit passages and rooms whose purpose is undisclosed – no names, numbers, or titles on the doors. The people who work there, including me, know enough of this information to do their jobs, and nothing more. There are security locks everywhere; doors that open only after biometric checks of four different features – voiceprint, retinal pattern, ultrasound skeletal scan, DNA swab. They stopped using fingerprints forty years ago: too easy to fake.

Tampling and a few other select officials have access to the four elevators that connect the ninth floor to the tenth. The tenth floor is smaller than the ninth, more open, and less crowded. It's also the real heart of the GU. You'll find my boss's second office in one corner. Like all the doors, it's not marked, but if you put your eye to the retinal reader, a hidden projector will briefly display his name and position. Sandford Dane, GU Secretary-General. The human face of this huge organisation.

It so happens that I'm one of the officials permitted access to Floor 10. Eileen Myazaki, pleased to meet you. Yes, I know I don't power-dress like Tampling, although I like to feel that my appearance is neat and tidy, and my pay grade seems too low for me even to *know* about those two extra floors, let alone have access to the ninth, never mind the tenth. But my role is one that Dane long ago realised was essential: to make sure he's fully prepped for every media event, scheduled or not.

I'm way down the food chain. I don't organise the events. I don't even deal with any of the technical equipment – the cameras, lighting, sound, editing software… Three sections on Floor 9 take care of all that stuff. I'm just there to make sure that Dane doesn't forget anything, that his suit has no specks of dust or hairs on it, that his tie is tied in the correct manner (he *hates* wearing ties, but always does), his hair is neatly combed (and, a few days ahead of major events, trimmed). Despite all the electronic gadgetry that stores his appointments and reminds him when they're due, he would sometimes forget things. The tiny things that could wreck his public image.

I make sure they don't.

Not that he'd be likely to forget this appointment, utterly routine though it might be.

* * *

As I checked Dane over for stray hairs and lint, I kept up a running commentary on the preparations going on above us. He knew the procedure, but I had an audio feed that confirmed its current status. As usual he gave it only part of his attention, but unless anything diverged from normal, he'd focus on the content of the coming broadcast. Assistant Secretary Sitraka Rakotomalala, sitting across the room, would be following the whole thing on his monitor.

The audio crackled in my ear. Large headphones muffled the noise so that it wouldn't bleed out into Dane's speech.

In one of the nameless and numberless rooms overhead, a technician checked his instruments for the third time and punched a code into a secured, dedicated terminal. The terminal connected to a concealed freewave transmitter somewhere in northern Madagascar. Even Dane had no idea where it was. This generated a profiled waveform, arriving at the same instant in cis-Venerian orbit, 0.513 AU, as a string of coded soliton pulses. Three orbital freewave antennas, each an enormous and expensive device in its own right, formed an equilateral triangle that circled the Sun in a plane at right angles to the ecliptic. This was the Deep Space Freewave Array, in constant communication with *Star Pyramid*.

More than two light centuries away, in the starship's command

and control Deck D, a violet light would be blinking on a remote panel. The duty comm officer would check the telltales meticulously and patch the signal through to the PA system, to be heard by the seventy or so crew that were currently animate. The rest would snooze on in their SusAn caskets at a positively tropical 77K until it was their turn to be defrosted and on duty.

A freewave link from Earth to cis-Venerian orbit requires a few megawatts of power and a few picograms of mahabhavium.

A freewave link across three hundred light years – and growing – requires gigawatts of solar power, antennas with a baseline of a hundred million kilometres, and one nanogram of mahabhavium. This precious element is used to coat a single component, a resonating cavity just under two centimetres across. The receiving antenna on *Star Pyramid* is 80 metres in diameter and its resonating cavity requires a further 23 nanograms of mahabhavium. The 24-nanogram total contains 93% of the solar system's current supply, and all of it is human-made. It had taken fifty years, and a substantial proportion of the industrial effort of the GU powers, to bring that element into existence, atom by atom.

In the bowels of the GU Tower a light of the same violet hue appeared on the Assistant Secretary's desk. He glanced my way. I nodded, gave Dane a final visual once-over, and smoothed back a strand of his hair that had gone AWOL. Then I stepped back out of shot as the Secretary-General composed his features into the paternal expression that never left them in public, and seldom in private. Flawlessly, he took his cue from the HV board and began to speak. It was a routine message, but *Star Pyramid* got nothing but the best: Dane always did the job himself, as had his predecessors.

It did cross my mind that although the audience on *Star Pyramid* was an assorted rag-tag of whichever crew happened to have been reanimated at that time, there was also a potential audience of fifteen billion here on Earth, and just *possibly* this performance was primarily for their benefit. Well, not exactly benefit: to remind them that Dane was not just *my* boss, but *the* Boss. GU Secretary-General, in charge of the entire Project.

* * *

In the early days after launch the audience for such broadcasts had usually been pretty close to twelve billion. Not that three billion missed it; they hadn't been born then to swell the human population to its current level. Demographic transition notwithstanding, humanity had failed to curb its urge to breed. Population growth had slowed down until the asteroid belt's resources became widely available. Then, with all restraints removed, it had exploded again. Now even this source was severely stressed: not by theoretical availability but by economic feasibility. Ever more extreme technology kept most of us fed and housed. The rest took their chances with the four horsemen of the apocalypse made real: the white horse of disease, the red horse of war, the black horse of famine, and the pale horse of death. To which we had added the grey horse of soil degradation, the blazing horse of climate change, and the yellow horse of pollution – an entire cavalry that Saint John the Divine had never dreamed of.

The GU coped as best it could. Local warlords were tolerated as long as they didn't attack their neighbours. If they did, the GU dispatched personalised assassin-drones. Food, water, and temporary shelter were distributed to affected areas, often too late for many, but better than nothing. Amid the burgeoning chaos, *Star Pyramid* remained a shining beacon of hope, but its shine was becoming tarnished. Now, maybe a third of the people on the planet watched these broadcasts, a drop of seven billion. The Project required an attention-span of four hundred years; few humans could sustain a span of four hundred seconds.

The people on board *Star Pyramid* were not informed of these depressing developments. The Psych Team had reasonably advised that any downbeat message content could lower their morale. They needed all the positive reinforcement that Earth could give them. The Psych Team had also advised that a small proportion of mildly negative news should be included to 'enhance credibility'. That is, stop them smelling a rat.

One dreadful truth that absolutely must not be passed on to *Star Pyramid* was the massive decline in audience figures. When the excitement of the departure for Karoubi's Star had died down, even the importance of the Project for humanity couldn't drum up much public interest in the spacecraft's snail-like crawl, in cosmic terms, towards that distant objective. Still, Dane saw these routine exchanges as one way to remind everyone on the planet that the Project was on time, on target, and remained vital to the future of humanity.

And to remind them who was in charge, of course.

His message, oft-repeated, was a mantra that drew on the years of training and conditioning of *Star Pyramid*'s personnel. It was intended to drive home yet again that they must remain committed to a single overriding objective, and to remind the billions on Earth that their many sacrifices would eventually pay off a billion times over.

Mahabhavium.

In sufficient quantity, it would open up the Galaxy. In the quantity that humanity could manufacture, there would be nothing but slow stagnation, decline, violence, and eventual collapse. Despite humanity's now centuries-long unification, driven by the Project and long solidified, signs of impending disaster were becoming increasingly evident.

Like most of us, I hoped that we could hold it together for another 175 years, when *Star Pyramid* was due to return with its unbelievably valuable prize. Even though I'd be dead by then, I felt that it would be awful if the ship came back with the goodies, only to find that the whole planet had died.

It was a message the ship's crew had heard before, one that they lived with every day of their animate lives. Yet, as it carried to those select few in the lonely, gigantic pyramid, it would have a profound emotional effect.

A message from home. I felt proud to be associated with it, however tiny my role might be.

* * *

Cynicism aside, there was a sound reason for these broadcasts, though not for their relentless content-free repetition of messages everyone had understood centuries ago.

Star Pyramid was a single-celled organism adrift on an unfathomable ocean, and none would know better than its inhabitants how frail and lonely she was. The regular broadcasts from Earth would help to preserve their morale, and, perhaps, their sanity. It would also help to ensure their adherence to the original plan, formulated nearly four centuries before, still with a century to run.

The freewave was a slender thread binding *Star Pyramid* to its home system, and the GU psychologists were well aware of the dangers inherent in such a tenuous link. The accountants were equally aware of the high cost of the equipment needed for such broadcasts, but that battle had been won long ago. *Earth first.* Emotional dependence would be encouraged by direct contact, and the freewave had been designed for that purpose as much as for its scientific and operational advantages.

In any case, *Star Pyramid* had to be able to phone home frequently to reassure Earth's billions that it still remained in existence, rather than having been wiped out by life-support failure or an errant rock. So there was constant two-way communication. Exchanges of technical data aside, Earth learned about life on board *Star Pyramid*, which was basically routine and boring, and *Star Pyramid* learned about what was happening back home, which was anything but.

Carefully edited so they didn't worry about the bad bits, as I just explained.

The regular morale-booster from the Secretary-General was just one strand in this tapestry of psychological reinforcement, but a useful one. It proved that their work was still being valued at the highest levels. So the ramrocket, loneliest outpost of humanity, remained tethered to the terrestrial apron-strings by the twin cords of duty and communion.

* * *

When the violet light went out, Dane leaned back in his chair and breathed a sigh.

"Thank you, Eileen," he said, polite as ever. "How did I do?"

He always asked that, as if my opinion mattered. Maybe it was his way of gauging how ordinary citizens would react. Maybe it was just another polite reflex. Maybe he actually wanted to know. I could never tell.

"Your usual flawless performance, sir," I replied.

I could have been telling him that even if it had been terrible, but Dane was a past master at spotting lies, and I'd come to realise that he did actually want the truth. That was one of the reasons he'd risen to his exalted position.

"I wonder how it went down with *Star Pyramid*'s crew," he mused.

I looked up the instant feedback questionnaire, routinely sent from the ship. "More of a morale boost than the opposite, sir. They value the regular contact and the reassurance you provide."

"Yes," he said. "But they would say that, wouldn't they, Eileen?"

CHAPTER 20
STATISTICAL OUTLIERS
Gayl Goodenough
Star Pyramid 2420

Rowley Pollard winced.

I was helping him to service one of the pipelines in the Hydroponics section when this week's pep talk from the Sec-Gen came through. Dane meant well. It was supposed to boost our morale. Clearly it wasn't having that effect on Rowley.

"Fuckin' bollocks," he said, but without rancour, brushing his over-long (in my estimation) ginger hair away from his eyes as he bent over one of the inlet sockets, inspecting the filter to see if it needed changing. The automatics monitored such things, of course, but visual inspection by a human being was useful backup. It also helped keep the animate among us occupied. Neither of us belonged to the Hydroponics section, but Rickart liked to shove us out of our comfort zones by assigning routine maintenance tasks in other specialities, ones that every crew member ought to be able to perform. So there we were on Q Deck amid the green goo, armed with an assortment of hand tools and limited knowledge.

We all knew *why* the GU kept sending these messages, and we accepted that from their point of view they were necessary. But they were really aimed at Earth's teeming billions, not the 68 crew who were currently animate. Every year about twenty or thirty of us were put back to sleep in one of the SusAn caskets on N Deck, chilled by liquid nitrogen, our residual bodily functions closely monitored for any sign of incipient failure. Within a day their replacements had been defrosted, given a very thorough medical check, and put through a short retraining programme. At that point I was twenty-nine months into my stint; Rowley only five.

"You know the GU might well have a recording of that," I said.

"They don' record *everythin'*, Gayl. It's the ship's tech systems they monitor, not personal behaviour. That'd be illegal."

"It was when we left Earth, but even then there were loopholes. By now they might have changed the law."

"We can't live our lives as if some GU goon is sittin' on our shoulders. Anyway, they swamped with system data, let alone personal. Even if they was listenin' to what we sayin', they'd never be able to analyse it all. I don' give a toss what the GU do or don' have. They's two hundred fifty light years away."

"You could be arrested when we get back."

"*If* we get back. You really think they'd prosecute one of the heroes who saved the Earth?"

"Stranger things have happened."

"Don' care. It's all very well remindin' us that *Star Pyramid* is a miracle of technology, engineered with multiple redundancy for our safety," he complained. "Course it is. Earth's future depends on our success. But the truth is, despite our faithful IAS being ever on the alert, we could hit a meteor swarm an' it'd gut the ship like a flyin' fish in a fisherman's kitchen."

Pollard had a penchant for elaborate metaphors.

"A cheerful thought, Rowley," I said.

The Impact Avoidance System was a laser barrage designed to vaporise incoming dust grains before they vaporised *us*. They wouldn't slam into the ship at lightspeed: the same fields that worked the ramscoop would slow them down, and the sorting system that selected hydrogen atoms would do its best to divert them. If any snuck through, the IAS would have five seconds to deal with them. In theory, that would be ample.

Anything bigger… well, Rowley was on the money. But we both knew – it had been drummed into us during training – that since a cubic centimetre of interstellar 'vacuum' contains one atom of hydrogen and precious little else, the probability that *Star Pyramid* would hit anything large enough to cause significant damage was a lot smaller than the chance of a lobster being elected to chair the European Assembly. Even though 'large enough' was pretty small in this context, given our speed of 300,000 kilometres *per second*. But at the back of our minds was the disturbing thought that hugely improbable events are still *possible*.

Neither of us pointed this out.

Rowley put the adjustable spanner back in his tool belt, and I swear a grin flashed across his face. He was an incorrigible Eeyore and I was convinced he *enjoyed* moaning about what could go wrong.

"A malf in the fusion plant'd smear us 'cross the heavens in an expandin' cloud of debris," he continued, in the same soft tone. He could have been talking about what was on the menu for dinner, for all you'd deduce from his voice. "A runaway infection in Hydroponics'd leave us without material for food printin'. Lateral jet failure'd lay us open to muscular degeneration in zero gravity. A breach of the antimatter containment vessel'd reduce us to a plasma cloud. We could fail and be dead before we know it. And that's just what could happen *before* we get there."

"We're probably safer here than anyone back on Earth," I said. "For a start, back there you'd be far more likely to be arrested for disseminating anti-GU propaganda. 'Earth first', remember?"

He grunted. "Now *you* need to be careful what you say."

"Don' care," I said, fake Bajan.

He laughed. "The official news reports are uniformly positive, but we all know they's a pack o' lies. The *real* state o' the planet's goin' to the dogs. Fast."

It was common knowledge on board the ship that someone – more likely a group – back on Earth was covertly sending short messages giving us the truth. What was *not* common knowledge was that this was common knowledge: the senior crew didn't know that the rest of the crew knew about it. Well, that's what the rest of the crew thought... Rowley suspected that a select group of very competent hackers, location unknown, names unknown – *everything* unknown – was embedding text messages in the colour coding of randomly changing HV channels in Earth's morale-boosting freewave broadcasts. But only the person receiving them would know.

It was widely believed, on no factual basis, that this subversive arrangement had been set up decades before *Star Pyramid* launched, because the space navy's top brass knew that whoever was in command of *Star Pyramid* would need an accurate ongoing picture of what we'd left behind, not a sanitised one. This tended to point the finger at Admiral Fiona Rickart.

The GU must have been aware that something of the kind was happening. It was obvious that a few of the crew would be Security sleepers, a rather literal description. We weren't supposed to know they were on board, ready to take command if we appeared to be going off mission, but it was a pretty sure bet. Our Earthbound masters would want as many power levers as possible, and would have no qualms about pulling them. What the crew knew, any animate sleepers would also know, and they must have some back door for reporting to Mission Control. But even if the GU knew about the messages, they hadn't been able to stop them.

Rowley carried on grumbling in his soft Bajan drawl, but he was a careful worker and he didn't let it distract him. Just his way of letting off steam, I reckoned. I had my own worries, less immediate but equally serious. I was worried about spectral discrepancies and inaccessible gas clouds. I was worried that we'd get to Karoubi's Star and discover that the entire Project had been pointless.

* * *

It was Georgina Maxwell who got me worrying.

George – we all called her that – wasn't an astrophysicist. She was one of the medical staff, a highly trained (but aren't we all?) nurse, whom I'd first met at ITU Guayaquil. As well as tending the sick, she was lead investigator in a long-term study of the crew's health. Perhaps the only study ever of people on a subluminal star flight.

It was one of my monthly health assessments. Basically, we'd finished, and she was packing away her instruments.

"No significant issues, Gayl," she said. "Keep an eye on your weight, though. It's gone up two kilos this month."

"That," I said, "would be Rowley's birthday party. But you're right, I'll do a bit more exercise."

"I definitely advise it," she said. "Astrophysics is a sedentary job. Not like mine. I'm wandering all over the ship every day."

That was a surprise. "I thought you spent most of your time here in sick bay." The official name was the Medical Care and Assessment Unit, but everyone called it sick bay.

She popped several instruments into a sterilising chamber. Dropped wads of used tissue into the recycling slot.

"Oh, no. There are accidents, which can happen anywhere, and the health study involves observing people at their work stations and when they're relaxing in the public areas, like the restaurants and bars."

"Ah. Keeping an eye on our food and alcohol intake."

"No, we measure those automatically. On your social behaviour, mostly."

"You're a snoop, George," I said. "I'd never have thought it of you."

She grinned. "You got me. Actually, Gayl, it's all anonymised. Medical confidentiality."

"Funny how we never seem to know what other people's jobs are like," I said. "My mother was a school teacher. The kids all got long holidays, and everyone assumed the teachers did as well. Actually, they spent most of the 'holiday' period preparing lessons for the next term."

George nodded. "I've read your record, of course. But that doesn't tell me what you really *do*. What your working day's like."

"No reason why you should," I said. "I haven't the faintest idea of what most of your kit does. Well, I can guess some, given where you've been poking it. But medicine's a mystery to me."

She sat down next to me. "To me too, sometimes. But I've got a few minutes before the next victim. I wish I knew more about stars and things. You must know an awful lot."

I made a face. "I suppose. What *really* interests me is what I don't know. What *nobody* knows. Research. I'm working on Karoubi's Star right now. Let me show you."

I pulled out my tab, activated its small dais, clicked up an image.

"Here's what we could see from Earth before we left. A tiny speck in a random starfield." I pointed to the star, much like the thousand others in the image.

George screwed up her face, puzzled. "But isn't it a neutron star? No way you could see one of those from Earth."

'See? You do know some astrophysics! That's right. That speck isn't Karoubi's Star. It's Karoubi's *companion*. The system's a binary: two stars orbiting their common centre of mass. One big star, one small; one moderately massive star, one much less massive."

"And from Earth we can only see one of them. The big one."

"Yup. Now, here's the best image we can get from where we are now."

"Oh! Not a speck any more. It's a definite ball. Looks a bit like an orange."

"That's its true colour. Karoubi's companion – koppa Leonis 662 – is an orange dwarf: a K-type main sequence star, to be formal. About 0.9 solar masses, burns hydrogen, and has a surface temperature of 4,500 K."

She squinted at the image. "I still don't see the neutron star."

"Nope. Even from here, it's far too small and faint for any of our telescopes to spot it."

"So how did anyone know it was there?"

"Because Karoubi's Star is a pulsar. Pulsar 7731Q. Much smaller than its companion, but its mass is twice as big."

"Is that unusual?"

"Not really. Pulsars are neutron stars, and about one neutron star in twenty is a binary. There are even binaries in which *both* stars are neutron stars. But Karoubi's Star is unusual in a different way. It's the only known star with mahabhavium lines in its spectrum. And that we *could* detect from Earth."

"Zelda Zimmermann," George said. "We learned about her at school in our *Star Pyramid* lessons. She was one of my heroes."

Mine too. "Then you'll know that a pulsar is a neutron star that emits a beam of x-rays. As the star spins – and boy, do neutron stars *spin* – the beam spins too. An observer in the right place sees a sharp x-ray pulse as the beam sweeps past. Now, a neutron star is exceedingly dense: a billion tonnes inside a sugar cube."

Her eyes widened. "I can't wrap my head round that."

"Me neither. I just do the sums and marvel at the answer."

She shook her head, not disbelieving, just awed.

"How can something so weird form in the first place?"

"Starts as a supergiant – a star about twenty times as massive as the Sun. Later, it collapses under its own gravity when the nuclear fires in its core can't put out enough energy to keep it inflated. When the shouting's died down you're left with a ball of neutrons ten kilometres across, one and a half times the Sun's mass. The rest is ejected as a supernova – a *ginormous* explosion."

"Did Zimmermann observe the explosion?"

"Nope, that happened ages ago. She knew about the x-ray beam from other people's work. What interested her was the surrounding gas clouds. They're much bigger than either star, so they're easier to observe, and they contain the mahabhavium."

I passed her the tab and she peered at the image. "Don't see any gas clouds."

"I'll zoom out and enhance the contrast." Leaned closer and waved a finger.

She sucked in her breath. "Oh! It's *beautiful!* All kind of filmy and swirly."

She gave me back the tab with a satisfied smile. "Now I see why you became an astrophysicist. And here's me thinking it's all high-powered math."

I decided not to spoil the illusion by telling her that what had really grabbed me was the high-powered math.

"That was part of it, yup."

"The gas clouds are remnants of that enormous explosion, then?" she asked.

It was a common mistake. "Oddly enough, they're not. It happened too long ago and the material has dispersed. That's one of things I'm looking at, we can get a far more detailed picture now we're so much closer. My main interest is like Zelda's: the gas clouds. They're concentrated around the pulsar."

She wrinkled her nose. "So how did they form, if not because of the explosion?"

"Good question. *Very* good question. Like I said, what interests me is what I *don't* know, and as far as your question goes, I know absolutely nothing. It's a complete puzzle why there are gas clouds, to put it mildly. But then, so is the mahabhavium."

"You're saying we know it's there, but we don't know why."

"That's right. Of course, we don't have to know why to scoop the stuff up. But I *want* to know why… and I don't."

"That must be frustrating."

And how. "Yup. But research *is* frustrating, most of the time. That's what makes it research. It's worth the frustration when the little light bulb above your head goes off.

"The best theory we've got explains both the gas clouds and the mahabhavium, but it's also impossible to test. The idea goes right back to an offhand remark Zimmermann made when she first spotted the mahabhavium. She wondered whether a near-miss with a passing black hole could have ejected matter from the pulsar. That would form a cloud of highly energised neutrons that rapidly produced a wide range of atoms via what astrophysicists call the r-process– sorry, I'm getting too technical. Uh– calculations fit the data *fairly* well, but we can't detect small black holes, so the evidence will always be circumstantial."

George nodded again. "I get the main point. Karoubi's star is a bit of an oddball, but not a total oddball."

"Yup."

"Aside from the mahabhavium."

"Yup. Let me show you how we know that's there."

I flicked up the latest high-resolution spectrum, far better than BEAST or EROS could ever have obtained. "This is the spectrum of the gas clouds. It shows which wavelengths of light are stronger or weaker. The gas clouds are lit up by the companion, so this is what we call an absorption spectrum. Elements in the cloud show up as *dips* in the trace, not as peaks, because their atoms block the starlight. And this dip here–" I pointed– "is the main spectral line of the lighter isotope of mahbhavium."

"That's fascinating," George said, sounding as if she meant it. "A bit hard to see like that."

"I'll flip it. Then the dips become spikes, like *this*. Much easier to see."

"Oh, yes. Much easier. It's very sharp, isn't it?"

"Yup. That's because of the high resolution we can get now we're closer."

"Thanks. Oops, the next victim's arrived. Tell me more next time, OK?"

"It's a deal. You can teach me some medicine."

I was half way down the corridor when I reran the last bit of the conversation.

It's very sharp, isn't it?

* * *

Fiona Rickart was animate, getting ready for turnover, but I knew she wouldn't have been listening to Dane's routine broadcast. If it actually contained any meaningful content, one of her staffers would tell her. Rickart had more important things to do. Despite looking like everyone's favourite auntie, prematurely grey and comfortably padded, she was in charge of more than seven hundred individuals, locked up together in a tin can for four hundred years, thrown to the star winds in a desperate quest for power. And, also despite looking like everyone's favourite auntie, she ruled the ship with a rod of iron. You never knew when or where she'd turn up, and woe betide you if you were goofing off.

"Where's Fiona?" Rowley said, glancing over his shoulder. "Shouldn't she be here?"

Seven of us were having lunch in the restaurant area, and the Admiral was scheduled to fill the remaining seat at the eight-seater table, but the seat remained empty.

"Taking reports from the duty medics," Michael Clapham said, spreading a thick layer of honey on a slice of sourdough. "When Fiona's animate and conventionally awake, she's always busy."

"Too busy, I feel," said Thomas Quatermain. He was part of the medical team, but right now he was off duty, so he wasn't involved in the reports Rickart was assessing. In any case he was technically a psychologist, though one with broad training in all areas of medicine.

"She's never off-duty," he said, expanding on his cryptic remark.

"Well, yeah… but every day is much like every other day. Dull, boring, and repetitive." That was our geneticist Valentina Krupka, currently running one of the long-term health surveys in the science programme.

"She's shielding crew and technists alike," Quatermain said. "Carrying more than a fair share of the burden. An unsafe share." He had a mournful bloodhound face, and it suited him down to the ground.

"That's why Dane keeps sending us those pep talks," Krupka said. "Moral and psychological support." Her expression belied her words. "And very effective they are, too." Her tone was sarcastic.

"You're right, they don't help," Quatermain said. "As a trained psychologist, I can admire their professional construction, but not their intentions. They're trying to inculcate a Pavlovian response. The GU rings the bell and waits for us to drool."

"And do we?" Krupka replied.

"No. But we try to convince Earth that we do. To stop them interfering." No one mentioned the sleepers, but we all knew what he meant.

I picked up my plate, now empty except for smears of sauce, and dropped it into the complex machine that we all called the dishwasher.

"Anyone know where Kyril is?" I asked. Kyril Pallendorf was one of the high-echelon scientists, currently the acting chief. His speciality was observational spectroscopy, and it was mission-critical in a way that most of our self-directed science programme was not.

"Somewhere on K Deck, I think," said Clapham. "Why?"

"I need to talk to him."

* * *

I wasn't looking forward to it.

Pallendorf was as much an oddball as Karoubi's Star.

Pallendorf the scientist was familiar to everyone: smart, efficient, energetic, with a breadth of knowledge spanning more major areas of scientific disciplines than ought to be humanly possible. His speciality was the dynamics of diffuse astronomical phenomena: planetary rings, galaxies, gas clouds. But his main role on *Star Pyramid* was administrative: Head of Science. Of average height with straggly hair, he wore sober suits, always with a jacket and tie and the tie was that of the Swiss Academy of Sciences. He was a hugely competent administrator if you ignored his evident awkwardness and inability to unbend. He also tended to get fixed ideas, and once he'd made his mind up it would have been easier to budge a recalcitrant elephant.

Pallendorf the man was an enigma. His public record, outside scientific publications, was unusually thin. He was formal, stiff, and stand-offish, which led many to think he must be of German origin: a stereotype that should have been a warning, since most Germans aren't at all Germanic in that way. Actually he was Swiss, with a German-speaking father and a Polish mother. There'd been some family tragedy when he was young, but no one knew exactly what.

A malicious rumour, not serious but horribly credible, maintained that he was a bot, but I always got the impression that inside Pallendorf there was a real human being struggling to get out.

Since I was under his direction until one of us was deanimated, I'd figured out ways to get along with him. But conversations were always difficult, and almost impossible if you disagreed with him.

I collared Pallendorf in one of the radial corridors on K Deck, which houses recreational facilities. He often played low-*g* racketball. He was out of breath and looked annoyed with himself.

Probably lost again. It's his own fault, really: he *will* play against people like Varadan. It wasn't the best moment to choose to disagree with his observations. But in my view it was urgent.

"Kyril? I'd like to discuss your readings on Karoubi's Star if you can spare a moment or two."

Pallendorf bridled. "You mean the pulsar *component* 7731FQ of what is unofficially the Karoubi *binary*."

Snappy today, I thought. But it was too late to back out.

"I'm sorry. Just being informal." *Damn. Now he'll think I'm telling him not to be so snooty. Oh well, guess I am.*

He glared at me. "What about my readings?"

Deep breath. "Actually, it's the gas clouds that I'm thinking of, Kyril. Not either star. I'm not sure about your estimates of their diameter."

He went into porcupine mode. "Not sure? Why ever not?"

Oh hell. "I'd've expected the absorption lines to be more diffuse for a cloud of that size. There ought to be local Doppler shifts that would reduce the coherence and blur the lines. They look too sharp."

He didn't quite sneer at me, but he came close. "Gayl, Gayl... I *have* thought of that, you know. But the plain fact is that interferometer readings put the diameter at a minimum of a billion kilometres. A billion. *Minimum*."

Before I could object that the interferometer readings wouldn't be accurate enough, he conjured up another reason to ignore what I was telling him. "We know it's a binary system: neutron star plus K-type main sequence. Those aren't at all unusual."

"Nope, I know that, but– "

"But it also has gas clouds. I admit, those *are* unusual *this* close to the neutron star. While not being totally convinced about Zimmermann's black hole theory, I find it plausible that something unusual happened a few billion years ago and the gas clouds are the remaining consequences. You agree?"

He exuded confidence, and took my ambivalent grunt as acquiescence.

"Given all that, anomalous spectral lines are very likely. Understanding how this system attained its present state is the least of our problems, Gayl. We need to focus on data that will help us secure the mahabhavium."

I persisted, though I could see that he wasn't ready to concede a centimetre. "But the sharpness of the lines..."

A dismissive wave of the hand showed he wasn't listening. "An anomaly. Perhaps due to focusing in the magnetic fields. Or greater structural integrity in the cloud than we'd anticipated."

Across a billion kilometres? It doesn't fit and he knows it.

It was my turn to say that I'd thought of that. "I've tried to use x-ray data to get an independent estimate. It comes to less than a hundred million kilometres. Preliminary data, of course. We need–

"I'll tell you what you need," he said, angry now. "You need a larger database for the statistics to become significant! What you've got is a bunch of freak statistical outliers. Keep measuring, and I guarantee they'll go away. You'll see. I'm sure you can get better data and explain the discrepancy."

Patronising bastard. If anything round here is a statistical outlier, it's you.

There was no point arguing with Pallendorf in this mood. I'd been wasting my time. But I had to *try.*

"I intend to. Damn it, Kyril, I *want* the cloud to be big enough! Just as much as you do. I just don't think it is."

He backed off, perhaps sensing I was ready to explode.

"Look... there's a faint chance you could be right, Gayl. I admit that. I doubt it, but I concede that you might be."

No you don't.

"But, as I said, right now it would be premature to jump to that conclusion. Now is not the time to cast doubt on vital data that were agreed long ago. It would be bad for morale. Suppose, just for a moment, that you're right. *What do we do then?* We can't go home empty-handed."

He looked directly at me. "Gayl, we're approaching the climax of four hundred years of effort by the entire planet. If people start to think it's going wrong, everything will come apart. On *Star Pyramid*... and on Earth. Because if you start putting out negative vibes, the GU will get to hear of it. They'll order us to put you back into SusAn, and bury anything you've said under a pile of bumf taller than the GU Tower."

"Everyone knew it was a gamble, Kyril," I began. "If I'm right, we just lost, that's..." My voice trailed off.

Oh, damn. He's right. Too much rests on the roll of the dice.

It was an object lesson in how stiff, awkward Kyril Pallendorf had secured – and deserved – such an influential position on *Star Pyramid*, and I suddenly realised that he was better at managing people than anyone gave him credit for. He just had a different way of getting us to do what he wanted.

I felt the blood drain from my cheeks. "OK, Kyril. I think you're wrong about the observations, *and* you're wrong about the science, but you're right about the psychology. I've been too focused on the technical problem to notice the human one. I agree, telling everyone we've failed before we even arrive would wreck *everything*.

"I'll do as you say. Keep my mouth shut. Collect more x-ray measurements. Refine the statistics."

He nodded, relieved to have won.

The battle, Kyril. Not the war.

"That's sensible. By all means keep me apprised of the data."

"I will. I hope I'm wrong. Hope the outliers go away. Hope the cloud is ten times as wide as I believe it is."

But hope won't change the spectral data.

* * *

"I hope after all this it doesn't turn out to be a Mare's *Nest!*"

I gestured airily at a hazy streamer of light spread across the big HV dais on K Deck. It was an outlier of the Karoubi gas clouds, a turbulent plasma streamer. Fifty years ago, when its filamentary structure had first been resolved, it had been christened the Mare's Tail.

I'd had a bit too much to drink, and I'd kind of overlooked my promise to Pallendorf. I was still accumulating data, but slowly; the statistical blip hadn't gone away like he'd predicted. Its significance, which had started out just below three-sigma, was now a little over four and heading relentlessly towards five. Even in physics, that counts as certainty: one chance in 3.5 million of being wrong.

I hadn't told anyone else yet but I was worried stiff, and perilously close to untying the bag and watching the cat hoof it into the distant reaches of the universe. Clapham inadvertently rescued me before I could shoot my mouth off further and do some *real* damage.

"The spectrograph says not."

"Yup. But that just proves the stuff's *there*, Michael. It doesn't prove we can get it."

Rowley Pollard butted in. "No need to get cold feet, Gayl. If it's there, we'll get it. One way or another. We carryin' jus' 'bout every possible kind of equipment; we got people with every kind of expertise and trainin'; we got instant access to all the brainpower on Earth. We–"

I gritted my teeth. As long as I didn't tell them about the data behind my scepticism, it could all be put down to being too drunk to hide my fears.

"I'm worried about extracting it from the gas clouds, Rowley."

"We got everythin' we need to scoop the stuff up, Gayl," he pointed out.

"Yeah. Funnel it in. Separate the atoms. All tried and tested tech," Clapham said. Pollard, towering above me, stared: inscrutable, silent.

After a moment, somewhat breathless, definitely tipsy, I said: "Sure, that's what we're expecting. The Project managers had thousands of simulations run, and we've got detailed plans for every contingency they threw up. We've got equipment for every viable method that Earth's finest could dream up. But…"

I let my voice trail off. Feeling the bag wiggling in my hand as the cat struggled for freedom.

"But what?" Clapham asked.

"But if those gas clouds were too close to the neutron star, Michael, we'd be in deep shit."

It's a hypothetical. Still on the safe side.

"*If…* yes," Clapham said. "Gravity's way too high, and the radiation zone would fry the electronics. But Pallendorf is sure the clouds are big enough not to worry about that. Reckons they're a couple of billion kilometres across."

I gaped at him. This was news. "A *couple*? I thought it was *one*."

"Um. I think it's 1.9 if you include the Tail."

"There's no mahbhavium in the tail."

"Oh. Anyway, the main central bulk is 1.1 billion. That's big enough on its own."

Oh hell. Fuck Pallendorf. Exit cat. "It's a lot smaller than that."

"Says who?"

"Says the spectral lines. They're too sharp. You just have to look at them closely."

"And you have?"

"I have. And they are."

"Kyril seems happy with them."

He used to be. But he doesn't like the way those x-ray outliers stay put. I think he's wavering.

"I don't care what Kyril says he thinks, they're not right. And I'm pretty sure he knows it."

Pollard gave me the same strange stare. "If the clouds really are smaller than Kyril claims, there must be a reason. The simulations been tellin' us to expect clouds a billion kilometres across ever since Jason Karoubi proposed an expedition to Pulsar 7731FQ."

I grabbed another shot glass of tequila, downed it.

"A reason," he repeated.

"There is," I said. "Well, *I* think there is. But you'll say I'm crazy if I tell you what I'm thinking."

"No I won't."

"OK, have it your way. I think there's a planet there, and it's scoured away the outer regions of the gas clouds, where its orbit passes through where they used to be."

"A *planet*? Round a *binary star*, one of which is a *pulsar*?"

I shrugged. "Maybe. Planets round main sequence stars are ten a penny. Two of the earliest exoplanet sightings were round pulsars. PSR B1257+12, in Virgo, 2,330 light years from Earth, now known to have three planets; PSR B1620−26, Scorpius, 12,400 light years. But they're rare, I admit."

"You've been bonin' up on the history. To beef up the case for your theory. Right?"

"Nope. I've got an eidetic memory, remember?"

"And does your eidetic memory know anything about exoplanets round binaries?"

"Yup. There are plenty of them, too. In some the planet circles both stars, a long way out; in others, it circles one star despite perturbations from the second star. I think that's what's happening in the Karoubi system."

Pollard shook his head pityingly.

"You crazy, Gayl."

CHAPTER 21

THE SLEEPER WAKES

Alfonsina Shegwada

Star Pyramid 2420

I woke up.

Put like that, it sounds normal and straightforward, but this awakening was anything but.

For a start, I'd been asleep for over seventy years.

Earth time, that is. I prefer to think in Earth time.

It was my third awakening from SusAn, but unlike the previous two, it wasn't consistent with the duty cycle that had been assigned to me when the vessel began its voyage to Karoubi's Star. On my previous reanimation my schedule had been changed, authorised by Commodore Nathan Clarke, who was the current Flight Director while Admiral Fiona Rickart was frozen.

Well, that's what the computer records said, and it was true. The records included the reason for the change, too: my skills were likely to be needed at turnover.

That was true as well. Though not in quite the way that Commodore Clarke had been led to believe when I persuaded him to change my SusAn schedule.

Everyone on *Star Pyramid* gets woken up about once a century for a three-year stint (ship's time) of normal human life – if living inside a metal pyramid light years from the nearest star, travelling almost as fast as a photon, grappling with two time scales, can ever be considered normal. Mind you, if you didn't think too hard about where you were, and stayed in the non-technical zones, it could have been just a basic but serviceable hotel with lots of rooms, very few guests, and no windows.

It had to be a three-year stint because the body needs time to recover fully from reanimation. Yes, it will *function* perfectly normally– until you're frozen again. If that's done too soon, subtle changes in cellular structure caused by the previous deanimation will interfere with the procedure, with a significant probability of dying when you're next reanimated, or waking up with massive brain damage.

I'd spent the last 74 years as a lump of frozen meat, wrapped in a casket far colder than anywhere on Earth, synapses firing once every few weeks. Meat that had once been a thinking, breathing individual, and – crucially – could become one again, if its awakening followed the prescribed protocol.

As mine did.

It wasn't sudden. A gradual slide from death to unconsciousness to strange and vivid dreams that you never remember, then to a vague sensation of being alive, a sense of deep cold, quickening of the blood, transient pains and muscular spasms. Then you start to remember what's happening.

I was disoriented at first, which is entirely normal. Your rebooted synapses don't always fire in their usual sequences. Your brainwaves surge across the visual cortex like being on hallucinatory drugs; you see (or imagine you see) multicoloured spirals spinning in front of your eyes like a child's toy top. But you're not seeing anything real, your brain is interpreting its own internal states as if they'd been created by external sensory input.

As I surfaced from this disturbing world of psychedelia, everything came flooding back. My father and mother. My plan for revenge. My single-minded pursuit of a place on board *Star Pyramid*, walking the tightrope that hid my true level of ability, so that no one realised I knew every system backwards, yet making myself indispensable in a vital but unglamorous area: food production. My deep sense of satisfaction when that ploy succeeded.

My even deeper anger–

Someone spoke. My train of thought interrupted, I became fully conscious. A medic was staring into my eyes and asking me if I remembered my name.

Oh, yes. And I remembered something else. Something I was sure I could never forget.

Mvua haina hodi.

But all I said was: "Alfonsina. Alfonsina Shegwada." Slurred but comprehensible.

The medic nodded and smiled at me. "Good." She called a pair of robonurses over. "We'll help you out of there, Alfonsina. Wash off the rest of that gel. Get you into a coverall."

Only then did it register that I was naked and smothered in slime. You're immersed in it during reanimation to start conditioning your skin.

"Your muscles may seem weak at first, but they'll soon get

stronger. We'll give you some more tests and some exercises to strengthen your body. You'll be as right as rain in no time."

As right as rain.

Absolutely.

* * *

Since I was going to be animate for three years, there was no reason to hurry. No human could ever know everything there was to know about a machine as complex as *Star Pyramid*, but I tell you now, without any false modesty, that if anyone has ever come close to that, it's me. However, *kulenga, si kufuma. One who aims, does not always hit her target.* So I would covertly familiarise myself with *Star Pyramid*, from A Deck all the way to Z Deck, inside and outside the hull. Just in case anything had changed since the design was supposedly frozen.

While I was doing that, I'd find the most effective way to disable the ship. The first step was a year away. The second– well, that would depend on whether they suspected me of causing the first one.

A year passed.

A year in which I followed a routine of three days on duty, two off, with military precision, except for an unexpected problem with one of the hydroponics troughs, which after six solid days of work we traced to an apparently unrelated error in the formatting of a memory bank at the other end of the ship. On my workdays I kept an eye on every stage of the ship's food cycle, and helped out with anything cleared for level W crew, mostly routine maintenance on infotech systems. That covered pretty much everything on board, from impact avoidance to life support to food preparation to table tennis.

I did these jobs to the best of my ability, giving no hint of my true purpose on board *Star Pyramid*. And counted the days until I could carry out that purpose.

Everything depended on the precise timing of turnover. And that wouldn't be firmed up until a week or so before it happened.

* * *

Eight days.

I could do it in eight hours, if I had to.

I'd spent years planning for this day, this hour, this minute.

Studying to develop my innate skills, concealing their true scope, worming my way into a system that I despised, concealing my true feelings so thoroughly that at times I fooled myself. And all the while, my anger lay hidden, deep inside me, a molten core of banked fire.

I smiled, remembering how my enemy had invited me into its inner sanctum. How I had ridden the shuttle to the L2 Lagrange point, strapped in alongside about a hundred other prospective crew members, not one of whom ever suspected that I didn't share their indoctrinated beliefs.

Had they known what I was contemplating, they'd have ripped me apart with their bare hands.

Yes, this day was the fruit of long, toiling preparation.

If it'd been possible, I'd've hacked into the antimatter storage rings and turned *Star Pyramid*, its crew, and me, into a burst of radiation. But I'd known all along that that was hopeless. Would you want to be sitting inside a very large bomb if someone could set it off just by running the right code on their tab? Everything to do with the MAD was so secure that even I, with my inside knowledge, my extraordinary hacking talents, and my many past opportunities to leave back doors and Trojans, couldn't break down the firewalls. The AM system was isolated from the rest of the ship, not just electronically but physically. The only way to disrupt its operation was to get into W Deck, and that was impossible without physical keys and authorised biometrics. Before leaving Earth I'd spent years thinking of ways to work round these obstacles, and reluctantly concluded that I could never succeed.

Instead, my plan would unfold in two phases. The first would disable communications between *Star Pyramid* and Earth. The second would disable *Star Pyramid* itself.

It had to be in two phases because, while the freewave was working, the Global Union would be monitoring every bit of computer code that anyone on *Star Pyramid* wrote or changed, instantly. They had thousands of highly trained infotech staff for just that purpose. From the moment the Project first poked its dirty little snout from behind the skirting boards, the GU had been paranoid about every facet of security – physical, proprietary, electronic.

To be fair, my presence on the ship proved the designers had been right. Just not very competent.

However, the GU's infotechnists could well be competent enough to spot the extensive changes I would need to make in mission-critical software, and I couldn't risk that. So, even though it might alert them to my interference, the first task was to disable the comm. I could do that without much fear of discovery because I'd already set the crucial parts of it up before *Star Pyramid* launched, hacking in from the ITU in Ecuador. All that remained was to bring the pieces together.

There was plenty of time, and it was important not to act too soon. The longer the interval between introducing my modifications of the control algorithms and their being activated, the more time there'd be for someone to notice what I'd done.

For the moment, all I needed to concentrate on was phase one. I was going to set it up so that it looked like a complete accident. A legacy coding error from the early days of the Project, which had unfortunately gone unnoticed despite all of the checks and tests. Anyone with computing experience would find that entirely convincing, so no one would suspect me.

And that would leave me free to proceed to phase two.

It wasn't actually necessary to destroy the ship – though that would be the most satisfying method – or even to stop it reaching Karoubi's Star. I just had to make sure that it could never return to Earth, or anywhere else for that matter, with or without its hoped-for cargo of mahabhavium. But destruction was a far more satisfying idea, the only thing I had to live for. My mind was set.

When *Star Pyramid* died, so would I. I'd factored that into my calculations from day one. I'd get no glory from my sacrifice. If everything unfolded as I'd planned, no one else would ever know that I'd been responsible for the Project's failure. But I wasn't interested in glory, and I had no fear of death.

I was dying the day the rangers killed my father.

I'd died the same day as my mother. My body, though far from pretty, still functioned, but my mind was *dubwana*.

Zombie.

All I'd ever wanted was vengeance.

* * *

Star Pyramid's electronics were dispersed all over the ship. Partly for convenience, but mainly to avoid everything being taken out by a single micrometeor strike or a systems malf. Whenever possible, the ship's systems had inbuilt redundancy. When it wasn't, they were designed for resilience and robustness.

A call, incoming, on my tab. From Infotech. I accepted it.

"Alfonsina, I have a task for you."

This wasn't actually a surprise. I even knew what it would be.

"One of the server banks on F Deck has crashed, and temporarily put a dozen food printers out of action. It won't reset. Trace the fault and get it working again, please."

I called up system information and located the server concerned. I already knew which one, but I had to make it seem as though I didn't.

"OK, I see it," I replied. "Leave it to me."

For the next four days I wandered all over the ship, opening cabinets to reveal the intricate wiring within them, patching in test equipment, searching for the underlying fault. I knew exactly what it was, you appreciate. I'd caused it. So, naturally, it took me *ages* to find it. I'd hidden it very carefully, and I doubt anyone else would have found it more quickly. Not *too* carefully, though: it had to be something you could find without knowing where and what it was.

The search gave me the perfect excuse to spend most of my waking hours on F Deck, where the ship's most important computers lived, and where they kept their prodigious memories. It also gave me the perfect excuse to spend hours rummaging in the files, leaving obvious access trails that looked entirely harmless, since all of them were, but concealed others that were not.

Eventually I traced the fault to a bad connection six decks away, and replaced several connecting cables.

Job done.

In the privacy of my personal cabin I made sure that – as we'd been assured but dared not believe – there were no security snoops able to spy on certain crucial activities. I compiled the last, simple piece of code that would break *Star Pyramid*. Then, back on F Deck, I surreptitiously loaded it into the system through the back door I'd engineered at ITU Guyaquil, seven months before I embarked on this criminally insane voyage.

An innocent query to a database of pizza recipes…

That's all it took.

Mvua haina hodi.

CHAPTER 22

TURNOVER

Fiona Rickart

Star Pyramid 2421

Dutifully, I listened to the latest worldwide broadcast from the GU Tower. It was inspiringly upbeat. Earth's teeming billions remained fully united behind the Project. They were all rooting for us, praying for us, praising us to the skies. We were an inspiration to every one of them, our mission the salvation of the planet.

Dutifully, I swiped the image of the latest Secretary-General off the HV dais.

"What utter crap," I said, not so dutifully. But I made sure no one on board would overhear. In public I toed the party line. In private… well. By the time *Star Pyramid* was ready to launch, it had become obvious to me that any news we received from home would arrive with large quantities of positive spin. To keep things credible there'd be a few disasters, of course; hurricanes, earthquakes, all the usual. But nothing to suggest that conditions on the homeworld were deteriorating in any significant manner.

So I'd secretly set up a system that would let a small but select group of hackers, among the best on the planet, bring me the *real* news. Them and the successors they would enlist. Their messages were short, simple, heavily encoded, and scattered in colour levels of occasional hoxels in the HV feed. Steganography, it's called: hiding a message in a way that humans could never notice. Works like magic, and in fact, that's pretty much where it started, way back in 1499 when Johannes Trithemius wrote *Steganographia*, a crypto text disguised as a book on magic. As one does.

Although only two other Flight Controllers knew the keys to the codes, the news had inevitably got out, as I'd always expected. Intended, even. It did little for our collective morale, but I believe in telling the truth. In the long run it causes fewer problems than lies, however comforting.

Earth was heading downhill fast. Famine, riots, and all other forms of lawlessness had been on the rise for fifty years. The failure to control global warming in the 21st and 22nd centuries had turned a broad belt of land straddling the equator into desert. In Africa an irregular wilderness of sand and rock, hundreds of kilometres wide, now linked the Sahara to the Namib. Almost a billion people had had no choice but to migrate to more tolerable climes, and this had not pleased those already living there. The North and the South had protected themselves against the Middle with fences, then walls, then minefields, and now patrolling autonomous shoot-to-kill AI weapons. A few million had made it through these multiple hells, succeeding only in being confined to vast refugee camps – in reality, prisons – in a state of advanced poverty, sickness, and hunger.

That was the good news.

The bad – and by now it was getting really bad – included widespread terrorist bombings and shootings, six wars with conventional weapons, and a skirmish that had threated to go nuclear, flattening Kashmir, Nepal, and much of Reunified Tibet, stopped only by threats of total annihilation from an unprecedented alliance of the major nuclear powers.

If you wanted a straw to grasp, that was it.

To be honest, I didn't expect much of the planet to be left by the time *Star Pyramid* got home with the goodies, if it ever did. But the barrage of accumulating disasters made us all even more determined to carry our task to completion. Far more so than the GU's over-egged and dishonest homilies. It was, quite literally, up to us to Save the Earth. Further encouragement was superfluous.

So we hoped for better news and stayed on mission.

It was all we had left.

* * *

In 2421, two thirds of the way into its 306-year coast, I set in motion the complex sequence of events that would turn *Star Pyramid* end over end, its lateral jets firing and stopping in a carefully orchestrated sequence. At the same time we would reconfigure the ramscoop field, which incidentally meant taking the Impact Avoidance System offline for several hours. Using their most recent observations, Astronomy had chosen a region of space that *ought* to be even more devoid of matter than usual, and the risk, though higher, remained tolerable.

With the IAS back on line, the ship's attitude now reversed and stabilised, and its spin restored to create the sensation of gravity, the giant freewave antenna would be perfectly positioned to send signals to Karoubi's Star, but there was no one there to receive them and that wasn't what the antenna was for. Temporarily, we'd gone silent. *Star Pyramid* had to re-establish contact with Earth, and that required a vital secondary manoeuvre that was now to be carried out for the first – and probably only – time. We had to reverse the direction of the freewave antenna.

The procedure was, in principle, routine. All the moving parts had been tested; any components that gave the slightest cause for concern had been replaced with new ones. Rotating the entire antenna would put too much strain on its mountings, so we didn't do that. I held my breath as the ship's freewave antenna split into 24 separate curved triangular petals.

Mission Controllers at Bayankhongor could only hold their breath too, or sit with fingers crossed, waiting for communication to be restored, while the petals twisted in unison like the blades of a variable-pitch turbine. When they'd completed a full half-turn and been reconnected, contact with Earth would resume.

It didn't quite go like that.

Until now, everything had pretty much functioned as the designers and builders had intended. There'd been thousands of minor failures, like the pasta machine that would only make spaghetti and the robocleaner that lost its way in half-*g* gravity and sprayed furniture polish all over the fire extinguishers on R Deck, but nothing remotely serious or unexpected. I guess we'd all become a bit complacent, so it was a shock when the entire ship rang with a huge *crash!*, which reverberated for the next minute. Red lights flashed all over the freewave control dais.

I was animate for the entire process, of course. So it was my call when disaster struck.

"What the fu–" Not language befitting an Admiral, even in the 25th Century. I was about to rephrase it as "What happened?", but had the presence of mind to try to find out first. After all, I had instant access to every system on the ship.

A meteor strike? The IAS was supposed to make sure we didn't hit even a grain of interstellar dust: at close to lightspeed a direct hit would be like a nuclear explosion. But even a football-sized rock would only have taken out one or two of the antenna's petals, because it would pass through them so quickly.

We were still alive, so nothing larger than a dust grain had hit the hull.

I breathed more easily when my instruments told me there'd been no hull damage. Full integrity. Whatever had happened, only the antenna had suffered.

There are procedures for such events. The first is: *don't panic*. The second is: *not yet*. Important though the freewave system was, it was Category B. Only mission-critical problems were Category A, and the freewave wasn't mission-critical. We could manage perfectly well without it, aside from possible psychological problems on board ship and political nervous breakdowns on Earth.

"What's the problem, Elise?" I said, trying to sound calm.

Elise Franck, currently in charge of comm, pointed mutely at her HV dais. She looked like someone suffering from PTSD. When I saw what she'd seen, that seemed a likely diagnosis. The image was the current configuration of the antenna, which by now ought to have reassembled itself into a parabolic dish. In between, it should have been looking more like a chrysanthemum flower, a symmetric ring of long thin petals. It didn't look like either of those. It looked like a cross between a gap-toothed child and a train wreck. Most of its petals seemed to be missing. The few that remained were bent or broken.

"Any chance we can get the pieces back?" Elise asked, her normally cheerful round face radiating anxiety.

I pulled up local radar. I knew what I was going to see. Big chunks of the antenna, sailing off into the wide black yonder. No time to waste, so I contacted Engineering. They were already on it, as expected.

Call you back.

"We were spinning when the antenna split," I said. "Angular momentum is conserved. They're already eight kilometres away — in about twenty different directions."

"That's a no, then." She thumped a console with her fist and burst into tears.

I felt like doing the same, I wanted to smash everything in sight, sit amid the ruins, and howl. But this is not Behaviour Becoming of an Admiral, and more to the point, it would make matters even worse. Which, I suppose, was why it was not Behaviour Becoming of an Admiral. In any case, we Rickarts are as hard as diamond-tipped drills. We never cry.

Not where anyone can see us.

"Let's not give up right now, Elise. We've got shuttles. Tow cables. The engineers are already looking for solutions as a matter of extreme urgency. Every minute we lose makes retrieving the broken parts more difficult. Maybe they can find a way to recover the pieces."

Maybe. I wasn't hopeful.

Meanwhile, I had other problems to deal with.

"Did we hit a rock?" I asked her.

Elise made a visible effort to pull herself together. Sniffed, wiped her eyes with a tissue. Sniffed and wiped some more. Brought herself back under control.

"No. The external cameras don't show any impacting objects." She ran through a dozen data sets. "As far as I can see right now, we did it to ourselves. Something went wrong with the sequencing of the origami-moves. One petal tried to go back into docking mode half way through swivelling on its axis. It smashed into its neighbour, and they started falling like dominos."

Docking mode, I knew, folded the petals flat against the hull. It was supposed to be activated only during the initial installation phase, and, in the event of an unexpected failure, for essential maintenance during flight. Anyone wanting to put the antenna into docking mode had to have all the right authorisation codes and make their way past a dozen safeguards and checks.

I shook my head, aghast. "Elise, that shouldn't happen." I wanted to say 'can't happen', but managed not to seem quite that stupid.

She was pale, her hands were shaking. "I know. *I know!* But it did." *Right. Find out why later.*

"Can you transmit anything at all with it in that condition?" I asked. "I want to let Earth know, even if it's just two letters in Morse code."

She touched icons, changed HV dais, fighting to find a way through the maze of disrupted algorithms and smashed machinery.

"No. Not at this point." She sighed. "Earth will think–" she began.

"–we're dead. Yes, they might well do that. But not yet. They'll start by assuming it's a temporary comm failure. Most likely somewhere on Earth or up in solar orbit. They'll be testing every system, especially on the cis-Venerian triple antenna. Could be something as simple as loss of signal lock."

She bit her lip and nodded.

"Only when they've checked out everything their end will they decide it has to be something our end," I added. *Cue panic in high places.*

She nodded again.

"Ideally, we need to get something working at our end before they finish checking everything out at their end. If that's not possible, tough. They'll just have to sweat it out until we can get through. We've got enough troubles of our own without wasting effort worrying about what the GU will think. I don't care how we do it or how long it takes. Liaise with Blanchet in Engineering.

Jury-rig something to get *one* signal back home, even if it blows every fuse on the ship. We can replace fuses."

She stood up, once more a functioning human being, albeit a tear-stained one.

"I'll get an inspection team on it straight away," she told me.

It would, I reckoned, take Bayankhongor about twelve hours to eliminate any Earthly cause of the comm loss. It took Elise's team three times that to patch together three welded pieces of the dish that might just be able to transmit a freewave signal strong enough to be picked up by the triple antenna. Michael Clapham helped, setting up an error-correcting code that would improve legibility provided the technists back home realised what he'd done.

I was confident they would. The GU's human resources were virtually unlimited.

I could only imagine what was happening in the corridors of political power during the latter part of those 35 hours 17 minutes of silence. Then Elise sent out a brief message: SP OK FW D732. You can probably guess most of that; D732 is a damage code.

Less than a quarter of an hour later, our improvised antenna picked up a return message. Decoded, it read, in its entirety: "QX."

A miracle of brevity. Some joker who was a fan of Edward Elmer 'doc' Smith's classic Lensman series must have contributed to the code book. It meant something like: *Understood.*

Elise sent notification of receipt, and we could stop worrying about premature reports of our demise.

Engineering had reported back. *Still working on it.*

That was bad.

* * *

The technists had traced the fault, but Lojo – Lorimer Ejército Jomari, the currently active software specialist – looked puzzled. A busy little man, with boundless energy, he had my almost total confidence. Almost, because in my job you can't assume anything.

"It was a coding error in the software that turned the petals," he told me. Then he started on what was clearly going to be a lengthy technical description.

"Executive summary, Lojo, please," I said.

It still sounded extremely complicated, but the bottom line was some sort of syncing issue in the operation of the motors. The error had been frozen into the design fifteen years before we left the solar system, but had escaped notice.

Not our fault.

As if Earth could do anything to punish us if it had been. Aside from cutting off communications, which would harm them more than us.

It bothered me when I realised I was viewing the GU as an adversary. *Have I been too long in this role? Or is it a sign of some impending general malaise?*

What else *is going to go wrong?*

My confidence was draining away, with almost half of the voyage still to go.

Lojo still looked worried, probably feeling the same way I did. I assured him that no one on board *Star Pyramid* was to blame, because whoever had made the original error was long dead.

* * *

I had some welders and other heavy engineering experts reanimated. Elise had devised some scheme to improve the improvised antenna.

"It should give us enough bandwidth for text messages," she said.

"Some good news at last!"

"Not entirely. The transmission rate will be about a hundred words an hour. At most. If we're lucky."

I was horrified. "Is that all?"

"It's fifty times better than we can manage at the moment." She pulled up some schematics, flicked them over to me. "The main issue is the error-correcting code. Our signal is so faint that plain text would arrive as total gibberish. Preventing that multiplies the bit-stream by a factor of about ten thousand. And that's with the most efficient codes available."

"Find me something better."

She shook her head. "Sorry, Fiona. Let me clarify: the most efficient codes that are mathematically possible. You're asking me to square the circle."

Yes, but the math depends on the assumptions you make. I was about to argue that we should try to change the context when Engineering, in the form of Salomé Blanchet, finally reported back in person with something specific.

She was out of breath and flustered. She also looked very, very tired and depressed.

"You asked whether we can retrieve the broken pieces," she said. "The short answer is 'no'."

"What's the long answer?"

"That's 'no' too."

"Expand."

"Um. They're too far away already for us to send out drones with tow cables, and even if we could find some way to do that the cables would snap the moment we put any tension into them. The only possible method is to send some shuttles after them."

"We've got eight shuttles," I said. "We can sacrifice a few if we have to."

She sighed. "Shuttles could chase them, but they were designed to carry passengers and collect mahabavium from a gas cloud, not to lasso chunks of metal ten times their mass. I suppose it would be *possible* to modify them for towing, but by the time we'd done that the fragments would be too far away for the limited range of a shuttle. In any case, they don't have enough power."

"Shit. Can we build a replacement antenna? We've got equipment for almost any eventuality."

"Almost, Fiona. Not this one."

"Why not?"

She spread her hands in a gesture of defeat. "I don't want to be too pessimistic. With another 150 years to go before we arrive, I wouldn't rule anything out. But there are two big problems. One is the size of the petals. There's isn't room inside the ship to fabricate them."

"What about outside? That's how they were put together in the first place. From smaller components."

"True. But that was done with all of Earth's resources. The real killer is the raw materials. We don't have any. The only suitable sources are now… two hundred kilometres away in every direction you can think of. And every second that passes they get further away."

I refused to give up that easily. "How about something lightweight? Something we could print?"

She sighed again. "We thought of that, Fiona. But the antenna was made from large bits of metal for a reason. It has to send a freewave signal hundreds of light years, and keep it coherent enough for Earth to receive it. Even with the Deep Space Freewave Array we have to generate a very precise focused signal *here*. Create a highly degenerate caustic in the k-field, to be technical. Nothing printable would be sufficiently rigid."

I thought about that. "And in any case, we don't have enough stuff to print it with."

"Yes."

"You're telling me we're screwed."

Her grim face was answer enough.

No video, then. No real-time transfer of data from the ship's computer banks, I suddenly realised. Until now, the GU had been privy to every bit of data we handled. Every report, every scientific observation, every medical event. Now they'd be permanently in the dark about virtually everything.

That feels good, I realised. *Never liked working with someone watching over my shoulder.*

The unedited news from home would now be much more succinct. The bandwidth was now so limited that the only covert messages in the bitstream – bitdrip – would have to be two-character codes, each assembled over randomly chosen days.

Every silver lining has a cloud. Earth wouldn't be able to send us detailed advice if anything else went wrong. No software updates; either we wrote our own or we didn't update at all. We could tap the combined intellect of fifteen billion people… but only at a hundred words of text an hour. From now on we'd have to rely far more on ourselves.

My gut reaction surprised me.

I found it liberating.

* * *

Lojo walked in, worries creasing his brow.

"Problem?" I said.

"I think so. You remember I said the syncing bug was an ancient error in legacy code?"

"Vividly. It was reassuring, in its peculiar way."

He grimaced. "I don't think you should be reassured. I should have said it had *apparently* been caused by legacy code."

I licked my lips, which suddenly felt dry.

'Apparently'. Weasel word.

"If *I* said 'apparently' when telling everyone else what you've told me, it would just mean that I hadn't understood all the details. But when *you* use it, it seems to me that it has to indicate a degree of uncertainty."

He nodded, reluctant, hesitant.

"There *are* things I don't understand, Admiral Rickart," he said. "But they're not any of the technical details."

"Then what?"

"I'm running some maintenance routines to rule out malware. Or other deliberate interference. I'm not convinced that the error is as old as the metadata file states. There's something odd about the access record, and I'm beginning to think it may have been hacked. I'm getting Lawson to check against older backups, but that's taking a while because they were put in storage on F Deck."

I felt a shiver creep up my spine. "You suspect sabotage?"

There. The word was out in the open.

He pursed his lips, sighed. "I wouldn't yet say 'suspect', Admiral. I'm investigating that as one possible contingency. But I'd bet a lot of money that the access record isn't accurate. Which suggests that someone's been tinkering and gone to extreme lengths to cover their tracks."

My stomach seemed to imagine we'd gone into zero gravity. It was somewhere down in my boots.

"What's the evidence?"

He spread his hands to indicate eloquent acknowledgement of ignorance. "It just... *feels* wrong. The statistics of the dates and times feel artificial. Can't pin it down, Admiral, but Lawson's report ought to clarify things when he's finished digging into some files that he's just realised are significant."

"You did a Benford's law check?" There's a surprising pattern to the leading digits of numbers in almost all real data. Goes *way* back – all the way to Simon Newcomb, an American mathematician of the late 19th century. So of course it's named after Frank Benford, a physicist who rediscovered it fifty years later. You'd expect all of the digits 1 to 9 to have the same probability of being the first digit in most real-world data: about 11%. Not so. On average, 1 occurs 30% of the time, 2 about 18%, deceasing steadily to 9, which happens only 5% of the time.

When people invent lists of numbers, the human brain instinctively tries to choose each digit with the same probability. We think that's what random numbers ought to look like. Tax authorities learned in the 20th century that they could catch fraudsters by spotting violations of Benford's Law in their tax returns.

He stared at me like a grandmother unexpectedly being presented with an egg to suck and a sheet of instructions.

"Of course, Admiral. And some similar patterns that might detect phoney data. Nothing showed up. But nowadays anyone faking data knows about those tests, so they take them into account. I sort of got the feeling that in this case the expected statistical regularities were not only all present, but they were a little too tidy. There ought to be fluctuations about the ideal values, and there were. But those were too tidy as well."

I thought about this. "You mean the fluctuations in the fluctuations didn't – er – *fluctuate* enough?"

He gave an emphatic nod. "Not a bad way to put it. I'll get someone on it, we can quantify that."

"It wasn't a serious suggestion, Lojo."

"It is now." He ducked his head a millimetre, turned, and left. Leaving me to mull over what he might find.

Sabotage.

On a spaceship centuries away from the homeworld, it was the Flight Director's worst nightmare.

* * *

While I waited for Lojo to report, I took some obvious precautions to protect the physical infrastructure of the ship. It would be idiotic to be so busy tracking down a saboteur that we let them plant a bomb in Life Support or Hydroponics. Or wherever else it could destroy the ship, which was pretty much anywhere. So I had forty of our Marines reanimated and deployed them to guard the most sensitive areas and patrol the ship on an unpredictable schedule.

They'd all been deanimate for a decade or more before the disaster, so none of them could be the saboteur. An accomplice? Possible, but unlikely enough that the immediate danger to my ship was more important. I had to trust *someone*.

There was no way to do that in secret, but I did manage to place several of the Marines in the most vulnerable areas – areas that no one would have any legitimate reason to visit without my approval.

I was fairly sure I'd done that without anyone else noticing, because so few of us were animate when the disaster happened. The kitchen staff would've noticed the increased numbers, though, so the Marines would subsist on their emergency rations for the time being.

* * *

Lojo visibly harassed, looked even more worried than before.

"Lawson has reported?" I asked.

"Uh-huh."

"And you don't like what he's found?"

He nodded, face glum.

"So you think it was sabotage?" I said. I managed to keep my voice sounding calm, no matter what I was feeling inside.

"No." Lojo shook his head, and for a cruel moment my heart

leaped. "I *know* it was sabotage." The leap turned into a cardiac belly-flop.

"How?" I wailed.

"Lawson found the backups. The bad code wasn't there. We dug deeper. Whoever had changed the code had covered their tracks extremely carefully. But these things are so complex, with so many files cross-referencing other files, that there's always going to be somewhere they slip up. The problem is to find it. One solitary microneedle in Haystack City. But, despite the odds, Lawson pulled it off. He found evidence of unauthorised access to an obscure file in the password verification routine for food preparation updates. A bug in the code – deliberate, he reckons – allowed anyone who knew about it to instruct the system to stream its short-term memory buffer to another location."

"Which did what?"

"Effectively, it let the hacker eavesdrop on high-level system access and steal an administrator status code. Then they used *that* to get into the control software for the antenna. Afterwards they erased almost all of their tracks, but the erasure created a discrepancy in the use of memory-space."

This is terrible.

"Any idea who it was?"

"No. They covered their tracks well enough to conceal their identity."

I shook his hand. "Good work, Lojo. Thank Lawson for me. Uh– don't tell anyone about this, except those on your team. Make sure anyone on your team who knows about it does the same."

"Understood."

"I'll get to the bottom of this, but I don't want to alert the saboteur that we're on to them – assuming they're still animate, which they should be, since the last change of shift was seven months ago."

"Will do. But what if the saboteur *is* someone on my team?"

"Then they'll already know we're on to them. Can't do much about that except keep an eye open for changes in behaviour."

I can do better than that. But I can't tell Lojo.

One act of sabotage had very nearly derailed the entire Project. We couldn't afford another. I had to assume Lojo's team might be compromised. I needed to set an undercover Security agent on it immediately. And I knew exactly whose sleep I was going to disrupt to do it.

CHAPTER 23
AIRLOCK HOLMES
Reynheiður Sigmundsdóttir
Star Pyramid 2421

Something bad has happened.

I knew this the moment the psychedelic spirals faded and my neurons ramped up their activity, dragged out of their ultra-slow-wave SusAn trance; knew it even before my eyes flicked open and reacted to the dim red light. I knew it because there were only two reasons to wake me: either we'd arrived at Karoubi's Star or something bad had happened.

The clock display on the faceplate above my head, helpfully synced to Earth time, showed we'd been voyaging for only 252 years.

Turnover.

Something's gone wrong at turnover.

And they've woken me up to deal with it.

It would, I told myself, justify my inclusion among the crew. And, perhaps, offer me some kind of redemption.

Reassured that my brain was, in fact, still in working order, I tried to haul myself out of the casket. Realised that my brain wasn't in working order at all, because the lid was still shut. Then the lid opened like beetles' wings and a current of warmer air brushed my face. Something loomed in front of me. Eyes, nose, mouth. A face.

Of course it's a face, dickhead. I deduced I was still woozy from a rapid reanimation. *Not only has something gone wrong: it's something serious. Something that has to be dealt with* immediately.

"Help me out," I mouthed. It came out slurred but intelligible.

The ambient lighting changed gradually into a more normal, but still dim, white. The casket tipped up to a slanted position, and several hands pulled me out. Pale green revival gel dripped from my naked body, to be sucked into funnels attached to flexible tubes resembling a hyperactive octopus. There was no true gravity at turnover, but the ship was spinning to create its semblance.

It felt... odd.

There were three of them, all wearing white medics' overalls, and a fourth in black coveralls. All her badge said was: Fiona Rickart, flight crew, Z. But this was false modesty – a meaningless and rather transparent gesture that tried to suggest that we were all equal, when everyone knew where they stood in the pecking-order. She might as well have been wearing an admiral's insignia on her shoulder. It would have been more honest.

Her presence did make one thing clear. *Definitely serious. Extremely.*

"Are you OK?" the lead medic asked inanely.

I wondered what they'd do if I'd said 'no'. Instead, I said "Uh-huh." Which could be taken either way, so I qualified it. "Give me a few minutes to get my balance back and I'll be as good as new. Well, as good as I ever was."

They sat me on a low couch and ran instruments over my body. Wrapped a gown round my pale, still wrinkly, skin. Clapped another octopus on my head and tapped into my brain. They must have been satisfied because, after a few minutes of this attention, they removed the helmet and the instruments, and left the room. Leaving me alone with the Flight Director.

"Admiral Rickart," I said. "What's happened that's so bad you have to wake me up?"

"The freewave antenna's been sabotaged, Reynheiður."

She didn't mince words. *Me neither. Not the time for small talk.*

"Partial or total failure?"

"*Almost* total. But we can send and receive very short messages. The bandwidth is minuscule. No voice, no video. Text only, and not a lot of that."

I tried to figure out why anyone would want to disrupt *Star Pyramid*'s communications with Earth.

"We think it was done to prevent Earth from digging into our software," Rickart said, anticipating my thoughts. "Whoever did it, they presumably didn't have enough access to wreck the ship, and they didn't want the best brains on Earth to trawl through our code looking for interference while they tried to get it."

I grunted. "Makes sense. And you know what it means."

"I think so. What's your view?"

"Whoever's behind this, they're planning something more deadly. But they need time to gain access to some critical system, unimpeded by the GU's vast resources."

"All *Star Pyramid*'s systems are critical," she said.

"Sure, but some are more critical than others. Juicier targets. I assume you've taken steps to protect those."

"I have, but I'm not going to give you any details unless you convince me you need to know."

No flies on this woman. "Of course. I'd say the saboteur was trying to cut us off from Earth altogether, to improve their chances of avoiding detection. It didn't *quite* work, but it worked well enough."

She nodded. "Our thinking, too."

"And it's my job to stop them," I said, sounding stupid.

"It's your job to stop them."

I could feel the blood surging through my veins. The cocktail of wakeup drugs, no doubt, but it made me feel *alive* in a way I hadn't felt for, oh god, more than 250 years. Even better than a gnathroprine hit. Less likely to kill me, too.

"Then you'd better get me off this couch and give me full access to every person, system, and location on *Star Pyramid*, Admiral," I said. "And make sure the Rip van Winkels keep snoozing– uh, that no one currently inanimate is revived until I give the word, or unless absolutely overriding circumstances demand it. If the saboteur's back in a casket, I want them solid as a corpsicle until we find out who they are. But I'm pretty sure the saboteur isn't back in SusAn yet."

She helped me to my feet and handed me a tab.

"Way ahead of you, Reynheiður."

* * *

Lorimer Ejército Jomari had sent me a list of the currently animate personnel, along with another list of everyone else who'd been revived within the last twenty years, ship's time.

"Anything that could narrow down the search?" I asked him. "There are 736 people to consider."

I'd already decided that it was actually a lot smaller, but I wanted to get his view without prejudicing it.

"The ship's complement is 737," he said. "Three deaths *en route* now."

"I know. I also know it wasn't me."

He shrugged. "*I* don't know that."

"No, but *I'm* the one who's in charge of sorting out this shitshow. If it's any consolation, I don't think it was you. Or the Admiral, for that matter. You were the one who detected sabotage, and Rickart had me reanimated to deal with it. So it's probably only 734. Which brings me back to my question, which you seem to be avoiding."

"Oh. No, it's my answer I'm trying to avoid. The question's fine. Uh– yeah. I think the chances are very high that whoever did it is animate *now*."

"Why?"

"They went to considerable lengths to give the impression that it was just a legacy code glitch. Something that was missed long ago, before launch. That makes me think that not only was it done later; it was done *much* later."

I was tempted to believe him – it would cut down the number of suspects dramatically. So I resisted temptation. I've always had an ascetic streak.

"That's a leap in the dark, Lojo."

On my HV dais his tiny image raised a finger and waved it. "Not entirely. There's more. The longer the perpetrator left hacked code hanging around, the more chance we'd have of spotting it."

I thought about that. "Makes sense. So it's recent."

"*Very* recent. So: they're animate. QED."

I got out of my comfortable chair, walked across to the bank of backup consoles, seeking inspiration. When it came, I didn't like it.

"We could deanimate everyone who was animate immediately before the disaster," I said. "Replace them with whoever has the necessary expertise. If you're right, that would solve everything."

He went pale, and his hands, normally steady, shook. "Yes, it would be the obvious solution. Aside from condemning innocent people to death or disability because they've been animate for less than the safety period. Including me, my team, you, and– Jeez, you don't *really* think Fiona would–"

I gave a hollow laugh. "I'd lay heavy odds that the GU would favour that over risking the entire Project."

"Wouldn't be surprised," Lojo said, and it wasn't a joke, black or otherwise. "But Rickart would have to authorise it, and there's no way she'd do that." He paused. "Madre de Dios, I hope not! Uh– you can ask, I suppose. Anyway, I could be wrong. Maybe the saboteur is a lump of frozen meat and the damage has already been done, lurking somewhere in trillions of lines of code. Then we'd be killing innocents unnecessarily."

"If that's happened, they'd die soon anyway, along with the rest of us. Unless you can find the malware. You're bot-tracing it, no doubt."

"Do you need to ask?"

He looked so mournful that I couldn't help smiling. "Not really. I like your reasoning, the saboteur's among the animate."

His clouded face became sunny. "Yeah." Then the sun went behind a cloud. "Now all we have to do is find out *which* among the animate, and stop them."

"Right. If so, they had to *know* they'd be animate for a stint that included turnover."

He nodded. "Sounds simple, doesn't it? Everyone knows the date of turnover. It was baked into the mission parameters before we left Earth."

"Pretty much everyone on the planet," I agreed. "The HV channels did it to death for years before launch."

It seemed like we'd hit a wall. A dead end. I fiddled with the console's controls, which had no effect because they were currently disabled. Well, no effect on the ship, but it had one on me, because the distraction activity reminded me of something.

"But what far fewer people know," I said, "is that–"

"The precise timing has to be decided a few weeks before we start the procedure," he finished for me. "To take account of small deviations in trajectory resulting from the flypasts, danger of meteorites, whatever. However, that won't cut the numbers down. We're still looking at everyone on board. Not to mention thousands back home if it was done long ago. And all of them are dead."

"OK, let's think it through. The saboteur needed to know the *precise* timing to choose the optimal moment to hack the code. But initially, they couldn't've had any idea whether they'd even be animate at turnover time. Those schedules can change at the drop of a hat, depending on what expertise the Flight Controller wants. So they had to fix that before they could do anything else, don't you think?"

"Um. No prob. A competent hacker – and I'm sure this one was extremely competent – would be able to make sure one of their cycles coincided with turnover, and protect it against future changes. We're looking for signs of that, of course."

I mulled that over.

"Thanks, Lojo, that helps a lot. I agree, they're still animate." I didn't say I already knew. He was smart and helpful and I wanted him to stay that way. "We could be wrong, but my gut says we're right. Anyway, it makes sense to start with the land of the living."

* * *

Lojo was right. Even though it was a logical step, Rickart refused to authorise mass deanimation. On the grounds of ethics and morality.

"If we lose those," she told me, "we don't deserve to travel between the stars."

* * *

While I played detective, Lojo's team was sifting through vast quantities of data looking for some kind of slip-up, something that would give us a clue to the identity of the saboteur. Focusing particularly on anything related to turnover and earlier interference with the SusAn schedule. Almost certainly indirectly related; the saboteur had to be extremely competent and wouldn't leave anything remotely obvious for Lojo to sift from the mass of onboard data that covered every tiny detail of every function of our complicated vessel.

I was the other claw of a pincer movement, looking at psychological profiles, searching for motive, opportunity, and method, the three pillars of detective work since Glug the troglodyte tried to figure out who had snaffled his mammothburger.

I always work better with real people than dry records. Records always tell you the same thing – assuming you're paying attention – and they don't get annoyed or embarrassed or upset if you ask the same question twice, or focus on some discrepancy. People do, and it can be very revealing in the hands of an expert profiler, namely me.

That's just one of my superpowers. The rest are more physical – armed and unarmed combat, explosives from firecrackers up to nukes. I can drive or fly just about anything that moves, and find a way past anything but the most sophisticated security software. I'm the thief they set to catch a thief.

At the back of my mind was what I believed to be the key question, one that might just blow the whole thing wide open before the saboteur blew *Star Pyramid* wide open.

What were they planning next?

It seemed clear they'd been buying time for something bigger. Much, much bigger. Something terminal. If we could figure out what it was, we could get one step ahead of them. Keep an eye open for any interference with whatever they were going to interfere with, knowing what it was.

We had plenty of guesses, but nothing concrete. Nothing I found convincing. So I kept myself busy with routine grunt work, hoping for inspiration, while Lojo's and Rickart's teams did their best to keep their eyes on *everything*.

I scrolled the list. Not counting the newly revived Marines, there were 87 people currently animate, a dozen more than the normal number because Rickart had revived a number of key personnel to help deal with the crisis before I'd told her to stop. I would work my way through them, one by one. Excluding myself, but including Rickart and Lojo.

You think I'm paranoid? No.

I'm far more suspicious than that.

* * *

I finished the 86th and final interview. I'd done them in two sets, each lasting 14 hours with short breaks, all of it repetitious and deadly dull. Everything was recorded, and I could review anything I wanted to within seconds, but the biometric readouts are the truly revealing items. Those and my innate talent for spotting lies.

I sat back. Stood up. Paced the room. Sighed.

So much for biometric readouts and my innate talent for spotting lies.

On the face of it, I'd eliminated every single one of them.

Two clearly had something to hide, but it wasn't sabotage, so I had no interest in digging deeper. The others had emerged from the interview with every appearance of being squeaky clean. Their biometrics showed no hint of falsehood. They all showed signs of distress when I asked bluntly whether they were the saboteur. Some strong, some milder, all within the normal response range for people accused of something nasty that they haven't done. Their accounts of their movements on the day of the disaster and two days either side were convincing, and – as far as I could tell – accurate.

Nevertheless, my nostrils were quivering. I'd been face to face with the saboteur, I was convinced of it. Just couldn't pin the feeling down to any single individual. The saboteur must have been a very competent actor. Deep training in a terrorist group, perhaps. They knew how to fool biometrics. Hell, *I* did.

It didn't worry me that whoever it was had somehow managed to get themselves on the crew list. For all I knew, the saboteur was part of a huge anti-GU organisation. They could have sent the GU hundreds of candidates; only one needed to survive the stringent vetting process. Maybe they'd hacked the hiring records. I could've done.

It did worry me that the interviews would give away our

suspicions. That was unavoidable, but it meant that whatever they had in store for us was going to happen a lot sooner. The longer they waited, the greater the chance of being discovered. The only good thing about that was that the more hurried they were, the more likely they were to make a mistake.

I did have a shortlist. A mix of personality profiling and technical expertise. I resolved to investigate my top ten suspects more deeply, delving into their pasts, as far as the records on board went. I would ask the GU to make their own enquiries, too: I just had to keep the request short and the answers 0 or 1.

The saboteur was a computer whiz, we knew that. It might not show up in their job description; anyone known to have a high level of infotech skill would be an automatic suspect. Very possibly it was a talent that they hadn't advertised.

On the other hand, they could've figured that we'd make that deduction, and gone for the double bluff. So as far as I was concerned, anyone with even a moderate level of infotech skill was an automatic suspect. There were three of them in my top ten and a dozen more among the animate. Those three were Izumi Ikari, Alfonsina Shegwada, and Abdülkadir Yilmaz. Ikari and Yilmaz had level Y security clearance, which certainly included everything to do with the freewave antenna. Shegwada's clearance level was a lowly W. However, when she'd worked for KarouBiz she'd been Deputy Head of Cryptography, which surely would have merited level X clearance, if not Y.

It bugged me. Shegwada was operating below her potential.

I flicked up her record and cast my eyes over the tasks she'd been performing since her most recent reanimation. I'd've expected a few issues where she'd needed to pass the job to higher authority, but there was nothing like that. She was highly efficient, versatile, and quick. And she specialised in food preparation, which, I remembered, was where Lawson had spotted unauthorised access.

My psych profiling nostrils twitched. Anyone's would've done. We needed to keep a very close eye on Alfonsina Shegwada. Never mind that her record showed high levels of commitment to the ideals and aims of the Project. That could be fake. She'd downplayed her ability to write top quality security code. And if you can write it, you can hack it.

The more I thought about it, the more I felt that there was something off about Shegwada. Had she volunteered? No, quite the opposite. When first approached she'd said no. Only after two months of persuasion did she change her mind.

Playing hard to get? I did wonder. *If it's her, she's* very *clever. And she's been planning this for a very long time.*

Now I mentally moved her to pole position. It wasn't that her answers had been vague or evasive. On the contrary, they were to the point, precise, clear, and calm. An Earthbound court of law would never have convicted her on what was no more than a hunch. But this wasn't Earth and I wasn't running a court. I was judge, jury, and executioner, all of it with GU authorisation. Something about Shegwada didn't ring true. Maybe *too* precise, *too* calm?

I didn't alert Security, in case someone gave away my suspicions. I wanted to give her enough rope to hang herself. But I did file a sealed report, to be opened in case I died or was incapacitated, stating that she was my main suspect, and why. No one wanting to wreck a starship with more than 700 people on board, and willing to commit suicide to do it, would think twice about a convenient murder.

I did tell one person: Lojo. I was as certain as I ever could be that he was on the level. He was already so well versed in the investigation's progress that he was bound to ferret it out for himself, and I trusted him to keep his mouth shut. Not to mention that he was in charge of all the ship's infotech, and I couldn't very well keep tabs on my prime suspect without his help.

Call it a calculated risk.

$* * *$

That evening, I'd ended up as the only occupant of a two-person table in one of the informal street-food places that had mysteriously appeared in H Deck's wider corridors. Corridor-food, I guess. I was half way through a burger – amazing what a hi-tech kitchen could do with nothing but green goop; the meat had the right taste and texture and there were even onion rings and a slice of pickle, all synthetic – when Gayl Goodenough came over, asking if I minded her joining me.

"Feel free," I said.

She picked up a food tray and drinks, wandered back to the table. Sat down, stretched her long legs. Forked cottage pie into her mouth. Passed me a beer.

The only time I'd met Goodenough before was when I'd 'interviewed' her. As a key person in the science team, her animate periods were spaced irregularly, depending on what events she was involved in, and we'd never overlapped until now. She told me she'd had an unusually long second period in SusAn, followed by two reanimations eighteen years apart. This was her third reanimation. We went through the usual where-are-you-from and what-do-you-do. Except that she already knew what I did, and that turned out to be why she'd chosen to join me.

Having demolished her meal in quick order, she looked round the room as if searching for someone. She was trying to appear casual but to me her body language was distinctly furtive.

"Looking for anyone in particular?" I asked.

She drained her glass, put it down. "Yup. I'm making sure they're not here."

Intriguing.

"You're a GU detective looking for whoever wrecked the antenna," she said.

I ignored the 'detective', happy to be mischaracterised. "I can't tell you anything about the investigation, Gayl. It's–"

She shook her head. "I don't want to know. I want to tell you something that I think *you* ought to know. I don't want the person I was looking for to overhear us, and for all I know she can lip-read."

Even if you're paranoid, they might still be out to get you. I took out my tab. "Tell me who you're worried about. I'll trace their whereabouts."

"Can I just type the name? More secure."

"Go ahead." I passed her the tab.

She typed, passed it back. I'd already seen the name as she typed it in.

A quick check: "You're in the clear. Shegwada's on M Deck." I erased the name.

Gayl let out a sigh of relief. "I'll keep this short. She was in the same group as me at ITU. Got to know her quite well. She's a definite oddball. Seems normal, but I think that underneath it all she's very highly strung. Not sure what about.

"A couple of things about her bother me. I hadn't put them together until I learned that the antenna had been sabotaged."

Trying not to look *too* interested, I said: "Go on."

"One time, when we were in ITU, I accidentally interrupted her while she was doing some infotech thing. At the time I thought nothing of it, but because you're obviously looking for any suspicious behaviour, I reviewed my memories–"

"Hold it. Reviewed your *memories*? Do you keep a diary?"

"Nope. Actual memories. Mine is eidetic. I can't forget anything. But I do have to… retrieve it."

"Go on." This was sounding interesting, with Shegwada already topping my list.

"She was examining a holocopy of some document. She had a stack of them."

"Unusual."

"It is, though there could be plenty of valid reasons for hard copy. Anyway, now that I've rerun things, she looked startled. Slightly… guilty.

"Now, that's not suspicious of itself. I only saw the document for a split second. To be honest, I was embarrassed, walking in on her like that. Making her jump. So half an hour ago I sort of wound my memory back, and read all the wording I could see. It wasn't much, but it does make me wonder."

This is wild. I wonder what it's like to have a mind like that. Probably awful. I know there are plenty of things I much prefer to have forgotten.

Can't remember what they are, naturally.

"What was it?"

"It was open at the cover page. I guess she'd only just started to look at it. It said 'Antenna Deployment', followed by the usual security clearance rigmarole and a red GU logo stamp. It was level W, so any trainee was entitled to access it. Couldn't read anything else."

"You sure of that?"

"One hundred per cent. Like I said, I never forget a thing. And I thought I should tell you, because it could've contained documentation about reversing the antenna at turnover."

"Very possibly," I said. "Level W documents only give an overview, but a skilled hacker could dig deeper once they knew what to look for."

I was definitely interested. It was circumstantial, but it reinforced my own hunch. I managed not to let the interest show on my face. For all I knew, Goodenough was in on the sabotage, fishing for information. Maybe the fish was a red herring. I didn't think she was, but I had to be careful.

"Did you notice what any of the other holocopies were about?" I asked.

"Nope. But, like I said, there was a second thing bothering me. Maybe it's related. About ten months ago I was passing her room and thought I'd say hello. When I knocked on the door it hadn't been closed properly, and it swung open. She was looking at some sort of schematic diagram on her tab, which she promptly closed down. I apologised for intruding, she said it wasn't a problem, and we had a long chat."

"She's not usually very talkative," I said. "Keeps herself to herself. That's a bit weird. Do you know what the diagram was?"

"Some sort of plan. I didn't recognise it, but I can dig the memory out and draw it for you. It shouldn't take very long."

"Please do. Flick it to me as soon as you have a reasonable sketch."

She nodded.

"Thank you, Gayl," I said. "I doubt any of this means anything, but I agree it's worth looking into. I'll add it to the rather limited amount of evidence I've accumulated."

She looked disappointed. Then smiled.

"I think you're much more interested than that, Reynheiður. I can read people's expressions. I think it's because I have such a huge database to work from. But I understand why you're not saying so. I'll disappear while she's not around. Thanks for listening."

As I watched her disappearing back, I thought: that *is one dangerous lady. If* she's *the saboteur, we're in trouble.*

But I didn't think she was.

* * *

I told Lojo what Gayl had told me.

"Not sure if that helps much," he said. "For a start, we don't know whether Goodenough's lying. Maybe *she's* the saboteur, and she's trying to frame Shegwada."

"Possible," I said. "Dangerous thing to try, though. Attracts unnecessary attention. Goodenough wasn't in my top fifty before; now she's number two, after Shegwada."

"Even if she's telling the truth," Lojo said, "it doesn't add much. The next step has to be something involving infotech, which already puts Shegwada in the hot seat."

"Goodenough's an astrophysicist, Lojo. They're very infotech-savvy. But I'm not sure we should focus exclusively on a hack attack. We need to consider other options, too. What about infecting the hydroponics? Releasing a tailored virus into the air supply? Poison gas?"

"Those are all vulnerabilities, of course," he said, but he didn't look convinced. "Spread our net too wide and we won't catch a thing. We shouldn't lose sight of the obvious. Whoever it is, they started out by disabling our comm. We've already decided they did that to stop GU infotech experts monitoring what the saboteur was going to do next. So their next step has to involve some kind of high-level hack."

"Shegwada does have impressive infotech qualifications and experience," I agreed. "Well above what her level W clearance merits. She's been hiding her light under a bushel. That in itself is suspicious."

"So we arrest her?"

"There are several other people with similar qualifications and experience, Lojo. And much higher clearance."

"Yeah. My team."

I shrugged. "I doubt it's one of them, but if it is, they could have set Shegwada up as the fall guy. And if we fling her in the brig and sit on our backsides, job done, we'll be playing into their hands."

"So what do we do?"

"Watch *all* the top suspects. Figure out what they're planning to attack, defend against it, and catch them *in flagrante delicto*. Which is Latin for 'with your pants down'."

"Easier said than done."

"Agreed. But you've made a start already. And you're right, it'll be something with the infotech."

Lojo sat back and stretched aching muscles. "Sitting too long at a dais," he said. "Feels better now."

"I know how you– "

I stopped as my tab alerted me to an incoming message. Gayl had flicked over her copy of the diagram Shegwada had been looking at, ten months ago. It was clearly something technical and complicated, but I couldn't place it.

"Lojo? Any idea what this is?"

He peered at my tab's tiny dais. "Too much detail, no context. I'll ask the Library."

I didn't hear the reply, he'd routed it to his ear implant, but I could tell when it came through because his face changed.

"You know, Reynheiður, there's one feature of *Star Pyramid* that's uniquely vulnerable, *and* involves massive computational resources," he said.

"Recycling? Life support?"

"Not what I have in mind."

"What, then?"

"Impact avoidance. And if Goodenough's story is true, that's what Shegwada was looking at."

Hell. Even at a small fraction of lightspeed, a collision with anything larger than a grain of sand would be fatal. At our current speed, we were vulnerable to matter as small as a particle of dust. So *Star Pyramid* had an elaborate multi-level system of lasers and other equipment to evaporate any particulate matter, ionise it, and use the ramscoop field and Da Silva linkage to shove it aside.

A big rock, say football-sized, would get through. Anything bigger wouldn't even notice. But space is *empty*, especially between the stars; not totally, but the chance of a collision between an object the size of *Star Pyramid* and anything larger than a sand grain was negligible.

Empty – except for fine dust and the occasional molecule of gas. We had those covered.

A conversation with Michael Clapham surfaced from my distinctly non-eidetic memory. "When a mathematician says something's negligible," he'd once told me, "they mean they'd like it to be zero, but deep down they're uncomfortably aware that it's not."

"And if an engineer says something's negligible?"

"It means they can't do anything about it but hope it won't happen."

The control room for the Impact Avoidance System was A Deck, right at the tip of the pyramid. Where the ancient Egyptians put their pyramidion, a miniature pyramid covered in precious metal; gold, perhaps, but better still, electrum. Our pyramidion was far more valuable than anything monetary.

If Shegwada could subtly subvert the IAS, we'd be a sitting duck. She wouldn't have to do anything more. We'd plough into the next patch of dust like a fighter jet hitting a mountain, shredded into a trail of short-lived fire.

While I was musing on what we knew, or might know, Lojo had been busy.

"There's no record of Shegwada accessing schematics for the IAS," he said.

"So you think Goodenough's lying? In that case, we ought to—"

"No, I think Shegwada hacked the records. The list of what she *did* access – well, what the records *say* she accessed – doesn't feel right to me. The amount of time she allegedly spent on different categories of file doesn't match the importance of the contents."

"Ah. Not exactly conclusive."

"No, but in the context of everything else—"

"Agreed. Do you think Shegwada's already done the dirty work?"

Lojo shook his head vigorously. "Security keeps an especially close watch on anything involving the IAS. Entry to Decks A–C and V–Z requires biometric ID and direct authorisation from the Flight Controller. No one except authorised maintenance crew have been in there since we left L2 in 2169.

"She can't have sabotaged the IAS physically. Not yet. It's impossible."

"What about a delayed-action software fault?"

"Nothing like it's been found so far."

None of this was remotely reassuring.

"Keep a close eye on every critical system, hardware and software," I said. "Keep ten on A Deck."

"Already happening. And we're watching Shegwada like a hawk."

"Make that ten hawks. I'll contact Rickart now."

After Lojo left, I buzzed Rickart, and told her of our suspicions and the evidence for them.

"As of now, she's under covert surveillance," she replied. "There's no way she can go anywhere without Security following her every footstep."

"It had better be invisible, Fiona. I don't want her spooked."

"Oh, it'll be much less obtrusive than that."

* * *

I was working my way through the personnel files of the other nine of my top ten suspects, wishing fervently to be back in Kong's bar getting drunk on hooch instead of numbing my brain with bureaucrap, when Lojo's avatar popped up on my dais.

"You clear?"

"All alone and secure, Lojo. I assume you have something sensitive to tell me."

"Sure do. You were right. The saboteur is Alfonsina Shegwada."

"You certain?"

"One hundred per cent. As soon as we found the evidence I alerted Rickart, and a squad's on its way to arrest her."

"What *is* the evidence?"

"Circumstantial, but compelling. Within a few hours of the antenna being wrecked, Shegwada tried to access a level-Z HV terminal that only three people are authorised to use. It's hidden away on G Deck in the backup control and command."

"Shegwada's security clearance is W. She had no business being there. Did she get into the system?"

"The records say not, but I don't trust them any more. She's very clever. But not quite as clever as she thinks. We can prove that she left her cabin, made her way to G Deck, and spoofed the biometric sensors to get in."

I stared at his avatar, worrying. It seemed too easy.

"You're not telling me she was so stupid she let the cameras film her?" I said.

Every corridor on *Star Pyramid* has small spy cameras, always on, and all their recordings are saved. Before the disaster they'd also be sent direct to Earth. After the disaster, they were still saved on the ship. There were no cameras in private rooms or common eating and recreational areas, though. We'd been assured of that, and on the whole the assurance was believed because the GU wanted us to succeed, and knowing every word was being spied on wouldn't be likely to help. The other reason we believed it was that we would have spotted anything of the kind long ago. Rickart had made sure that the ship was swept electronically from stem to stern once a week. After all, there were plenty of organisations, other than the GU, that would be interested in what we were doing. Semi-legitimate ones like media outlets; illegitimate ones like terrorist groups, political lobbyists, and conspiracy wingnuts.

Lojo gave me a quizzical stare, telling me I hadn't needed to ask such a silly question. I forbore pointing out that it was my job to ask questions, silly or subtle. In my experience it's often the silly ones that turn out to be strokes of genius.

"That's right, I'm not telling you that. She hacked the cameras so that they'd substitute previous footage whenever she sent them a particular signal. When she'd finished on G Deck and returned to her room, she sent it, erasing all traces that she'd ever left."

"You told me that was impossible," I said with some heat.

"I was wrong. Her ability to subvert electronic surveillance is out of this world. If the freewave was still working the GU might have spotted it, but we don't have the manpower or the analytical software to monitor cyber attacks in real time. That confirms why the antenna was wrecked."

"So how do you know it was her?"

"Carbon dioxide levels."

"*What?*"

A hopeful smile illuminated his face. "Like I said a while ago,

Star Pyramid is very complicated. Everything interacts with everything else. All of it's recorded.

"In particular, there are continuous records of the levels of all gases in all parts of the ship. Among them oxygen, nitrogen, and carbon dioxide. They give very precise readings every few seconds, *everywhere*. It was Izumi who thought of it."

"That's Izumi Ikari?" Another in my top ten.

"Yes. She has a way with numbers, very smart, on the ball. Realised that with the right math, you can detect the effects of people breathing. It's a rhythmic pulse of carbon dioxide superimposed on the main trace, and it's concentrated near their location. She wrote the code, some sort of Fourier–wavelet hybrid; tried it. Discovered that when the ship's quiet, with very few people moving around, you can track individuals. Once you've locked on to their breathing pattern, you can follow their progress through the ship. And you can follow *past* movements using archived data.

"You'd already placed Shegwada at the top of your list of suspects, thinking that her low clearance level was a red herring. So Izumi analysed *her* movements, for the past month, and cross-referenced them to what the cameras had seen. That night, the two failed to match. Someone came out of Shegwada's cabin, unseen by the cameras. No one came out of any other cabins. It had to be *her*. And that, Reynheiður, was the tiny mistake that will seal her fate."

"Well done, Izumi. Have a gold star. But it's not sealed yet, Lojo. Not until Shegwada's shoved back in a casket and frozen, so she can't do any more damage. Not until we've made sure she hasn't set up something fatal already."

* * *

I strapped on a flechette gun and left my office in a hurry. Shegwada's cabin was where all crew accommodation was: on H Deck. Very convenient for access to G Deck, I belatedly realised. That was backup Command and Control with direct access to the fore shuttle bays.

Before I got there, the commander of the arrest squad buzzed me.

"Forelli here. The bird has flown the coop, Ms. Sigmundsdóttir! She left her room in a hurry a few minutes ago, as soon as we received the order to arrest her."

Shit. "Must've tapped our comm."

"Seems likely. She left a message."

"What does it say?"

"Some gibberish. *Mvua haina hodi.* Maybe a code?"

"No time to investigate right now. Put someone on it later, if we're still alive by then. Any idea where she's gone?"

"No. She's played the same trick and the cameras aren't tracking her."

"Carbon dioxide levels? That's what she fell down on last time."

"Too much activity with everyone rushing around. But we still think she's targeting the IAS. Lojo says she was trying to access the IAS controls from her room, but that failed when we shut off all the terminals in her area of the ship. She took off straight after that."

"That's one thing off my mind," I said. "Leaving a worse one. Now she's spooked, she'll act immediately. Not the subtle software tweak I've been expecting; something crude and obvious now her cover's blown. She's going to attack the IAS physically. A bomb, probably."

"Where would she get hold of a bomb?"

"We know she can move around the ship without the cameras seeing her. M Deck, probably. Give me an hour in there and *I'll* make you a bomb."

I buzzed the Admiral.

"Fiona, I hope you've got an armed squad on A Deck. One of the ones you said you wouldn't tell me about."

"Yes. No. Well, not exactly."

My heart sank.

"The IAS compartment is little more than a closet. They're spread out around B and C Decks. They know she's probably coming. They'll stop her."

"I think she's got a bomb. What happens if it blows up just outside A Deck?"

Salomé Blanchet, listening on the same channel, butted in. "The bulkhead would withstand the blast. The only way to do serious damage is to get inside."

"The door is sealed," Rickart said. "I have four armed Marines guarding it. There's no way she can get through that door. She's not going anywhere inside this ship."

I was getting a little bit tired of being told what Shegwada couldn't possibly do.

"What about *outside*?" I said.

* * *

They'd shut down all the airlocks, but I didn't think that would stop someone with Shegwada's capabilities and determination. It's the combination that worries me most: fanatical genius.

The one point slightly in our favour was that Shegwada had been forced to act prematurely. She'd be improvising. If we were lucky, that might trip her up. Though it seemed a faint hope. I decided on pessimism. Not just glass half empty: no glass at all.

When Forelli said one of the vacsuits was missing, my pessimism was confirmed. It had been taken from R Deck.

"That's where the aft shuttle bays are," he said.

I know that. "Did she steal a jetpack?"

"No. Probably didn't have time to get to the storage compartment."

Good news, for once. "That will slow her down." Clambering about on the exterior hull is slow work in a vacsuit, especially on a spinning ship. You have to use the cat-rails and hook up a safety cable. If she'd managed to grab a pack of attitude jets she'd already be outside A Deck and we could kiss *Star Pyramid* goodbye.

By then I'd grabbed the nearest vacsuit and started the tricky process of inserting myself into it. Ignoring all the usual checks, I slapped the faceplate shut and headed straight for the main concourse. In the near-zero gravity of the ship's axis I could *fly* to A Deck. And *I* had a jetpack.

Their use inside the ship is strictly forbidden. So is flying along the concourse. But I figured no one would mind if I broke Rule 897.5.2b. Or any others, for that matter.

A horrible thought struck me. "Did she steal a shuttle?" *If she did, we really are screwed.*

"No. All present and correct."

I breathed a sigh of relief. "Then she went out through the access port beside one of the main shuttle doors. That gives us more time than I'd feared."

Less than I'd like, though.

"Lojo here. I've got the cameras back. She was in a rush and didn't have time to cover her tracks. But we can't see her anywhere in the ship."

"That's because she's outside, on the hull. Show me the external camera feeds."

A series of images appeared in front of my eyes, projected by the suit's helmet. A flicker of movement caught my eye.

"Did you see that?"

"Yes. She's got as far as M Deck."

"Can't see a bomb," I said. "What's that strapped to her back?"

"A class 5 laser."

Class 5 was used for welding thick slabs of metal. And cutting them. And suddenly everything became clear.

"She's not heading for A Deck! That attempt to access the IAS controls was a ruse, and we've fallen for it. She's going for the secondary ramscoop field generators outside J Deck!"

In a way we'd been right: she was, in fact, targeting the IAS. But indirectly. The secondary generators modified the ramscoop field in conjunction with a laser barrage and the Da Silva linkage to ensure that if the ramscoop couldn't swallow the ionised dust created when the lasers evaporated a particle of matter, it would be whisked away from *Star Pyramid*'s path. They were one of about a dozen of the ship's subsystems that had to be mounted outside the hull.

We could rebuild the secondary generators, but that would take weeks. On average, the IAS deflected one killer sand grain every two days.

Not good odds.

"On our way," Forelli said. "We've got this. Leave it to us."

Like hell I will.

* * *

The view from outside the ship was awe-inspiring. Against a backdrop of the darkest skies you could ever see, stars sparkled like frost in moonlight, a billion pinpricks of light. It wasn't the time for stargazing, but the dramatic spectacle sharpened my senses. The ship cut a dark triangular slice out of the bright cloudscape of the Milky Way. And no more than forty metres ahead of me, Alfonsina Shegwada was using a welding laser to cut a slice out of the support structure of one of our four secondary ramscoop field generators.

Even disabling one of them would put the ship in deadly danger.

The laser wasn't just a tool. It made a highly effective weapon, as was confirmed when the bracing strut behind which I was hiding started to melt. The only upside was that while she was shooting at me, she wasn't cutting into the field generator support, its weakest component.

I didn't have a laser, but I had my faithful flechette pistol. The problem was to get a clear enough shot to ensure that the spray of tiny darts hit their target, without getting my head burned off.

All vacsuits have a common band for radio comm, which she hadn't switched off. But I didn't waste time talking to her. You can't talk a fanatic out of the embedded beliefs of a lifetime. This was the supreme culmination of her sad little life, and she'd see it through to completion whatever anyone said.

She'd probably kill herself after that. Use the laser… or just unfasten her safety cable. For a brief moment I wondered why she was so determined to destroy *Star Pyramid*. Some childhood trauma? Very likely. There was nothing like that in her file, but given her hacking abilities I'd have been amazed if it was a true record. She had a twisted kind of courage, and there was no doubting her commitment to her cause. In different circumstances I might have been sympathetic. If I'd experienced whatever it was that drove her, I might even have done the same thing myself. But right now my job was to stop her, not psychoanalyse her.

And I couldn't see how to do that.

She finished severing one support. With the ship still spinning, centrifugal force would be putting a severe strain on the other three. I couldn't do anything about that – it takes two weeks to spin the ship up or down because of the huge angular momentum involved. If another support broke, the rest would snap and the field generator would spin off into space, suffering the same fate as most of our freewave antenna.

The supports had been built with plenty of spare strength, but if she managed to cut another–

Then I realised what was stencilled on the hull, just behind her.

You've made a mistake, Alfonsina.

I flicked off the common band and buzzed Forelli. "Where are you?"

"C Deck. But she must have done something to the airlock. We're cutting our way out."

"Don't bother. Stay clear. Fiona, you there?"

"Yes."

"Full control of the ship?"

"Yes."

"OK. On my count of three, wait *exactly* ten seconds, then perform an emergency dump for RCU 11." That was one of the recycling units on J Deck, which dealt with hydroponic sludge. If any of that ever got too contaminated to recycle, it had to be ejected. "But *don't* open the hatch. Override the safeties."

To her credit, she didn't ask why. She'd probably worked it out. Rickart had always been quick on the uptake. She just said "Got it."

I watched the camera image on my faceplate. Shegwada had gone back to cutting the field generator support. Still oblivious.

I counted to three.

A countdown appeared, superimposed on the image. Starting at ten. When there were three seconds to go, I poked my head out from my shelter and aimed the flechette pistol.

You have to be careful: in a spinning reference frame the ammo follows a pseudogravity ballistic trajectory. It's a straight line in a reference frame that's stationary relative to the fixed stars, but from my point of view the stars were anything but fixed. However, flechettes move so fast that very little correction is needed.

I took careful aim, fired a long burst…

…and missed her.

I flicked the common band on again and her voice rang in my ears: "–need to be a better shot than that."

The hatch of the emergency recycling ejection tube that she was standing on blew off its mountings and a powerful stream of semi-liquid sludge pushed Shegwada and the hatch off the hull. She was tumbling erratically away from the ship, thrown by its spin; firing her laser but unable to aim. Its even more erratic beam might've hit me if she'd got lucky, but she didn't.

"I didn't miss," I said quietly. "I was cutting your safety cable. I wasn't shooting at you.

"But now I am."

I didn't want to, but she still had the laser. Aiming through the sludgy fog at the point her whirling form was about to occupy, I fired another burst.

I've always been good at skeet shooting.

* * *

Its comms crippled, its damaged field generator support now welded back and reinforced, an otherwise intact *Star Pyramid* remained on course and on mission.

Life on board would never be quite the same. We'd had a chastening lesson in the fragility of our enterprise. We knew we'd been lucky. For months it was impossible not to keep looking over our shoulders, wondering what the next disaster would be. But people are resilient, and we slowly became accustomed to the new normal.

The apron strings to Mother Earth were now hanging by a thread.

We're on our own.

Thoughts turned from a chaotic present to a more ordered

future. The eka-Bussard remained on standby. Although we were coasting, we were still well above ramspeed, so it could be restarted if necessary. We would continue capturing mass and using it to create antimatter. Earth wanted us to bring back as much antimatter as we could manage, and we had plenty of spare storage capacity for that. Since collecting it would cause resistance, slowing us slightly, the ramrocket engines would be restarted every few months for a brief burst.

Once we commenced the deceleration phase, powered by the antimatter we'd been creating *en route*, the ramrocket engines would be mothballed. The only time they'd be returned to working order was if we couldn't get the Da Silva drive working, and had no option except to turn round and spend a century crawling home using the MAD as a booster for eka-Bussard ignition.

We'd keep the ramscoop fields working, though. They fuelled our fusion power and they were a crucial component of the Impact Avoidance System and antimatter creation.

Deceleration Phase would start in 2506, after a total flight of 89 years, ship's time.

Colloquially known as *braking point*.

PART SIX

KAROUBI'S PLANET

CHAPTER 24

SMALL RED DOT

Gayl Goodenough
Star Pyramid 2553

Braking point had come and gone. For the past 47 years, devoid of spin, *Star Pyramid* had been pointing away from Karoubi's Star, antimatter engines blazing to slow it down. The eka-Bussard's ramfield and its Da Silva linkage remained active, but only as part of the Impact Avoidance System. The artificial gravity had changed its vector from radial to axial, the technists announced – their way of saying that the roles of walls, ceilings, and floors had changed dramatically. But the only people who'd had to adapt quickly were those who'd been animate at the time, and I hadn't been one of them.

It did seem a bit odd at first when, having emerged from my casket, I was allowed once more to roam the corridors and decks, and everything looked different. But you soon adjust.

Another change I noticed was a new fashion. People were wearing what looked like six-pointed silver stars below their insignia.

"What are those?"

"Snowflakes."

This wasn't terribly informative, so I enquired further. The stars recorded how many stints their wearer had experienced. One snowflake for each deanimation. I found out where to get them and shortly had four pinned in front of my collarbone – about average.

It also seemed odd to be working with many of the same people again after 150 years, ground time, but it wasn't coincidence. Now that we were close enough to Karoubi's Star to do some serious science, Rickart had revived most of the science team. You can't make good astronomical observations through the flame of an antimatter engine, so we were deploying drones a few kilometres from the ship. The instruments weren't quite as good as the ship-based ones, but they were the best we could use.

I tracked Pallendorf down in the instrument suite. He'd been observing the Mare's Tail, a turbulent stream of superheated gas ejected from the spinning neutron star at much the same speed as *Star Pyramid*. The only visible sign that a pulsar was present.

"*Four hundred years*," he said, mostly to himself, though he'd noticed my arrival.

"Ninety-eight, allowing for time dilation," I said.

"Whatever. Thing is, Gayl, we still can't see it. After all that time. Not from Earth, not from here." He meant the pulsar. The orange dwarf delighting in the name koppa Leonis 662, now mercifully dubbed 'Karoubi's companion', had been visible from Earth, with the right telescope, before we left.

"Too far away even for BEAST to see it," I agreed. After more than 400 years in operation the Big Earth-orbit Aperture Synthesis Telescope was still Earth's most powerful astronomical instrument, optical or radio. Commissioned in 2124, it comprised twelve huge beryllium mirrors stationed in two sets of six at Earth's L4 and L5 Lagrange points, 60 degrees either side of Earth in essentially the same orbit. Installed into halo orbits around these neutrally stable points, BEAST's mirrors were two multifaceted insect eyes getting a stereoscopic view of the star field. Their effective resolution was that of a mirror 250 million kilometres across, and although they had a far smaller light-gathering capacity than a complete mirror that size would've had, they could see clouds and oceans on the nearer exoplanets.

But they couldn't see Karoubi's Star, the pulsar formerly known as 7731FQ.

Text messages told us they could see the Mare's Tail. *We* could see the Mare's Tail. But we couldn't see Karoubi's Star, either. It would be tricky enough to spot it when we got there.

"However, there are senses other than sight," Pallendorf said. He rearranged icons on his HV dais and an image sprang to life. Composed of millions of coloured hoxels, it showed the density of neutrino flux emitted from the area around the Mare's Tail. The Tail glowed faintly in shades of deep blue against a neutral grey background, luminous green along filaments, edged with yellow where the gas molecules were piling up in shock patterns. Towards the base of the tail was an irregular yellow ring, with a single red pixel at its centre.

The red dot was Pulsar 7731FQ. A spinning neutron star. Karoubi's Star. Its orange dwarf companion was off the edge of the dais.

The yellow ring was the shell of gas that had been thrown off when the ancestral star's iron core had turned to helium, triggering gravitational collapse. The red dot was the compacted mass of degenerate neutronium, ten billion tonnes of neutrons to every cubic centimetre. In reality it was some ten to twenty kilometres across, spinning once every 1.47 milliseconds.

Next to the red dot two tiny purple rectangles jutted out, one on each side, with ragged edges because they were inclined at an angle to the dais's hoxel boundaries. Zimmermann had been right: these represented traces of the black hole that, some half a million years before, had careered into the neutron star's gravity well, shaved its crystalline surface, and whirled past, back into deep space.

What a sight that must have been.

In those jutting arms, the building blocks of atoms were squeezed together in new configurations. According to BEAST's version of a spectrograph, one such configuration contained 126 protons, 126 electrons, and 184 neutrons. The lighter isotope of mahabhavium. Sole reason for our 400-year voyage. According to theory, this infinitely desirable substance would no longer be confined to the purple rectangles that had spawned it. It would have diffused throughout the surrounding gas clouds. These had been large enough for the less powerful EROS to pick up the characteristic spectral lines. Without those observations by Karoubi's group, we would never have left home. BEAST added further confirmation.

More theory, and – so he claimed – Pallendorf's observations, indicated that the clouds were large enough for some of the shuttle craft stashed in *Star Pyramid*'s bowels to scoop up enough mahabhavium to send the people of Earth into paroxysms of delight, without being sucked into the star's fearsome gravity well.

* * *

Seven months after I was reanimated, it was my turn to be one of the people who had to adjust rapidly.

As the MAD slowed the ship, we got ever closer to free fall. That was gradual, giving us all plenty of time to adjust. But now, slowed to a fraction of lightspeed, its antimatter drive in standby mode, *Star Pyramid* was coasting towards Karoubi's Star. Walls, which had previously been floors, had reverted to floors as the lateral jets once more spun the ship. And that was harder to cope with. It wasn't the centrifugal force as such; more that you had to change how you got around the ship. And to remember where doors and corridors and furniture had moved to.

I didn't mind. Coasting provided a huge bonus for the entire

Science team. We could go back to using onboard instruments, which were superior to those on drones. We could *see* again, right across the electromagnetic spectrum. And what we mostly looked at was the Karoubi system.

The pulsar was still invisible to the naked eye. Even with a powerful telescope it was hard to spot across a gulf of half a billion kilometres. But the distortions that its powerful gravitation imposed on light rays from the starfields behind it were easier to see, at least with time-lapse imaging. The background stars rippled, as if a tiny lens had passed across them. As, indeed, it had. A lens made from warped spacetime.

Even better, Karoubi's Star was now very distinct in neutrino images, and its gravitational field, computed from the stellar displacements and correlated with neutrino density maps, was a spectacular sight on the HV daises, where its exact position could now be pinpointed. The presence of Karoubi's companion had been factored in from the start; its orbit was outside the gas clouds so it wouldn't cause trouble. The calculations for orbital insertion had been performed, checked, and were constantly being updated. The MAD was prepped for reignition and the automated burn had been simulated as a further check.

I went looking for Pallendorf and found him talking to a few of the crew, among them Michael Clapham. Kyril had just finished his latest observations of the star's spectrum. There was no mahabhavium in the star's crystalline crust, and there never had been; just naked neutrons in a superdense packing. It wouldn't have helped us if it *were* present in the star; anything stupid enough to get close to the surface would be smeared out into a layer one atom thick before being converted to neutrons and radiation. But there were gigatonnes of mahabhavium in the surrounding gas clouds, just as predicted centuries ago on Earth. The plan was to scoop some of it up, and it was clearly there to be scooped. That should have been reassuring; well, it *was*, to some extent, because we'd be in deep shit if it wasn't. But I wasn't reassured, because the supposed outliers in my x-ray data were still doggedly refusing to go away.

"Enough mahabhavium, Kyril?" I asked him.

He nodded, glumly. "No problem with the mahabhavium. Sharp spectral lines."

Something was wrong, and I was pretty sure I knew what it was.

"Too sharp?"

He nodded.

"Gas clouds not where we hoped?"

"No. They should be quite extensive, because neutron stars condense from overcrowded regions."

I know this.

"All the simulations of near-collisions between a black hole and a neutron star produce a range of heavy elements, among them mahabhavium, in clouds that project well beyond the region where tidal effects would be unsafe."

I know this, too.

"Unfortunately," he said, "no one seems to have told this to Pulsar 7731FQ. The clouds are there, but too close to the star."

I was hoping I didn't know this. But I know why.

"A planet," I said.

He stared at me, mouth clamped flat.

"I wish I'd been wrong, Kyril."

He nodded, swore without passion. "I should have listened to you. It would have given more time for contingency planning."

We could all feel the weight of his depression. A wave of nausea ran over me, and I made a rapid dash for the nearest sanitary facility. When I'd wiped away the vomit and felt able to stand on my feet again, I rejoined the stricken group staring at the HV displays.

Pallendorf was swiping fingers across a terminal. The main dais flickered as he switched its feed, a flash of cyan as the signal format changed.

"Preliminary only," Pallendorf said. "Poor definition, but good enough."

A red dot – bigger, now, but it was obviously Karoubi's Star – sat at the centre of a yellow halo representing the gas clouds.

"The boundary of the safe zone," Pallendorf said, swiping again, "is *here*." A green ellipsoid popped into view, surrounding the star.

Murmurs, suppressed groans. It also surrounded the gas clouds.

"And the planet?" Clapham asked.

"Here's its orbit." A blue ellipse popped into sight above the dais, surrounding the orange ball of the companion. It strayed close to the green ellipsoid but didn't intersect it. A darker blue dot showed its current position.

I willed the dot to go away. It didn't. In an irrational way I felt it was my fault. If I hadn't predicted its existence, it wouldn't have existed.

"I'm sorry, Kyril. Sorry I was right."

He divined my feelings. "Don't feel guilt, Gayl. Never feel bad about being right."

Clapham put an arm round my shoulders. I reached up for his hand and gave it a squeeze.

"It's an oddball, too," Pallendorf said. "I guess any planet in a neutron star system would be. It's about the size of Titan. Revolves once every 450 days; rotates every nineteen hours."

"That ellipse can't be right," I said. "Not in a binary system. The orbit will be all over the place."

"It's right *now*," Clapham said. "But it won't stay that way. The pulsar will perturb it." He flicked up a graphic. "I've been running simulations, and it's just as I expected. A chaotic orbit. Sometimes round the pulsar, sometimes round the companion, in rough ellipses that slowly change their orbital parameters. Every few million years it transitions from one to the other in a trajectory that looks like spaghetti, passing through where the gas clouds *ought* to be. Here's a typical transition." Another flick and the graphic changed.

Yup, spaghetti all right.

He waved his hands in agitation. "That erratic motion is what scoured out the gas clouds. Just like you predicted, Gayl."

CHAPTER 25

DECISION TIME

Fiona Rickart

Star Pyramid 2572

I had a decision to make.

The deanimate personnel of *Star Pyramid*, now sleeping the peaceful sleep of a frozen log, were going to suffer from an almighty anticlimax when they were reanimated, but that wasn't the decision. I'd already decided to put that off because there was nothing for them to do, yet. According to the original plan, they'd be reanimated once we were in orbit around Karoubi's Star. All of them. At that point they'd be needed to carry out the operations required to scoop up the mahabhavium, store it, complete the construction of the Da Silva drive, test it, power it up, go home. Right now it was simpler to let them sleep on.

We were approaching orbital insertion. The original plan had been to orbit the pulsar, but that was pointless now, so we were going for an orbit round the planet. I'd already set in motion the reanimation of fifteen specialists in orbital dynamics and control. They were awake, healthy, and ready, and our trajectory was on track.

There was no point in trying to hide the truth; the air of depression was all too tangible. That wasn't what I had to decide.

No, the decision I had to make was what to tell Earth.

They knew the schedule. They'd know pretty soon if I didn't send reports confirming we were still following it. But right now—

Earth doesn't know.

Before the freewave failed, they'd have been downloading real-time records of everything from the composition of our atmosphere to the number of times anyone sneezed. If it had still been working, they'd've known the gas clouds were too small long before Kyril grudgingly admitted it. They'd have known the Project was in bad trouble.

Not any more. Now all they ever knew was what I decided to tell them, and even that had to be short and simple.

Never put off till tomorrow what you can put off till the day after? An old joke, bang on target.

I chickened out and waited.

Item one: restore morale.

That was urgent, before the ship copied our homeworld and fell apart. I could see how to do that. I had a story to tell. A plausible one. It might even work, but for now it was just a temporary stopgap to offer a glimmer of hope.

The story was this:

The bizarre planet was only a setback. To be sure, the original plan had called for a simple operation, with specialised equipment carried for precisely that purpose. But the planners had foreseen the possible failure of their plan, and instead of providing for specific contingencies, they'd equipped *Star Pyramid* with tools for every conceivable task – except, as we'd discovered to our dismay, repairing the main antenna. More importantly, they'd equipped us with personnel with a breathtaking range of basic skills.

If *Star Pyramid* couldn't improvise, nobody could.

I ordered a select team of experts to be reanimated; people who might be able to find a way out of our predicament.

Slowly the outlines of a plan began to materialise.

Since the planet had scoured the gas clouds clean, a large proportion of everything that used to be in them, mahabhavium included, had to be down on the planet. In the atmosphere, on the surface: that was for us to find out. When we knew where it was, and in what form, we'd work out how to get our paws on it. Whatever we needed, P Deck ought to be able to provide it. Or provide something to make something to provide it. Or some iteration.

I had no idea just how hazardous that game would be, but it was the only game in town.

It did pose new problems, though. In quantity.

Instead of a simple scooping and sifting operation we'd have to mount a planetary expedition. Nothing elaborate: we'd grab what scientific data we could, in passing, but the prime objective was mahabhavium. At least ten kilos; preferably fifty. More, if we could get it without undue delay.

The bright side was that this story, played cleverly, really would restore morale. The technists and scientists would have a whole new planet to play with. Once we'd secured the mahabhavium and delivered it to Earth, we could always come back to do some serious science.

Item one ticked.

Item two: tell Earth.

That would set the pussycat firmly among the GU pigeons. Panic in high places, no question. I was quite pleased to be 378 light years away, with only a communication link that Thomas Alva Edison would have sneered at to tie us to home.

I'll get round to it real soon.

Item three: Forward Planning.

My story was so loosely structured that it would've been a gross exaggeration to call it a plan. I had to set up a proper committee to examine the likely needs of a planetary expedition, and get P Deck ready to give it to them. Right now we didn't know what conditions on what inevitably was now called 'Karoubi's Planet' were like, but we could extrapolate from the physical data we'd already got. The temperature would be reasonably comfortable over most of the planet, for instance; our suits wouldn't melt or freeze solid. But there was so much we didn't know…

Somewhere in the recesses of my brain I sensed a tiny, mewling ball of panic. A rising sense of foreboding, of defeat. With a conscious effort I quelled the growing fear. I'd lived with this tension since *Star Pyramid* first set out. I couldn't afford to indulge in too much hope; hopes are all too easily dashed. I had to remain detached.

For someone saddled with the burden of command, such introspection was ingrained habit. So was the facility for self-control. Yet, even as the panic subsided, I sensed the traitor within, gibbering mindlessly to itself in subdued but terrified whispers. For a moment I slumped across my desk, devoid of energy.

Then, shaking my head like a spaniel emerging from a pond, I straightened my back. *I must show strength. Rickarts never refuse a challenge.*

Everything was going to change, now. Our customary routines had run their course, and what had been planned to replace them no longer applied.

I turned on the Public Address system, adjusted the throat microphone.

Deep breath.

Here goes nothing.

CHAPTER 26

WATER WORLD

Hjördis Sigmundsdóttir

Karoubi's Star 2572

For the first time since its launch from Earth's L2 point, everyone on board *Star Pyramid* was animate. Not necessarily *awake*, you appreciate: about a third would be asleep at any given time. But as warm sleeping bodies, not frozen blocks of meat.

Rickart had taken the decision to wake everyone up because the mission was now far outside its original parameters, and there were difficult decisions to make. The more minds there were to focus on our predicament, the more likely it was that someone would find a solution. Anyway, a democratic decision would be far more likely to attract lasting support when things got tough. And they would.

We hadn't failed *yet*, but unless we could get very creative, we soon would. And then we'd have to decide whether to try firing up the antimatter drive to get us up to ramspeed, and either risk another 400 light year journey and slink back to Earth with our tails between our legs, or... whatever we decided collectively to do instead.

I reverted to my administrative role, which was to oversee the technists by keeping an eye on system integrity. It wouldn't be great if any vital equipment failed. I didn't do the tests or analysis myself, just made sure anyone who did was up to scratch.

They were doing fine. I moved people around from time to time, pawns and knights and kings and queens on a pyramidal 3D chessboard, but it was a desultory kind of stalemate, waiting for something to change the strategy of the game. Mainly I wanted to stop them getting bored, which would risk getting sloppy. Not too much, though: I had to give them time to wrap their heads around new challenges.

Some tasks were prosaic. Bots kept the ships' rooms and corridors clean, but someone had to check the bots out and make sure they weren't developing any problems. On a grander scale, Hydroponics and Recycling were still in good order, and in principle we could keep ourselves and any descendants alive for thousands of years.

Our gene pool was large enough for us to reinvent ourselves as a generation ship. We could explore the Galaxy. Seek out new worlds. Boldly whatever. But that decision would come later. If there was a way to get hold of mahabhavium *here*, it was our duty to try it.

They'd woken us up in small groups over a period of weeks. After the usual post-awakening rituals and medical checks, we were told officially that we were in trouble. They'd had lots of practice in breaking the news gently, and it hadn't worked for anyone. *All that effort, no reward.* Now we were stuck in a tin can 400 light years from home, wondering what the fuck to do next.

I've seldom felt so wretched.

Still, we weren't beaten yet. We had over seven hundred high-quality brains to put to work on the problem, plus whatever Earth could cobble together through the minuscule bandwidth of our jury-rigged freewave antenna, once Rickart got round to telling them we were in trouble.

It was strange, wandering around the ship and perpetually running into people. Previously you gathered in small groups for common tasks, and the corridors were nearly always empty. Now they weren't exactly crowded, but on any trip between different parts of the ship you usually met at least one person coming the other way. The dining facilities, previously three quarters empty, were running meals in six shifts, non-stop. The recreational areas also had plenty of spare capacity; all the more so because hardly anyone was using them. We had more important things to do.

* * *

Rickart had insisted on proper democratic procedures for all significant decisions and discussions. We were a tight little community and anything authoritarian would have put people's backs up and made everyone's lives unpleasant, not that we were currently living in a bed of roses. A formal structure would also drive home the point that our lives had irrevocably changed.

This discussion, more properly a brainstorming session, could make the difference between abject failure and spectacular success.

We assembled in the main auditorium on K Deck, the only public space that could hold us all. There were a few unoccupied seats: a few of the original crew members were dead, and some of the living had important tasks that couldn't be put off.

As always with a crowd of people, everyone was chattering away to everyone else, until Rickart walked in and most of us promptly shut up. The usual few who hadn't been paying attention kept right on chatting until their neighbours shushed them.

There were only two items on the agenda, but each was substantial. (1) Briefing on the current situation. (2) Open discussion of what to do about it.

For the moment we were still approaching Karoubi's star, which was now about 500 million kilometres away. The original plan had been to take up an orbit around the star, close to or even within the gas clouds, which would have made a suitable base orbit from which to launch the shuttles. The current plan was to orbit Karoubi's planet instead, if only as a temporary measure until we decided what to do next. We had antimatter aplenty for further manoeuvres.

Rickart said she hadn't yet told Earth about the gas cloud issue. "I fobbed them off with the not-quite-lie that there'd been a minor technical delay in readying the first shuttle to scoop up mahabhavium. I did that to buy us time to figure out a solution before the GU jams what little freewave capacity we still have with non-stop instructions and questions."

"They might think of something that we don't," Pallendorf pointed out.

"They might, yes. But we're on the spot, fully informed, and smart enough to find an answer if there is one."

I was optimistic that we would. At least, that's what I kept telling myself.

She then gave everyone a brief summary of the salient points, the main one being that our existing plan to secure mahabhavium was a dead duck. Pallendorf and Goodenough gave a joint presentation of the scientific evidence that the gas clouds were well inside the radiation zone, so they weren't accessible. Quatermain and Clapham did a double act.

"The problem isn't that the radiation would kill anyone piloting the things," Quatermain said. "It could, but if a suicide mission would save the day I'm sure there'd be enough volunteers. I would've signed up."

"Me too," Clapham said.

I thought about this. So would I. We hadn't come all this way to give up, whatever the cost.

"However, that's not feasible. The radiation is so intense that the shuttle's systems wouldn't be able to function. And there's another problem too, isn't there, Michael?"

"Sure is. That close to the star, its gravity is too strong for the shuttle to escape and return with the prize. Not at the slow speed needed to collect the atoms, not against the friction of the gas cloud. The second problem means that we shouldn't waste time trying to solve the first. And we shouldn't waste time trying to solve the second, either, because you can't break the laws of physics."

"So we have to get hold of the stuff some other way," Rickart said, rounding off the briefing and disposing of agendum (1). "And in general terms it's kind of obvious what we have to do. The gas clouds aren't where we expected because the planet had swept them clean. No one knew there was a planet when we first set out; it didn't transit Karoubi's companion and its gravitational effects were too small. But that actually gives us some hope, because some of the material must have ended up on the planet.

"We just have to find out where, go down, and get it."

She paused.

"Of course, it may not be that easy. Kyril: fill us in, please."

Pallendorf took over again. "Right now we just have preliminary surveys from distance. Karoubi's planet is about the size of Titan back home, with similar gravity. Right now it's in a standard elliptical orbit round the orange dwarf, but in the long run the orbit's chaotic, swapping between the pulsar and its companion on a timescale of tens of millions of years. It has a surprisingly thick atmosphere, mainly nitrogen, ammonia, and methane. There's liquid water at the surface, and plenty of water vapour in the air. Much more than I would have expected, to be honest. It's created a thick cloud layer. That leads us to believe it has an ocean. No idea how deep or how extensive. The ocean is liquid during the phases when the planet is close enough to Karoubi's companion, and freezes when it's not. The pulsar doesn't put out enough heat to melt it.

"However, it does put out radiation, especially x-rays. The planet's orbit stays away from the main jets and the Mare's Tail, but over the years it will have accumulated radioactives. Mahabhavium itself isn't radioactive, but anything containing it might be. The background radiation level is mild, but we'll have to decontaminate anything we bring back to the ship. Salomé Blanchet says that won't be difficult with the right precautions.

"In true colour images the planet is mostly pale brown – the ocean – with light grey areas of cloud." He flicked up an HV image. "Where the cloud cover has cleared we can see lots of small dark brown spots, which we're pretty sure are islands."

"So the rest is ocean?" Clapham asked.

Before Pallendorf could answer, someone said:

"Any sign of larger land masses?"

I didn't recognise the speaker, but my tab identified her as Avira Stote, a SusAn reanimation specialist.

"Not yet, Avira," said Rickart, without consulting a tab. The Admiral knew *everyone*. "But right now we can't detect any clear surface features. We'll be able to see through it with infra-red and radar when we get closer. So the picture will get more detailed.

"There's one point in our favour. It's been said before but I'm repeating it, because it could be the key that unlocks the Galaxy for humanity. All the evidence points to the planet having scoured out the gas clouds, so any mahabhavium it scooped up ought to have been distributed fairly uniformly across its surface."

Pallendorf nodded, looking avuncular. In a good mood today, then.

"That's what I'd expect," he said, "but it probably happened a billion years or more ago. There are plenty of ways the stuff could have been redistributed over that long a time period. So it's no more than an educated guess until Gayl and I can get better data. Which I'll make accessible to everyone as soon as I'm confident it's correct.

"Any questions?"

There were, of course.

Few answers.

* * *

Weeks passed.

With its MAD on standby, *Star Pyramid* was now coasting towards Karoubi's planet at the right speed and on the right trajectory for orbital insertion, so there was no reason yet for the GU to suspect that the mission was in trouble. The crew had settled into a slightly awkward routine. Waiting for more information on Karoubi's Planet, waiting to learn of our likely fate.

When information started to trickle in, it was ambivalent.

The Project's inner circle had gathered on D Deck for a brainstorming session.

"The good news," Pallendorf announced, "is that we're starting to see through the clouds."

"And the bad news?" I asked him.

"The *bad* news – well, it's fairly bad – is that most of the planet is covered in water, as we feared. One gigantic ocean, basically."

"How deep?"

"So far the deepest part I've seen is about two kilometres down. There are plenty of shallower areas, but nothing like a continental shelf, though: no continent. Roughly 99 per cent of the surface is underwater, and of that, about six per cent has a depth of ten metres or less. We can't land anything in the sea, that goes without saying. Which leaves the land. And that's… tricky."

"What's tricky about the land?" I said.

"There isn't any."

Turned out that wasn't quite true. There was land, but it didn't come in usable chunks. There were hundreds of thousands of small islands, none more than half a kilometre across. All of them pretty flat: no more than 80 metres above sea level at their highest. All of them liberally strewn with boulders, and no doubt smaller rocks, pebbles, and grit.

Shuttles aren't designed to land, let alone take off, and with that sort of terrain there was no prospect of modifying them to do either. "Can you land an OWLL?" Pallendorf asked.

Salomé Blanchet pursed her lips. "With care, yes. We've got to avoid the rocky areas, but some of the beaches are big enough. However, that comes later. First step is to drop a bunch of drones, take a close-up look at what's down there. And that could be tricky, too."

"Why?"

"Weather, basically. The clouds contain a lot of water vapour, which implies rain. The parachutes aren't designed to work in heavy rain. Fortunately most of the vapour stays in the clouds, but sometimes it precipitates out as a fine drizzle, with occasional heavy showers. A few thunderstorms, so there could be occasional flash floods. There are signs of that kind of erosion on some of the larger islands.

"The winds are another problem. They're light most of the time, but there are random gusts, presumably turbulent flow round the bigger outcrops. The parachutes aren't designed for gusty winds, either. Given time we could strengthen them, but there was a big safety margin anyway. If we keep away from the rain, most of them should survive the landing. Some, I predict, won't."

"How many drones have we got?"

"Two hundred and six, Kyril."

"OWLLs?"

"Four."

Blanchet had picked an area near the planet's equator, since *Star Pyramid* was in a roughly equatorial orbit. All we could see with the unaided eye was bank after bank of pale clouds, but the HV daises displayed full-colour images of the terrain. The ground was variegated, in shades ranging from reddish brown to pale buff. The sea was light brown. The images were true colour but enhanced for brightness. If we'd been down there in person it would have been on the dark side of twilight – very little of the star's light penetrated. Enough to see shapes and shadows, not enough to figure out what they were.

Our electronic eyes, however, could dispel some of the gloom. And what we saw, aside from clouds, was a random scatter of brown-buff speckles in an ocean of light brown, uniform except for the intricate wave interference patterns created by the interminable scatter of islands, islets and rocks. They were too numerous even for a computer count; not because we couldn't process the data, but because any distinction between islands and rocks would have been arbitrary. At a rough estimate, including anything down to a metre across, there were 200 million islands. The largest 40,000 were between half and a quarter of a kilometre across. And every large island was horribly rocky terrain, except for what looked like narrow sandy beaches round the edge.

The ocean – well, despite all the islands, we couldn't think what else to call it – was criss-crossed by millions of shallow waves. At the moment, the weather was reasonably calm; the highest winds were no more than a stiff breeze. Waves broke on the beaches, much like terrestrial ones but moving more slowly.

Build a spaceport, and Karoubi's star would make a fantastic holiday resort. Aside from the thin unbreathable atmosphere, permanent twilight, and unending rocks.

The target for landing the drones was centred on one of the larger islands, with an area of beach that was much wider than usual. Salomé had chosen that with a view to a later OWLL landing. The drones – she was dropping ten to begin with – ought to end up within two or three kilometres of that; maybe closer if the winds behaved themselves, but that was unlikely. Their cocoons would float and we could crack them open and fly the drones to the target site.

We could make new drones by the hundreds, if necessary. We had so much tech on board that we could probably build ourselves a new OWLL, given twenty years of uninterrupted development, but there was no point worrying about that now.

Rational scientists and atheists we may have been, but I noticed many crossed fingers as the bundle of cocoons with its cargo of drones floated slowly out of Bay A on G Deck, the further forward of our two shuttle decks. The designers had located the shuttle bays at two corners of the square decks, to avoid the danger of collision with the spinning ship, small though that was. Each corner contained two shuttles and one OWLL.

The bundle drifted away, ignited its tiny engines in a quick burst that separated it from *Star Pyramid* and its orbit, and sank towards the cloud layer. The cocoons would split up and hit atmosphere 34 kilometres above the clouds. We'd be able to watch the fireworks as friction did its best to burn through the heat shields, but only the telemetry could tell us whether the parachutes were doing their job.

* * *

We lost one drone to atmospheric friction and two more when their parachutes tangled, but the other seven were undamaged. All of them landed in the sea. We took advantage of the current calm, rain-free conditions near the ground to make our first close-up explorations of the surface of Karoubi's Planet.

In the cameras the ocean was darkly forbidding, but that was probably the diffuse lighting. The waves seemed oily and sluggish: in the lower gravity they moved and broke in slow motion. There was no reason to doubt that this was an alien world.

With the surviving drones safely down and assembled on the target beach, our xenologists had a chance to survey the immediate locality. And almost as soon as they switched on the near-field cameras they were jumping for joy and screaming their heads off.

We all were.

We already knew that the islands were covered in rocks. Now we could see that between the rocks some sort of plant-like organism sprouted in profusion. It looked like a turnip bedecked with seaweed, glutinous and straggly, with bunches of round protuberances like grapes, and lines of blisters down the centre of each frond.

Alien life.

"Not especially exciting, compared to what the HV channels served up on a daily basis," Carolina said.

"But hey," Sandy added, "it's the first genuine alien life form anyone's ever found. Bacteria would've been astonishing; life this complex is literally out of this world. Well, provided 'this world' is Earth and you mean 'literally' literally."

It was Nobel Prize material. Carolina and Sandy were ecstatic.

We promptly named the stuff 'seaweed', despite Carolina's protests.

"We shouldn't use the names of Earth organisms!" she said. "Could prove misleading."

"Can you suggest anything better?" I asked.

"Well, no," she said. But as a matter of principle… Oh, hell. Call it what you like."

The edges of the leafy parts were scalloped, and close examination suggested that these indentations were signs that some organism was using them as food. We hadn't actually seen anything eating them. Or eating anything else, for that matter.

"That turnip-like bulb at the base seems untouched," Carolina said. "Curious. Maybe too tough–"

"We're looking for mahabhavium, not alien vegetables," Rickart interrupted, a trifle sourly.

I wondered why she was so negative. Probably realising that life forms generally make everything more complicated. She and I both knew that from long experience.

* * *

While seven hundred people carried out jobs ranging from overseeing the cleaning bots through gardening duties to maintenance of essential equipment, most of the key players were closeted together on D Deck: Command and Control.

Kyril was carrying out remote operations with five drones, which gave him close-up views of their immediate surroundings. Carolina and Sandy were allowed one each. I was observing the planet on a larger scale.

Sylvia Gregory, duty meteorologist, was scanning the planet, gathering data for the next weather forecast and generally watching out for anything interesting. I kibitzed over her shoulder as she zoomed in on a region of clouds that was turning dark grey. At first the change was almost invisible, and the region was small, but within an hour it had grown bigger and darker, and it was starting to show signs of spiral structure.

She flicked the image to our tabs. "I think you need to take a look at this."

Kyril grunted in irritation at the interruption, but as soon as he saw the spiral patch of dark cloud he changed his tune. "Thanks, Sylvia. Whatever that feature is, we can expect high winds."

"That's the last thing we need," I said. "It all looked so peaceful from orbit. Until now. How high should the winds be to damage the drones?"

"They're military spec," Kyril said. "Not like flimsy civilian ones. But I wouldn't risk flying one in gale force winds, let alone anything stronger. I'll keep them well away from that thing."

"What do you think it is, Sylvia?"

"On Earth it would look suspiciously like a hurricane. Maybe a tornado. More likely something peculiar to Karoubi's planet. A karoubicane. I'll take a closer look."

Kyril nodded. "Copy anything interesting to me. Keep me posted on where it's going. Or if you see any others."

"Will do."

He gave us a wave and focused back on his drone controls. Then he changed his mind.

"Hjördis? You're in charge of overall planning. Tell someone to bounce a laser off it and get its composition. I'd like to know whether it's just atmospheric gases and water vapour, or something more dangerous."

"Khloe and Ray can handle that," I said. Klohe Mandrapilias was the duty laser expert. Raymond Jacobson was Chief Chemist, reanimated along with his entire team, still coming to grips with operating in a cosmic village that was, to employ a timeworn cliché, a hive of activity. It was certainly buzzing.

The grey swirl had grown larger and darker, even as we were talking. At a rough estimate it was now twenty kilometres across. Khloe said the laser could be rigged to give me Doppler readings on the wind velocity, so I told her to get that sorted as well.

Twenty minutes later she flicked a summary to my tab. I passed it on to Kyril immediately. Copies to Admiral Rickart and Wazmakai, a female engineer in charge of mechanical equipment. Like most Afghans, she had only one name.

"Wind speeds up to 150 kilometres per hour," Kyril said. "No drone would survive being hit by that."

"The chemistry is interesting, though," said Jacobson. "Lots of water vapour, as you'd expect, but there's also a lot of silicon."

"Sand?" I asked.

"The beaches are predominately silicates, so basically, yes."

"A sandstorm, then," I said.

"That's the closest Earth ever gets to it. But it sounds more like what the astronomers call a silicate storm. Quite common on exoplanets. But they're usually calmer than this. More like drifting smoke, tiny particles. Judging by the signals, this one has bits of grit in it. It'll be extremely abrasive."

"If the storm hits the drones," Kyril said, "It'll grind down their lift surfaces. Smash them apart. There's nowhere they can–"

He stopped as Wazmakai came into the room. A diminutive bundle of compressed energy, she didn't so much enter as materialise.

"I got here as fast as I could," she said, somewhat out of breath, "as soon as Sylvia added Khloe's observations to the weather report. Thought you might need some help."

"Very much so," Kyril said. "As I was about to say, there's nowhere they can shelter."

"The drones?" Wazmakai asked, not having heard the previous conversation but making an informed guess. "Well, you might be able to wedge them between rocks if you can find anywhere suitable. But they're not built for anything above gale force winds."

"We've got plenty of drones," Rickart reminded her.

"That's not the problem," Wazmakai said. "If these storms are common, they'll make it much harder to collect mahabhavium and bring it back up. Assuming we find any to collect."

"We'll find it," Rickart insisted. "How, where, I don't know. But it's down there somewhere, and there's no time pressure. Only what we inflict on ourselves by being impatient." She gave a hollow laugh. "But you're right, Wazmakai. It doesn't exactly improve our chances."

* * *

The storm abated without coming within a thousand kilometres of the drones. No new ones started up. We considered this a hopeful sign.

Pallendorf and the xenologists resumed flying their drones. One of them was scooting along a particularly broad and lengthy section of beach on the western side of the largest island we'd yet seen. Suddenly, Pallendorf gave a yell.

"What the fuck is *that*?"

CHAPTER 27

CALTROPS

Carolina Moreira

Karoubi's Star 2572

On a stretch of sand on the rocky foreshore, something was moving. Not a wave, and not just a seaweed frond flapping in the breeze. It looked…

"*Alive*," I said. "First seaweed, now this. And it looks a lot more interesting. I think it's an animal. Well, an alien equivalent."

I'm Carolina, one of precisely two xenologists in *Star Pyramid*'s crew, the other being Sandy Horrocks. Xenology isn't the primary role of either of us, but second strings to our bows helped both of us survive the rigorous selection process, back in 2169. We were slotted in at the last moment when someone high up in the GU got it into his demented head that the ship might encounter aliens; perhaps during its two flypasts, at Karoubi's star, or just somewhere along the way. And once the idea was in there, no one could winkle it out again. To prevent organisational gridlock, one specialist astrophysicist and one cosmologist got bumped to make way for substitutes who didn't know quite as much but also had training in (hypothetical) alien life forms.

Why xenology? Well, when I was a kid I read a lot of science fiction, which was full of weird, and mostly unbelievable, aliens. I got interested in astrobiology until it dawned on me that most of the research assumed that 'life' was just like life on Earth. Searching for copies of our own planet, basically. That seemed unimaginative, in a subject that cried out for imagination, since we didn't actually have any aliens to study. Not *too much* imagination, mind you; science fiction is about entertainment, not science.

Being overtly critical wouldn't butter any parsnips, as my old granny used to say, so I vowed to be constructive and write scientific papers about the possibility of unorthodox life forms. This as a definite sideline to my astrophysics, you appreciate.

I got lucky. The astrobiology community had finally twigged that even Earthly life was much weirder than they'd been thinking. Suddenly I was in demand for meetings and editorial boards, and –

as I said – that was what got me on *Star Pyramid*. Sandy's story was very similar, except she first got interested in aliens through the visual arts. It pays to stand out from the crowd, as long as you do everything else in the orthodox manner like the rest of the competition.

Accidentally having a complete dork on your side helps, of course. Provided he's extremely influential.

Pallendorf brought me back to reality. "An animal?" he said, voice sceptical. "On a world like this? Impossible."

"Tell that to this beastie, Kyril," I said.

"When the planet's circling the neutron star instead of the companion, the ocean must freeze! Plants are one thing, but how can complex life evolve under such conditions?"

"It evidently *did*," I said. "And plants are just as complex as animals. We share half our DNA with a lettuce."

"Yes, but most of those are bookkeeping genes for cellular –"

"That's not the–"

Sandy came to my rescue before I lost my temper completely.

"There are lots of possible answers to your question, Kyril. Off the top of my head: the deep ocean probably doesn't freeze at all; creatures down there might not even notice any change in orbit. Maybe creatures here go into some extreme form of hibernation when the planet switches to the pulsar, like bears, but sleeping out a Pulsar Winter for a few million years. Some bacteria can survive for at least fifty million years in spore form. Why not these guys? Maybe they *need* a big freeze to reproduce. After all, some trees on Earth need forest fires to germinate their seeds. Not great for us; essential for the trees."

Pallendorf looked unconvinced, so she added: "Just a few hypotheses, Kyril. It would take decades to do the research, and now's not the time."

"The thing about aliens," I said, "is: *they're alien*. Trite but true. You have to set aside all prejudices about earthly life."

He grunted reluctant assent.

Clapham said: "It has to reproduce *somehow*. Can't be the only one."

"Definitely not," I said. "Reproduction is a basic characteristic of any form of life. It can't evolve unless it reproduces."

"Mind you," Sandy said, "there are an awful lot of ways to reproduce. If aliens turned up and discovered how *we* do it, they'd never believe it."

The alien was a bit like a twisted starfish a metre tall. But instead of five arms, it had four, symmetrically arranged. There were openings at their tips; suckers, maybe, or eyes, mouths, anuses – possibly one of each. Probably none of the above. It was a delicate shade of blue, covered in a network of fine green lines that got finer and more numerous near the tips of the arms. Or whatever they were.

"It's like a tetrahedron," Clapham said. "But its faces have been sort of *sucked in*. Giving four– well, dimples. Separated by four... spikes. Tentacles. Whatever."

Rickart ignored him, moved closer to the dais, peered at the creature. "This thing's... let's call them tentacles... are stumpy, not spikey."

"Maybe it's a mineral formation," Pallendorf said, but he didn't look as though he believed it. Just trying to keep an open mind, which was unusual for him. "Or a machine," he added, looking even less convinced.

"If it's a machine," Clapham said, "it's technology. Tech is itself a sign of life. So either this thing is alive, or whatever made it is. And that would require greater complexity, and be even more of a surprise. So – Occam's razor – it's alive."

He looked immensely pleased with himself, though whether by the discovery of an alien animal, or by the logic of his deduction, I couldn't tell.

Then I realised. *He's a mathematician. It'll be the logic.*

"In some sense," Rickart pointed out. "No reason for it to be Earthlike life."

"Every reason for it not to be," I said. This was Xenology 1.01. "Occam's razor is a dangerous instrument, like any edged weapon. Simple isn't always right."

"True," Clapham, said. "But redundant axioms should be eliminated."

"Fair enough," I said, "if you're sure they're redundant. This environment isn't remotely Earthlike, so whatever adapts to it won't be Earthlike either. Wrong atmosphere, and significant levels of ionising radiation. So what counts as machinery, and what counts as life, is somewhat moot."

From their expressions, a bit more Xenology 1.01 was in order.

"That said, I don't believe it's a machine. What's always hard to wrap your head around is that for this beastie, what we have here is not an extreme environment. This creature isn't struggling desperately to survive in circumstances inimical to life. It's *comfortable* down there, however awful it might seem to us. Its species must have adapted to this environment over tens of millions of years. Maybe billions."

"What we think of as harsh conditions," Sandy said, "might even stimulate evolution by increasing selection pressure. On Earth, global catastrophes like asteroid strikes were generally followed by an explosion of biological diversity as evolution explored a new possibility space."

"You're saying it likes it here," Clapham said.

Sandy nodded. "Feels right at home. Because it *is* at home. Just like we're at home in molten ice – ice is a rock, you realise – in an oxygen atmosphere that combines with our bodies if ignited by fire, which was highly toxic to the bacteria that were around when it was being generated as a waste product. These guys wouldn't last five minutes on Earth."

The creature was perched on a rigid tripod of tentacles, the fourth one pointing skywards, waving slowly in random directions.

"It looks fairly static," Pallendorf said. "Are you sure it's not just another plant?"

Just. How quickly we adapt to novelty.

At that point the upward-pointing tentacle started to flex downwards, and the two that were now below it buckled as if it was trying to kneel. Suddenly the creature tipped over with a flop-suck-splashing noise. The fourth tentacle was now pointing upwards, while the animal rested on the other three. The knee-bends straightened, and once more the creature stood upright, a rigid tripod with a fourth leg on top. Same pose, different tentacles.

"Not static," Pallendorf corrected himself, before anyone else could. "I concede. Animal." He paused, shot me a glance. "Uh. Animal-*like*."

"Interesting form of locomotion," I said. "Not any of the usual quadruped gaits."

"That's because its legs aren't positioned like those of an earthly quadruped," Clapham said. "It's got four legs – or whatever – but it's not a quadruped."

"So what is it?" Rickart asked.

"Whatever we want to call it," I said. "Quadpod?"

"Tetrapod would be better," Clapham said. "'Quad' is Latin, 'pod' is Greek."

"No it wouldn't," I said. "Already in use for Earth animals. Four-limbed vertebrates forming the superclass *Tetrapoda*, living or extinct. All descended from the fishes that crawled out of the ocean on to land, often called tetrapods themselves."

"Then it's a quadpod?" Sandy asked.

"No. It's a caltrop," Rickart said.

"A what?"

She shook her head and grinned like a Cheshire cat that's just spotted a dozen Cheshire mice who are so busy with a giant Cheshire cheese that they haven't spotted the grin creeping up on them. We were all on a high, and Fiona was no exception.

"Ah, Michael, you mathematicians need to learn some ancient military history. A caltrop is an area denial weapon. Used as far back as ancient Rome, if not earlier. A metal device with four spikes, shaped so that one of them always points up, however you position it. With barbs on it like a fishhook. Tread on one and it's too painful to move, you can't easily get it out again, and you're an easy target for slaughter, whether you're a man, a camel, or a war elephant."

"They had *war elephants*?" Clapham squeaked. "Do those count as area denial weapons too?"

"Well, you'd be wise to stay clear of them, but technically they'd be armoured vehicles," Rickart said.

I looked at Sandy and she nodded. "Caltrop it is," I said. "Executive decision by the xenology team."

"And the way it moves?" Clapham asked.

"I'd call that a topple," I said.

We watched as the creature zigzagged its way towards the beach, one topple after another. Clouds had come over and it was starting to drizzle. The caltrop ignored it.

"There's another one!" Pallendorf interrupted. "Coming out of the sea! I've never seen anything remotely like this."

Another caltrop emerged from the waves and toppled up the beach after the first one. Then another. All of the newcomers were smaller than the first, about half its height or less. They were similar shades of blue, some paler, some darker.

Within ten minutes there were six of the smaller ones, arrayed in a rough circle round the big one on the damp sand.

"Fascinating," I said. "It looks like they have some sort of social structure."

"'Be careful not to make assumptions'," Clapham quoted me.

I can take a joke, and he had me dead to rights. Even so, I had a defence. "I don't think I am, Michael. Sociality is a universal, not a parochial. Still, you're right. We need to study them much more extensively before drawing any conclusions."

"And one day we will, Carolina. But not today," Rickart said. The cat had regained dominance over its grin. "We have to focus on getting mahabhavium. It has to be *somewhere* on this planet."

"Seventy-five million square kilometres of it," Clapham said. "Nearly all of it ocean, so that's where the stuff has to be."

"Barring anything we've not thought of that could concentrate it or transport it to the land," Pallendorf pointed out. "There should be some traces in solution, but some of it could have precipitated out. There are simple solid plutonium compounds that won't dissolve in water, and mahabhavium probably follows a similar pattern. I'll get Jacobson to investigate, he's got some fantastic software for predicting chemical properties."

"There's salt in our blood, and we haven't lived in the sea since *tiktaalik* and its tetrapod relatives crawled out of the ocean 400 million years ago," I mused, thinking aloud. "Since the caltrops *live* in the sea, there could well be traces of mahabhavium in *them*."

Clapham gave me a funny stare. "I kind of wish you hadn't said that, Carolina."

* * *

Rickart had called together the heads of all the Science, Engineering, and Technists sections to decide how best to proceed. The breakout room was jam-packed.

Some steps were obvious. We knew – circumstantially but convincingly – that there had to be mahabhavium somewhere on Karoubi's planet. Lots of it.

We didn't know where it was.

The scientists were convinced that it had to be in the sea, since Karoubi's Planet was mostly sea. As it scooped up material from the gas clouds over endless aeons, most of it would have fallen into the sea. Any that fell on the land was likely to have been washed into the sea by the persistent rain showers and occasional flash floods.

If it was in solution, we could figure out a way to evaporate the water and extract it. If not– think again.

"We need samples of the seawater," Pallendorf said. After a moment, he added: "Actually, we need samples of everything we can grab. Caltrops, vegetation, rocks, sand... even the air. We might get some idea with laser ablation, evaporating the water and trying to detect which atoms are present."

"I'd get better data if I could do the analysis *here*," Jacobson said.

"We'll have to send an OWLL down some time," I said. "It could bring stuff back."

"I'd rather not risk an OWLL at this stage," Rickart said. "We've only got four. Can you do remote analysis, Ray?"

"If we can get the right equipment in place, I guess so. It'll be a bit crude, though."

"I know you," Clapham said. "By 'crude' you mean 'possibly inaccurate in the fifth decimal place.'"

"If you tell me what you need, Ray," Wazmakai interrupted before they started bickering, "I can fix something up and get it down there. The drones are already equipped for sampling. Getting water from the ocean is easy: let down a flask or even a sponge, pull it back up. Solids… well, the drone has to land, and its robotic arm can pick stuff up, stash it in a container, fly it back to the module."

"How long will that take?" Jacobson asked.

"Three hours for prep and drop, two to collect the samples, twelve to analyse them."

Rickart gave the go-ahead and Wazmakai left in a hurry.

"We should do some brainstorming on possible contingencies," Clapham said. "What-ifs. What if it's dissolved in the sea? What if it's not? Can we break bits off rocks, if they contain it? How much stuff can we transport back to *Star Pyramid*? We need to get ahead of the game. Those of us who don't have enough to *do* should spend their spare time thinking."

"I have a request, Admiral," I said. "Sandy and I are willing to think, but we should also be allowed to study the caltrops. I don't know what we'll find, or whether it'll be useful for getting mahabhavium, but that's the point. *I don't know.* We need to find out. We're the only people here who have the right training."

"We can think about other things as well," Sandy said. "While we're doing it. During the boring, routine bits."

"Sounds good to me, Sandy," Rickart said. "If I change my mind, you and Carolina will be the first to know."

* * *

Jacobson ran through a set of HV visualisations of data from the chemical analysis module. He pursed his thick lips, flicked back through the sequence, refined the image.

Grunted.

Whether out of satisfaction or frustration wasn't clear.

"Well," he finally said. "There *is* some mahabhavium in the sea.

Plutonium nitrate dissolves in water, and now we know that mahabhavium nitrate dissolves as well, which is what I'd've predicted."

He always came over as slightly pompous, but when you got to know him you realised it was just the way he spoke. Measured, confident. Privately, I was convinced that his manner masked an unwarranted feeling of inadequacy.

"Give me two hours and I'll have its molecular structure. I'd expect its crystalline form to be $Mb(NO_3)_4.nH_2O$ with n between 4 and 6, just like plutonium."

Satisfaction, then.

"But extracting it from solution could be a problem."

Maybe frustration, after all.

"Why?" Rickart looked puzzled. "We can evaporate the water and collect the residue."

"It's present in very small amounts," Jacobson said. "Too small. It would take centuries to extract the amount we want."

"Is that because mahabhavium nitrate doesn't do what you expected, and dissolve readily in water?" Pallendorf asked.

It was Jacobson's turn to look puzzled. "No. Not at all. It conforms surprisingly well to Mendeleev's extrapolation technique, anomalous stability aside. The computations predict that it should dissolve without any difficulty. At the temperatures on the planet, which are pretty close to a warm day on Earth, plutonium nitrate dissolves easily in water. And in nitric acid; even in acetone and ether. Mahabhavium nitrate should, if anything, be *more* soluble."

"So where's it gone?" Rickart asked. "If it's not in the gas clouds, it must be on the planet. It can't have been expelled from the system entirely, can it? Or sucked into the visiting black hole, now long gone?"

"Hard to see how. But right now, your guess is as good as mine."

"Maybe the caltrops gobbled some of it up," I said. "Sucked it in. Along with whatever they feed on. Life forms often concentrate heavy metals."

Clapham gave me another funny stare. "I *really* wish you hadn't said that."

* * *

Drone 5 found a dead caltrop in a crevice between rocks. Picked it up – well, scraped most of it up, it was partially decayed – and brought it back to the module for chemical analysis.

Jacobson stared at the data. Kept staring. Not moving a muscle. Eventually Rickart tapped him on the arm. "Something wrong, Ray?"

"Uh– no. Yes. Well, both."

"Are you going to let us all in on the secret?"

"There's a slightly greater concentration of mahabhavium in the dead alien than there is in the sea. Mainly in bodily fluids. Their version of blood or lymph."

"In principle, that's great news," I said. "How many dead aliens would we need to get fifty kilograms of mahabhavium?"

Jacobson waved up a computation. "About four billion. The concentration is about 25% greater, so not much of an improvement on seawater."

"I was about to order an intensive search for more caltrop carrion," Rickart said. "Until you came up with that figure. Still, let's have a good look around. Maybe there's a caltrop cemetery somewhere."

Six hours passed. "How many dead aliens have the drones found?" Rickart asked.

"Three, so far," Pallendorf said. "And that's not for lack of searching."

"That's a relief," Clapham said. "I'd've been very unhappy if you'd allowed a massive caltrop hunt."

"Yes, that would be terrible," I said, suppressing a shudder.

Pallendorf's laugh was more like a cackle. "There's not enough mahabhavium in the ocean: too dilute. There must be thousands of kilos in the caltrops. We don't need *that* much!"

"No," I said. "We just need four billion of them. How long do you think it would take to catch that many?"

"Hmmm… half a million a year… 1600 years," Clapham said.

"Yes, but like I said, we don't need that much. We can fire up our Da Silva with two kilos. That would only take 30 years."

"We'd need more than that," Clapham said. "Enough to build at least one more ship. Two would be better. That's 90 years."

The Admiral stared blankly into space, shook her head, rejoined the rest of the universe.

"We could do it, Michael. Life support, hydroponics, recycling… they could all last that long. Longer. Earth could wait." She pushed her hair away from her forehead. "I'll ask them. It's about time we filled Earth in on what's gone wrong."

Clapham snorted incredulously and shook his head. "You know what the answer will be, Fiona! Earth's already waited for four centuries, and we all know everything's falling apart. It's not so much lurching from one crisis to another as struggling through one interminable crisis in which everything is going to hell in a handbasket at the same time. Not just a vicious circle: a vicious network. Earth can't afford to wait another 90 years! It can't afford to wait *ten* years, from what the uncensored newsfeed's telling us."

"No. In any case, the GU won't accept the risk of our systems collapsing unexpectedly," Hjördis said. "Not now we've arrived. They'll want us to move fast."

"I'll ask them," Rickart repeated. "And when they reply, we can all decide what we're going to do."

Clapham stared at us, distraught. "I can tell you now what the answer's going to be."

No one was willing to look him in the eye.

* * *

"There is no way," I said, "that we can kill off the first alien life forms humans have ever encountered!"

It felt like a nightmare. But this was real.

"A caltrop hunt would've been awful," Clapham said. "But *this* is worse!"

"The GU says our mission parameters leave them no choice," Rickart said. "It's horrible, it's disgusting–"

"It's obscene," I said. "It's unspeakable, literally. There are no words. We can't get at the gas clouds, so they're ordering us to make our own. Use some of our antimatter to boil off the oceans and the atmosphere, then collect the resulting gases using the original plan of a shuttle equipped with ramscoop. Incidentally slaughtering not just the caltrops, but everything else living here, but that's of no consequence to the GU.

"It's a crime against– well, not humanity. Inhumanity."

"The GU knows exactly what the decision involves," Pallendorf grumped. "I'm sure it understands the consequences. It won't have taken that decision lightly."

"No. And when King Egan III kicked off the European Secessional Wars, he didn't take that decision lightly either."

"I'm not convinced it will even work," I said. "Any clouds we make will be tiny compared to the existing gas clouds, let alone what they should've been."

"Sorry, Carolina. I wish you were right, but it will," Wazmakai said. "And the GU knows that. It won't be easy, but it's feasible."

"What makes you think that?" I said, grasping at straws. "You've only just heard of the plan."

She shrugged. "Oh, Salomé and I worked it out *ages* ago, as soon as we realised the stuff was on the planet. It was an obvious possibility. Drop dozens of AMbottles into the ocean, timed to shut down simultaneously and let the antimatter make contact with ordinary matter. Repeat if necessary. We didn't bother to work out an optimal sequence or the best locations and depths, but it's easy enough. The resulting cloud would be tiny compared to the star's gas clouds, but the concentration of mahabhavium would be a million or more times greater. Then all we'd need to do is tighten up the ramscoop fields and program the Da Silva linkage accordingly."

No straws, then. I was drowning.

Clapham, obviously as distressed as I was, shook his head; out of denial or bemusement I couldn't tell.

"It's not just the nature of the instructions," he said. "It's the haste. Why all the rush? Why not give us time to come up with an alternative?"

"What they *say*," Rickart replied, "is that we need to exploit our safe arrival. *Earth first*, that's their overriding principle. If we could've kept to the original plan, we'd have been scooping up mahabhavium by now and stockpiling it by the kilogram. If we hadn't encountered any snags, we'd have been on our way back within a month."

"We'd be *back*," Clapham said. "There's no 'on our way' with a Da Silva."

"Back, or stuck," I said. "Back if the drive works, stuck here if not."

Rickart nodded, but continued explaining the GU's reasoning.

"They're terrified that the longer we hang around here, the more chance there is of something going wrong."

"Oh, for god's sake. *Star Pyramid* has survived the entire voyage," Clapham pointed out. "It was built to an extremely high standard, it had to be. There are *no* signs of any vital system beginning to deteriorate, let alone fail."

"Aside from the wrecked antenna," Rickart said. "And that's the issue. We had a saboteur on board. There could be others."

"I suppose," Clapham said, wavering.

"Fiona's right," Wazmakai said. "They wouldn't have put all their eggs in one basket if they could avoid it."

"That's what worries the GU," Rickart said. "They don't care whether it's true; they're not willing to take the risk. Every hour we spend here increases the opportunities for more sabotage. For all anyone can tell, *Star Pyramid* could be destroyed as we speak. So they're telling us not to faff around, but to put into action a new variant of the original plan."

"No matter the consequences," I said.

"No matter the consequences." Rickart sighed, began pacing the room. Perched herself on a nearby seat. "I don't like it any more than you do, Carolina."

I wasn't ready to concede. Never would be, whatever anyone else thought.

"All the evidence shows that Shegwada worked *alone!* Getting one saboteur on the ship was almost impossible. More would've risked blowing the whole thing wide open. The GU's being paranoid. If there'd been a second saboteur, we'd all be dead by now. Shegwada was a lone wolf.

"Anyway, what the GU proposes is immoral. Unthinkable. Also totally unnecessary! There's no rush, and they shouldn't pressure us like this. If the human race behaves like that, it doesn't *deserve* the keys to the Galaxy! It's not the caltrops that should be exterminated. It's *us*."

"On balance, I think Carolina's right," Clapham said. So I'd convinced one of them.

"No," Pallendorf objected. "She's wrong. *Earth first!* It might be different if we knew these things were intelligent." His voice was a growl, his expression pugnacious.

I looked him in the eye. "Kyril, we have no idea about their level of intelligence. But do you really think the GU would have issued different instructions if they *had* been intelligent?"

He stared at me, then at his feet, a sheepish look on his face. Said nothing.

"Hypotheticals won't get us anywhere," Rickart said. "Our instructions, from the very top, are perfectly clear. We may not like them, but it's not our decision. The GU says it's them or us."

I couldn't keep my mouth shut. "And you agree with that?" I shouted.

"I didn't say that, Carolina." She straightened her back, military posture. "I agree it's them or us. But I'm not sure that means it has to be *them*."

Pallendorf's face was red with anger. "So you're saying it's *us*? Humanity will never get its mahabhavium?"

She made a wry face. "Not saying that either, Kyril."

"Then what? You're not making sense!"

"I just said it's not our decision. But think about it. Actually, it is. We're not obliged to respect the chain of command. The *realpolitik* is that Earth has no control over what we do. They can scream and shout and threaten, but they can't make us obey. Not from 400 light years away."

She took a deep breath. "There has to be another solution. And we're going to find it. The risk of further sabotage is small. The risk of accidental failure is smaller by far. So I'm going to tell everyone that we're pausing the GU solution for a week, while we seek a less drastic alternative."

I nodded. "So what will you tell Earth, Fiona?"

"Not that! They'd have a fit. No, I'll tell them exactly what they want to hear."

CHAPTER 28

EARTH FIRST

Reynheiður Sigmundsdóttir
Karoubi's Star 2572

I'll tell them exactly what they want to hear.

Rickart still had people sweeping the ship for electronic eavesdropping, but I had access to devices they'd never be able to spot, courtesy of my GU handlers. Only I knew where they'd been hidden.

The Admiral's words were tinny in my ear, courtesy of an implant connected to my eardrum, but clear as a bell. And they rang a bell, too. A warning bell.

The other three sleepers were already animate. My duty was clear: assemble them, brief them, and do what the GU had placed us on board to do.

That's the problem when you play *realpolitik*. The other side gets to ignore the rules too. And the GU's advisors had been centuries ahead of Rickart's cabal of traitors.

Jurisdiction wasn't the issue.

A well-trained force of four would be more than enough. Shit, I could probably do it on my own. But you should never start a fight unless you're certain you can win it.

Damn it, I *liked* Rickart. I didn't like the GU's decision. It was the kind of thing Rutzkoi would have signed up to, but he was long dead, along with Krantz and all the other people that had made my life a misery.

Earth first. A clarion call that had motivated the Project from the day it was first conceived. Earth first, and to hell with the rest of the universe, if that's what it came to.

And it had.

* * *

Everyone on *Star Pyramid* had known there must be covert GU security personnel on board from the day the embarkation process was complete. It was a no-brainer, the GU wasn't going to hand over control of the most expensive and most critical project ever to an assorted bunch of citizens, even if they had been chosen for their loyalty as well as their expertise. But only I knew the names. The rest knew about themselves, and no one else. They didn't even know about me, not by name. They knew someone was in command, and they knew it wasn't them.

It was a bit like those logic puzzles where everyone has either a red mark on their forehead or a white mark, and anyone who can see a red mark has to put their hand up. The first person to deduce what colour their mark is wins. Except that the marks weren't visible. The personnel files wouldn't help, because they didn't say 'GU security'. Except mine, and even then it was only Rickart who was supposed to know about me. To everyone else I was a specialist in human relations. Which, in a way, I was; just not the sort of relations that the term suggests.

The rest of my team knew one thing, though: a short cut through the puzzle logic that would identify me to them. Trite and low-tech but tried and tested from at least the time of Julius Caesar. A code phrase. One by one I let them know I was the one in charge. I did this quickly but carefully, so that no one outside our little group realised what I was up to.

I also had the codes to a weapons locker on U Deck, which everyone else thought contained spare parts for the hydroponics gardens.

There were four of us: a compact group, but highly trained and experienced. The other three were Lynton Jacobi, Hassan Qarabaghi, and Emily Xu, all RAG veterans. Jacobi was an expert on improvised explosive devices. Qarabaghi had been personally responsible for the arrest of 63 members of an Islamic hit squad. Xu had spent six years under cover having infiltrated a high-level cell of the Daughters of Baal, who had revived an ancient religion of the Levant and used it to attract fanatical followers dedicated to the breakup of the GU and the re-establishment of what they fondly believed to be ancient national boundaries. They had their own Holy Book, the *Wisdom of Baal*, and believed it to be the literal word of their god. Actually it had been written as a training exercise by a chatbot coder, who had accidentally released the file into the UnderNet. In the ensuing years it rewrote itself a dozen times and evolved an enhanced ability to attract devotees.

Within five hours of my snoop picking up Rickart's fateful words, all four of us were armed with compact automatic weapons, stabilised gyroscopically against recoil and capable of firing up to a thousand rounds of 1.3mm soft-headed mini-darts at a rate of fifty per second, either singly or in bursts. Each of us also had two grenades the size of walnuts that packed a punch big enough to slaughter a rhinoceros.

I'd handed out the weapons when we assembled in one of the shower cabins on K Deck, having just finished a game of low-gravity mixed doubles tennis. No one was around – *Star Pyramid* may be just a starship, but its combined deck area is more than 80,000 square metres, which divided among 740 people works out as 108 square metres per person.

* * *

I decided not to inform the GU at this stage. To do so I'd have to take advantage of a back door into the freewave message queue and send six short code groups, but we might be discovered if I tried. It would be better to wait until I could access the freewave overtly and report success.

I waited until the Admiral – for so I still thought of her, even though she was a traitor to humanity – was closeted with a small group of co-conspirators. Risking the failure of 400 years of global effort just to save a bunch of weird, slimy animals like distorted starfish.

Mad.

It was a relief to put a plan into action. We'd sat too long on our butts already. Time for the GU to take back control. Show the fucking traitors who's boss.

We marched along the corridors, weapons at the ready. The corridors cleared miraculously ahead of us, pale-faced people scuttling into adjacent rooms, securing doors, terrified we were coming for them. They knew we were trouble; just not for whom. The atmosphere in the ship was electric; that is, a state of shock.

We knew exactly what trouble we'd cause, and to whom.

Pallendorf had left; Pollard and Goodenough had joined the meeting, along with three others whose names I didn't yet know; that made eight people in the room. They'd presumably been warned we were coming, because they'd secured the door, but a well-placed mini-grenade blew out the locking mechanism. I saw the horrified looks on their faces. Their ears still ringing, they were frozen with shock. Couldn't comprehend what had happened.

One face was very familiar. *My sister.* As deluded as all the others.

Only Rickart had figured it out. Military training, you never lose it. She held up her hands just a bit above waist height, to show that she was unarmed and not intending to start any trouble. With four mini-dart sprayguns trained on her head that was a wise move, albeit a trifle obvious.

Hjördis opened her mouth, then thought better of it and just stared at me.

"Don't shoot, we're unarmed," Rickart said.

"I know," I told her. "I know everything you've done and said since you had me reanimated."

"Then you'll know why I decided to take the action I have."

That's a laugh. "You haven't taken any action, Admiral. That's why we're here. To make sure you do what the GU has commanded."

One of the women, a short mousey creature who I recognised as Carolina Moreira, glared at me. Foremost among the alien-lovers.

"What the GU has commanded, you miserable bitch, would be the worst crime humanity has ever committed," she yelled. Well, at least one of them was showing some kind of defiance.

I gestured at her to shut her mouth. We weren't there to argue the GU's case with weak-minded snowflakes. We were there to enforce its orders. I wasn't going to waste my breath trying to talk these idiots into doing what they'd been told. They'd already proved themselves untrustworthy. No second chances.

As far as I was concerned, we'd have been well within our rights just to shoot the lot, but our orders were very clear: bring them back unharmed so they can be put on trial for treason.

"Face away from me and put your hands behind your backs," I said. I told Jacobi and Xu to bind the conspirators' hands together with cable ties. Qarabaghi kept his weapon trained on the group, switching it slowly from head to head, as the electronics identified faces and kept it aimed between the eyes and two centimetres up. I walked up to Rickart, who they'd bound first.

I didn't catch what happened, because I was focused on Rickart. I heard a scuffle, the unforgettable high-pitched whines of bursts of mini-darts, like circular saws cutting sheet metal.

A thud as a body hit the floor.

More thuds.

The remaining conspirators started screaming and yelling, despite having just been told to keep quiet. Fucking civilians, no discipline. I turned to see who had died.

Shit.

It looked like someone had turned on a fire hose full of blood. Three bodies were crumpled on the messy floor.

One of them was Hjördis.

I swivelled round, to see Qarabaghi taking his finger off the trigger. Something broke inside my head, and I lost it. "You shot my *sister!*" I screamed.

I knelt beside what was left of my twin and burst into tears. *What am I doing?* My mind was disintegrating.

I got to my feet, waving my gun erratically. Next thing I knew, something hit me on the head and I lost consciousness.

* * *

I was lying on the floor, some sort of rough carpet. My head was aching, but that was nothing compared to my heart. I put my hand to feel where someone had hit me. There was a painful lump, and my hand came away bloody.

"Sorry about that," Emily Xu said. "You looked like you were about to shoot Hassan."

"I was," I said. "He killed my twin sister."

"I didn't know who she was," Qarabaghi said defensively. For once, he looked distinctly unhappy. "She attacked me, tried to snatch my gun. It was a reflex action."

"There were *three* bodies," I said, still groggy, wondering what the fuck to do now. "Who shot the other two?"

"I shot them as well," he admitted. "They wouldn't stay still to let Emily and Lynton bind their hands."

I found myself fervently wishing that Xu had let me kill him.

"You idiot. Of course they wouldn't, not when you were hosing my sister down with mini-darts. They were probably only trying to get out of the field of fire."

Qarabaghi shook his head. "Didn't look that way. They were going to attack as well. Reynheiður, I'm really sorry your sister got shot, but it wouldn't have mattered who it was, I'd have done the same thing. *Earth first.*"

Blood was pounding in my ears. "You're telling me it was *her* fault?"

"All she had to do was stay calm and do what she was told."

I glared at all three of them. "This is a total fuck-up. You weren't supposed to harm anyone. Leave that to the GU authorities when we get back."

"Let me bandage your head," Xu said.

"No!" I didn't want any of them touching me. "I'll do it myself, later. What have you done with the others? Did you kill Rickart too?"

"No one else has been harmed," Jacobi said. "They're locked safely away. We've closed down the entire ship, everyone confined to their quarters."

"You won't be able to keep them like that. There'll be essential maintenance to do, food to prepare and eat."

"I'm well aware of that. It's temporary. We'll let key personnel out in small groups, each with one of us on guard. Later we can keep them under control by taking hostages. Rickart as the prime example."

"Sure," Jacobi said. "They'll do what we tell them; if they don't, we start shooting hostages. Shoot *them*, too." He looked eager to begin.

So much killing. Despite my training, what had happened revolted me.

He took a step in my direction.

"Stay away from me, Hassan!"

"Just wanted to look at that head wound."

"Stay away. Right now, all of you stay away. I need to come to terms with what you've done. What we've done."

He made sympathetic noises.

"What *we've* done," Jacobi said, "is save the Earth. Those traitors were going to disobey a direct order from the GU. An order that would secure the mahabhavium we were sent here to get."

My head throbbed. "Save the debating chamber speech for later, Lynton. There's more important work to do."

* * *

Admiral Rickart had always been brimming with confidence.

Now she looked defeated.

I was watching the five prisoners from Rickart's seat on D Deck, lord of all I surveyed. I'd bandaged my head, taken some painkillers, and instructed Xu, Jacobi, and Qarabaghi to round up three work-gangs from the crew and start preparations for releasing antimatter into the oceans of Karoubi's planet.

It wasn't really necessary at that stage, but I wanted them out of the way, giving me time to think.

On the HV dais a tall black guy, who I recognised as Rowley Pollard, was wandering around the empty store room on L Deck that currently served as a prison for the five traitors who'd survived the massacre. Looking for some way to escape, no doubt.

Waste of time.

"We need to find a way outa this mess," he said. "We can't let that bunch of murderers wreck Karoubi's planet, mahabhavium or not."

Unnecessarily, the computer was telling me who was whom. Admiral Susan Rickart, Flight Director. Rowley Pollard, Comms. Michael Clapham, Mathematics. Gayl Goodenough, Astrophysics. Carolina Moreira, Xenology.

There should have been three more names.

I felt tears welling in my eyes. It had all gone horribly wrong. Krantz and Mardeen had *used* my dead twin to sucker me into this. I didn't even agree with the orders we were blindly obeying. But: *Earth first.* I was here to do my job, which had now become mission compliance. The Project must succeed. No matter what.

"How can we make plans," Clapham said, "when they're listening to every word we say and watching everything we do?"

"Don't care what they watchin'," Pollard said. "Gotta find a way. Can't let Earth kill off the caltrops."

"If we could get loose, we'd find a better way," said Clapham.

I sighed. These were good people. Good, but naïve. Pity they were so misguided. I tried not to think of the innocent alien animals, soon to become nothing more than collateral damage.

"If we avoid specific plans," Goodenough mused, "it won't matter what they overhear." She raised her voice. "You! Listen up and listen good! You'll never control seven hundred people– and you'll need them all to scoop up that mahabhavium! Some time, you'll make a mistake, and then it's seven hundred of us against four of you."

It should have sounded pathetic, empty posturing. It struck me as raw courage.

"You do realise they could just leave us here," Moreira said.

"Use us as hostages," said Clapham. "Threaten everyone else, make them carry out the procedures to secure the mahabhavium."

"Hostages won't do them any good," Rickart said. "W Deck is more secure than the GU Tower basement. Right now, I'm the only one who can operate the controls, let alone release any antimatter."

"Susan, they'll hear you."

"They know it already."

"They'll torture you until you tell them the codes."

"There aren't any codes. They need *me*. In person."

"But– what if you were dead?" Clapham asked. "Then no one could get access."

"There are procedures." She didn't elaborate and no one asked.

"So what do we do?" Moreira said.

"Wait for them to come to us."

* * *

The Admiral, I felt, wasn't thinking clearly. We weren't going to use the traitors as hostages. We were going to use *Star Pyramid's* crew. Shoot a few who weren't needed for scooping mahabhavium, and Rickart would eat out of our hands. Leave her alone to calm down; she'd still have to do exactly what we wanted.

What the GU wanted. But was it what *I* wanted?

I ordered Xu, Jacobi, and Qarabaghi to return the work-gangs to their quarters, seal their doors, and accompany me to L Deck.

Time to interrogate the traitors, I told them.

Qarabaghi and Jacobi couldn't hide their pleasure. Xu seemed unmoved by the prospect. Just doing her job, however distasteful.

We marched along the deserted corridors, arrived at the storage room, and Qarabaghi unsealed the lock.

The five remaining traitors were huddled together on the floor at the far end of the room. They looked scared but defiant.

"Get them out," I said, gesturing with my mini-dart gun.

Qarabaghi took two steps into the room. His gun flicked from face to face, lining up with their foreheads. Getting all his ducks in a row.

I followed him in, gun at the ready. "Out!" I said.

Reluctantly, they got to their feet. Qarabhagi waved his gun and they walked out of the door ahead of me, between Xu and Jacobi, who were standing either side of the door. Qarabhagi followed, turning to reseal the door.

This gave me the opportunity to whirl round and put twenty mini-darts into his brain. Then, before the other two members of my squad could react by shooting *me*, I shot them both.

I was about to turn round to face the prisoners and explain when everything went black.

Again.

* * *

"The brain-scan shows no serious trauma," a voice I couldn't identify said.

"The coarse-scale nervous activity looks normal," said another. "You can interrogate her, but I'll have to stop you if she shows any signs of deterioration."

I wondered who they were, and who they were talking about.

"She's coming round," said the first voice. And I realised they were talking about me.

I groaned. "Where am I? What happened? Who are you?"

"I'm Jacinda Wilson, trauma nurse. You're in the sick bay." She didn't tell me what had happened. The scan might not be showing trauma, but my head didn't feel like that. It felt like a hangover from the hooch in Kong's bar, except that acquiring it had been less fun. And marginally more dangerous.

Ah. Bashed on the head. *Twice.* Once with justification, once not. As memory returned, I understood where I was, and why.

"Sigmundsdóttir, I need to ask you some questions."

That voice, I recognised.

"Give me a moment, Admiral Rickart," I mumbled. "I'm still confused."

"So am I. Your murderous thugs shot three of my people! Just because one of us made a brave but misguided attempt to resist. I thought they were about to shoot *me*. Then one of your squad hit you on the head. The others took us away and locked us up. After which, you shot all three of them and set us free.

"I won't apologise for hitting your head again, though I'm glad there's no brain damage. We had no idea where you stood. None of it made the slightest sense. It still doesn't."

I tried to sit up, failed, and realised I was strapped down on some sort of stretcher-cum-trolley. Someone – no doubt the nurse – did something to the trolley and part of it swung slowly up, moving me from a reclining position to a sitting one.

"Why am I strapped in?" I asked.

"Well, you did smash your way into my meeting with a grenade and storm it brandishing an automatic weapon," Rickart said drily. "With three others, also heavily armed, one of whom promptly killed three innocent people with sprays of mini-darts."

"It was Qarabaghi. Disobeying orders. The other two held their fire. I didn't fire my gun, not then. I haven't got one now."

"That's because we took it away from you, though I'm not sure that's adequate protection, as your comrades would no doubt point out if they were still alive. You're an unknown quantity,

Sigmundsdóttir, and right now that's something I can well do without. 'Loose cannon' doesn't even come close. We've just seen you shoot three members of your own squad in cold blood."

"Dammit, Admiral: *I just rescued you!*"

"You did. And I have no idea why. Anyway, we'll take that into account when it comes to your trial. Right now I have more important things to do than argue with you, or listen to your stupid excuses.

"Someone call Security. Tell them to come here, take her away, search her *thoroughly*, including scanning for implants, and lock her up in a holding cell until I decide what to do with her.

"Oh, don't look at me like that. I did wonder about sending you to R Deck. Count yourself fortunate that I changed my mind."

"That's recycling."

"Correct. Standard procedure with corpses."

I didn't protest that I wasn't a corpse. That could be arranged. To be honest, I was surprised they hadn't done it already.

I said so.

"I thought about it, but I decided you warranted slightly better treatment than that. I'd give you more credit for killing Shegwada if it hadn't been done to preserve the GU's plans. Now, for some mad reason, you've shot your squad and set us free. My opinion of you is distinctly ambivalent.

"However *Star Pyramid* is going to need every live body it can get, so it's stupid to waste a perfectly serviceable one."

She spun on her heel to cross the room to the main HV dais, then stopped. Half-turned, staring at me. Despite my psych training, I found her expression unreadable.

She inclined her head, stroked her chin.

That, I *could* read.

"I've been a leader for most of my career," she said slowly. "And I realised long ago that people's true character comes to the fore in times of stress. I'm getting the distinct impression that you're more committed to your family than to the GU's plans for Karoubi's planet."

This, I felt, was pretty obvious, but it was encouraging that she'd noticed.

"Hjördis is the only family I've– *was* the only family I had." I wriggled, trying to get more comfortable. "Can you take these straps off? My leg itches, just behind the right knee."

"Not yet. Maybe not at all."

"Not even if I say please?"

"Nurse Wilson? Scratch her knee for her, will you?"

Nurse Wilson complied. Not exactly a major surgical procedure, but a highly successful one.

"Thank you, nurse," I said.

"I'm here for your welfare, Ms. Sigmundsdóttir," she said. "You can choose not to believe me if you wish, but I assure you it's true. We have a sacred duty to *all* of our patients. Even the worthless shitty ones."

"In a way, that applies to me, too," said Rickart. "Now, tell me why I shouldn't change my mind *again* and have you recycled."

"Because you need every live body you can get," I said.

"*And?*"

"And because I *didn't* carry out my orders." I licked my lips. "Yes, I did at first, but I didn't like it. Not that you can be sure of that. It all happened so fast, I didn't have much time to think. When the order came through–"

"How? The bandwidth on the freewave is pathetic."

"One brief code, embedded in the sentence structure. They trained us to respond without hesitation, me and my squad.

"I already knew what the GU wanted, and what you were planning to do instead."

"You can tell me where you put the bug later, and how it evaded the sweeps," Rickart said. "You clearly know more than I do. Right now I have no idea what I'm planning to do instead."

"You're planning to lie to the GU and tell them you're following orders."

"No, I've already done that. And you've no doubt told them about it."

"Actually, Admiral, I haven't. Too busy putting the squad together and arresting you."

Rickart flicked something up on the dais and peered at the display. "Hmmm. No complaints from the GU yet. You're telling the truth.

"What do *you* think I should do?"

The sudden change of tack floored me. I wasn't expecting to be asked for advice. I shook my head, as much as the restraints allowed.

"No idea. No, that's not true. The death of my sister had made my mind up. I had to conceal it from my squad until I was ready to act on it, but that's why I rescued you."

"And what has your made-up mind concluded?"

"I think you should continue to lie to the GU and tell them you're following orders."

She gave me a piercing look, not disbelieving, just… *wary*.

"And then?"

I grinned, despite my aching head. "And then… you need to come up with a way to get your hands on a decent supply of mahabhavium that *doesn't* involve mass slaughter of the first alien life forms humanity has ever encountered."

It was dawning on me that I'd been on the wrong side, causing the deaths of six people, one my twin. I'm not from a shame culture, but I might as well have been.

A smile lit up Rickart's face, just for an instant.

"Then you're willing to disobey the GU and help us?"

"I've already disobeyed the GU by killing three RAGs. If we went home now they'd have me arrested and jailed for life, or worse. As for helping you: that's a no-brainer. It would help *me*, and maybe go some way towards atoning for what I did.

"Shit, Admiral: Hjördis is *dead*. And it was my squad that killed her. I'm damned if I'm going to add the slaughter of countless weird aliens to my crimes."

Rickart turned to Nurse Wilson. "Is she telling the truth, nurse?"

Wilson pursed her lips, ran a hand across a smaller HV dais that was standing in a corner, just within my peripheral vision.

"According to the analysis of these readouts, she is."

Rickart leaned close, stared into my eyes.

"What do you say about that, Sigmundsdóttir?"

"What you already know. People like me have been trained to fool brain scans. Shegwada managed it, and she was an amateur. There's no objective way to find out whether I'm lying."

Rickart nodded. "Very good, very honest. All part of the training, of course. But I think there's a *subjective* way. Experience. To get to my level you have to be a good judge of character."

Still staring. Neither of us blinked.

She stepped back. "You've *almost* convinced me. Nurse Wilson: please remove the headset and undo those straps. Sigmundsdóttir: behave yourself and I might just scrap that trial. The facts are clear; what matters is where we go next. But I warn you: you'll be confined to your quarters until the psychologists can put you through a more thorough examination. And we'll keep a 24-hour watch on you after that.

"Until we give you more freedom, I suggest you turn your mind to the only serious problem we currently face: how to get hold of enough mahabhavium without destroying every living thing on Karoubi's planet."

CHAPTER 29
MEET THE ALIENS
Carolina Moreira

I wasn't shaking any more – well, not much – but I'll never forget the horrible rasping noise the guns made as my friends were slaughtered, and the blood spraying everywhere: walls, floor, ceiling, my friends, me.

It could have been me.

And then we were locked up, then rescued, and three more people died. They were the criminals who'd murdered my friends, but I take no comfort from that.

I've washed the blood off a dozen times, but in my mind it's still there.

There was no way to conceal from the rest of the crew what had happened, and it was pointless to try to hide the reason. *Star Pyramid* was now on a war footing. War with the Global Union. War with the people of Earth.

The atmosphere in the corridors and public spaces was tense and gloomy. The GU didn't know we were disobeying orders: Reynheiður Sigmundsdóttir hadn't told them. But they soon would. We'd have to tell them ourselves when the delay became obvious and the excuses ran out.

We also knew the GU couldn't do a thing about it. Sigmundsdóttir said there were no other sleeper squads, and she had no reason to lie. Anyway, if there were, they'd have been activated by now.

We existed in a strange sort of Limbo.

* * *

Sentiment on board the ship was changing. Previously, the majority of the crew had followed the GU plan without demur. We knew what we had to do, and why, and we were determined to carry it out. We'd been preparing for it all our lives. But now many began to feel brainwashed.

Ironically, Shegwada had always seemed exceptionally committed until she revealed her true feelings, but she was a one-off. There'd always been a few who were openly less committed, but they showed little more than a lack of enthusiasm. Everything had changed now everyone knew that our taskmasters back home had ordered us to exterminate the caltrops, merely because it was expedient. Because it would guarantee a supply of mahabhavium *immediately*. They hadn't been willing to wait, to find a better way. Everyone knew that when we failed to obey those appalling orders at once and without question, the GU's gut response hadn't been rational argument, but violence. So now, many more of us were finding it much harder to reconcile our commitment to the Project with grim reality.

We felt lost, abandoned, betrayed. *Used*. We'd willingly given our lives to the Project, and now we found that our opinions *didn't matter*. Our goddamned *lives* didn't matter.

Maybe half of us were still loyal to the GU, and that would have made life on board very awkward, were it not for a virtually universal condemnation of the extermination order and the attack on our people. On those issues, there was consensus. And the more we talked it over with each other, the more another consensus was emerging.

We're free agents, and it's time we acted that way.

* * *

I'd be astonished if anyone at the GU had ever expected *Star Pyramid*'s two xenologists to get the slightest chance of practising their profession – except for the dork who got us on the programme, you appreciate. Certainly Sandy and I had never expected to exercise our skills in that direction. I had thought there'd be a good chance that I'd be able to do something useful in astrophysics, as part of the science team, because we'd be up close and personal with a neutron star. One with very strange spectral lines in its gas clouds. And it seemed likely that Sandy would get some interesting results on gravitational curvature, neutron stars being not that far removed from black holes.

Life seldom works out the way you expect, and our lives certainly hadn't. Here we were, only a few billion kilometres from said neutron star, and neither of us had made a single observation of it. We were much too busy observing the first alien life forms humanity had ever encountered. We lived and breathed caltrops. Excitement isn't the word. We were on some sort of intellectual high.

It was almost enough to make us forget the killings.

The GU's botched attempt to take over the operation had been a warning, and Sandy and I were determined to take as much advantage as possible of the chance to study the alien ecology of Karoubi's Planet before it turned out that there actually *was* a backup goon squad, and it all went belly-up again. Rickart seemed confident that there wasn't, but Sandy and I didn't want to take the risk. Not that our work would count for much if there *was* a backup team and Earth got what it wanted, but the opportunity was just too good to miss, whether or not we'd ever get to publish our results in a professional journal. Research is its own reward.

That the GU's coup attempt had failed was largely down to luck. No one who had seen Reynheiður Sigmundsdóttir's service record would have expected her to trash her orders and kill her support team, even if one of them had shot her sister. She and Hjördis weren't even particularly close.

Families are strange things.

Alien families are even stranger, as Sandy and I were documenting, snatching an hour's sleep here and there, doped on wake-up drugs, not wanting to miss a thing.

Not that caltrop families were definitely families, or the spectacle especially... well, spectacular. All we really knew was that the caltrops tended to form groups, with a single large one and anything from two to fifteen smaller ones, of numerous sizes. The purpose of these groups – maybe 'function' or 'functions' was a better word, since we didn't know whether caltrops had a sense of purpose – was unknown, and likely to stay that way for a long time yet. We had lots of guesses, ranging from plausible to wildly unlikely. In xenology, the unlikely explanations are more likely to be correct than the plausible ones. Like I told Michael, Occam's razor doesn't always cut it.

Sandy and I formulated hypotheses, which were ten a penny, and collected data, which was tedious but rewarding. Everything we did was overshadowed by the uncertain state of *Star Pyramid*'s mission, but that wasn't our problem at that moment, so we did our best to ignore it and concentrate on our research.

At first sight, all caltrops were alike save for a continuous range of sizes. The smallest we'd seen had tentacles nine centimetres long, the largest were around 1.4 metres. They tended to congregate in orderly groups around a single large one, emerging from the sea and coming together for most of the planet's 19-hour day. By the following morning they'd all dispersed – the largest one to more distant areas of its island, the rest presumably back into the sea.

We suspected that the caltrops were responsible for the scalloped edges of the seaweed, but for now that remained unproved, like most of our hypotheses. The smaller caltrops were very similar to the bigger ones, but they weren't exactly the same shape: allometric ratios worked the same way on Karoubi's planet as they did on Earth. Larger creatures had to be bulkier and heavier to support their own weight, even though the gravity was lower than Earth's. So the bigger ones had proportionately thicker tentacles and were generally fatter.

On closer inspection, each caltrop was an individual. The markings towards the ends of their tentacles seemed as varied as human fingerprints. With good optics we could distinguish them easily, especially when the onboard computers had done enough pattern analysis. Which is how we'd realised that there were clear signs of significant relationships.

One of the first hints of structure that we'd seen was when six small caltrops emerged from the waves to surround a big one. Whether this was a family group – mother or father with kids – or a bunch of small caltrops ganging up on one big one, we still didn't know. Maybe it was an alien birthday party, or a pre-funeral gathering to say goodbye to an elderly relative while they were still alive. Like I told Kyril weeks ago, there's one overriding rule in xenology: *the thing about aliens is, they're alien.* Their behaviour might look like patterns typical of Earthly life, but that means nothing. Assuming it's what it looks like is a dangerous trap. So we had plenty of hypotheses, and very little definitive evidence for any of them.

This was no surprise. It was straight out of the first lecture in First Contact 1.01. I'm not religious, but… by God, it was fun.

The more we studied the caltrops, the more we began to recognise that they weren't as boring as they seemed. Yes, the big ones spent a lot of time standing still. Yes, the smaller ones kept wandering in and out of the ocean and huddling round a big one. The frequent showers of light rain and drizzle didn't seem to bother them. Most of their behaviour was repetitive, but that applies to all forms of life. Observe a human being and most of what you'll see will look very familiar after a few days. Sleep, wake, eat, drink, urinate, defecate, fornicate, walk, talk, stare goggle-eyed at an HV dais… We're not really as interesting as we like to think. Most of the rich experience of human living lies beneath the surface. Much of it happens internally, in the mind.

* * *

We were the xenologists, but it was Clapham who alerted us to signs of ritual behaviour.

He noticed that, dotted around the islands, on the beaches just above the waterline, were curious collections of grey stones. One day the beach would be empty, the next there'd be one of these collections, and the one after that it would be empty again. He'd assumed they were just stones washed up by breaking waves, arranging themselves at random. The shapes they formed were highly variable – lines, curves, irregular hexagons. Sometimes a few of them had been placed on top of the rest; mostly they were all lying on the sand.

We'd all noticed them, and dismissed them as inconsequential random piles. Until, two days after the GU's abortive attempt to take over the ship, he suddenly said: "I'm an idiot!"

Sandy looked at me and grinned.

"Can we quote you on that?" I asked him.

"You damn well can. I can't think why no one's noticed it."

"Noticed what?"

"Have you counted the stones?"

I shook my head. "Should I have?"

"Do it now."

I instructed the computer to display a dozen piles, chosen at random. Counted the first one: six. The second: ten. The third: nine.

"The numbers are all over the place, Michael. No patterns."

"Yes, that's what it looks like. Now pull up footage from the day before, for each area where there's a pile."

We were now gazing at a dozen pairs of images. One of each pair was a pile of stones. The other was a group of caltrops.

"Count the caltrops," Clapham said.

I counted one group: seven. The second: five. The third: four.

"Just as random."

Clapham nodded. "That's what I thought, too. But you're not counting them in the same order. Compare the number of stones with the corresponding number of caltrops."

"Six, seven. Ten, eleven. Nine, ten. Three, four... Oh."

Sandy was staring at me, a mixture of astonishment and excitement. We'd both seen what Clapham had.

Every pile, whatever its shape, had one stone fewer than the corresponding group of caltrops. A few seemed to have a few stones missing, but if you looked closely there were always the requisite number, half-buried by windblown sand.

"That can't be coincidence," Sandy said. "I wonder... no, that's ridiculous."

"Wonder what?"

She blushed. "I'm embarrassed even to mention it."

"Don't be."

"OK. Here goes my reputation as a logical scientist."

Clapham had been the first to see it. I'd been a bit slower, but hesitated to say something so obvious, yet so impossible.

"The smaller caltrops," Sandy said. "One big one, on its own; then a number of smaller ones topple out of the sea and up the beach, surrounding it." She sucked in a deep breath. "A number identical to the number of stones."

"Are you suggesting that the smaller ones are *responsible* for these arrangements?" I asked her.

"Something is," Clapham said.

"Well, yes, but the numbers might just be coincidence. We've never seen the small caltrops pushing stones around."

Something does," he said. "And it's *not* a coincidence." He paused. "Trust me, I'm a mathematican."

"We've never figured out why they group together, either," Sandy pointed out. "But they do."

"Have you observed them at night?" Clapham asked.

"Well… no," I admitted. It was a major omission, I knew, but with so much going on we'd been going for the low-hanging fruit. "Not exactly ideal observing conditions," I said. "We don't have any lights down there."

Clapham shook his head, wonderingly.

"Then I strongly suggest you get some."

* * *

We weren't sure how the caltrops would respond to light, so we sent down a drone bearing lights with adjustable wavelengths, from ultraviolet to infrared. The caltrops stayed away from them except when they were operating in a range of bluish-purple. Those, they ignored, so we finally got some night-time footage.

And what a revelation it was!

By day the caltrops were at best sluggish, at worst inert. But as night fell, Karoubi's planet came alive. The 'seaweed', which we had thought were plants, started crawling around, pursued by the largest caltrop in its group. It ripped pieces off the edges with its upright tentacle, whose end opened up to reveal… well, a mouth, and a throat down which it sucked the pulpy tissue. Presumably to digest it somewhere towards its middle, where the tentacles met.

As the temperature fell, a persistent drizzle set in. Strange threadlike worms, metres long, emerged from the sand. Reacting to the rain? Too early to tell. Whatever had brought them to the surface, the caltrops were quick to exploit the result. The smaller members of the group clambered over each other in a feeding frenzy, sucking the worms down like spaghetti though *all four* tentacles. Meanwhile the worms wrapped themselves round the peripatetic plants, tightening their grip like a strangler fig attacking a tree, but much faster.

But that was just the overture.

After a time, the action quietened down. The plants stopped moving and once more looked like an exotic form of seaweed. The worms remained on the surface but settled down, with just an occasional wriggle. The group of caltrops reassembled, the big one in the centre, the others ranged around it in a ring. Then–

They danced.

The largest caltrop flexed its upright tentacle, as if conducting an orchestra, and the others toppled busily around it, moving in a coordinated circle, like a weird version of a folk dance. After a time, their direction reversed. They stopped, and one of them broke away from the ring, toppling down the beach and into the sea.

The others waited.

So did we, but less patiently.

Then the caltrop that had gone AWOL reappeared from the sea. It toppled up the beach to where the big one perched on a tripod of tentacles, the fourth waving slowly, seemingly tracking the approaching caltrop.

The smaller one fussed around, and scrabbled at the sand with the three tentacles that were in contact with it, making a smooth patch.

Its upright tentacle bent, and the orifice at the end opened wide.

A bulge began to travel down the tentacle, from the central junction towards the tip. When it reached the tip, a round grey object began to poke out.

A quick contraction, and what was obviously a new stone was deposited on the cleared patch.

"Holy shit!" Clapham said.

"I know what it looks like," I cautioned him, "but we don't have remotely enough information to conclude that it's defecating."

"No, I didn't mean–"

"Yes, you did."

Now a second one broke off and headed for the ocean, emerging several minutes later to deposit another stone. Followed by a third, a fourth… until every caltrop except the largest member of the group had collected a stone and brought it back to the group. Then they pushed and pulled and tugged at the stones, bringing them together in a cluster. Move them around like someone arranging flowers in a vase, stopping occasionally to see if the effect was right.

Of course we had no idea what they were really doing.

As the pale light of Karoubi's star's gas clouds rose above the horizon the rain eased off, then stopped. The caltrops headed back into the sea, all except the largest. That one disappeared between the rocks. We secured samples of the worms before they, too, vanished.

Now all that was left on the sand was an enigmatic arrangement of stones.

Sandy and I were in raptures. The performance had answered one question: what do caltrops eat? But so many new questions remained unanswered that we didn't know where to start. Was it a caltrop party? A ritual mating dance? Were the stones excreta? Religious offerings? Art works?

We already knew that the stones would be gone by the next morning. Presumably pushed back into the sea, ready for the next…

… whatever.

* * *

So of course we had to put an overnight watch on one of the piles that were still there next morning, after all the caltrops had departed, to see how they disappeared.

That was another revelation.

This time there was no big caltrop, no peripatetic seaweed, no worms. But, at apparently random intervals, a small caltrop would topple up the beach and *pick up* a stone with its upright tentacle. Once more a bulge would travel along the tentacle, but in the opposite direction, towards the middle.

"Either they have very strange habits," Sandy said, "or those stones are neither faeces nor food."

"No. They just seem to… Well, I'm not sure *what* they do with them."

"Pick 'em up and put 'em down," said Clapham.

Neither Sandy nor I found this observation helpful.

"Ritual," Sandy said.

The age-old sociological and archaeological phrase for 'no idea.'

CHAPTER 30

WHERE HAS ALL THE MAHABHAVIUM GONE?

Raymond Jacobson

Karoubi's Planet 2572

When the xenologists told the other members of the science team what they'd seen, and showed us edited footage, we all started talking at once. Eventually everyone calmed down enough for an orderly discussion.

"Those stones clearly have some significance for those creatures," I said. "Maybe the chemistry will give us a clue as to what it is. Have the technists picked up any samples of the stones?"

Wazmakai flicked through her tab's HV dais. "No."

"Why not? I thought they were picking up samples of *everything*."

"They are. But the caltrops keep moving the stones. So they were given lower priority, to avoid wasting time searching for their new positions."

I glared at her.

"I'll authorise immediate top priority," she said.

I thanked her with elaborate courtesy, to avoid screaming at her like a maniac.

* * *

When we watched the drone trying to pick up some of the stones, I began to have more sympathy with the energetic little engineer's position.

"Sorry, Wazmakai," I said. "I was expecting it to be easier than this."

"So was I," she said.

No sooner had the drone appeared near the assemblage of stones that we'd identified as the easiest to access than three of the large caltrops appeared from nowhere, toppling along at high speed, and converged on it. They huddled up next to it in a protective triangle.

"That's why it's harder than expected," she said.

"Buzz them," Rickart said. "Try to shoo them away. Rev the drone's motors."

It quickly became clear that we were more likely to damage the drone than to persuade the caltrops to move. They were stubborn little critters.

"Does any of the drones have an ultrasound projector?" Rickart asked.

Carolina shook her head. "No. We've not seen any sign of the caltrops responding to sound, anyway. We have very little idea of what senses they possess. Response to light, certainly. Other than that, they probably have *some*, no idea what. We've been told not to waste our time on xenology research."

Rickart pursed her lips. "I stand reprimanded, Carolina. Politely, but pointedly."

"The thought was never further from my mind, Fiona."

Sandy suddenly yelped. "Oh! That might work!"

Rickart's head turned. "Do tell, Sandy."

"*Response to light*... We know they ignored light in the blue-purple range, right?"

"We do. But we need something they don't ignore."

"Precisely. At that point we wanted light that *didn't* affect them. How did we find it?"

Carolina and I got it at the same moment, but she beat me to the punchline. "By trying all the *other* wavelengths! They stayed away from those. Maybe we can find something they actively avoid."

"Worth a try," Rickart said.

Wazmakai made some adjustments, tried a few combinations. A bright orange flashing light sent the caltrops toppling away in apparent panic.

The rest was routine. The drone secured several stones, deposited them in its sample return box, and headed back to base.

* * *

After three hours and twenty-seven minutes of remote chemical analysis I had the first result. I contacted Rickart.

"Admiral? I think we may have found the mahabhavium."

"In the stones?"

"That's what it looks like. Not a lot, but I think it could be enough, provided we can get hold of enough of those stones. Give me another two hours to check, and I'll confirm or deny."

"We can predict mahabhavium chemistry by extrapolation from plutonium," I said. "That's what Mendeleev and his successors did, and it's how I predicted mahabhavium nitrate in the ocean. With extra help from some powerful molecular dynamics software, of course. Remember?"

"Perfectly," Rickart said. "But you also told us there isn't enough."

"Not enough to extract, no. The solution was much more dilute than I expected. Which raised an interesting question. *Where had all the mahabhavium gone?*"

"Into the caltrops," Carolina Moreira said

"Some, yes. Again, not enough. Nowhere *near* enough! And that tells me there must have been some kind of mahabhavium sink that sucked most of it out of the ocean. A chemical sink, you understand. Some kind of lower-energy configuration that would attract mahabhavium atoms and bind them to something else."

"You told me you might have found the mahabhavium," Rickart said.

"I have. In the stones. They're actually mineralised nodules, and a significant part of the mineral content is mahabhavium silicide."

I flicked up 3D models of the two mahabhavium compounds with colour-coded atoms. No one but an expert would deduce much from them, except that they were similar but different, but they were impressive works of art in their own right.

As the others admired them, the Admiral went for the jugular.

"How much?"

"Ten per cent, roughly. It varies from one nodule to the next."

"And the other ninety per cent?"

"Carbonates of sodium and calcium, plus a tiny proportion of organic materials. Probably contamination by things like that seaweed. But they contain more than enough mahabhavium to complete our mission."

"That," Rickart declared, "is fantastic news, Ray." She squared her shoulders and suddenly looked ten years younger.

"The main problems will be collecting enough nodules and bringing them up to *Star Pyramid*," I said. "In the lab up here, I can extract the mahabhavium a lot more easily than our mass spectrometers could ever have extracted it from the gas clouds. I'll have to develop a purification process, because we won't be sorting the atoms as we collect them, but that's simple basic chemistry."

"Could the metal be extracted on the surface?" Rickart asked. "It would make transporting it into orbit easier."

I shook my head. "It would be very difficult to carry out all the necessary actions. Especially remotely."

She stroked her chin. "Earth wants us to bring back fifty kilograms. Of the pure metal."

"That would be around 1300 kilos of the nodules," I said.

"Let's review the options," Wazmakai said. "Drones can *transport* them, in small quantities, but – as we all know – they can't return to the ship, even without a payload. Shuttles can't land. Cocoons can land but not come back. So it has to be an OWLL. Unless…"

"Unless what?"

"Unless we decide to custom-build something else."

"Could we?" Rickart said. "I'd prefer not to risk an OWLL if we can avoid it."

"With what's on P Deck? Definitely. But it would take a year or so."

"That's too high a price."

Wazmakai nodded. "An OWLL it is, then. Payload 1500 kilos. That's a single flight, with or without a pilot."

"Do we need a pilot?" I asked her.

"No. But we might need a human to load it. Mind you, I'm hoping we won't. Conditions down there aren't great for a human being. The radiation levels are tolerable with suits, for a few days at least. It's not a problem if the OWLL picks up radiation—we can decontaminate it when it comes back, or just moor it outside the ship. My biggest worry is a karoubicane. Human pilot or not, we'd have to lift the OWLL, and then it would need to return to *Star Pyramid* to refuel before going back down. On top of that, the silicide dust in the air will play havoc with the mechanics if it has to make repeated trips. It'll be bad enough with *one* trip."

"I don't want vague hopes," Rickart said. "*Can you do it?*"

She licked her lips, narrowed her eyes. Frowned. "Yes."

Smiles all round, except from me and Carolina. Rickart nodded. "OK, that's a promise. I'll authorise– "

"Not so fast, Fiona," Carolina said. "That's not the bottleneck. The problem is, how big is the accessible supply? The caltrops get the nodules from the sea, but then they *take them back*. The next set of nodules they bring may well be the same ones, recycled. Or they may be accessing a fairly small stash. We can steal their nodules, but if that's the case, the supply would quickly run out.

"No, we need to collect them *ourselves*, in quantity. At an informed guess they're probably on the sea bed. The caltrops suck them off the bottom, just like they do on land. We need to do the same – *if*, and it's a big if, there are enough of them down there."

"Then we'd better check that out before we jump to conclusions and waste a lot of time and effort. Wazmakai?"

"I'm sure we can put together some suitable submersibles. They can communicate via the drones if we include a basic radio device. Doesn't need to be anything sophisticated. Lights, cameras–"

"Action," Clapham joked.

Rickart ignored him, stared at Wazmakai. "How long?"

"To build one? Two days. It needs to be light enough to be carried down in a cocoon and robust enough to survive the experience. That's not the easiest combination. But we can do it."

"And to deploy it?"

"A few hours. A drone can lower it into the ocean if we rig up suitable cables."

"OK, get a team on it. Now."

Wazmakai spoke rapidly into her tab.

"I wasn't being entirely facetious, Fiona," Clapham said. "We do need action, not just planning. We don't want to waste time if the submersible finds enough nodules. We need to modify an OWLL *now* to make landing less of a gamble."

"On it already, Michael," Wazmakai replied. "It'll take some cutting and welding, but it should be straightforward. The main problem, oddly enough, is getting the nodules loaded into the OWLL's cargo bay. It ought to be easy, but everything is designed for standard cargo-bots, and we don't have any."

"I thought we had pretty much everything anyone could think of," Clapham said.

"We do. Apparently no one thought of cargo-bots. It's a nightmare."

Rickart gave her a long, thoughtful look.

"Nightmares, we can handle," she said. "Face it, we've already had plenty of experience. Improvise. There has to be a way."

Wazmakai nodded and shot out of the room. Rickart plonked her sturdy form down beside an HV dais. "I'm ordering everything to be released to everyone on board. We need every brain cell on *Star Pyramid* working on this."

* * *

"You won't believe this," Sandy said.

"I probably will," I replied. "My credulity has been stretched so far that my mind is open to almost anything."

"You *still* won't believe this," Carolina said. "Play it, Sandy."

On the medium-sized HV dais in one corner of the main ops room, lights began flickering in a cube of darkness.

"Footage from the sub," Sandy muttered. "Before we turned on the lights. Same bluish-purple that worked on land. So I did some colour-shifting to make things more visible.

"The lights should come on about… now!"

The dimness faded up to what looked like normal daylight. Everything took on a yellowish tinge.

Strewn across the sandy seabed were thousands upon thousands of small, round stones.

"Are those nodules?" I asked them.

"Yes."

"All of them?"

"Probably."

"The ones that contain mahabhavium silicide?"

Sandy shrugged. "They have the same reflection spectrum, allowing for attenuation by the seawater. I'm pretty sure they contain plenty of MbSi."

"I'll set up a remote chemical analysis," I said. "But I agree, it looks like we're in business."

"Finally, yes," Sandy said. "But keep watching."

At the edge of the dais, something moved.

A caltrop. One of the smaller ones.

Five others followed it. They moved along the seabed using their strange toppling gait, until each straddled a nodule. Then they bent their upright tentacle down inside the tripod formed by the other three, and used it to suck up the nodule.

"The nearest shore is about forty metres to the left," Sandy said. "That's where they're all headed."

Their position relative to the HV dais segued sideways as the camera changed direction. A procession of caltrops toppled off to the left. The image cut to the land, where one of the large caltrops was waiting. The procession made its way out of the sea, deposited the nodules, and arranged them in a tight bunch.

"That," I said, "is wild. So the caltrops really do collect nodules from the seabed."

"Yes," Sandy said. "And they return them in a similar way. We have footage of that, but you can imagine what it shows."

"I think the nodules are some sort of waste product," Carolina said. "That does explain the traces of organics that you found, Ray. They *were* from the seaweed, just not contamination. But this is an alien ecosystem, and we shouldn't equate the nodules with Earthly animal waste."

"Waste product from what?" I asked her.

"Something that lives – or lived – in the deep ocean. We know that living organisms can concentrate particular elements and compounds. Think of the thick beds of chalk on Earth, deposited by tiny coccoliths that extracted dissolved carbon dioxide from the oceans, combined with calcium to make their skeletons, and then died, falling to the sea bed. All the other shelled creatures that did much the same.

"I think that long ago, maybe billions of years, this ocean had lots of dissolved mahabhavium salts. Then *some* living thing sucked it out and turned it into mahabhavium silicide. For some reason it formed nodules. They've been around ever since – and that's where all the mahabhavium went."

"Sandy. Carolina." I said. "You're the xenology experts, and that's a good theory, but living organisms aren't the only things that can do chemistry on a planetary scale. I have a suggestion I'd like to run by you."

"Then run it, Ray."

"This planet has a lot of mahabhavium. It also has a lot of nitrogen in its atmosphere. Hydrogen and oxygen in the water. There are massive silicate storms that generate powerful lightning flashes, which would help to produce more complex molecules.

"Mahabhavium nitrate dissolves in water, so it should exist in the ocean. It *is* there, but in far lower concentrations than I'd expect. But we do find it in these nodules, in proportions that would send any earthly miner into ecstasy.

"Plutonium combines with silicon to form plutonium silicide, formula $PuSi$. A simple two-atom molecule. It's grey in colour, and it precipitates out of solution because it's not soluble in water. Extrapolating, mahabhavium silicide – $MbSi$ – ought to be similar, but even less soluble. Similarly grey, though a different shade. Karoubicanes are storms of silicate sand. I'm wondering whether they've been dumping huge amounts of silicon into the ocean, and it's reacted with the nitrate. Probably been going on for billions of years, so now there's hardly any nitrate left in solution."

"All of it converted into insoluble mahabhavium silicide?"

"Exactly. I think the nodules were precipitated from the ocean by purely chemical action. They start as a small seed; then other stuff accumulates on it. I bet if we sliced a nodule open we'd see lots of concentric layers." When Rickart frowned, I quickly added: "Not that it matters.

"Chemical deposition doesn't explain the ritual dances, of course," I said.

"No reason why it should," Carolina said. "I agree, your theory would explain the rest just as well as ours. And it's probably more plausi–"

"All very interesting, I'm sure," Rickart interrupted. "But all we need is the bottom line. The stuff we want is spread all over the ocean floor. In the shallows, thankfully. Easy to grab. Ten kilos of the pure metal would make the GU delirious with joy, whatever our mission parameters call for. Fifty are entirely within our reach. All we need is to build submersibles than can trawl the nodules off the seabed and load their catch into an OWLL. Then we can bring it up. When we decide we've got enough, we can complete the Da Silva drive and scoot for home."

Wazmakai grunted and rushed off out of the room. Her voice floated back along the corridor.

"On it!"

CHAPTER 31

SEND AN OWLL

Fiona Rickart

Karoubi's Planet 2572

My faith in the ingenuity of *Star Pyramid*'s people turned out to have been justified, though not without a few false turns, dead ends, and other obstacles along the way. The corridors were buzzing again, but this time buzzing with ideas. Most of them sensible, though few worth taking any further. Of those, two or three were gold dust.

For a while it seemed as if every solution we found caused new problems, the Lernean Hydra raising its ugly head once more. Though its ability to regenerate several heads when one was chopped off was a later addition to the myth, Gayl tells me. First appearing in the works of Euripides. (Is there *any* subject that woman is ignorant about?)

Fortunately, Wazmakai, Salomé Blanchet, and their people in Engineering started to get on top of the proliferation of difficulties, and the ocean of Karoubi's Planet ceased to play the role of the Lake of Lerna where the terrible Hydra made its lair. This train of thought did make me worry that there might be real monsters in the ocean, since we knew so little about the planet's ecology. After all, we still knew very little about what was in the *Earth's* ocean. But there wasn't much we could do about it if they were there, and it was pointless to worry if they weren't.

Anyway, so far things were working out pretty well.

I won't bore you with a detailed account of exactly how we (I say 'we' but it was mainly the engineers) put everything together, dropped it safely to the surface in the right place, assembled it remotely, but I will say that we made heavy use of a lot of stuff on L, P, and T Decks.

All of the activity centred around one of the OWLLs, now sitting serenely on a sandy beach with the strange slow waves of the alien ocean lapping just down the beach from its landing gear. We had chosen that area because it was close to the heaviest concentration of nodules that we'd been able to find, near any flat space wide enough to land an OWLL. Better still, the locality showed no sign of previous flash flooding. It wouldn't be great if there was a heavy storm and our equipment got washed into the sea.

Getting the OWLL there hadn't been straightforward. They land on a tripod of shock-absorbing legs designed for firm ground. Wazmakai and Salomé were worried about landing on, and taking off from, sand. Possibly damp sand. They sent down a modified drone to test how firm the proposed landing zone was, and the results were encouraging. The sand was mixed with larger stones, which formed a firm layer underneath, consolidated by smaller particles trickling down between them. Rain and wave action had compressed the sand and this underlying layer. It would support the weight of the OWLL and its eventual cargo.

This wasn't good enough for either Wazmakai or Salomé, so it wasn't good enough for me.

They drew up a plan to modify the OWLL. They (well, their team) cut apart the landing strut supports and welded in new sections to give the tripod a wider base. They removed the pads on which the struts would rest, built new ones with three times the diameter, and attached them in their place. Now the OWLL ought to be stable even on less compact sand.

They were also worried about the engines churning up the sand, so they fitted baffles to divert the exhaust sideways. Normally that wouldn't have been feasible, but the gravity on Karoubi's Planet was low, even lower than on Earth's Moon, so the reduction in thrust was tolerable.

The mods had done the trick. The OWLL was down, upright, and the exhaust had made an irregular crater around it far enough away for safety, instead of digging a big hole right underneath it. The equipment we'd sent down smoothed the sand again to get rid of the crater, which would have impeded loading, and we were all set.

Out in the bay, amphibian surface craft were taking advantage of the calm weather to hoover nodules off the seabed and deposit them in their none-too-capacious holds. When they'd filled the holds to the maximum safe level they returned to the beach and rolled straight up on to it on wheels with wide inflated tyres, designed to spread the weight and avoid getting bogged down.

They then lined up beside the OWLL, where a conveyor belt under a rainproof canopy directed the nodules into the cargo bay. Once emptied, they returned to the sea for another load.

We'd already loaded 1140 kilos, 75% of the OWLL's capacity

and enough to provide the GU with 44 kilos of pure mahabhavium, nine times what they'd happily settle for. There was no shortage of accessible nodules. I'd been worried that the caltrops might interfere with operations, and we had the drones ready for laser patrols, not that I liked that option. However, they were staying away. Scared by all the activity, Carolina and Sandy reckoned, but that was no more than a guess.

Everything looked rosy.

We could have brought the OWLL back up and sent it or another one back for more, but it seemed better to carry on while the weather held, because any interruption to loading now would mean we'd have to set everything up again. So I ordered the nodule collection to continue.

"All our eggs in one basket?" Clapham protested.

"They're not eggs, Michael, and OWLLs are more reliable than baskets."

That was true.

Even so, it was the wrong decision.

* * *

Worried about karoubicanes and flash floods, I failed to take other natural disasters into account.

We did have a few seismometers, placed by the science team using drones. They hadn't turned up anything remotely alarming; Karoubi's Planet was remarkably quiet, seismically speaking. Until the earthquake. Well, karoubiquake.

Even then, we didn't worry. The epicentre was on the far side of the planet from our OWLL operations, and the 'quake was low-magnitude. There would be some disturbance of the ocean, but with the bigger islands damping down the waves, the ocean couldn't support a sizeable tsunami over distances of thousands of kilometres. Even so, I was about to order the OWLL to lift off, just in case, when Meteorology noticed that a distant karoubicane had stirred up a huge cloud of sand in the upper atmosphere, smack in the flight path. With a nearly full load and limited fuel, the OWLL couldn't return to *Star Pyramid* without running into thick clouds of abrasive sand. And there was no point in moving it, since the conditions where it went would be much the same as those where it already was. So we decided it should stay put.

By the time Clapham figured out what was going to happen, it was too late.

What none of us had realised was that because nearly all of the surface was water, shallow waves from the 'quake would travel right round the planet. The islands were so small that the waves would just diffract past them, starting to pile up at the antipodal point.

About a hundred and twenty kilometres from our precious OWLL.

It's a well-known effect. It created a jumble of rough terrain at Mercury's Caloris basin when a large meteor smashed into it and the planet in effect focused the seismic waves on the opposite side.

"How high will the focused waves be?" I asked.

"Not very. About a metre when it gets to the OWLL."

"Speed?"

"Slow, like all the waves here."

Didn't sound dangerous. "The OWLL's engines are three metres off the ground, well above the waves. The water will just wash harmlessly round the landing struts," Wazmakai said.

The waves did exactly that.

Except for the 'harmlessly' bit.

* * *

"Stuck? How can it be stuck?"

"Karoubi's Planet has no moon," Wazmakai said.

"What's that got to do with it?"

"No moon means no tides."

"So?"

"No tides means the sea level hardly changes, so the sand doesn't consolidate as uniformly as I'd expected. The rain's too gentle to have much effect." She hit her head with her hand. "*Idiot!*"

"Don't blame yourself. No one anticipated this."

She shot me a tearful look, as if to say 'That doesn't let me off the hook'. So I placed both hands on her shoulders.

"Wazmakai, it's *not your fault*. It's this whole fu– godforsaken system! It's crazy."

She made a wry grimace. "I still feel guilty."

"Maybe we're not *meant* to have mahabhavium," I said.

That brought her out of her self-pitying wallow. "Don't be stupid, Fiona. I don't believe in destiny, and neither do you!"

I grinned.

"You set me up!"

I did. It worked.

"It was firm enough to hold the OWLL," I said. "We checked."

"Was. It still is. But in between, when the waves rushed past, it wasn't. The sand beneath the landing strut bases swirled around too, and they sank into the sand. Not far, but the sand was softer under one of the struts and the OWLL has tilted. If the tilt had been four degrees or less it would still be safe for takeoff, but it's six degrees."

"So we send down another OWLL. Transfer the nodules into it, keep going."

"Of course. One snag. Dumping them in is easier than heaving them out again. Oh, for a cargo-bot! The equipment down there can't handle that."

"So send down something that can."

"That will take too long. The OWLL might sink further. If it tips over it could explode. We need to act fast or we've got a huge mess and we're out one OWLL. There are probably going to be aftershocks. And Sylvia's Meteorology group says there's a fair chance of that karoubicane hitting if we take too long to complete the job."

"Oh, great. What about sending a cable and a winch?"

Wazmakai was already gesturing at an HV dais. "That's exactly what I'm setting up, even as we speak. But the situation is too delicate to deal with remotely. Machinery could disturb the sand."

"You're saying…?"

"Our hands are tied. We've got to send some people to sort it out. We'll need volunteers."

Way ahead of you. "Already got them."

* * *

Wazmakai was livid. "You're sending *Reynheiður Sigmundsdóttir*? After what she did? We can't trust her."

"Quatermain says we can. The Psych Team's done brain scans, truth tests, everything. They know the methods RAG uses to get round brain scans, and they've had enough time now to rule them out. Anyway, she did *two* things, remember?"

"Sure. Saved our arses. *After* three of us were killed by her goons."

"I didn't mean that. I was referring to how she dealt with Shegwada. But you're right, she did those things too. She's desperate to make amends. Since I have to risk *someone*, I'd rather risk *her*."

"I still say we can't trust her."

I raised a finger, school-marm style. "I know what I'm doing, Wazmakai. She's not going on her own. Janice Leiter has volunteered to go with her."

"Who's Janice Leiter?"

"She's on the list as a recycling specialist. Which I suppose she is."

"Suppose? Not following you."

"Her real name is Suzanna Mardeen, usually known as Zanna; her rank is Colonel. She's a RAG enforcer. She recruited Reynheiður."

Wazmakai blew her top. "A *RAG enforcer?* Operating under a false name? I thought Sigmundsdóttir and her squad were the only GU goons on board. Now you tell me there's another one. RAG people are seriously scary. Closest thing the GU has to secret police."

Oh, no. There are some much closer than that.

"That's why Mardeen is perfect for this task. The only other person on board I'd not be upset to lose. The only people who know what she really is are me, you, and Reynheiður Sigmundsdóttir. She doesn't know Mardeen is on board, but of course she'll recognise her when they meet. Mardeen was kept on ice until a week ago. When everybody was reanimated I made sure she remained tucked away out of sight, off the official crew-list. She's combat-hardened, knows Reynheiður backwards— and she'll have weapons. Reynheiður won't."

"It just gets worse, Fiona. A GU sleeper and an *armed* RAG enforcer. Are you mad?"

"Calm down, Wazmakai. I believe we can trust Reynheiður to carry out this task. Her sister was committed to the Project, and she feels guilty about Hjördis's death. She'll do everything in her power to make the sacrifice meaningful. As for Mardeen, she's now under orders from the GU to assist us in every way she can. They're bowing to the inevitable and accepting that our plan is the only way they'll ever lay their grubby little paws on any mahabhavium."

Wazmakai clearly remained unconvinced, but it wasn't her call. "I've got a horrible feeling that something will go wrong."

"Wazmakai: I can't run *Star Pyramid* on feelings."

Perhaps I should've done, because she was right.

But it wasn't what any of us had been expecting.

* * *

They'd taken a second OWLL down and landed half a kilometre along the beach from the first. There hadn't been time to modify its landing struts or attach engine baffles, but it didn't have a heavy payload, reducing the risk. It did blast a bit of a hole in the sand, but Mardeen was an excellent pilot and was ready to take off again if the landing proved unstable.

"I don't like the look of this," Sylvia said, peering closely at a series of false-colour HV grids, annotated with arcane symbols.

Not words I particularly welcomed. "*Another* problem?"

"Not yet, but brewing. Potentially. The karoubicane's on a heading that's much too close for comfort."

"Will it hit the landing site?"

"Hard to tell, sorry. Hurricane paths are notoriously unpredictable, and it's no different on an alien planet. But my gut feeling is, it's quite likely."

I did the prudent thing. "OK, Sylvia, point made. We'll cut our losses and settle for the current load of nodules. When back on board and refined, that'll produce almost 44 kilos of mahabhavium."

Enough already.

Mardeen and Hjördis had persuaded Reynheiður to sign up for the voyage, so Mardeen had always known she was on board. Reynheiður showed little surprise that Mardeen was. They made a good team. They'd worked together before, and they gave every appearance of having put their past differences behind them for the greater good. They'd inspected the damaged OWLL, taking care not to disturb the sand around it, and attached a strong cable to one of the mountings used to strap it down during the voyage. The other end was wrapped round a powerful winch, bolted firmly to solid bedrock and secured by a dozen other cables splayed out on the far side to take the strain, also bolted to bedrock.

It had been hard work, especially in suits.

They checked everything twice, and Wazmakai did the same from the remote readouts. She'd simulated the whole operation, and it ought to work provided the sand underneath the OWLL held no more surprises.

"Weather forecast, Sylvia?" I said.

"The karoubicane's strengthening and the wind's rising. We're within the computed safety margin for time, but it's very tight now. Getting tighter by the minute."

I didn't need to tell them this made the whole operation far more perilous. All we could do now was hold our collective breath, hoping the cable wouldn't break, the winch would hold, that it wouldn't jam. Sweat trickled down my spine.

It was working. So far. Millimetre by millimetre, the OWLL's sunken strut began to rise. Imperceptibly, the craft began tilting back to the vertical. Wazmakai's instruments were giving us the exact figures.

Already fine dust was swirling around, obscuring the view. The waves were changing their pattern, longer gaps between them, slightly higher peaks. Strange beat patterns.

Wazmakai signalled the all-clear. "Near enough to vertical. OWLL-1: you are cleared for takeoff." Even now she hadn't lost her sense of humour, and it broke the tension.

We can do this.

The next step was the most crucial, and the most likely to fail. She prepped the pre-programmed sequence on her dais.

There was no time to shore up the raised strut as originally planned. We didn't dare put a pilot inside, because the change in weight could disturb the delicate balance of forces, but we didn't need to. The plan had always been to take off under remote control. The difficult bit was that the cable had to keep taking the strain until the OWLL had started to lift off and its rockets were supporting its weight. Then, and only then, would an explosive bolt disconnect the cable. It was basically a standard manoeuvre, common throughout the era of spaceflight, though performed in unusual circumstances.

Mardeen and Sigmundsdóttir beat a rapid retreat, far enough away to be safe from an explosion if the heavily loaded OWLL toppled. As soon as they reached a safe distance they hunkered down behind the rocks. Wazmakai activated the automatic sequence, the rockets fired, and after a heartstopping wobble the OWLL stabilised and began to rise. With a sharp *crack!* the bolt detonated. The cable, under huge stresses, whipped back, and the winch was pulled out from its fastenings.

But the OWLL was on its way!

Half-hidden behind the dustclouds of the approaching silicate storm, its rockets flaring, it rose steadily, taking its precious cargo with it.

"All systems on OWLL-1 nominal," Wazmakai said calmly. "Bit of a wobble at plus 2.3, but the gyros dealt with it. Rendezvous with *Star Pyramid* in 7 minutes 11 seconds."

While all this was going on, Mardeen and Sigmundsdóttir had emerged from their protective rocks and climbed into OWLL-2. They would launch under their own control, although Wazmakai could step in with automatics if necessary.

"What the hell is taking them so long?" I said.

"Dunno," Wazmakai replied. "Nothing's wrong, they're just delaying takeoff."

"That's a very bad idea when there's a karoubicane heading their way." I sent a verbal order. "Lift off immediately!"

There was no reply, and no sign they were complying.

"Do you have visual feed from inside the cabin?" I asked Wazmakai.

"No. It's not been activated. No audio either. That's a bit strange. But they don't have time to run through the usual checklist, they're omitting anything inessential."

"Then why are they still on the ground? The wind is getting really nasty now."

"No idea– ah, there she goes!"

The video from one of the drones showed OWLL-2 lifting off as sand swirled crazily around it. Then the video went black.

"Drone out," Wazmakai said. "Smashed by the wind, I imagine. But OWLL-2 is out of the danger zone. Some clever piloting there, the wind was shoving it all over the place."

"They're both brilliant pilots," I said. "I wonder which of them was flying her."

"Neither," Wazmakai said in a puzzled voice. "It lifted on autopilot."

* * *

OWLL-1 acquired low orbit, matching our position and velocity, and we readied Shuttle Bay 3 to receive her.

With the mahabhavium nodules now safely within our grasp, we were past the danger point, and I started to relax.

"No comm from OWLL-2," Wazmakai said.

"There wasn't before they lifted. Could be just a fault. Bring it into Bay 4, and we'll find out what happened."

I left it to Jacobson to deal with OWLL-1 and its precious cargo. I was much more concerned about my crew, and hurried over to Bay 4.

The bay doors shut, air flooded in.

Wazmakai opened the main hatch. No one came out.

"I'll go in," said one of the security guards. A few seconds later: "One of them's here. Let me– ah, the tag says it's Colonel Mardeen."

"What about Sigmundsdóttir?"

"Only the one. She must still be down on the planet."

In the middle of a silicate storm? No one can survive that.

We got Mardeen out. She was alive but unconscious. I had her sent straight to sick bay.

* * *

"Knock-out gas," Doctor Raphson said. "Someone sprayed it into the Colonel's suit using one of the emergency air nozzles."

"Sigmundsdóttir," I said stupidly. *Who else?*

"Must've been."

"But why?"

"Colonel Mardeen may be able to tell us more when she wakes up. It was xenofluorane, by the way. Standard issue. We have a lot of it on board."

Not quite as much as we did. "How long till she comes round?"

"Best to let her sleep it off. Ninety minutes. But she'll be woozy at first. I'd wait at least two hours."

I waited three. As Rowley Pollard often says, 'there's no rush'. But events moved faster than that. I'd hardly left sick bay when Pollard buzzed me.

"Sigmundsdóttir left a recorded message on the computer, to be released when she failed to return. You need to hear it. Shall I flick it over?"

"No, I'll come to you."

It was a short message, recorded in haste. I'll just give you the gist.

Reynheiður Sigmundsdóttir was suffering from a huge guilt complex. Not just from being instrumental, however inadvertently, in the death of her sister; not even for the others who'd died. From the lies she'd had to tell, the secrets she'd had to conceal.

She'd been right all along when she hid away in Shuidaoyuanzhongchang, wherever the fuck that was.

She'd tried to redeem herself by volunteering to go down to Karoubi's Planet. But in the end, that hadn't eased her guilt. So she'd decided not to come back.

* * *

When the high winds had died down, I sent OWLL-2 back, just in case Reynheiður had survived. She was resilient and resourceful, one of RAG's best. Miracles can happen.

Not this time.

The body had probably been blown into the ocean. It could be a hundred kilometres way.

Rickarts never weep. Not in public.

CHAPTER 32

TECHNOLOGY TRAP

Carolina Moreira

Karoubi's Star 2572

Fiona had invited fifteen of us to her luxurious private quarters for a quiet, informal chat.

This was highly suspicious. Rickart seldom did informal, and even less often did she let anyone into her personal space. So I was expecting something important, disguised as an informal chat, and I wasn't disappointed.

"Before we start the main business of this – uh – chat," she said, "I want to assure you that this room is bug-free. If the GU still has snoops on board – which, by the way, I'm confident they don't – it will *not* be informed of this discussion. Though it will be informed of what it may lead to. I'll make sure of that."

That did kind of confirm my suspicions.

"As a precaution, RAG Colonel Suzanna Mardeen – some of you may know her as Janice Leiter – has been confined to quarters under close observation. I don't want to risk any interference from the GU at this stage, and she understands that. Not why, though; not yet."

More confirmation. Something incendiary was afoot.

"I want your candid opinion on an issue that can't fail to be highly controversial. I'd like to pick your collective brains before I run it past all the other Flight Controllers. If they're amenable, I'll put it to a vote of all the crew."

What the hell is she up to?

Rickart didn't *look* nervous. She seldom did. But I was watching her hands, and she kept interlacing her fingers and parting them again. She also hesitated before expanding on her opening remark, which was unusual for someone so decisive.

"I don't think I'm exaggerating when I say that humanity stands at a crossroads. This may be the most significant event in human history."

"I just *love* these informal discussions," Pollard said.

Fiona waved a hand. "Sorry, Rowley, but I didn't want to arouse suspicion."

"If that was the aim, it failed," said Quatermain. "No one's talking about anything other than the Admiral's mysterious meeting."

Rickart grunted. "I rather expected that. Still, I had to try.

"Despite everything that Fate threw at us, our mission has been a success. Jacobson has decontaminated both OWLLs and the nodules, and his team has already produced enough pure mahabhavium to complete *Star Pyramid*'s Da Silva drive. Salomé Blanchet is overseeing the fabrication of the necessary cavity as we speak."

"Then we can go home!" Gayl cried.

Rickart nodded. "We can. The question is—"

"Whether we should," Clapham finished for her.

Shocked faces all round.

As Rickart glared at him, he ducked his head. "Sorry, Fiona. But you're not the only one with misgivings about the Project. I shouldn't've interrupted, but it sort of slipped out."

"But surely, the whole point of this mission is—" Pallendorf began.

"The point *was*," Clapham said. "Doesn't have to be, now."

"But—"

"I very much regret having to say this, but Michael's right," Fiona said. "A lot of things have happened since we set out from Earth, and the word in the corridors is that many of our people are losing confidence in the GU and questioning the purpose of our mission."

Too right. The doubts have been growing for years.

"You've all heard the unofficial but uncensored reports of events back on the homeworld. When we lost most of the freewave antenna all messages had to be short and snappy, but those reports are still trickling in, one steganographic bit at a time, and the story they're telling is dire. Earth is going to hell in a handbasket. While the GU's *still* sending us compact versions of those cheerful little homilies, having just about got over its snit when we refused to exterminate the caltrops, the reality is even worse than you've heard.

"I know that these unofficial reports are being leaked. Bound to, I'm the one leaking them. But I haven't leaked the worst ones."

She waited for that to sink in.

"Such as?" Quatermain asked.

"Two border skirmishes have gone nuclear within the last three months. One in SouMerica, Paraguay-Uruguay. The other between India and Pakistan. Over Kashmir, as always."

More shocked faces. Shaking heads. Mine among them.

"How bad?" said Pollard.

"Tactical nukes only, so far. But they've caused three million deaths in SouMerica, five million on the Indian subcontinent. Three times as many casualties – burns, radiation poisoning. The fallout will destroy millions of hectares of arable land, making the famines even worse. Global temperatures have already dropped two degrees.

"Worse, there's a growing danger that the Democratic Republic of Free China will be dragged into the conflict. Radioactive fallout has already caused the evacuation of several cities in Reunified Tibet – which, fortunately, has no nukes – and the provinces of Yunnan and Sichuan. If the DRFC starts firing off ICBMs it'll be Armageddon.

"The inner Solar System is now a Balkanised patchwork of mutually hostile militarised zones, as far out as Jupiter. Several nations have armed fleets, patrolling to protect their interests in the asteroid belt. Clashes are inevitable, and each one has repercussions back on the homeworld. Basically, the politicians are all screaming at each other and making wild threats. Most nations have degenerated into repressive police states. Democracy is just a sham.

"*That*, people, is on top of the catalogue of disasters that have been happening almost every month for the past 150 years. Droughts, famines, floods, hurricanes. Crime levels up everywhere. Mass shootings at record levels. Riots, looting, kidnaps, murder. Plagues, some new, plus many that we thought had been eradicated, now back in force thanks to anti-vaxxers, religious extremists, overpopulation, poverty, and sheer bloody stupidity. Not to mention suspected biowarfare."

"But that's the *point*, Fiona!" Pallendorf said, angry and loud. "Of the Project. To provide easy access to unbounded resources, so that Earth can tackle all those problems!"

Clapham laughed. "That's what they told us, Kyril, yes. But the problems were never really about resources as such. More about resource *distribution*. But above all, about *power*. God, guns, and greed: three political axes that *ought* to be orthogonal, but have always been aligned, because they represent three mutually reinforcing paths to power over one's fellow humans."

"I'll say no more," Rickart said. "Michael has summed it up admirably. We need to decide where to go from here. Can we trust Earth with mahabhavium? Can we be sure they'll use it wisely?"

I put a hand up. I'd been thinking along the same lines myself, and Fiona's stark description was far worse than anything I'd suspected. It tipped me over the edge.

"Michael and Fiona are right," I said. "But Fiona asked the wrong question. It's not about doubt that Earth will use mahabhavium wisely. It's about the certainty that they won't. The first alien life ever found, and they wanted to kill it. When we refused, they started to kill *us*. We have to ask ourselves: do we *really* dare release such creatures into the cosmos?"

Several people started to argue with us, all shouting at once. Gustav Schröder, one of the support staff, said: "You're only saying that, Carolina, because you're a xenologist. Worried more about your precious caltrops than–"

"You're out of order, Schröder," Fiona said. "You're *all* out of order. Shut up!"

I'd never seen her so angry. Normally she hid her emotions.

"I *said* I wanted us to *discuss* this. Not fight about it. Look at yourselves! Then multiply by a billion. You're making Michael's point for him."

"Let me get this straight," Pallendorf said. "Michael and Carolina are suggesting that after 450 years of global effort by most of the human race–"

"Fifty years effort, 400 going to the dogs," Clapham said sourly.

"Michael: you shut up, too," Rickart said. "Let Kyril speak."

"Sorry, Fiona. Sorry, Kyril."

"–now that we've finally laid hands on the mahabhavium, we *don't* give it to Earth?" Pallendorf finished.

Clapham nodded. Waited a second to see whether anyone was going to answer. When no one did, he said: "That's exactly what I'm suggesting."

"Seconded," I said.

"Not just them," Rickart said. "It's what I'm suggesting, too, as I'm sure you've already deduced."

"Admiral, you can't mean that. This is treason." Pallendorf had gone red in the face, fists clenched, jaw thrust out in a parody of the alpha male.

Jessica Wilson, one of our anaesthetists, covertly pointed a finger at Pallendorf making an exhibition of himself. She gave a brief nod and poked her neighbour in the ribs. Whispered in his ear.

Pallendorf didn't realise it, but the more he behaved like that, the more his case would crumble to dust.

Rickart tried to calm him. "Kyril, please stop shouting. You won't advance your viewpoint that way. Quite the reverse.

"The nearest law court is 378 light years away, and no one can get closer than that unless we give them the means to do it. We're on our own out here. If you insist on bandying points of legality around, Earth has no jurisdiction outside the Solar System. Even there, the treaties are not universally recognised. We're free agents in the most intense meaning of the phrase. Only *we* have the power to decide humanity's future. It can either be the same as its present, spreading uncontrollably across the entire Galaxy, or it can be different."

Pallendorf sat down, face still red, but possibly for a different reason.

"Could we – er – *persuade* Earth to change? Tell them we're withholding the mahabhavium until they demilitarise?" Quatermain said. When everyone stared at him he backtracked. "Just playing Devil's advocate. People like that can't be trusted."

"Actually," Rickart said, "something along those lines might be possible. About two centuries from now."

"But what gives *us* the right to decide?" Khloe Mandrapilias said.

"*We*," Rickart pointed out, "have the mahabhavium."

Khloe clenched her fists in anger. "Just now you complained about power! Now you want to exert it yourself!"

She nodded. "*Realpolitik*, Khloe."

"I wasn't asking about power. I was asking about rights."

Rickart hesitated; Khloe's point had struck home.

"I'm sorry. You were, and you deserve a proper answer. We have the right because *someone* has to face up to this issue, and we are the only people in the universe who can actually affect the course of history. You all know the GU slogan, it's been dinned into us. *Earth first*. I've got a better one: *Humanity first*. Not just in the sense of *Homo sapiens*, but in the sense of compassion towards our fellow creatures. And right now we are humanity, in both senses, because Earth's leaders have forfeited any right to that title and the rest have no say any more.

"I don't want us to be responsible for doing even more damage to the lives of billions of honest, ordinary people. I don't want our efforts – humanity's efforts – to be squandered by greed and arrogance. The Project, as presented to the public, was always a fraud. Look at how the GU reacted when we refused to use antimatter to vaporise the oceans of Karoubi's Planet!"

"Woke up a bunch of thugs, killed three of us," said Schröder. "Plus three of their own."

I hadn't expected that from him; it was an interesting straw in the wind.

"They would've killed almost everyone on board if they had to," I said. Apparently we were now both on the same side. *The side of the angels?* I hoped so.

"Mahabhavium in the hands of people like that will do *nothing* for the majority of the citizens of Earth," Clapham said. "The ruling elite *always* had the power to improve everybody's lives, but Gustav's just reminded us of what they've actually done. The only thing that giving Earth mahabhavium will achieve is to put immense, unstoppable power into the hands of those who are currently abusing it. That's what the Project was *always* for, it's why it got the go-ahead in the first place. It wasn't some supreme act of altruism. It was too *expensive* ever to be that."

Pallendorf pursed his lips, let out a deep breath. "It's a point of view, Michael." He breathed in, sighed. "You've half-convinced me, to be frank. I've had such misgivings myself, but I kept telling myself that I was over-reacting. However, we can't just abandon Earth's people, Fiona. That would be to join their oppressors."

It was her turn to nod. "That's not what I'm about to propose. We've abandoned them for four centuries, and we'll have to continue for a few more. There's no way round that. But in the longer run, we will have a golden opportunity to *save* the Earth."

I've learned to be wary of politicians who claimed to be handing out golden opportunities. Somehow the gold always flows towards *them*.

But this was Fiona.

"All I want from you," she continued, "is a straw poll. Should we do that? Should we withhold the mahabhavium until we can find a way to use it wisely? And what I also want is to hear as many arguments as you can brainstorm about why we should and why we shouldn't. I'm only going to put this proposal to a vote if I have a solid idea that it'll fly. So I need to hear the best arguments, both ways.

"You want us to follow GU orders? Convince me that we should. Ditto if you don't.

"Now, get your brains in gear and advise me. Do I tell everyone we're taking the mahabhavium back to Earth as planned? Or do I tell them we should go against the GU and use it to save the Galaxy from the human race, and the human race from itself?"

* * *

The rumours spread around the ship like wildfire. No way to stop that, and none of us wanted to. It would cause trouble, but people had to work their way through it. Announcing it and immediately putting it to a vote would just elicit gut reactions. We wanted those out of the way before the vote was taken.

There were fights, verbal and physical. A dozen people ended up in sick bay with broken bones. One had been stabbed with a steak knife, fortunately missing anything vital. The perpetrator was locked up until they calmed down. There'd have to be a trial eventually, but now wasn't the time. Security squads prowled the corridors, trying to anticipate violence and squash it before it snowballed. And every time there was a violent act, it strengthened the anti-GU argument: if *we*, the cream of the crop, behave like this, what would Earth's leaders do?

* * *

Clapham had been digging into the archives. He'd found a transcript of an old meeting between Joel Krantz and Thekla Maury. Circulation had originally been limited because it cast doubt on the motivation behind the Project, but since the GU could no longer interfere he'd put a segment of it up for public consumption, with added commentary.

Maury had been telling Krantz that the Project was just one gigantic boondoggle, albeit one with a worthy aim: unifying the world. But that wasn't the part Clapham wanted to emphasise. It was their discussion of transformative technology.

Her recorded voice sounded as fresh as if she'd said it yesterday. So was her message.

"It's a common thread throughout human history. Transformative tech always looks wonderful at first when all its advantages strike home. Then, just when it's infiltrated its seductive way into just about everything, we discover we've made a bargain with the Devil."

Clapham's comment was succinct and pointed.

"Mahabhavium is transformative technology."

Later he posted another segment.

"At first the new gizmo can do such fantastic things that no one asks the hard questions. What are the side effects? How can it be abused? So regulation is light, on the grounds that anything heavier would stifle the nascent industries at birth. The gizmo corporations flourish, spread, take over their competitors. By the time the government decides to start regulating them, they're too big to control. By the time the downsides become inescapable it's impossible to get rid of the tech, even when it becomes virtually unusable."

"Thekla Maury was a prophet," Clapham said. "Think of fossil fuels. Think of the OuterNet, ruined by malware. Think of the UnderNet, a powerful resource for criminals that we inflicted on ourselves.

"Think what will happen with mahabhavium. Don't just think about the good it might do: think about the potential harm it *will* do.

"I call it the technology trap.

"Let's not fall into it *again*."

* * *

The auditorium could hold 740 people. Twelve seats were empty: Rickart on the podium and eleven deaths; two medical, one an accident, *seven* by violence, and one suicide. Not a pretty ratio, as the empty seats, deliberately collected into a block, mutely emphasised.

The discussion was 'lively', as they say.

Pallendorf wanted a compromise. Why not return to the Solar System, leave a package of mahabhavium and tell Earth where it was, and jump back out before anyone could show up? But this amendment was voted down. The argument against seemed to be that it would weaken us without solving the underlying problem; the vote was much closer than I expected, and a lot of people voted against it because they wanted us to go home and hand over the goodies. The rest voted against it because they didn't.

I glanced at Rickart, made eye contact, shook my head. She knew what it meant. *Too close for comfort. This could split us right down the middle.*

I needn't have worried. As always, Rickart was on top of things.

"There's a viewpoint that hasn't yet been aired," she said. "Colonel Mardeen: I believe there's something you wish to tell us."

I could feel the sudden tension in the air. *Ask a GU goon what she thinks about betraying Earth?*

Mardeen stood up. Her air of confident arrogance had long faded. She looked tired, yet determined.

"You all know that I was a RAG enforcer for the GU. That gives me a different take on the situation we're in.

"You're expecting me to side with the Global Union. That's my job. Rather, it *was* my job. I could bang on about how the incessant catalogue of disasters, on Earth and on this ship, awoke something in me that I hadn't known was there. About realising that the GU had been exploiting me all along, just as it had been exploiting everyone it touched. That the real criminal isn't so much GU officialdom as the GU itself: the organisation, not the people. It's like a religion started by fraudsters that acquires its own momentum, so that the priesthood, originally in on the scam, end up believing all the nonsense themselves. And when the fraudsters die, they leave a self-perpetuating meme."

The auditorium was a babble of noise now, with some shouting. *This wasn't what anyone had expected.*

Rickart called for order. Mardeen waited patiently for the hubbub to cease.

"I *could* tell you that," she said. "I guess I just did, but how *I* feel isn't what I want you to understand. During my time in RAG I've seen *exactly* how the GU operates. I warn you now: if *Star Pyramid* returns to Earth, *every single one of you will be in deadly danger.*"

More noise, eventually dying down of its own accord.

"What do you imagine awaits you if we go back? I know, it's been brainwashed into you from the day you were assigned to the Project. You're expecting a hero's welcome. Interviews, parades, awards, all the usual razzmatazz. After all, you're the courageous people who battled against all odds and saved the Earth.

"I'm telling you now, it won't be like that.

"The moment *Star Pyramid* arrives back in the Solar System, you'll be surrounded by military vessels. You can jump away, but then, you might as well not have gone there to start with. If you don't, they'll board the ship and take control of everything. You'll never come within a million kilometres of the media. If you're lucky, they'll spirit you away somewhere you'll never see the light of day. More likely they'll kill the lot of you, once they've interrogated you to extract every gram of information."

Total silence.

Rickart broke it. "Why do you think that?"

"I don't *think* it, I know it. Let me tell you why. In the GU's eyes we're all traitors. We lied, disobeyed a vital order, risked the future of the planet, killed GU operatives... the list is long. More significantly, the GU will be desperate to conceal the order to exterminate the caltrops, and what their hit squad did when we disobeyed. They can't allow a single one of us to reveal the truth."

"I don't see how that can be right," Pallendorf said. "They'd have to make it public that *Star Pyramid* had returned with mahabhavium, or they couldn't take credit for the success of the Project. So some of us, at least, would have to appear in the media."

Mardeen snorted in disbelief. "Some *actor* would appear in the media, claiming to be one of us. Spouting whatever lies the GU found most convenient."

She sat down.

Rickart gave me a meaningful glance.

"I move that we adjourn this meeting for a hour, to allow discussion of this new information," I said. Clapham seconded the motion, and it was passed by an overwhelming majority on a simple show of hands.

At the appointed time, with the auditorium once more full, the personnel of *Star Pyramid* assembled to decide the future of the human race.

Mardeen's speech had struck home. Of the 729 people still surviving, only six voted to continue the mission as planned. Another six abstained. None of them complained when they were outvoted: they could see which way the wind was blowing.

Now that we'd decided, there was an air of anticlimax. Rickart was about to declare the meeting closed, when a quiet, unassuming woman, sixteen rows back, plucked up the courage to ask what I'd always considered to be the most important question of all but hadn't found the right opportunity to ask. Her insignia showed that her name was Sereana Reddy and she worked on L Deck, checking minor equipment in and out.

"If we're not going back to Earth, Admiral– where will we go? What will we do?"

Rickart didn't reply immediately, probably because a dramatic pause was more effective.

"We'll go back to Earth, eventually, Sereana. Maybe sooner than I think, if everything works out the way I hope. By then we'll have our own fleet of Da Silva drive ships. Nowhere near as big as this one, of course. *Star Pyramid* is so huge because we didn't know enough to make it smaller. The first sub-cee starship… and almost surely the last. A dinosaur."

"How can we possibly build a fleet?" Sereana asked. "We haven't got the space or the resources."

Rickart squared her shoulders. "We're going to find the right star system, and found a colony."

That got a reaction. A huge collective sigh; then everyone talking at once.

Rickart let the chatter continue until it died down of its own accord.

For the first time in a long while, we knew where our future lay.

"Where are we going to find a suitable planet?" Sereana asked. Before Rickart could answer, she blushed and said: "Oh, I suppose we'll be able to explore anywhere we want. I keep forgetting that, it's so hard to get used to."

"You're right," Rickart said. "There's space enough, all around us. But not the raw materials and equipment to build a fleet. So: yes, we'll explore."

"Would 729 people be a big enough gene pool?" a greying man six rows back asked.

Rickart gestured towards a thin-faced man in the audience. "Dr Amblesyde?"

The Chief Medic rose to his feet. "Big enough," he said. "Especially since we're not closely related to each other."

It was encouraging how the discussion was coming round to the practicalities of disobeying the GU, not the disobedience itself.

A Maori woman in the front row interrupted, identifying herself as Huhana. "I don't see how a colony could work, not in the long run. Oh, I know, Hydroponics provides food, and we can make more using the recyclers – but we can't do that indefinitely. A self-sustaining colony can't rely solely on advanced tech! We'd need sperm and ova for food animals, and many more plant species. All sorts of machinery that we *don't have!* Well, maybe we could make some machines, but surely not everything. And we can't build a fleet of ships out here. Not enough metal, mahabhavium aside."

"Those," Rickart said, "are serious objections.

"At least, they would be, were it not for two things I know but you don't.

"First: we won't be searching for a planet."

Murmurs all over the auditorium, but I could see that a few of them had already worked it out.

"Second: you don't know what's on Decks I and O."

"But there aren't any Decks I and O," said Huhana.

Rickart donned her inscrutable look. "Are you sure of that?"

PART SEVEN

NEW BEGINNINGS

CHAPTER 33

STARFOLK

Michael Clapham

Star Pyramid 2573

I'd figured it out. In fact, it was partly my idea. But only Fiona had known about I and O Decks, which made it a sensible idea.

Star Pyramid's builders had gone to great lengths to conceal those decks. They didn't reach all the way to the hull, or to the main concourse. They protruded in cunning ways into the surrounding decks, and they were equally huge.

Each of them contained everything you needed to start a colony. In duplicate: one set on I Deck, a larger one on O Deck. Everything from crayons for children to construction equipment and fabrication devices. Sperm and ova for agricultural animals, with the necessary machinery for *in vitro* fertilisation and subsequent development. Cocoons and parachutes to drop them to the surface of a planet or a moon. Six more OWLLs: four with five times as much carrying capacity as our current ones, plus two giants with ten times as much. No use at Karoubi's planet, unfortunately: 'some assembly needed'. Human sperm and ova, to expand the gene pool. Even though it was probably big enough already.

Lots of other useful stuff. All of it loaded covertly at L2.

This might seem impossible, but everything that came on board *Star Pyramid* was in opaque containers. Had *been* in opaque containers since it left whichever factory had made it. The containers were labelled, but the only way to check whether the labels described the contents was to open the container, and that was sealed, only to be opened by authorised personnel. The sheer quantity of containers was daunting, and the people making random checks to keep away bombs planted by terror groups were in on the deception.

Once *Star Pyramid*'s skeleton had been assembled, it had been draped in thick green plastic sheeting. Ostensibly to keep out prying eyes of the media, who had made several unauthorised flights to film the action; also to stop errant tools and components flying off into space, potentially damaging the stream of vehicles making rendezvous with the ship. Behind the green drapes, the interior structure could be changed without much difficulty. Most of the assembly was by bots, who don't ask awkward questions.

When three-metre thick toughened steel replaced the plastic sheets, all sorts of covert design changes could be implemented. And were.

I'm not saying it had been easy. But it had been done.

Why?

According to Fiona, the GU had realised that *Star Pyramid* might end up on its own. Not for the reason that had actually happened, but because they knew full well how precarious Earth's social structure was becoming.

A dozen different scenarios would easily end all life on Earth. If any of those happened, *Star Pyramid* would be a tiny cradle containing the whole of humanity, adrift on a cosmic river. But, given the opportunity, humanity could regenerate from that tiny population. Provided it could get a good enough start.

Thus began the covert Colony Programme, with the apparent stupidity of there being no I and O Decks, so stupid that no one suspected that they existed, so no one would wonder what they contained. Their presence, and the reason for it, couldn't be revealed; it was the best-kept secret of the entire Project. Public confidence would be wrecked if the GU seemed to be forecasting the End of the World. Ironically, this one decision conferred a degree of redemption on the GU. In this one respect it had shown wisdom, humility– and humanity, in the compassionate sense.

Our future now resided in those two decks.

It was only when I told Fiona my idea that she told me about them. Only then did the idea make sense. It could work!

Oh, yes. My idea? Here's a clue.

Almost every book, film, or HV about colonising space assumes that you start on a planet.

Actually, that's the most ridiculous place to choose. Stuck at the bottom of a gravity well, hard enough to get down to, almost impossible to get back up again. Why go there at all, when you're already out in space?

So what do you choose instead? A ship?

Even *Star Pyramid* was too small for that. We could use it as a long-term hotel, and grow a certain amount of food, but we couldn't manufacture big things like more ships. We couldn't farm animals. Crucially, our population couldn't *grow*.

Not a ship, then.

An artificial colony? Not a bad idea, but it takes the resources of a planet, which you don't have.

No, what you do is what Earth had already done with its furthest-flung colony.

You colonise an asteroid belt.

It's perfect. All the raw materials you'd ever want, close at hand. Well, easy to get at, even if the average distance between large bodies in an asteroid belt is a million kilometres. There are lots of smaller rocks, many more convenient for mining. Just drag them to the refinery. And we had an advantage Earth's belt hadn't. Moving stuff around is easy with a Da Silva drive: point and go. A million kilometres is next door. And there's no need to wrestle with gravity in an asteroid belt; there isn't any, not enough to worry about.

You make inflatable domes, fill them with breathable air. Mine and smelt metals. Solar panels provide all the energy you'll ever need. Hollow out an asteroid, spin it up, melt it, and create a huge habitat, like blowing glass.

The possibilities are endless.

And, yes – eventually you can find a nice planet, send stuff and people down there, and found the kind of colony that every sci-fi *aficionado* expects. But you don't *start* that way. In fact, you don't have to create ground-based colonies *ever*, but it would be a crime to waste all those juicy planets, lurking among the myriad stars.

* * *

There was one further decision to make. We'd put it off too long already.

"What are we going to tell Earth, Fiona?" I asked.

She shrugged. "Do we have to tell them anything? Why not just go silent?"

I didn't believe she meant it, it was a rhetorical question. "I'm not sure we could live with that," I said. "There's enough guilt as it is."

"Why not tell them the plan failed?" Carolina suggested. "That we couldn't get any mahabhavium? That we're trying to return home without it – see you in four hundred years?"

"That's one possibility," Rickart said. She didn't look enthusiastic.

"We should tell them the truth," I said. "We're withholding mahabhavium until they sort themselves out politically and militarily. That way we give the ordinary people hope and put

357

pressure on the leaders and the rich corporations. *Get your act together.*"

Fiona nodded, but I didn't think she was agreeing with me. She was just registering receipt of the message.

"Don't be naive, Michael" she said. "It's not what we tell the GU: it's what the GU tells everyone else. They can spin it any way they want to, and no one will be the wiser. Not until our descendants go back and renew contact. The GU could tell everyone we're traitors, I suppose, but they'd gain very little aside from deflecting some of the blame. No, I think they'll announce that they've lost contact with *Star Pyramid* and try to give the impression that the ship's been destroyed. *We* failed, *they* did everything they could.

"They certainly won't announce that we're holding a gun to their heads until they start to behave like sane adults. And since what we tell them will make zero difference to anything that happens back on Earth, we may as well tell them the truth."

* * *

The GU's pleasure at being told we had secured the mahabhavium lasted just long enough for them to send congratulations, before the next trickle of binary digits explained what we planned to do with it.

It would be an understatement to say that the GU was not pleased.

It also discovered that you can't rant effectively over a channel with severely limited bandwidth, and there's no point in doing so because nothing you can threaten will impress people 378 light years away whose close family all died more than 300 years ago. But in case they started making threats to twelfth-generation descendants, Rickart had the freewave switched off.

* * *

There's only one way to test a Da Silva drive: turn it on and see if it works.

Two main things can go wrong. You can end up in the wrong place, the *k*-field's existence wave peaks disrupted by what the theorists were calling *k*-weather. Or the ship can blow up.

The astronomers had chosen the target: a main sequence star with not just one but two lovely, dense asteroid belts. It was 1,837 light years away: three and a half times the distance that *Star Pyramid* had covered in 400 years.

On a nod from Rickart, Wazmakai pushed the big, purely symbolic, green button. Green because red was too reminiscent of nuclear launches. A button because– well, there had to be a button.

Before her finger came off the button, we were there. Loon and Kylie had been right.

The computers recorded the star's position. Began to catalogue its planets, asteroids, comets. Analyse their composition. But we weren't intending to found a colony yet.

This was just the beginning.

We celebrated. Things got pretty raucous and everyone disgraced themselves.

Then we chose the next target.

Time to explore.

Freedom.

* * *

I don't know who started it, but by the end of the tenth Da Silva location-swap (going from A to B but not passing anywhere between – there *is* no between in a karmabhumi field) we'd acquired the habit of referring to ourselves as Starfolk.

To distinguish ourselves from the rest of humanity.

I doubted the name would stick.

* * *

"So the GU loses out," Gayl said.

We were having a quiet drink in one of the bars on H Deck. Right now, *Star Pyramid* was orbiting a beautiful gas giant about 170,000 light years from Earth in the Large Magellanic Cloud. They'd see it as being in the constellation Cygnus, or rather, they would if it hadn't been hidden behind the dark clouds of the Cygnus Rift. The bar's HV dais now displayed glorious images with characteristic bands of cloud and occasional oval swirls the size of the Earth. Nothing much happening, but that was OK, it was still spectacular viewing. Relaxing, too, and we could do with some of that.

Lovely as the gas giant was, we weren't planning to stay there. This system, the 23rd we'd explored so far, didn't have an asteroid belt. But one day, its five largest moons might provide comfortable places to live.

I'd taken my time answering. Didn't want to spoil the moment. But reality has a habit of intruding, and we were still coming to terms with what we'd done.

"Loses out? That's putting it mildly," I said.

Gayl and I had partially overlapped during training, but had hardly noticed each other. Unusually, we'd been animate together several times during the voyage. Over those years we'd formed a close bond, and now that the prospect of a colony was imminent, it had got closer.

We weren't the only ones. *Star Pyramid*'s crew were pairing off, ready for the day their contraceptive implants came out. Ready to be pioneers. The founder Starfolk.

Gayl sipped her drink, a mocktail concocted from the juice of an imaginary fruit, invented by the dispenser.

"Four hundred years, Michael! *Four hundred!* All wasted. We're betraying our entire race!"

I gave her a very direct look. "We are. But the alternative is to betray the entire Galaxy. The GU was always going to lose out with that attitude. The first alien life we encounter, and what did it tell us to do? Genocide!"

"According to Sandy and Carolina's latest assessment, caltrops aren't intelligent."

"Xenocide, then. Anyway, they're more intelligent than bureaucrats. The GU didn't even hold fire while we looked for another way to get the stuff. First sign of a problem and they woke up a goon squad and killed three innocent people. And why? Because they were scared. Too scared to wait even a few days. Just in case something unexpected happened to *Star Pyramid* while they were waiting. It had lasted 400 years. A few more *days* wouldn't've hurt."

"Michael, they were desperate." She sounded sad. Rightly. The silence grew uncomfortably lengthy before I replied.

"Don't you see? That makes it *worse*. What would happen the next time they got desperate? And the time after that? Every alien lifeform would create a conflict of interest for the GU. Not to mention the bankers and politicos and industrialists and generals and priests... and all the other power-seekers. It's an unavoidable consequence of expansionism.

"The GU had its chance and it muffed it. Earth showed her true colours. And we just can't permit that attitude, out among the stars. Conquering Earthmen, plague of the Galaxy. Spreading like vermin and destroying everything we touch. We wouldn't want it inflicted on *us*, so we shouldn't inflict it on anyone else."

Deep sigh. Gayl nodded. "Yup. And now you're going to add: 'just like they did to Earth'."

"Just like they did to Earth." I pulled her closer. "Face it, Gayl: humans started wrecking the planet the moment they evolved, and they've been at it ever since. Overpopulation, pollution, the forests, plains, glaciers, oceans... even the very air we breathed. Wrecked. Wrecked by greed, by superstition, by selfishness... by sheer unadulterated stupidity."

"They did wonderful things too. Medicine, art, science... Even *Star Pyramid.*"

"But like Fiona said, the Project was a fraud from the start. It was never about resources. Yes, Earth was running out, but the Solar System had more than we could ever need. Why go to distant stars for what's in our own backyard?"

"I don't think 'fraud' is quite fair," Gayl said. "The main aim of the Project was to unify the people of the planet. And to stop everyone fighting to get hold of Earth's tiny supply of mahabhavium. That worked."

"It worked right up to the moment when *Star Pyramid* headed off into the wide black yonder," I said. "Then it started to fall apart. And unification was at best a secondary aim. Think of the slogan: *Earth first.* Rank hypocrisy. They *never* put the Earth first. The true slogan was *Wealth first.* More wealth for people who already had far too much. They wanted unity because anarchy would be bad for business. And that attitude goes way back. Think what they wanted to do to Federico Berrios. And why."

Gayl nodded. "You know... speaking of Berrios... Is there any chance of rescuing him? Now we've got the Da Silva drive it would be easy to track him down. The main problem would be to match speeds. I suppose we could use the MAD to accelerate *Star Pyramid* to near-lightspeed, and *then* switch on the Da Silva–" She stopped. "No, we can't. He's going too fast. *Star Pyramid* is so massive that it's limited to 98.41% lightspeed. *Tyger* has no such limit. It must be at 99.99% or more by now."

I swallowed hard, took a deep breath. Recovered my ability to speak, albeit shakily. "It's very tricky, Gayl. Given time, we can build something that could rescue him. But that's a long way off."

I managed a faint smile. "On the plus side, there's no need to hurry. On his timescale, a thousand years is the blink of an eye. But when it becomes possible, it has to be done. Future generations owe it to him. Whatever it costs–"

My voice trailed off, I could hardly speak. Gayl took my hand in hers, gave it a squeeze. I swallowed, on the verge of tears.

"It's really got to you, hasn't it?" she said. "I never figured you for an emotional type."

"Me neither. Mathematicians have emotions, too."

Gayl brushed away tears from her own eyes. Changed the subject back to the earlier one.

"You were saying that we've seen all this before, throughout Earth's history."

"Yes, I was. But this time there's a difference. Not *us*, as such: the position in which we find ourselves. We can *stop it*. And that's what we've decided to do."

Gayl gave an unhappy nod. "Whether some of us like it or not."

"Would you prefer us to head back home and hand faster-than-light travel to the current rulers of planet Earth? Knowing what they're bound to do with it?"

She said nothing. I put an arm round her shoulders. "It's a fresh start. The slate's been wiped clean. With care, we can keep it that way. I agree it was a horrible decision to be forced to make, but it was the GU that pushed us in that direction. They showed us the monster we were about to unleash, red in tooth and claw, jaws dripping saliva."

"You have a very vivid imagination."

"Not vivid enough, I'm afraid. Think about it. How would Earth behave if we ever found *intelligent* aliens? A civilisation? Do you think they'd settle down to discuss mutual respect over a cup of tea? Hell, we don't do that to most of our *own* race! Never have done.

"No, appalling though it may seem, it was the right decision. The *only* responsible decision."

I almost believed it myself.

She licked her lips. "Even if I don't agree, the decision's been taken. I can't reverse it. I really don't know what I'd do if I could!" Another sigh. "But now *we're* going to exploit mahabhavium. To explore. To travel. To find places like this. To spread human culture. We're going to colonise the stars. Asteroids first, then moons and planets. Take out our contraceptive implants, reproduce. Found empires.

"Doesn't that sound familiar, Michael? *What makes you think we're any better than they are?*"

It was a good question. Not a new one, *Star Pyramid*'s crew had debated it endlessly. Most agreed with the answer we'd hashed out. Those who didn't, grudgingly accepted that they were going to have to live with it. Gayl was still wavering.

"*We,*" I said, "respected the caltrops' right to live their own lives, even though that got in the way of what we wanted. We didn't issue instructions to slaughter every single one of them. We didn't awaken secret assassins to kill anyone who failed to toe the authoritarian line. We found another solution.

"I know it sounds arrogant, Gayl, but it's like Fiona said. Earth chose us because we're its best. We have to *do* what's best."

"It *is* arrogant, Michael."

"Only if I'm wrong."

Maybe I am. I looked down at my feet, suddenly unsure of my ground.

"Aren't we tainted by our own ancestry, Michael?" Gayl persisted.

I raised my head so that her eyes met mine. "I don't believe in genetic determinism. I do believe in creating an honest and compassionate society. This is the human race's chance for a fresh start. Not just Starfolk: everyone back on Earth. I'm not claiming we're superior beings. Just that we're in a unique position to grasp that opportunity. Humanity will never get a better chance."

I stopped for breath. This was getting too combative. "Do *you* think I'm wrong?"

She sighed. "No. With *that* track-record—"

"There are billions of people on Earth who are more compassionate, more loving, more honest, more selfless than we are. But they're not in charge. They're the victims, not the criminals. Whereas *we* are the only people who have an opportunity to change that. To stop this insanity once and for all."

"By abandoning them."

"No! Earth has been an endless planetwide clusterfuck for centuries. *It has to end.* We'll do what we can to help, but for now the people of Earth must stay inside the Solar System. A blockade."

She tilted her head, it looked good, not that that was her intention.

"Blockades are mainly about goods, Michael. What you're proposing sounds more like quarantine."

"Yeah, you could put it that way. Best way to stop a disease spreading. But when the time's ripe, we'll go back and rescue the survivors. On our terms."

"Survivors? What about those who won't survive because we refuse to interfere?"

"Giving the GU mahabhavium won't help a single one of them. It will just make the oppression worse."

She bit her lip. "Do you think that's what motivated Shegwada? According to the records, she came from a poor family. Both parents died when she was young. It's all a bit thin. I rather think she hacked the official files from that period of her life. She probably did it early on, before the GU's analysts had any interest in her."

I thought about that. "Could be, yes. She certainly had a deep-seated hatred for the Global Union and everything it stood for. There must have been a cause." I thought about that, too. It was uncomfortably like my own attitude.

"You know she left a message?" Gayl said. "Just before Reynheiður killed her. *Mvua haina hodi.* Someone in Security looked it up. It's Kiswahili for 'rain does not wait to be invited'."

I was only half-listening and I didn't think it through. I just said: "Rain? In the dark between the stars? What the devil did she mean by that?"

Gayl gave a wan smile. "I think I've figured it out. It's a proverb, and what it really means is that trouble will come in its own time, even though you don't want it."

I realised I was being obtuse. "That fits. Shegwada was hell-bent on making trouble. Destruction of the ship, no less."

Gayl brushed a strand of hair away from sad eyes in an unconscious reflex, her mind clearly elsewhere. "I wonder if, at the back of her mind, she was also thinking of trouble that had happened to her. She must have had what seemed to her to be a good reason, Michael. Something deep and dark. Given her level of hatred, something truly awful. She hacked the records to bury it. We'll probably never find out what it was."

"We can guess," I said. "The Project certainly trod on a lot of people's toes. I think it must've wronged people she loved, when she was a child. That kind of thing leaves deep scars."

"Close relatives. Her parents, maybe. She was orphaned when she was eight, assuming we can believe the records."

"Probably," I said. "Births and deaths are hard to conceal. Other records are easier to modify."

Gayl nodded. "Of course the GU always portrayed public enthusiasm as being strong and unified. And it was, mostly, because so many people bought into the stated objective."

"But there was plenty of opposition, too," I said.

"Yup. Just not very effective, and kept from public view."

"Trod on our toes, too," I mused. "Not surprisingly, we didn't like it. We finally worked out the GU's *real* reasons for the Project.

It completely reversed our attitude. Maybe Shegwada was right all along."

"Nope," Gayl said. "We can sympathise with her attitude, but not with how she intended to express it. She chose the wrong target. *Star Pyramid* isn't the GU."

"Not any more," I said.

"Good point. But even when it *was*, taking the ship out wouldn't have helped the ordinary people either."

"On that," I said, "we agree."

She leaned closer, clamped a hand on mine. "Michael: there must be something *positive* we can do. I *hate* this dog-in-the-manger attitude."

"Me too, but I can't see an alternative. Can you?"

Her breathing quickened, her face became more animated. "We could go back, Michael. Explain. Apologise, maybe. The bandwidth for freewave must be wider if we're closer. We could use radio, even."

I shook my head. "That would be lovely, but it wouldn't have any effect aside from making us feel less guilty. Anyway, the risk to *Star Pyramid* is too great."

"We've been jumping all over the place."

"Ah. It's not the risk of using the Da Silva drive that I'm worried about. It's how the GU will react. Mardeen went into all that. The last we heard, Earth was embroiled in nuclear conflicts. There were military vessels all over the inner Solar System, all spoiling for a fight. If we went back now, they'd board us and take over by force. Kill us, she said, and I believe her."

Gayl was nothing if not persistent. It was one of the many things I liked about her. "I know all that, Michael. I have an eidetic memory, remember? I didn't mean we should get *that* close to Earth.

"We've got enough mahabhavium to build more powerful transmitters and receivers," she pointed out. "Rowley's been designing some for us to use once we've built some smaller Da Silva ships. We could call Earth from a safe distance with one of those."

"In the distant future… maybe. Right now: Rickart still says 'no'. All Earth would do is harangue and argue. We've burnt our bridges. But later, when we've got enough Da Silva ships, we can risk sending some of them to renew contact and offer support. The threat will probably have gone by then. The military types will have wiped each other out."

"Maybe they'll have wiped the whole planet out."

True. But we can't stop that. Nothing can.

"I doubt it," I lied.

"I suppose we could rebuild the freewave antenna, once we get our asteroid industries working," Gayl said. "Then we could get in touch with Earth properly, from a safe distance. Assuming they're still listening." She blinked back tears. "Assuming anyone's still around to listen."

"There will be. And you're right, we could."

"Maybe we could melt a small metal asteroid, spin it up really fast and blow it like glass, Make a flat ellipsoid, slice it in half, and there you have it: an antenna."

"Not a bad idea," I said. "You should mention it to Kyril or Fiona. When we *do* go back, once we've got the ships, we can provide Earth with resources. Enough for a sensible sized population to live good, meaningful lives. Not enough to reach for the stars. Not yet. Eventually, we'll be able to lift the quarantine. But for now, we have to be cruel to be kind."

Gayl looked sceptical. "You really think we have that level of wisdom?"

"I hope so. I also think that when it comes to the crunch, it's more than Earth's rulers deserve. *We* didn't decide to destroy all life on an entire planet."

The warning buzzer bleeped. One minute to the next Da Silva jump.

We secured our drinks and strapped ourselves in. It was probably an unnecessary precaution, but it was early days and the technology was still being tested. Entwined our fingers for reassurance. For human contact. For love.

A series of stills flashed through my mind. Crowded cities. Depleted lunar mines, their spoil littering the moonscape. Accessible resources in the solar system rapidly diminishing. Threats of all-out war as human rats scrabbled for what was left. Divided and weak politicians clinging to power by promising humanity the Galaxy. Now denied them.

Gayl must've been having similar thoughts, because she stared at her feet, unable to look me in the eye, and in a tiny voice whispered–

"Didn't we?"

MAP OF THE
CONSTELLATION LEO

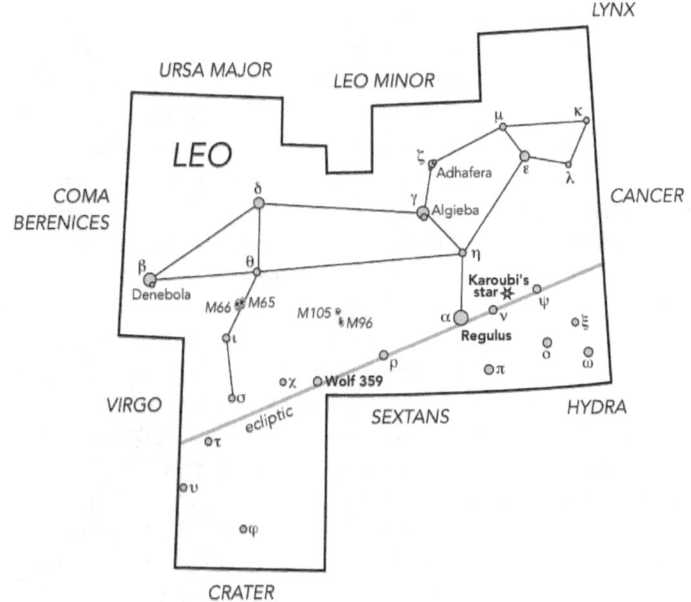

TECHNICAL NOTE

There is no star named koppa Leonis 662. 'Koppa' is a letter in the ancient Greek alphabet, but so ancient that astronomers never used it. Along with two others, 'stigma' and 'sampi', it had gone out of use by Mediaeval times. Its symbol survives as the Latin letter Q, and it's sometimes spelled 'qoppa'.

Gayl Goodenough would tell you a lot more, naturally.

Science *fiction*, OK?

AUTHOR'S NOTE

In 1979, Tim Poston and I started planning a science fiction novel, *The Vegetable Connection*, and within six months we'd written about a third of it and drawn maps of the planet on which the main action was located. Tim, like me, was a mathematician, and the central McGuffin was a curious piece of topological trickery that Tim had invented, based on a disc having two sides. Being devotees of the 'invisible book' approach to SF world-building we devised an entire timeline as context for the story. But Tim was travelling the globe in a series of short-term positions, the material was either handwritten or typed, and there was no internet. The book went on the back burner for 36 years.

In 2016 Tim was in Bengaluru, India, and it occurred to me to type everything we had into my laptop. This finally gave us the chance to tinker with it, mostly by exchange of e-mails. Within six months we'd written the remaining two thirds, and ReAnimus Press published it under the title *The Living Labyrinth*. Total writing time: 37 years. Of which 36 produced exactly nothing. The sequel, *Rock Star*, took us a mere six months.

Back in 1979 we'd also made some preliminary plans for a prequel, *Star Pyramid*, which explained the origin of the Starfolk and the Concordat of Habitable Exoplanets, a key part of the background for *Living Labyrinth* and *Rock Star*. But in 2017, before we could develop the ideas any further, Tim died unexpectedly.

As time passed, I got to wondering about *Star Pyramid*. I still had a pile of notes and letters, a list of characters, a solid start and a plausible ending. But what happened in between? On this the notes were fragmentary, contradictory, and – to put it politely – incomplete. The only way I could find out was to write the book. It turned out to be rather different from anything in the notes, aside from characters, start, and ending. Elsewhen Press agreed to publish it.

Peter Buck of Elsewhen Press and I wondered whether it would be possible to publish *Living Labyrinth* and *Rock Star* as well, to obtain a series in a uniform format. I also wanted to revise those books in the light of the events in *Star Pyramid*, which had caused several changes to the original timeline and created some minor inconsistencies that ought to be straightened out. Andrew Burt of ReAnimus Press kindly reverted the rights to those books to permit this.

While negotiating these contractual complexities, I started trying to fill in the gap between *Star Pyramid* and *Living Labyrinth*, and a fourth book in the series hove into view: *Lost in Translation*. It would be easy to extend the series – what happened during the Vegan uprising? The revolt of the Centauri bubble cities? How was Inferno colonised? What were the origins of the Vain Vaimoksi? But those books are still just 'hay in the kay', as Starfolk say.

Meanwhile, Elsewhen Press will be publishing the four existing books. Their order within Concordat chronology is: *Star Pyramid*, *Lost in Translation*, *Living Labyrinth*, and *Rock Star*. The first two are new; the other two have been rewritten, both for consistency and because I now think I have a better idea of what I'm doing.

Welcome to the *Chronicles of the Concordat*.

Ian Stewart, May 2025.

Elsewhen Press

delivering outstanding new talents in speculative fiction

Visit the Elsewhen Press website at elsewhen.press for the latest information on all of our titles, authors and events; to read our blog; find out where to buy our books and ebooks; or to place an order.

Sign up for the Elsewhen Press InFlight Newsletter at elsewhen.press/newsletter

ABOUT IAN STEWART

Ian Stewart is Emeritus Professor of Mathematics at the University of Warwick and a Fellow of the Royal Society. He has six honorary doctorates and is an honorary wizard of Unseen University. His more than 130 books include *Professor Stewart's Cabinet of Mathematical Curiosities* and the four-volume series *The Science of Discworld* with Terry Pratchett and Jack Cohen. His SF novels include the trilogy *Wheelers*, *Heaven*, and *Oracle* (with Jack Cohen), *The Living Labyrinth* and *Rock Star* (with Tim Poston), *Jack of All Trades*, and *Loophole*. Short story collections are *Message from Earth* and *Pasts, Presents, Futures*. His *Flatland* sequel *Flatterland* has extensive fantasy elements. He has published 33 short stories in *Analog*, *Omni*, *Interzone*, and *Nature*, with 10 stories in *Nature*'s 'Futures' series. He was Guest of Honour at Novacon 29 in 1999 and Science Guest of Honour and Hugo Award Presenter at Worldcon 75 in Helsinki in 2017. He delivered the 1997 Christmas Lectures for BBC television. His awards include the Royal Society's Faraday Medal, the Gold Medal of the IMA, the Zeeman Medal, the Lewis Thomas Prize, the Euler Book Prize, the Premio Internazionale Cosmos, the Chancellor's Medal of the University of Warwick, and the Bloody Stupid Johnson Award for Innovative Uses of Mathematics.